DREAMS THROWN AWAY

DREAMS THROWN AWAY

Outskirts Press, Inc.
Denver, Colorado

DILSA SAUNDERS BAILEY

Dreams Thrown Away
All Rights Reserved.
Copyright © 2009 Dilsa Saunders Bailey
v4.0

Cover Photo © 2009 JupiterImages Corporation. All rights reserved - used with permission.

Outskirts Press, Inc.
http://www.outskirtspress.com

ISBN: 978-1-4327-4222-5

Library of Congress Control Number: 2009927993

Outskirts Press and the "OP" logo are trademarks belonging to Outskirts Press, Inc.

PRINTED IN THE UNITED STATES OF AMERICA

I dedicate this book to my family – Jimmy, Kristina, and Lisa who have endured the many adventures and changes I have sought with grace, support, and much love. And, to the Ladies who supported me in my efforts – my sister Sara L. Williams and my cousin, Betty Saunders, I thank you.

INTRODUCTION

Kalina hugged her pillow even tighter as the bright sunshine invaded the darkness of her room. She buried her face in it to hold onto the peace that enveloped her just before the bright intrusion of the spring morning. The sun's warm rays streamed through her lace curtains creating psychedelic patterns on her pale blue wall, teasing her to get up and get going. It was Sunday, and, as usual, her day was already lined up with activity. She wished she could be like many of her friends who didn't have to get up and go to church every Sunday.

If only her dreams had already come true, getting out of bed would be a moot point on Sunday morning. The man of her dreams would be delivering her favorite breakfast in bed on a tray with a red rose across the silverware. She would sit up, smile at him, and give him a loving kiss as he joined her in bed – their bed. It would be huge in a fabulous room overlooking an amazing city skyline. They would never consider living far out in the boondocks. They would be much too sophisticated. Kalina had dreams, big dreams. Her dreams were way too big for the little rural town of Roebuck, South Carolina. After all, it was 1978, and the world was changing everywhere, except in Roebuck.

She heard her mother's slippers flopping and sliding down the

hallway, so she dug her head even deeper into the pillow. She wanted to hold on to her vision of lying next to a warm, strong, and
wealthy man who took care of her. She tried to ignore the sound
of those awful slippers and the shrill sound of her mother's voice
that followed. She shifted below the covers hoping her mother
couldn't tell that she was no longer asleep. She closed her eyes
gently and tried to steady her breathing.

"Kalina Denise Harris. Get out of that bed." Charlotte stood
in the doorway of her daughter's bedroom with her arms folded
across her flat chest. "You're going to be late for Sunday School!
You know you promised Mrs. Flowers you were going to help her
with the babies this morning."

Kalina didn't move.

"Kalina, you hear me! I know you can hear me." Charlotte
stepped inside the doorway heading for the young girl, but a strong
brown hand gently caught her arm.

"Oh, Charlotte, nobody wants to awaken to such a harsh tone
of voice. It's okay. She will get up on time." Preach pulled his wife
back into his arms and hugged her.

"I'll get her up," he whispered and lovingly kissed his wife on
her freckled forehead.

"You spoil her, Preach. You let her get away with murder. She
shouldn't have been up all night watching television. But, no, you
gave her permission anyway." Charlotte pulled her lavender nylon
robe close to her long, thin, tan body and went sliding back down
the narrow hallway in her white terry slippers.

"Thank you, Daddy." Kalina opened her eyes and smiled sweetly
at her father as soon as she knew her mother was out of earshot.

"Your mother wants to make sure you keep your word. Your
word is important. Right?" He sat on the side of her bed and
smoothed back her thick, wild curls. Kalina had one curl that would

always fall right between her eyes no matter how hard she would try to tame it. He smiled as he watched the curl escape again and land front and center of her hazel eyes.

"I know. I'll be ready for Sunday School. I promise." She sat up and looked around. Kalina was proud of her room and her white four-poster bed. She had begged and begged until her father had finally bought her the perfect bedroom set. It was white, trimmed in gold, and absolutely perfect. She had long outgrown the mismatched furniture that had once crowded her room. She was becoming too refined for the leftover furniture from her grandmother's and her parents' rooms. Now the room had become her kingdom, bringing her closer to her dreams of grandeur. And as Queen of her kingdom, whenever her mother set foot in it, she wanted to exile her forever. She sighed with pleasure as she imagined the house empty of her mother and her high nagging voice shouting commands and making demands. She and her father could live there happily ever after. Kalina would even be willing to go the local university to make her father happy. But, she knew that would never happen. That is why she had applied to schools as far away as possible.

Preach kissed her on the forehead and left her sitting in the bed staring at nature's psychedelic patterns. Though the art of the sunlight intrigued her creative soul, the previous night had drained her of any energy or desire to set foot out of her comfortable bed. The movie about zombies she had so eagerly watched had really frightened her. Going to bed after midnight normally would not have bothered her, but last night she had had trouble falling asleep. There was a scene with blood splattered on the walls that really bothered her. She couldn't shake it. It was as if she were expecting to see blood on her walls when she awakened. She shook her head and shrugged her shoulders. Either way, she was ready to crawl back under the cover. But, she knew how important it was to keep her word. Her mother was right about that.

Kalina got up and started her routine. She said her prayers quickly, asking God earnestly to forgive her for hating her mother. She made up her bed, making sure the sheets were neatly tucked and the ruffled pillows were balanced just right, almost picture perfect. She then headed for the bathroom to get dressed. A half hour later, after stuffing a couple of pancakes in her mouth, Kalina was ready, keeping the promise her father had made to her mother.

She rushed to the long black Lincoln that sat in the driveway.

"Daddy, can I drive?" she asked as she ran to the car with a choir robe hanging over her shoulder.

"Of course, you can." Preach handed her the keys. As her mother reached for the front door of the passenger side, Preach's hand covered Charlotte's and then kissed it.

"I'd better sit up front with her. You know how nervous you get with her driving," he said, grinning and graciously holding the back door open for Charlotte. Charlotte sat hard in the spacious back seat, plopping her sheet music and materials in her lap.

Kalina looked back at her mother triumphantly as Charlotte turned her head to look out the window at the trees lining the road. That was their little rural haven, nothing more. Trees or an occasional house or pasture would fade quickly as they made their way to church. Kalina glanced in the rearview mirror and saw her mother's eyes look forlorn and watery, as if she were fighting back tears. Charlotte met her daughter's eyes and sneezed then pulled out a tissue to clean her face and pat the moisture from her eyes.

"Look both ways before you pull out onto the highway. You know there's a blind spot over that hill," Preach instructed.

Kalina followed her father's instructions, but immediately thought about her mother's tears. There was an unbearable tension between them. That was another good reason for her to go away to school. She could not comprehend another four years of whatever it was that kept the two of them at constant odds. The car moved slowly down the narrow rocky and dusty driveway to the two-lane highway as the young inexperienced driver tried to keep her mind on the road and not on her mother in the back seat looking lost.

After Sunday School, Kalina took her place in line with the choir saying her hellos, then standing quietly waiting for the procession to begin. She repeated the words to her solo in her mind. She wanted to remember where to emphasize the words as her mother had taught her so the song would emerge flawlessly. She peeped through the doors as the ushers let people into the sanctuary. She saw her mother sitting at the piano playing softly. Her mother was beautiful. Kalina had never seen her look so beautiful before and wondered why she had not noticed this morning as they left for church.

As she listened to the piano, Kalina wondered if there was something about her father being the only male in the house that made the two of them appear to compete for his attention. She tried to think of what it was her mother had done to make her dislike her so much, but nothing came to mind. After all, her mother had tried everything to make peace with her – gifts, hobbies, and most importantly, she had shared her love for music. Now Kalina was 17 years old, ready to go away to school, and could probably count on one hand the number of times she and her mother had had a civil conversation.

———— ((●)) ————

Kalina's solo did awe the congregation as her mother had told her it would if she followed the right inflections. Her voice was both angelic and graceful as it resonated throughout the sanctuary. Kalina could see tears in some of the church folks' eyes and admiration in others. She loved singing, she loved music, and she loved this moment.

Like it or not, that was the gift she had inherited from her mother. Her mother was playing the piano with such emotion, evoking an even more passionate performance than she could have envisioned. She looked down and watched her mother's long, slender and tan fingers glide across the ivory keys. She couldn't help but smile. Their eyes met and she saw her mother's eyes well up, and a sad, almost haunting, smile returned.

She continued singing and turned to her father who was on his feet with his usual big, proud grin. She finished and then ran into his arms. The church roared. She looked back to her mother to thank her, but the piano bench was empty.

Kalina was impatient for the service to end. In the midst of the song, she realized that she didn't really hate her mother and wondered if she ever had. She sat in the choir stand watching the piano bench. She had never wanted to talk to her mother so badly before. She wanted to find out why her mother had left the piano when her song was over. She wanted to know if her mother was all right. Kalina was genuinely concerned for the first time in her life, especially when Mrs. Flowers took the bench to accompany the last two songs of the service.

There had been something sad in her mother's eyes that frightened Kalina and made her heart race as the service seemed to close slowly. The guilt of her own indifference and divisive manner was bugging her as she kept searching the sanctuary for her mother's reappearance. She began to worry that God was about to punish her for being so mean to her own mother.

After church, she took her usual spot at the top of the steps of the large brick church standing between her mother – who had suddenly appeared beside her – and her father. The church members of the largest Black church in the county would file out of the church shaking their hands and complimenting them for their messages and music. Some Sundays the ritual caused Kalina to feel like a superstar. Other Sundays the attention made her want to throw up. This Sunday she was beginning to feel anxious and unbalanced. She had only an urgent desire to go home.

Kalina stood in the line shaking the usual hands and smiling her prettiest smile. She made sure she looked each person in the eye and responded to each a relevant comment the way her mother had taught her. The thought made her turn to look at her mother. A tall dark man that Kalina had never seen before – or at least never noticed – was holding her mother's hand and speaking softly to her. Kalina instantly wanted to snatch her mother's hand from the man and scold her. She didn't know why, but there was a look of pleasure in her mother's face that was not familiar to her, and this made her uncomfortable.

Finally, the church was emptying out and Kalina was free to talk to her mother, or so she thought. When she ran into the choir room to talk to her, she wasn't there. Disappointed, she strolled across the dusty churchyard to the car to wait for both of her parents.

"Hey, Miss Stuck-up," said Mandy. Kalina turned to see her friend Mandy on the other side of the car.

Kalina responded by holding her head back and pointing her nose to the sky. Both girls laughed.

"We get out early tomorrow," Mandy said as she slid on top of the hood of the car. Kalina joined her, knowing that her father would chase them off as soon as he saw them.

"It's great being a senior, isn't it?" Kalina wrapped her arms around her knees.

"It sure is, Miss Proper," Mandy laughed. "You practicing for University of Penn?"

"I always speak that way. You know my momma would kill me if I didn't." Kalina reflected on the word *momma*. She was always using her mother's words or using her mother as an excuse. She had never thought of that before.

"Yes, your Momma and Daddy think you's perfect," Mandy said and shoved Kalina, and they both giggled some more. "My brother is going to let me borrow his car tomorrow, so I don't have to wait for the bus. You want to go to town? I have to buy my dress for the baccalaureate next Sunday." Mandy was playing with a white straw hat, bending it and twirling it. Kalina had seen her wearing it in church.

"Your momma made you wear that thing?" Kalina took the hat and started molding it.

"You know she did. I hate that damn thing. But, she says a respectable woman keeps her head covered in church," Mandy sighed. "I don't think she thinks I'm respectable."

"I guess me neither. Nor my mother, nor most of the women in the church. Only the old folks keep wearing those crazy hats," Kalina said. She knew her grammar was poor, but she had to talk that way a little to make Mandy feel more comfortable.

"You mean like that pheasant looking thing Ms. Aubrey had on her head?" Mandy said. She laughed holding her sides. "I coulda sworn I saw a beak on that sucka."

Kalina looked up and saw her parents coming down the church steps.

"Jump," she said quickly. Both girls jumped and ran to the other side of the car.

"See you tomorrow." Mandy ran off toward the road. She lived across the two-lane highway from the church. They waved at each other.

"I'm going with you tomorrow," Kalina yelled. "I need some shoes."

"You need what?" her father asked, handing her the keys.

"I need shoes to match my dress next Sunday." Kalina smiled at her mother who looked surprised. She handed her father back the keys.

"I'm okay, Daddy. I'll drive another time." She opened the back door and got in, folding her robe across her lap.

"Okay, Kitten." She watched her father hold the door open for her mother. He always did that. Even when she, herself, was being off-handed with her mother and even if her father agreed with her, he would always take an extra step to show her mother his respect. Kalina wondered if her mother had ever noticed that.

That evening as her father sat in front of the television watching a variety show, Kalina ventured upstairs to her parents' room. Her mother was sitting at the vanity rolling her long auburn hair into huge pink sponge rollers.

"Don't they hurt when you sleep on them?" Kalina said, walking up behind her mother. The two of them stared at each other in the mirror for a few seconds.

"No, you get used to them." Charlotte eyed Kalina suspiciously.

Kalina was extremely pretty. Her skin was the color of pecan pralines and her hazel eyes were dazzling. But, what made her even more exotic and beautiful than most was her bronze and black hair. It was as if nature had used her head as a canvas to create the perfect highlights.

Charlotte had once told Kalina that she was a little jealous of her beauty, but more proud than anything. She had even told Kalina how she used to love carrying her around as an infant because people would say, "That's the prettiest baby I have ever seen."

And they were right. She was an absolutely beautiful baby, but a baby who acted as if she hated her mother even then, and Charlotte had confided as much to Preach.

"Momma," Kalina took a seat on the bed behind her. "You played beautifully today. I mean, it was just way cool. Like you had so much feeling! I had never heard you play that way before. I mean...It was different than in any of the rehearsals or anytime. The way you played, it was just mellow and touching, Momma."

Charlotte put down the hair roller and turned toward her daughter.

"Are you all right? I know one of your and Daddy's favorite television shows is on. I know he's downstairs perched in front of his new toy. What are you up to?" Charlotte smiled as she asked the question. She reached over and touched Kalina's forehead. Kalina giggled.

"I'm fine, Momma. Are you?" her eyes became more serious.

"I'm fine, Child. Why would you ask?" Charlotte turned back to the mirror and began parting her hair for the next roller.

"You seemed sad. The music seemed sad. And you left as soon as I finished singing." Kalina started pulling at her rogue curl.

"How do you know when I am sad?" Charlotte asked tenderly.

Kalina got up and took the comb from her mother's hand. She began to part it and put the rollers in the thick, coarse hair. She followed her mother's directions on what to do with the hair grease and the papers that shielded the hair from the sponges. The two of them chatted until the rollers were gone. Then Kalina sat in front of the mirror as her mother detangled and braided her curly hair.

Kalina went to bed thinking her mother wasn't sad anymore and that she had made a difference. But, she was wrong.

CHAPTER ONE

"You are so quiet. You're scaring me," Kalina said, taking a big bite out of her burger. "Aren't you going to eat?" Kalina stuffed a few of the hot, salty fries into her mouth.

"I don't feel so good. The smell in here is making me sick." Mandy covered her mouth as her eyes began to water.

"You are really acting strange. Are you sick or something?" Kalina was enjoying her McDonald's burger. She didn't get a chance to come here often. Her mother had had a run in with one of the White teens that worked there. After that, she didn't trust them touching her food. So they never went to McDonald's.

"I'll be back," Mandy jumped up from the hard plastic seat and walked quickly toward the bathroom.

Kalina sighed. She began to greedily eat Mandy's left over fries. She was enjoying all the grease and salt. Her mother's food didn't have as much taste as the McDonald's food. There was a running joke at church that she and her father had to agree was the truth – that her mother could not cook. Although, Kalina had to admit she appreciated her mother's Sunday morning pancakes. They were the greatest.

Kalina ate hastily having the feeling that Mandy was going to be ready to go as soon as she got back. Mandy didn't look too well as she ran toward the bathroom.

"Let's go. I can't take this place any longer," Mandy said as she walked up behind her. "I hope you're finished shopping. 'Cause I need to go home."

"No problem. All I wanted was those really bad shoes. My God, they are the baddest things this town has ever seen!" Kalina was talking to dead air. Mandy had snatched up her things and was on her way out of the door.

Kalina had to run to catch up to her at the old yellow Volkswagen Beetle. She waited while Mandy reached over and unlocked her door. Kalina got in and placed her feet carefully on each side of the hole in the floor that had a loose board slightly covering it.

"When is your brother going to get this floor fixed? I don't like seeing the road underneath my feet," she complained as Mandy shifted and struggled to get the car running.

"Kalina, stop complaining. If you're not complaining, you're bragging. And if you're not bragging, you're complaining. You wear a person out," Mandy backed the car out of the parking space, and it jerked under her command of the steering wheel and the gas.

"You need to learn how to drive," Kalina said and winced as they just barely missed another parked car.

"I am driving. I have a driver's license and a car. My brother is going to give me this car when he gets another one."

"When's that going to be? Never," said Kalina. Giggling, she was in the mood to joke, but Mandy wasn't having any of it.

"You are really, really stuck-up and I'm not playing. You just don't have a clue about life. Your parents have just spoiled you rotten." Mandy's mood was becoming foul.

"What did I do to you? What the heck happened?" Kalina

started holding onto the tattered cloth seat with both hands. Mandy was making the little car speed along the two-lane highway out of town.

"Nothing happened. It's just that…" Mandy stopped talking and took a deep breath. "It's just that I was going to tell you something today and you wouldn't shut up. If you say one more thing about those ugly green shoes, I'll just scream."

"Since when do you not say something when you want to say something?" Kalina was hoping Mandy would slow down.

"Since Rudy asked me to marry him after I told him I was pregnant," With that announcement, Mandy really floored the Volkswagen, and it was groaning loudly as it took the curves.

Kalina started laughing. She was laughing so hard she forgot how fast they were going.

"What the hell are you laughing about?" Mandy screamed, with tears now flying out of her eyes, and her hair flapping wildly in the wind from the open window.

"You and your jokes! My God, you are not going to sit there and tell me you are ruining your life by marrying Rudy. That's hilarious," Kalina started laughing harder.

"I should just throw you out of this damn car," Mandy said. She turned her eyes toward Kalina who finally got the message.

"You're serious," Kalina said as she slowly realized that those were real tears and a real look of terror in Mandy's eyes.

"Yes, damn it!" The young girl was gripping the steering wheel so tightly her knuckles were whitening.

"You can't be serious?" Kalina wanted to cover her ears.

"I'm serious. Rudy and I are getting married the weekend of July 4th. Your damn daddy has already agreed to marry us. My momma is going to let Rudy come live with us in my room. Rudy's already got a job at the mill," Mandy blurted out between wet sobbing gulps.

Kalina was looking at her in disbelief.

"What about college?" she asked, bewildered that her friend had had sex and she hadn't known about it.

"I wasn't ever going to college. You know that. I ain't as smart as you," Mandy said, her voice calming down a little bit. "Besides, I'm going to be happy with Rudy and our baby."

"Don't be silly," Kalina chided. "There's no way you're going to be happy living in your little bedroom with Rudy and a baby."

"We won't be living there forever," Mandy answered, her anger returning.

"Yes, you will. Where else are the three of you going to live off the salary from the mill? I may be only graduating high school, but I know it costs a lot more to live off than what they pay you."

"That's why when the baby's big enough I'm getting a job there, too. People do it all the time. Besides, what do you know? Your momma's a teacher and your daddy preaches and sells insurance. Not everybody come from folks with college educations."

Mandy was pressing down on the gas pedal again as she spoke.

"I knew you wasn't going to understand. I listen to you talk about everybody like we all such ignorant hicks, because we are from a little town down south. People who look up to you and care about you… but you are always talking down about them. You always laughing at Ms. Rosemarie's turned over shoes and Mr. Parker's chewed up cane. Don't you know they think the world of you?

"All you see is southern hicks, somebody to make fun of. Hell, you probably won't even speak to me once you get your northern college education. You already said you was never coming back, except to visit. Those words hurt the most. I was going to ask you to be my baby's godmother, but what good is a godmother who isn't there?

"You don't know shit. You think you know everything. That's why I didn't tell you nothing. You would have started looking down your nose at me a lot sooner." Mandy was crying again.

"It must be that hormone thing they talk about with pregnant women. You are really acting crazy," Kalina said, glad to see her gravel covered driveway up the road.

The Volkswagen skidded up onto the gravel and stopped.

"Get out my car!" Mandy yelled. "Take your damn things and get out my car!"

"I hope you clean up your mouth when the baby comes," said Kalina. Her hands were shaking as she reached for the door handle. "I really hope it works out for you, Mandy. But, I hope you realize you are smart enough to go to college."

Kalina quickly got her bags out of the backseat and stood by the car.

"I hope you don't marry that jerk, either!" Kalina yelled and then ran up her driveway hoping Mandy wouldn't mow her down for calling Rudy a jerk. Then she had a vivid, ugly picture of the two of them without clothes having sex. She shook her head quickly tossing the image out of it. Why in the world, she wanted to scream, would Mandy have sex with Rudy? He was so ugly. And why didn't she tell her about it? She had thought they shared everything.

Kalina watched fearfully as Mandy backed into the highway without looking and took off.

"God, please let her get home safely." Kalina watched the Bug disappear down the highway. She went back to the edge of the driveway and picked up her bags. She had dropped some while she was yelling at Mandy. Her feet scraped against the speckled granite rocks as she walked up the hill to the carport. She noticed her father's car was home. She started to go inside but thought it was too nice outside. She dropped her packages on the garage doorstep to the kitchen and went to the swing set that sat invitingly next to the apple trees. She sat down and started swinging gently in the warm spring air. She was going to miss that swing, but not all these people. She couldn't wait to get away from Roebuck, South Carolina. The only person she was going to miss was her father and maybe her mother.

Kalina began to shift in the swing when she heard a loud booming sound. She jumped and looked around frantically.

"Was that a gunshot?" she asked herself. She stood up still looking around. She couldn't remember if her father had mentioned whether it was hunting season or not. During hunting season, she always stayed close to the house. There were so many woods surrounding them with so many poor hunted animals. She heard her heart pumping. She didn't want to become one of those annual hunting mistakes. She thought about the rednecks on television saying, "I thoughts its was a deer," and she grinned. Her father and mother would correct her right away for the racial stereotype as well as the bad grammar. Neither would make a difference if she were the latest victim mistaken for a deer.

She sprinted across the grass and gravel toward the garage. First, she ran past the Lincoln with its trunk standing open. She thought her father must have forgotten that he had left it open, so she went back to close it. As she shut it, it made a loud noise or did it? She jumped again and ran for the door leading into the kitchen. Something was wrong.

Kalina's skin was crawling with fear. She pushed the kitchen door open and heard another loud boom. She froze. The noise was coming from inside her house. Her hand held the doorknob tightly as her mind raced madly. What was going on and what was she supposed to do? The kitchen was empty and neat as always.

Her mother would never allow a dish or a glass to sit dirty and un-washed, not even for a second. Everything was in its proper place. Everything looked normal. The white metal chairs with the yellow cushioned seats were in their proper places. The salt and pepper shakers sparkled in the afternoon sunlight that crept past the bright yellow kitchen curtains.

"No!" she heard her mother scream. "No, Preach! No!"

Kalina let go of the doorknob and ran through the small cramped living room. She had always complained that the furniture was far too big for the room. She bumped her knee squeezing past the coffee table and the console television set her father had just bought. Then she heard another piercing scream.

Kalina's feet hit the bottom stair, and she stood still as she heard her mother pleading. Then Kalina moved up the stairs toward her mother's voice as silently as she could.

"I did it for you and for her!" Charlotte's voice choked with tears and dread about the money in the drawer she had just earned.

"I did it for you. Preach, listen to me. He paid me. Put the gun down, Preach. Please, Preach! Put the gun down! Let me explain!"

"Once a whore. Always a whore. That's what Momma told me when I brought you down here. She said you would make me rue the day I laid eyes on you!"

Kalina heard him clearly. Her parents' bedroom door was open. She was less than ten feet away. She stood stock-still and listened.

"Preach, Preach. Come on, Preach. Think about our baby. Think about Kalina. You don't want to ruin her life because of our mistakes," Charlotte reasoned.

"What do you care? She could have come home and been the one to find you with that man in our bed. Charlotte, how could you?" Her father's voice was calm as it echoed through the hall-

— 7 —

way to her standing on the stairs of the small brick cottage. Then Kalina heard the sound as Preach primed the shotgun.

"Preach, you made her promises you couldn't keep. We can't send her to school in Pennsylvania. That scholarship money won't cover enough, and you know it. I was just trying to help," Charlotte offered. "Put the gun down, Preach! We need to get Deke some help. He's losing a lot of blood."

"He's already dead, Charlotte," Preach said so calmly that Kalina's entire body shivered. "I never ever would have thought you would have betrayed me – not trusted me. I had faith in you, Charlotte. Why didn't you have faith in me? I took care of you, of Kalina, the church, my job, all my obligations to everybody. What was it that made you do this to me?"

"I was lonely, Preach. You didn't look at me with that love in your eyes no more. The only loving eyes you have are for Kalina. But, that's not why I did it. I wanted to make sure she didn't have to want for anything. Not the way I did. That's how I ended up down the wrong path. I didn't have anything. Nothing. My parents weren't there for me. You know that. You helped me. Preach, you know I always loved you for that," Charlotte was measuring her words.

Kalina absorbed everything, but she didn't want to understand what she heard.

"I took you off the street, and after all these years you bring the street to my bed, my home that I built for you." Kalina heard her father take a couple of steps.

"You built it for us," Charlotte's voice became shrill, "for us! For Kalina. For us. Don't throw it away, Preach! Not like this. We have got to stay strong for our child. You have to help her reach her dreams, Preach. Don't throw those dreams away. Please don't throw us away!"

"I could have asked the same of you, Charlotte. I can't let you destroy me like this. You're right. That's why we both have to go. Kalina. She'll be all right," Preach began to sob, and Charlotte began to moan loudly.

"No!" Kalina tried to yell as her feet became unglued from the landing of the stairwell, and she started toward her parents' bedroom door.

"No!" she tried to scream again, but nothing was coming from her mouth, or maybe it did but was drowned out by the deafening sound of the gunshot that silenced her mother's excruciating cries for mercy.

She reached the door just in time to have it blown shut in front of her. She heard the impact of her father's body slam against the door as he had put the second shot to the bottom of his chin. Kalina was thrown against the wall by the force of the door. She slid onto the floor and sat there for a few seconds. The house was deadly still. The smell of sulfur permeated the air.

She found it in her to jump up suddenly and started pushing frantically against the door. She used all the strength of her one hundred pound frame to get the door slightly open. She saw her father's legs stretched out across the carpeted floor. They were sprayed with blood.

"Daddy!" she screamed. "Daddy, let me in!"

Kalina kept pushing until she was gradually able to slide through an opening. When she did, her knees weakened. The entire room and the walls were covered in blood. Her mother sat naked in their bed. She looked down and saw a bloody mass above her father's shoulders. She didn't know which one to go to first. Her mother's eyes were still open with an understated terror captured in time on her face. Kalina crawled across the bed hoping her mother would look in her direction. She didn't. Kalina hugged her mother's lifeless body and became covered in the blood from the large, gaping wound around her heart.

Kalina reached for a pillow to put over her mother's chest and saw a man lying naked and bloodied on the floor. She couldn't say for sure, but he reminded her of the man holding her mother's hand in church. Deke was what her mother had just called him. Kalina hated Deke even more than she had on Sunday morning. She wished she had taken her mother's hand from his. She sat in the bed and called her father, but he didn't move. Kalina got out of the bed and squeezed back out of the door. She went down to the living room and sat in her father's favorite recliner. She fell asleep.

———————⟫«(◉)»⟪———————

"Y'all ain't right," said the little old man sitting at a table near the back of the funeral home. "That child been through too much to be putting her on some train to live with someone she don't even know."

"Now, Mr. Parker," said Ms. Rosemarie as she pulled at her neckline. She hated dresses with lace around the collar, and this one kept sticking her in the neck and making her itch.

"Now, Mr. Parker. We done asked everybody in da church and not in the church to take her in. But, everybody so mad at Preach for stealing the church money, and then on top of that killing his whoring wife, that they don't want the child."

"But, that child ain't done nothing to nobody." Mr. Parker steadied himself in the fold-up chair with his cane. "You could, at least, let the child live in her own house then.

"Mr. Parker, by the time the church sells the property – that is, if anybody wants to buy a house with three haunts in it. You know they gone be walking them halls with agony till that house is gone,"

Ms. Rosemarie said, rubbing her eyes.

"What about Glynda? Wasn't she a good friend of Charlotte's? You would think she'd take in her daughter." Mr. Parker shook his mostly bald head that had a few gray strands standing out on the side.

"I asked her, too. But, her own daughter Mandy is pregnant and moving in her soon-to- be husband. Plus, sounds like the two girls had a falling out. Glynda said she won't have the room for her. Besides, she was planning to go to Philadelphia anyway to school. She had gotten into the one of those big business schools up there. And another thing, the girl is kind of stuck up. Seems like don't nobody really like her that much. And I show can't keep her. I can barely afford myself," Ms. Rosemarie shook her head.

"So what's the plan?" Mr. Parker sighed.

———«()»———

Mount Tabor Church was packed. Ms. Rosemarie had picked up Kalina from the hospital earlier that morning. Somebody else had brought her a black dress and some shoes. Kalina walked into the church beside Mr. Parker as he limped down the aisle. She saw the two caskets at the front of the church. They were both closed. She looked around to see familiar faces, but she didn't see any. There was no other family. Her mother's only sister hadn't come to the funeral. Her father had no one left when his mother died. She was the last of Preacher Harris' clan. There was no one else.

The funeral was long and dry. No one cried. Everybody just seemed to be looking at her with anger and disappointment in their eyes. Kalina stared at the two black caskets with a little spread of flowers on each one. That was it. There were no other flowers. She began to think about all the people her father had helped, and not one of them had even sent him a rose.

Kalina's mouth was parched. She couldn't remember the last time she had eaten or drank anything. The multitude of faces around her became a blur. She barely experienced the funeral before being whisked to the gravesites and the lowering of the caskets into their graves. It was already starting to get dark. She felt the bony hands of Mr. Parker holding her by the arm on one side and holding his cane to balance himself on the other. No one shook her hand or hugged her. Kalina was scorned and stared at without pity. She caught the eye of a classmate who was actually smiling snidely. She thought about Mandy. Her eyes scanned the heads and hats, some with lowered eyes, some with daring eyes, but she didn't see Mandy or Mandy's mom.

She thought about Ms. Glynda and what her mother had said.

"These people are different, I give you that," Charlotte had said that last Sunday night as she braided Kalina's hair. "I have been living here for almost twenty years, and I don't feel like I have made a true friend yet."

"But, what about Ms. Glynda?" Kalina was enjoying her mother's long narrow fingers in her hair.

"That's what I'm trying to tell you, baby. I love Ms. Glynda, but I don't know if she returns the love or just wants to be known as my friend. I haven't quite figured that out yet."

"But y'all been friends for years," Kalina wanted to bite her tongue as soon as she said the words.

"Kalina, we do not talk like that in this house. Y'all is not a word," Charlotte watched her daughter mouth her words in sync in the mirror and smiled.

"Kalina, Mandy's like her mother in so many ways. I'm sorry you don't have any really close friends. Preach being Preach, and me being who I am." Charlotte didn't say anymore.

Kalina understood. Most of the kids in school merely tolerated her. Her parents had always put her on a pedestal and pushed her to be the best at everything. That was because they believed she could be the best. It was funny to her that because of her parents, she believed it, too, and so did the kids that merely tolerated her. They separated themselves from her. Little did they know that they were responsible for making her feel the way she did, like she was in a higher place in life than they were allowed. That's how they treated her, like she was better. For that reason, their perception of her had become her mindset.

Kalina later sat in the car with Mr. Parker. His chewed-up cane sat between them. It kept sliding toward her, and she tried to move out of its trajectory. Noticing her discomfort, he reached for the cane and slid it onto the back seat out of the way.

"My old dog chewed on this thing when he was a puppy. But, I love this old cane. It reminds me of when I wasn't hobbling around so bad and when old Duke was brand new and lively. That old dog has always kept me company. More than I can say for my own family. They have all moved away from this place. Can't say that I blame them.

"You gon' be better off up there with your aunt. She didn't have the money to come down, but a few folks got together to send you to her. Ms. Rosemarie packed you a few things, a couple of pictures and such, so you can remember them. She put Preach's family Bible in the bag, too."

"Where are you taking me, Mr. Parker?" Kalina could feel her stomach churning from hunger and now from apprehension of the unknown.

"I's been told to take you straight to the train station. We didn't want you to miss today's train. We got a few hours though. I'll stop and get you something to eat if you're hungry," the old man said sorrowfully.

"Why can't I go home?" Kalina asked, trying to stop the flood of tears as they began pouring down her cheeks.

"Well, the church is taking over the house to recover some of the money. I don't know who is going to buy it though. Most people don't want to move in a place where something that tragic happened," Mr. Parker guided his long weathered car down the two-lane highway to Spartanburg.

"The train you catching gon' take you to Washington, DC, and sit awhile. I hear you won't have to get off. It changes tracks or something, then it'll take you to Philadelphia," he began to explain.

"Why would the church sell my house, Mr. Parker?"

"They seem to think your daddy took a lot of money from the church. Some say it was to send you to school in Philadelphia. Maybe you can still go when you get there," he kept his eyes fixed on the road.

"For what it's worth, I don't believe Preach had anything to do with that missing money. I still think it's funny how nobody missed it until Preach was dead.

"My father never stole anything from anybody. My mother used to fuss because he used to give everything away. She said we could never have anything because Daddy would just give it away. That doesn't sound like my father," she protested.

"I has to agree with you on that one, young lady. But, the argument is that what Preach did two weeks ago didn't sound like him either."

The tears continued to flow, but her heart was stiffening up with courage. If no one in this town wanted her, she didn't want them either.

"I wishes you well, child. I hope you can make a good life for yourself. Find yourself a good man. Trust me. If you find a good man that loves you more than life itself, you will want for nothing.

That's what hurt your daddy so much. He loved your mother more than life itself. He would have done anything for her. You'll do good to find someone like that and have your own family. Then you won't be alone. It ain't good being alone. I can tell you that."

Kalina thought about Rudy and Mandy. Was that the kind of love Rudy had for Mandy? He was going to marry his baby's mother and work in a mill to take care of her. Maybe Mandy was the lucky one. But, then Kalina wondered if she wanted a man that would love her enough to kill her the way her father had murdered her mother.

Her stomach was no longer growling as she sat anxiously on the train holding onto her belongings. She was afraid to get up to go to the bathroom, eyeing all of the other passengers with distrust. She didn't want to lose any of what she had left. Her foot tapped the floor furiously as she tried to stop thinking about it. She was still in shock. The church folk had not only kicked her out of her home, but they wouldn't even let her see it one last time – not the red and blue swing set that sat between the apple trees, nor her white four-poster bed with the white bedding and the beautiful lace curtains on her window. What about her father's new toy, his console color television? What about all the pictures in the trunk under the window in her parents' room? What about her mother's antique vanity? Kalina flinched as she had memories of blood splattered on the mirror where she had last seen her mother rolling her hair for the next day. The next day her mother had left early for work. Though she worked at the same school that Kalina attended, they had missed each other due to early dismissal.

Kalina understood how Mr. Parker felt and why he carried his cane scarred with the love of a growing, teething puppy. Old Duke was all he had left to show him some love. Kalina had no one. She fought back the impulse to scream. She opened the shoebox

Ms. Rosemarie had given her for the train ride. It had pieces of crispy fried chicken and slices of pound cake. Kalina nibbled on a chicken leg. She decided to save the rest for later.

Waiting in Washington had tired her out pretty well. She had fallen asleep by the time they left the country's capital. Before she knew it, the conductor was nudging her.

"You've got two more stops after this next one, young lady. We'll be arriving in Wilmington in about 20 minutes. From there, we'll stop at 30th Street Station in Philadelphia, and then a few minutes after that we'll be stopping at North Philadelphia. Do you have any bags checked?"

"Yes, sir, I have one," Kalina answered the tall skinny Black man with the big hat.

"Well, let me give you a little advice. Get downstairs quick and get it. Things have a way of walking away from that place. Is someone picking you up?" he asked politely.

"Yes, sir," she answered, not sure if she should have.

"Good. That's not a station a young girl should be hanging around. You understand?" He smiled and she nodded. He then tipped his hat to her and went rocking down the aisle chatting with the other passengers as the train sped along..

Kalina turned to look at the landscape. There was a lot more movement of people than she had ever seen before. There were more buildings, more cars, and the air was getting grayer and thicker. Kalina's excitement about moving North had been sapped right out of her. With all that had happened, she kept wondering why a stranger would warn her about the station. She could only hope that was the least of her worries. Her Aunt Mazetta was picking her up from the station. She wrapped herself in her own arms and longed to be hugged by someone else. Maybe she wasn't totally alone after all.

CHAPTER TWO

Kalina found her way down the stairs of the busy station. There were people everywhere, some bumping into her without so much as a glance. Kalina held onto her little canvas tote bag and shoebox hoping she would find the bathroom before she had an accident. Her stomach was hurting from holding her urine so long. The redcap had told her where to find it and her luggage. His voice had been kind, but the way he looked at her made her feel dirty. She couldn't explain why, but she knew there was no need for further conversation with him. He might have taken it the wrong way.

She went through a big room with long benches. People were scattered everywhere. She noticed some greeted each other with hugs and smiles. She noticed others who hurried in and out of the station. It looked like everyone had some place to go. She walked across the marble floors and marveled at the huge antique clock in the middle of the station. She found the area where there were trolleys of baggage being unloaded into a corner. A man was standing among them looking at tickets, but some people were just grabbing the bags and leaving. She wanted to get her bag, but she had to go to the bathroom really, really bad.

She found the ladies room at the other end of the baggage area.

As she opened the door, the stench made her stop momentarily. There was an old woman whose clothes looked like they had never been washed. She grinned at Kalina with a toothless grin. Kalina scooted by her warily and checked the stalls. The first two were too filthy for her. The third was just bearable. She stepped in on a floor that was wet. She was hoping it was from a splashing toilet and not one that had overflowed. She carefully hoisted herself over the toilet and let a stream out that seemed to never end. She was beginning to feel the relief in her aching loins as she waited for the stream to finally stop. She hurried out of the stall and to the sinks that were old and dirty with rust spots. She looked for the soap, but the dispensers weren't working. She felt grimy. She rinsed her hands in the water and saw linen towels hanging in large loops. She started to dry her hands, but she noticed the towels were stained. She shook her hands dry and hurriedly went to the baggage area.

At first she couldn't remember the color of the bag Mr. Parker had brought with her. She stood staring at the pile of luggage that had dwindled quite a bit since she went to the bathroom.

"Which one?" a man from behind her asked. "Which one is yours?"

Kalina turned to see he had on a uniform like the man she had seen earlier. She turned back to the bags and tried to remember. She only knew the bag she had come with had not belonged to her or her parents. Then she spotted it. It was an old rectangular greenish-blue bag that was bulging.

"That one," she eagerly pointed to it.

"Let me see your ticket," the man said.

She gave it to him. He stepped across other bags and compared the ticket.

"That ain't it," he answered.

"Mine looks like that, I think," Kalina said indecisively.

"You think. You don't know what bag you packed?" he asked suspiciously.

"No, sir. I didn't pack it. My neighbor did," she answered as panic began to rise in her throat.

"It looks like that, though?" The man shook his head.

"I think so," Kalina was trying to fight tears. The man looked at her and then back at the leftover baggage. He started comparing tickets.

"You can look, too," he said. "This is your ticket number." He showed her the red numbers in the corner of the ticket.

"You from the South?" he said, more of a statement than a question.

"Yes, sir," Kalina said, beginning to look at every bag.

"Yeah, I could tell by the way you are drawling," he stopped at a big green suitcase that was just as beat up as the first one she had pointed out.

"This it?"

Kalina recognized it.

"Yes, sir. That's it." She was relieved not to have lost something else.

He looked at the ticket and then looked back at her and nodded. He lifted the bag and put it in front of her.

"You need a cab?" he asked.

"No sir. My aunt is picking me up." Kalina looked around for a familiar face and didn't see any.

"Well, you need to move on from here. Another train is coming and they gon' be bringing more baggage real soon." He walked away and began to put the rest of the bags in some sort of order.

Kalina lifted the bag as best she could and moved out of his way. It was heavy. She was hoping Ms. Rosemarie had packed some of her favorite things. She was hoping she put, at the very least, one of her dolls in it. Kalina loved her dolls. She sadly imagined how lonely they must be sitting in a dark room all by themselves with no one to touch them and keep the dust off them.

Kalina dragged the bag to the big area with the benches and found a bench where no one else was sitting. She opened her shoebox and nibbled on a piece of pound cake. She wondered if Mazetta had forgotten she was coming.

"Lord, have mercy!" a woman said, approaching her. "You have to be Kalina!" The woman had on tight red pants and a loose polyester blouse with crazy red and black designs. Her hair was bright red and so was her lipstick. Kalina thought she looked like a bad cartoon character.

"I'm your Aunt Mazie. Don't you remember me, child?"

"Yes, ma'am." Kalina recognized the freckled face and her pointy nose as the woman walked closer.

"Look at you. All grown up," Mazetta said as she hugged her tight. "And pretty, too. I'm going to have to keep the boys away from you."

Kalina was happy to be hugged, but she didn't enjoy the saturated odor of cigarettes and the alcoholic perfume on the woman and in her clothes.

"What you got there?" Mazetta took the shoebox from her. "Something in here smelling good. Who packed you a lunch?"

"Ms. Rosemarie," Kalina answered eyeing her shoebox. She suddenly wanted to take it back from Mazetta.

"Ooh, I can't wait to taste what's in here. One thing I did like about the South when I visited your mother was the food. Not hers, of course. We all know Charlotte couldn't cook worth a darn," Mazetta laughed.

"Are you all right, child? I couldn't believe it when they called to tell me she was dead. And I sho' couldn't believe it when they told me it was Preach that killed her. Now that's a man I never thought would a killed her. There was one or two up here that woulda gladly did it, had she not married Preach and moved out of Dodge.

"Is that your bag?" she asked.

Kalina nodded wondering why men would want to kill her mother.

"Well, get it and come on. Here, I'll carry this little bag for you. I can't help you with that big bag. My back wouldn't like it. Plus, I gotta go to work tonight and I'm not pulling no night shifts with a bad back." Mazetta took the tote bag off Kalina's shoulder and left Kalina to try to lift the big bag by herself.

"What you got in that thing anyway?" Mazetta grinned. "The whole house? Girl, I know you must be upset. Preach had built you and your momma a nice little house. You had some nice things, too. I guess they gonna sell it all to get they money back, huh?"

Kalina kept struggling with the bag, following Mazetta through the huge revolving glass doors.

"You got some money, child?" Mazetta asked.

Kalina thought about the two twenties in the tote bag. Ms. Rosemarie hadn't thought to give her one of her pocketbooks, not unless they were in the luggage.

"No, ma'am," she answered.

"Then, I guess we gon' take the bus." Mazetta led her past the taxi stand and down to the street.

"We gotta cross over. We better wait for the light since you dragging that big old thing. You bring some of your mama's things for me? She had the prettiest clothes. Every time I came down there, she would give me something. I still got a few of those things. She had so much stuff. I bet them old church gals having a ball with them now."

Mazetta was talking while Kalina was trying to catch her wind.

The bag was heavy. She could have used a little help. She followed her aunt across the wide street and noticed the sign that said Broad Street. She had heard her mother mention that street.

"Ever heard of Joe Frazier?" Mazetta asked.

"Yes, ma'am. He's a boxer, right?" Kalina asked between breaths.

"He works out right over there. That's his gym."

"For real?" Kalina looked around at the dirty street and wondered why someone that famous would work there.

"For real," Mazetta said. "We got lots of famous people around here. They love Philly. You gonna love it, too."

"I hope so," Kalina was beginning to understand why her mother had been so opposed to her coming here. The C bus came and a boy that was getting on behind her helped her with the bag. She turned to thank him, but he stepped over her and kept going.

Mazetta had dropped some coins into the metal box and the driver had given her two strips of paper. She handed one to Kalina.

"Hold on to your pass. We gon' need it for the next bus. We'll be home soon, though."

After the second bus, Kalina followed her aunt down a narrow downtrodden street. Now she understood what her mother had referred to as rowhouses. They were all attached. Some of them looked dangerously empty. There were people everywhere. There were lots of cars, old cars that looked abandoned parked on the sidewalk. There was trash everywhere. Kalina was relieved when Mazetta produced a set of keys and started up three marble slabs that were no longer aligned. She was about to put a key in when an old woman stuck her head out of a street level window next door.

"That your niece, Mazetta? The one from down south?" the dark wrinkly face woman with the wiry gray hair asked.

"This her. Kalina, this is Mrs. I'm in Everybody's Business. 'Cause, I didn't tell you nothing about my niece. Beware of this old coot. She busy selling moonshine and numbers from this window.

"Where your customers at? Ain't you got nobody to keep you busy?" Mazetta went ahead and stuck the key into the lock on the smudged and grimy door that used to be white.

"You be careful, child, of that old drunk she married to. He probably gonna try to climb on you as soon as her back is turned," the old woman yelled. "And my name is Lizzie. You need something, you come over here. You hear?"

Kalina nodded and dragged her bag in behind Mazetta. The first thing she noticed was the smell of urine and old grease. She covered her mouth as her eyes widened with disgust and amazement. There was trash and clothes everywhere. She saw something small darting along the baseboards.

"Come on in," Mazetta said cheerfully. "It ain't much, but it's your new home. It'll be good to have another woman in the house. You any good at cleaning?"

Kalina was afraid to leave her tote bag opened. She saw Mazetta drop it on one of the sticky filthy couches that was crowded into the living room. She grabbed it and tied the handles together tightly. The place was crawling with roaches.

"Have a seat," Mazetta said, looking around for a space that wasn't covered with something. Then she pointed to the kitchen. "Take a load off. I know you're tired from all that traveling. You didn't leave 'til late last night, right?"

"Yes, ma'am." Kalina dusted what looked like sugar off the wooden chair. The spokes in the legs were hanging out of it, so she sat down gingerly. She was exhausted, but too afraid to relax. She looked at the pile of dishes in the sink and saw leftover food and food wrappers stacked on top of each other.

"You know, Doc and them boys don't do no chores around here. And those little ones, all they do is make a mess. You'll meet them all soon. School will be out in a little while. They used to want to follow me down south to meet your mama. I guess they never will now," she said sadly.

"How you feeling, Kalina?" Mazetta touched her shoulder. "I know this a lot for someone like you to take in. But, you gon' meet some people been through a lot worse around here. I don't know if Charlotte told you, since she had gotten so uppity with her college education, but our daddy got killed right out there in that street. Some nigger shot him in the head arguing over a bottle of liquor. I'll never forget that. I guess we just got tragedy in our blood, is all."

Kalina sat silently as the roaches crawled freely over the kitchen table. One looked as if it was perched and drinking from a bowl of soggy cereal and spoiled milk. She wanted to jump up and run, but she didn't know where she would go. The people outside didn't look too friendly. She had heard more curse words in her short walk down the block than she had heard in her whole 17 years.

As if reading her mind, Mazetta told her where to find her room and the bathroom.

"We only got one bathroom, so if you want to take a bath or something you better do it before everybody gets home. They start getting in around 3 or 3:30. The older boys, well, they come in anytime. Jamal out of school, but Shandie still sticking with it. He says he is going to college like his Aunt Charlotte. I hope he does it. I hope Jamal don't drag him down. Shandie's smart like you. I hear you got a bunch of scholarships. You might get more now that you an orphan. You can at least get your social security check while you in school. When you get settled, you need to call them colleges and find out what you gotta do."

— 24 —

"Yes, ma'am," Kalina answered, getting the strength and the courage to go upstairs. She walked up the stairs gingerly through a path of clothes that were stacked on either side. She kept her tote bag tucked tightly under her arms. She went down to the end of the hall of the tiny house and found the door to her room. She could barely get it opened. There was a bed in the way.

The stench from the room hit her hard in the face. She saw the urine stained sheets on one of the beds. There were two twin beds stuffed into the room together. The only saving grace she found with the room was that it had built-in bookshelves that went from top to bottom on one side. But, they were lined with junk and toys and food and more junk. She shook her head.

Mazetta had acted like she was rich whenever she came to visit. Kalina had thought by the way Mazetta had behaved and had dressed that she lived in some real fine place in Philadelphia. She would have never guessed she was coming from something this poor, filthy, and insane. It was unbelievable that anyone with a right mind existed like this.

Kalina, still holding her bag, walked across the hall to the bathroom. The toilet, which appeared to have never been cleaned, had turds in it. She took some of the cheap toilet paper and used it to touch the handle, flushing the toilet. The waste flushed slowly down though some of it still floated back into the bowl. She shuddered.

The sink was a lot like the one in the public bathroom at the station. Where there should have been bright stainless steel, there were rust spots, and the porcelain sink was a big yellow and brown stain with scum and bits of toothpaste. She jumped when she saw a roach crawling across one of the toothbrushes that sat in a dirty glass. She looked in the mirror at her own expression and it was clouded with scum and splashes that had hardened with time. She decided at that moment that God was punishing her for her hateful ways in the past. She promised Him at that moment that if he delivered her, she would never look down on anybody else.

"Kalina, Kalina," she heard her Aunt Mazetta call from the bottom of the stairs.

"Yes, ma'am," Kalina walked rigidly back down the dark, smelly hallway across carpet that had stiffened with grime beneath her little black heels. She wanted to take those shoes off so bad, but she was afraid she would either step on a roach or get some dreaded fungus if she did.

"I have got to go to work soon, and ain't much food in the house. There's a corner store that sells sandwiches if you want something. I'm going to eat the last of your chicken so I won't be hungry when I get there. You only got one piece of pound cake left. I guess I'll eat that, too."

"Okay," Kalina said, not really wanting to let go of the food, but not feeling like she had much choice.

"You got money for a sandwich?" Mazetta asked.

"I might have a couple of dollars," Kalina answered, remembering she had told her Aunt that she didn't have any money. She was going to have to get better at lying.

"That's enough. You should be able to get a pop, too. Don't stop and talk to nobody. Everybody around here wants something. And I wouldn't wear them pretty clothes back outside, they might think you got more money than you do. Take only what you need with you, just in case somebody decides to take it," Mazetta advised.

"Yes, ma'am," Kalina answered. "Aunt Mazie, do you have a washing machine?"

"Yes, it's downstairs in the basement. There's a dryer down there, too. There might be some soap powder left. Doc and me gotta go shopping. We've just about let everything run out. But, you welcome to use it."

"Thank you," Kalina went back down the hall and squatted over the toilet. This time she found soap, but it was dark and grimy and hard like it hadn't been used in a while. She let the water run over it until it softened, washing away some of the grime before washing her hands. She looked around for a towel to dry her hands, but they were all dirty.

Keeping her clothes on, she made her way down into the basement passing her aunt at the kitchen table greedily eating her day old food. It looked as if there had been a century of junk collected down there. She started thinking about rats. There was one light bulb and it hung over the washer and dryer. She pulled the long string hanging from the chain and the light came on. She was thankful for that. She opened the washer and found it empty. She looked in a big brown bag sitting next to the dryer and found an unopened box of soap powder. Finally, luck was on her side. She went back upstairs, pulled the linens off both beds and carried them downstairs. They were going to take two loads, so she started the first one. She was happy to hear the water running into the washing machine. It was working. She went back upstairs and looked underneath the bathroom sink. There was a container of Comet and a piece of a blue sponge. She cleaned the sink as best she could.

Going back to the top of the stairs, she said, "Aunt Mazie, do you have a clean towel?"

"No, but I got a new pack of those dish towels. You can use one of those if you want to."

Kalina cleaned herself as best she could and came back downstairs to get her suitcase. She still didn't know what was in it. She dragged it upstairs and placed it on the bed that didn't have pee stains and opened it. Ms. Rosemarie had placed her father's bible on top. She picked it up and kissed it.

"Thank you, Ms. Rosemarie," she whispered. She found a pair of jeans, some underwear and a t-shirt that said "I Am Somebody". She went back into the bathroom still wearing her little heels. She came back and went through the bag. It looked as if the woman had stuffed as much as she could into the bag of clothes from her dresser and the front of her closet. She knew what she had and what she didn't have. She had packed her a pair of sandals, a pair of slippers, and a pair of tennis shoes. Kalina couldn't fuss about that. At the bottom of the bag were five framed pictures that had once sat on the mantle piece in the living room, and that was it. That was Kalina's life in a nutshell – no yearbooks, no snapshots, no mementos from vacations, no souvenirs from school.

"I'm not going to be here, forever," Kalina encouraged herself. "All I have to do is go to college. I can live on campus somewhere." Maybe Penn she thought, as she fought not to hear her mother's dying words about affording the school. Kalina was afraid her mother had died because she had chosen such an expensive school.

"It was all about me," tears trickled down her face, "about me, Momma. That's what you said."

Kalina put her socks and tennis shoes on and went downstairs to check the clothes. The first load was finished, so she started the second. As she was coming back up the stairs, she was met by two wide-eyed, snotty-nosed kids.

"Are you our cousin from down south?" the little girl took her hand. "My name is Alina. My mama says she was naming me after you."

"It's good to meet you, Alina," Kalina wanted to take her hand back. The little girl's hand was clammy and sticky. "How old are you?"

"I'm six," Alina grinned. She was missing her two front teeth. This made Kalina smile and forget her little cousin's sticky hand.

"What's your name?" she looked at the little boy who was searching the kitchen table as if he were trying to find something to eat.

"Mike," he said curtly. "I'm eight. So don't be treating me like I'm some kind of baby."

"What grade are you in, Mike?" Kalina asked, expecting a smart answer from the dirty little boy with bald spots in his head.

"What's it to you?" he said.

"He's in the first grade," Alina said. "We're in the same class."

"She's lying!" he shouted accusingly.

"Then, what grade are you?" Kalina put her hands on her hip trying to be feisty as her mother would have called it.

"So, I'm in the first grade. I didn't start school on time," he sat hard in the chair and stared at the table hungrily. Kalina knew he couldn't find anything edible there.

"Are you hungry?" she asked him.

He nodded his head.

"Me, too," Alina said.

"What do you normally eat?" Kalina asked.

"Cereal," Mike answered. "But, there was none left this morning. Sometimes Jamal will bring us something from McDonalds or Roy Rogers. He'll be home soon. He always comes home to check on us."

"Okay," Kalina looked around helpless. "Why don't we ask your mom what's here that you can eat."

"She gone, fool," Mike answered, his voice dripping with rudeness.

"What did you call me?" Kalina was offended and walked toward the little boy who didn't back down.

"I called you a fool. Momma been gone. We saw her getting on the bus while we was walking home," Mike laughed.

"We were walking home," Kalina corrected him.

"You was walking nowhere, fool."

Kalina turned her head and thought this was getting better every minute. She started back up the stairs and Alina took her hand again.

"Can you get us something to eat?" Alina asked. "I'm hungry."

Kalina thought about the twenty dollar bill in her pocket. She only had one more and she didn't know how long she was going to last there without any money. She was going to have to apply for Social Security as soon as possible like her Aunt Mazie had advised. Then she looked into the little ones' eyes and saw hunger, real hunger, for the first time in her life. She had always turned the television channel when they had shown those starving little children from Africa. But, now she was staring at real hungry children in America, and they were related to her.

"You and your brother stay here," she pointed at Alina and then Mike. "I'm going to the corner store."

She opened the door and realized she had no key to get back in.

"Don't you lock me out," she said. "I'll knock four times and you let me back in."

"What?" Mike shook his head.

"I can count," Alina volunteered. "One, two, three, four."

"That's right," Kalina said cheerfully. "You are a smart girl."

Kalina stepped out onto the slanted marble step and pulled the door behind her. She heard one of the kids put the chain on the door.

"Well, how you like living in filth?" Kalina was startled by the voice from the window.

"It's me, Ms. Lizzie," the woman hung out of the window. Kalina noticed it didn't have a screen.

"What do you mean?" Kalina was not going to get caught talking about her own aunt with a stranger.

"You know what I mean. Look at you, clean and pretty. Don't let Mazetta bring you down to her level. She's trash," the woman made a clicking sound.

"Could you tell me where the corner store is?" Kalina thought it best to change the subject.

"It's right there. Be careful with your money. Most of these idiots you see out here is druggies. They will knock you over the head for a nickel. So don't be flashing nothin' in that store over there. Keep it to yourself."

"Yes, ma'am." Kalina crossed the tiny street and maneuvered between some old cars; one was sitting on some concrete blocks. She walked past a couple of older men. One whistled at her as she walked passed them to the store's door.

"I got something for you at my store," someone yelled. She kept walking. She squeezed into the small store past a bunch of children counting out pennies for candy. She followed the smell to the side of the store where a man in a dirty white hat and apron was standing behind a counter. She looked up at a sign that listed hoagies, cheesesteaks, and fries. Mazetta was right. They were cheap enough to feed her and the kids for less than five dollars. She ordered hoagies and fries and picked up a couple of Frank's orange sodas. On the way home, she stayed on the side of the street opposite the man who had whistled at her.

She knocked four times, and an excited Alina opened the door.

"I counted the knocks," Alina squealed. "I counted all four of the knocks."

"So what," Mike strode into the room. "Just give me something to eat," he demanded.

"Hold your horses," Kalina said forcefully. "Nobody eats anything until you wash your hands."

"What?" both kids looked shocked.

"Wash your hands," Kalina commanded.

"Where? With what?" Mike was bewildered.

"You do know what soap is?" Kalina asked in amazement.

"Yeah, I know what soap is, you down south fool," Mike said.

"You keep talking to me like that little boy and you are going to starve to death," Kalina said, not believing her ears.

"Where's the soap?" the little boy answered.

"In the bathroom. Now go, both of you," Kalina pointed up the stairs. "You have to shake your hands dry."

While the kids were upstairs, she cleared the table. She tried to find a dishcloth, but could only find some napkins from a previous fast food meal. She used them to wipe the table off scooting the roaches in the process. She wet the ones left over and tried to make the table look clean. It was almost hopeless. She opened the sandwiches and sodas just as the children came down stairs. Alina was all grins.

"Look at the table," she told Mike. "Have you ever seen all of the table at one time before?"

"Stop acting silly, girl! You seen the table clean before," Mike sounded embarrassed. The two children pulled their chairs up to the table and were about to grab the food.

"No," Kalina yelled. "You have to say grace first. Now bow your heads."

The two children looked at each other.

"Don't you go to church?" she asked. They both shook their heads.

"Oh," Kalina was surprised. "At any rate, let's take ten seconds and thank God for the food."

"God, thank you for this food that we are about to eat for the nourishment of our bodies. Amen," she looked up and motioned toward the food. She watched the kids eat it hungrily. Neither of them had complained about what she had ordered, they just ate. She ate hungrily, too. The vinegar and oil, the salt and pepper and the oregano and onions weren't usually what she had on a sandwich, but it was good. She ate the whole thing, and hers was big. She had split one between the kids and they had eaten their half sandwiches. The fries weren't bad either. When they had finished, she made them help her clean off the table and put it all in the trash bag that sat in the middle of the floor near the sink. They looked at her with bewilderment, but did what she told them to do. Then she went back downstairs to check on the clothes.

"Where are all the towels?" she asked them. "Go get them." When they saw her coming up the stairs with clean sheets and blankets, they ran to get the towels. For the next few hours, Kalina and kids cleaned their room. She learned a lot about the other household members, and she learned which one of them had the loose bladder. It was Mike. For some reason, Mike didn't start school until this year and one of the reasons was because he had problems going to the bathroom.

Kalina wasn't looking forward to sharing a bed with the kids, but at least she could put the little girl between them.

Kalina was going down stairs with a load of the kids' clothes. She was planning to bathe both of them before sharing a bed and wanted their clothes to be clean. That's when she ran into Jamal and Shandie.

Jamal was tall and lean. His clothes didn't match his environment. He was clean. His pants had starched creases in them. His shirt was stark white. He wore a green baseball cap that had the

Philadelphia Eagles logo on it. "He is fine," thought Kalina. Her cousin was real cute. The girls in her class would have fought over him.

"What's your name?" he said in a deep baritone voice.

"Kalina," she smiled, but he didn't return the smile.

"Well, Kalina," he said, neither friendly nor unfriendly, but very seriously. "I've got one rule."

"What's that?" she said, trying hard not to let him know that she was thrilled by his looks.

"You and your nappy headed little cousins, stay out of my room. I have to share it with Shandie, but he knows the rules. What's mine is mine. And my room is my room and off limits to everybody. You understand?" His dark brown eyes were cold. Kalina suddenly forgot about his looks and decided that he wasn't a very likeable person.

"I understand," she said. He walked past her, and then turned around. He walked into the kitchen and saw that the table was cleared.

"You did that?" he asked.

"Yes," she almost followed it with sir, but thought he's not much older than she.

"Good, good. Maybe you can do something about those kids. Keep them away from me, you hear," he pointed his finger in her face.

"I thought you liked them," she said. "They said you feed them after school."

"I do. Doesn't mean I like them," he went up the stairs.

"I'm Shandie. I'm not as mean as my older brother," the fifteen-year old boy stood taller than Kalina, too. He had braids in his hair.

"I like your braids," she said lamely.

— 34 —

He touched his braids. "My girl does my hair. She can braid yours, too. If you want," he said. "Jamal put some food in the fridge if you hungry. But, from the smell of things you already have that covered."

"I went to the corner store," Kalina smiled, feeling proud that she had ventured out on her own the first day.

"Don't be doing that," Jamal said, coming back down the stairs. "You stay out of those streets. It ain't safe out there for no country bumpkin." His eyes scaled her entire frame. Kalina held onto the laundry tightly and went into the kitchen.

"Why you gon' call the girl out of her name for?" she heard Shandie talking to his brother.

"She better learn fast, this ain't the country. The girl's living in the Badlands now. This ain't no joke. You can't be giving her no false impressions. Not around here. And, you, you keep her out of my room," she heard the door close as she was going down into the basement.

Kalina came back and sat down at the kitchen table as Shandie made himself a peanut butter sandwich.

"Trust me, I don't have any need to come into your room," Kalina said. Shandie nodded his head and began to eat his sandwich.

As the day progressed, Kalina learned quickly that Jamal wasn't the only one with special rules. Doc and Mazetta had a unique relationship. She worked long hours in a cafeteria-styled restaurant garnering meager pay and tips. He drank and smoked up the money she made. The kids went without, and the last thing on Mazetta's mind was anything or anyone but her man.

The next day when Kalina met Doc, she wanted to throw up. He grabbed her and kissed her on the mouth with his stinky, chicken-poop smelling breath. She pushed him away. Then he grinned at her a huge toothless grin. He was light-skinned, like Aunt Mazetta, with a huge Afro. He wore a polyester suit that used to be white and a pair of black shoes that had never seen shoe polish. She wiped her mouth and ran up the stairs as quickly as she could.

"Now why you go and do that?" she heard Mazetta ask Doc. "Now the girl gon' be afraid of you. That's just what old Lizzie want."

"It was just a friendly kiss, Mazie. Baby, you know I didn't mean nothing by it. Just trying to make the girl feel welcome. Tell Lizzie Bitch that," his words were slurred as he swaggered toward Mazetta with his arms open. She ran into them like he was golden.

Kalina went into the bathroom to brush her teeth and wash her face. The fact that he was in the house at all made her skin crawl. She instinctively knew that she was going to have to avoid him at all costs, which was going to be hard in this little house.

Kalina walked into the kids' room to find them sitting there quietly.

"What's wrong?" she asked sitting next to Alina and giving her a hug.

"Daddy's home," Mike said, staring listlessly at the wall.

"Yeah, he is," Kalina looked from one child to the next. They had both changed completely.

"Why don't you go say hi to him?" Kalina wasn't sure if that was good advice, but he was their father.

"No," they both answered emphatically.

"Why not?"

Alina pulled away from Kalina's hug and began rocking back and forth on the edge of the bed.

"He hurts us," Mike said. "He's going to hurt you, too."

"What do you mean?" Kalina saw tears in Mike's eyes.

"I wish he was dead," Mike said.

"Don't say that, Mike. Don't ever say that," Kalina thought

about her own father.

"Does he spank you?" Kalina thought Mike deserved a spanking every once in awhile.

"He just needs to be dead," Mike said and laid his head on his pillow. Alina crawled up behind him. She had laid her head on the same pillow.

"Are you hungry?" Kalina noticed how late it had gotten.

"We'll wait 'til Jamal gets home," Mike answered.

Kalina walked over to the window and saw the garbage strewn street before her and heard people yelling and cussing at each other without any thought or consideration. She wondered what she was doing there. What lesson was she supposed to learn here? Her mother had always told her every difficult situation was another lesson learned.

She went back to her bed and lay down, too. She watched the kids stare off into nowhere quietly. She wondered what they were daydreaming, though she knew what Mike was thinking – he really wanted to see his father dead.

Kalina began to follow suit with the kids. When Doc came home, which was only two or three times a week and most definitely on payday, she stayed in her room. Jamal and Shandie disappeared when he was in the house, too. The only exception was that Jamal still brought them food every day whether Doc was there or not.

One day, one Doc-free day, Mike came down with a fever. School was out, and the three of them had stayed locked up in the house all day. Shandie and Mazetta had kept promising Kalina that one of them would take her to the Social Security Office on Broad Street and even show her where the library was on Erie. But, it had been almost four weeks and neither of them had had the time. The only store Kalina knew of was the corner store, and her forty dollars had dwindled down to about twelve and she desperately needed aspirin or something to break the boy's fever.

When she asked Mazetta about it, she said the boy needed Tylenol and that she would bring some home after work. Kalina was surprised that Mazetta didn't even go upstairs to check on Mike. Kalina found herself comparing Mazetta with her mother a lot. Her mother would have taken care of her before going to work. Her mother would have had Tylenol in the house. Kalina was beginning to hate Mazetta and beginning to hate herself more for not respecting and appreciating her own mother when she had her.

Kalina tried her best to keep Mike cool, but he was going from chills to fever too quickly. The boy was sick, really sick. She heard Shandie come in and ran down the hall. She was a few steps behind him when she heard the door close. She knocked on the door.

"Shandie," she called. "I need your help Shandie. Mike is sick. He's running a fever."

Shandie opened the door and Kalina stepped inside determined to get Mike the help he needed. She was shocked. It was like stepping into another world. The room was freshly painted in a warm beige color. There were bunk beds on one side of the room with matching quilts and pillows. On the other side of the small room was a leather sofa with matching end tables and lamps. In the middle of the floor was a heavy oak coffee table with little African figurines in the middle. Kalina looked up, saw an old style, but classic, ceiling fan, and in the window that faced the alleyway was an air conditioning unit. She looked down on the floor, which was tiled and clean, and saw an oriental rug in its middle. She gasped. The closet door was slightly open and there sat a huge garbage bag of what looked liked twigs and dried leaves. Shandie saw her eyes on the bag and hastily closed the closet door.

"You don't have roaches," she said.

"We do, just not as many as the rest of the house. We try to keep it clean and sprayed down," Shandie took her by the arms and started to escort her out of the room. As he opened the door, Jamal was coming in with a brown grocery bag.

"What the fuck is she doing in here?" Jamal took one hand and shoved Shandie back.

"Let me explain. Let me explain," Shandie was holding up both hands. Jamal put the bag down and reached for Kalina. Shandie grabbed him first.

"Mike is sick! She was looking for some help. Just give her some Tylenol. She be gone. She ain't got nobody to tell and nothing to say," Shandie spit all that out in one breath.

Kalina watched Jamal as his breathing began to calm down. She wondered if he had actually grabbed her, would she still be alive?

He walked past both of them and opened a drawer. He pulled out a bottle. "I don't know if you supposed to give these to kids, but Mike is a big guy. Try giving him one. Now get out."

Kalina took the bottle and backed into the hallway. She wasn't an idiot. There was definitely something illegal going on in that room. She had never seen it, but the kids at school had joked about smoking weed. That must be it. How else could he afford all those nice things?

Kalina was on her way down the stairs to get Mike some water when she heard Doc come in the door. She wanted to go back and knock on the door again to ask Shandie to go get the water for Mike. But, Jamal was in there and he had just literally put the fear of death in her. She decided to take her chances with Doc.

"Hi," she said as she walked down stairs. He leaned against the back of the living room sofa, and a slow toothless grin overtook his face.

"Hi, yourself, Luscious," he cupped his crotch with his hand.

Kalina tried to ignore the lewd gesture. She went straight to the kitchen and took a heavy plastic cup out of the cabinet.

"You keeping it pretty clean in here," Doc said, following her into the kitchen. "Your daddy shoulda killed your momma a long time ago. I ain't afraid to eat in here no more. My other bitches keep a house a little better than Mazie."

Kalina ignored him. Ms. Lizzie had already told her one day as she was coming in from the store why Doc wasn't home every night. It appeared that other women, not just Mazie, thought the man was a great catch.

"I said…" She felt his breath on the back of her neck first, then his hardness as he pressed himself against her pinning her against the sink. She let the cup finish filling up with water and turned swiftly throwing the water in his face. She pushed past him to run upstairs taking the cup with her so she could get water from the bathroom.

"Bitch," he yelled. "You gon' be mine, you little hussy! You gon' be mine!"

Kalina nursed Mike back from the fever, but he was still a little gray around the gills. She told everybody in the house that something was still wrong with Mike. She asked her Aunt Mazetta to take him the doctor. But, nobody listened.

That Friday she was struggling to get Mike to eat something. He was eating less and less each day. She was really worried and was wondering who could help her. She decided to go to Ms. Lizzie. She opened the front door and there stood Doc. She turned to run up the stairs and she could hear him running behind her. He grabbed her right foot and she fell up the stairs hitting her chin, but that didn't stop her. She took her left foot and kicked him. It landed in his face. Though her foot landed pretty hard, he was so drunk it didn't faze him. The only thing he wanted was her. The two of them struggled on the stairs. She fought him as he ripped at her clothes. Finally, she kicked him where it really hurt and he let go. She ran up the stairs and barricaded herself and the kids in their room.

Kalina sat there for hours waiting to hear her Aunt Mazie come in the house. She could always tell when she was coming in because everybody on the street knew her and everybody had something fresh to say to her. Kalina stood up and peered out onto the simmering hot street. It was even hotter in the room where she and kids sat with the door closed and no fan at all. She considered the comfortable room down the hall, but knew that was completely out of the question. Kalina stripped down to a pair of shorts and a loose pajama top. She reasoned she would dress back in her jeans before going back down stairs. She had already stripped the kids down to their bottoms. She fanned them and herself to keep some kind of breeze going in that hot darkening room.

She lay her head down on the pillow and the heat lulled her to sleep. She was startled awake by a loud noise.

"Kalina. Kalina. Bring your ass out here now," Mazetta was pounding on the door.

Kalina sat up rubbing her eyes. She automatically walked to the door to let her aunt inside. As she opened the door, her aunt snatched her out of the room.

"Aunt Mazie," Kalina tried to remove her aunt's hands from her collar, but the woman was stronger than she looked. She dragged Kalina down the hall and shoved her toward the stairs. Kalina was able to grab the banister and balance herself before she fell forward. She looked up just in time to capture her aunt's fist in her right eye.

"My God, Aunt Mazie!" Kalina put her hands up to block the fury of fists coming her way and ran down the stairs straight into Doc.

"You put your hands on my man. You little, bitch. I brings you in here and gives you a roof over your head," the woman started bouncing around in a stance not too unlike Joe Frazier or Muhammad Ali. Kalina ran for the door. At first, the door didn't want to cooperate, but she finally managed to get it open and ran down the marble slabs.

"Run, child, run," Ms. Lizzie yelled at her when she hit the steps. "They's crazy. I told you they's crazy."

Kalina ran down the street as fast she could to get further and further away from the nasty curses her aunt spewed from behind her. She must have run five or six blocks before Kalina realized she had no money, no shoes and no bra. She looked around the dark streets and kept moving. She was afraid to stop and stay in one place for one second. Cars blew at her. Men tried to stop her to talk to them. Some tried to grab her, but she was quicker than they were. She was scared. She was lost in a city, and the farthest she had been since getting to her aunt's was the corner store on Second Street.

Kalina made it to what looked like a major street and picked a direction. Although her feet were now bleeding from running across broken glass, she kept walking until she reached Broad Street. She stood at the light and chose a direction. She wasn't going to stop until she found a church.

CHAPTER THREE

"What you doing out here? It is cold out here. I don't care if it is summer. Where your clothes, child?" the old woman asked as she struggled up the concrete steps. Kalina had found refuge inside the darkened archway outside the big red church doors.

"Ain't nobody in there. It's in the middle of the night. And when those righteous ones show up tomorrow morning, all they gon' do is chase us off."

The old woman had newspapers coming out of her socks. She reminded Kalina of the scarecrow in the Wizard of Oz. Her hair was uncombed and sticking out from underneath a dirty baseball cap. Kalina couldn't really tell, but it looked like the old woman wore multiple layers of clothes.

"You actually in my spot. I sleeps here often. It's easy to hide up here in this alcove. Don't nobody be looking all the way up these stairs to bother nobody. That is, not usually." The old lady turned to see a man in a suit coming up the church steps.

"Oh, hell, Billy! What you want?" The old woman stood between him and Kalina.

"Etta, why don't you go back to the state store and get you

something to drink?"

"The state store closed. It's late. But, you wouldn't know nothing 'bout that," the old woman said facetiously. "Who you looking for?"

"I am not looking for you," he said.

"Leave that child alone," Etta took a step toward Billy as if she would protect her.

Billy pulled out a wad of money and let it drop on the church steps. Etta forgot Kalina and went chasing the dollar bills.

"Are you all right?" Billy offered Kalina his hand. "I'm not here to hurt you. I just noticed you on the street. I passed you a couple of times. I was trying to see if you were in trouble. And when I saw you come up here, I figured you were in trouble. Am I right?" His hand was still extended.

Kalina stared at him trying to figure him out, but she didn't know what kind of choice she had. She could continue to sit on the cold church steps in the dark or she could take this man's hand. She tried to see his eyes or even his face clearly, but it was too dark. His voice was all she had to go on and it sound kindly and genuinely concerned. She took his hand and he pulled her to feet. He looked down at her feet and shook his head. He picked her up and carried her down the stairs.

"Don't trust him. He ain't no good!" the old woman yelled.

"Don't listen to her," his voice was deep and mellow. His breath blew in her face, but it wasn't offensive. He walked to the white Mercedes. It was the same one she had noticed several times when she was walking. It had frightened her so she had kept heading toward a church, any church. He put her down and opened the door. The car was clean and smelled new. She worried about getting the blood from her feet on the carpet and the grime from the church steps on his upholstery.

"You're fine," he said, as if reading her mind. "We need to get those feet taken care of."

The music on his radio was jazz. She heard the announcer mention Temple University just as they were passing the school. She looked up at the tall buildings hovering over the neighborhood and wished she were in one – in a dorm safe and sound, anywhere but here, vulnerable and scantily clothed.

They kept driving until they turned down a street with huge older homes. The street was wider than her aunt's street and there were no cars on the sidewalks and no people outside. He pulled into a parking space and got out of the car. He opened the door for her and lifted her up the stairs and onto a porch in front of a door with a gold knocker. He didn't use the knocker, he rang the doorbell.

A beautiful, dark-skinned woman with long straight hair opened the door in a pink silk nightgown. At first, her eyes were filled with a smile, but when she saw Kalina, the smile faded.

"Look what I found," Billy's voice was upbeat. "Baby, I couldn't leave her on the street."

"Of course, not," the woman led them to a brightly lit kitchen.

"What happen to your feet?" the woman went into a room off the kitchen and came back with an old dishpan. She stuck it in the sink and began to run water.

"Go upstairs and get the witch hazel," she said to Billy in a deep and sultry voice. He left the room as ordered.

"My name is Elle," she said as she put Kalina's feet into the soothing warm water. "What happened to you?"

"My aunt beat me up," Kalina said, trying to choke back her tears of shame.

"Why?" Elle asked.

"She didn't say. But, I think she thinks it was because of her husband." Kalina bit her lip. She didn't want Elle to think she went after other people's men. "But, she was wrong," Kalina added. "He was trying to rape me and I fought him off. I think he told her it was the other way around."

"You think he told her you tried to rape him," Elle smiled just a little.

"No, I think he told her that I wanted him," Kalina answered. "No," Kalina added quickly. "I would never do that. Besides, he is twice my age, a drunk, a pothead and a tobacco fiend who hasn't had a bath in decades."

"He sounds real attractive," Elle brought Kalina a pack of frozen vegetables and held them to her face lightly. "Your aunt throws a really good punch."

Kalina nodded and let the cold bag mold itself to her face.

Billy came into the room with the witch hazel. Ms. Elle poured it into the water.

"Sit there a spell, and I'll go run you a hot tub of water. I guess this is it on the clothes?" Elle folded her arms.

"This is it," Kalina said as tears flowed freely, blurring her vision.

"I'll help you with the bath water," Billy put his arm around Elle and they walked out of the room all hugged up.

Kalina sat in the kitchen sobbing. She grabbed the napkins on the table to clean herself up. That was the first time she had cried so freely since she had come to Philadelphia. As she was mopping up her tears, the happy couple reappeared. Billy picked her up again and carried her up the stairs. He deposited her in the doorway of the bathroom. She looked around and cried even harder, this time from relief. The bathroom was covered in black and white tile with red, black, and white accessories. It was clean. The towels that lay across the radiator were clean. There was a brand new toothbrush still in the packaging. There was lotion and deodorant on top of the towels. And there were clothes, a brand new bra and panties, a pair of jeans, socks, a pair of slide-on slippers, and a t-shirt.

Kalina bathed and washed her hair. It had been weeks since she had felt that clean. She didn't know how she was going to re-pay this lovely couple. They didn't appear to need a housekeeper. Maybe they would let her cook for them. Then she realized how hungry she was. She stepped out of the bathroom with her dirty clothes rolled into a tight ball. She started down the stairs wondering what was next and she smelled it – hot food.

"Are you hungry?" Ms. Elle met her at the bottom of the steps with a paper bag. She held it out and Kalina deposited her clothes into the bag.

"We'll wash these tomorrow. Come on in and eat. Billy was running late for dinner anyway. I don't normally eat this late, but since it's Friday, I was giving him the benefit of the doubt," she kissed him on his head as she walked past him.

"Okay," Kalina liked hearing the word "tomorrow". Maybe that meant she had a place to sleep tonight. With that, Kalina dived into a real meal – roasted chicken with rice, greens, and cornbread. The food was so good she began crying again.

Neither Billy nor Elle mentioned the tears. They continued talking as if it were normal. Kalina cleaned herself up again and got up to clear her plate.

"Never mind the dishes. You have had a hard night. We'll talk things through tomorrow. You can sleep in my niece's room up-stairs on the right as soon as you go up the stairs. You were lucky. The two of you wear the same size clothes. I just bought those things for her. She's going away to school in a few weeks.

"I'll pay you back," Kalina offered. "If you could tell me how to get to a Social Security office, I can start collecting a check."

"Aren't you a little young for Social Security, sweetheart?" Billy's eyes were twinkling like a Santa greeting card.

"Both my parents are dead and I'm going to school in the fall, so I'm told I can collect Social Security benefits," Kalina wanted them to know she could carry some of her own expenses if she could get to the office.

"Well, let us worry about that tomorrow. Go get some sleep," Elle walked her to the bottom of the steps. Kalina stepped inside the niece's room, and it looked a lot like her room at home. The furniture was very similar. She walked over to the bed to find a big nightshirt with Yogi Bear on the front. How did they know she loved Yogi Bear and Boo Boo? She slid into the nightshirt and then slid into the bed. The sheets were soft and smooth and welcoming. It was another first for Kalina in a long time. God had sent her a pair of angels.

The next morning Kalina awakened to the smell of bacon, and even though she had eaten just before going to bed, she was famished. She ran into the bathroom and freshened up. She put on the clothes given to her the night before and tried not to seem too eager as she made her way into the kitchen. Billy was in a suit again, a different one from the night before. Elle was dressed in a pair of expensive slacks with a matching suit jacket, and some of the most beautiful jewelry Kalina had ever seen.

"Good morning," the happy couple greeted her. "Did you sleep well?"

"Yes, I did. Thank you so much. You don't know how much I appreciate your help," Kalina said, her eyes fogging up again.

"We were glad we could be of service," Billy put a plate of pancakes with strawberries, cream, and bacon in front of her. Her mouth watered. She dug in, and then looked up to see them watching her.

"I'm sorry," she said. "I forgot to say grace." She dropped her head and said grace.

"It's okay," Ms. Elle said. "We were just wondering..." She looked at Billy.

"We were just wondering if you would be willing to keep an eye on my father for me," Billy looked from Elle to Kalina.

"Of course," Kalina was happy to hear that she could contribute something.

"Don't be so quick to say yes," Ms. Elle answered. "You may regret it. He's a handful to say the least."

"What's he like?" Kalina asked. If it meant she didn't have to go back to Mazie's, she was willing to do just about anything.

———— ((•)) ————

Kalina was thrilled to see a different part of Philadelphia. She was impressed by the tall buildings downtown and all the people going here and there. She was especially awed by the number of people coming up the stairs from the underground trains. She had read about this Philadelphia, and this was what had attracted her to the University of Pennsylvania. There was William Penn standing atop their City Hall reigning over the masses of busy people and traffic. She was amazed as they drove around in a huge circle to get to his father's street. They went down a wide one-way street and turned into a small park area that was enclosed by a large u-shaped building. Billy pulled his white Mercedes into a small driveway and a man in a red suit with gold braids hurried to open her door. She smiled from ear to ear, no longer thinking about the dark bruises and cuts on her face from the night before.

Ms. Elle had tried to help her cover them up with makeup, but it only made it look like she was trying to hide something. She didn't care anymore. She wasn't down in the Badlands any more. She was in the upper crust section of Philadelphia. She could tell by how quaint and how clean the surrounding area was. She could tell by the high-end stores they had passed. They looked like the stores in the millions of magazines she had read growing up. She had arrived black, bruised, and orphaned, but she was here.

Billy said something jokingly to the doorman who tipped his hat to her and opened the glass doors to the building.

"Good morning, Mr. Sperling." A man from behind a tall desk nodded his head in their direction.

"Good morning," Billy said, waving at the man while moving toward the elevator to the far right. It had only one door, as the others on the left were doubled. He pulled out a key and stuck it in below the button. It opened immediately. As they stepped into the elevator, Kalina could hardly contain herself. The elevator was covered in mirrors with a small chandelier above them. Kalina covered the bruised part of her face and smiled at the other half of her face as she looked at her own reflection.

"Your father lives here?" she asked.

"Yes," Billy pushed the button that said P.

"I had no idea Black people lived like this," she stopped suddenly and looked back at Billy. She had automatically assumed his father was a Black man. Billy had that White look, but his voice was definitely that of a Black man. After all, she concluded, that although he was a very pale man, only a Black man would be with Ms. Elle.

Kalina looked at the fourteen numbered buttons below and decided to keep quiet and to stop assuming. Her mother had always scolded her for assuming and not getting the facts.

"Does that mean penthouse?" she asked giddily, beginning to feel like a silly little schoolgirl. She didn't want to give whoever this man was that impression. She was afraid he would reject her immediately.

"That it does," he smiled down at her. "Philadelphia doesn't have many high-rise residential buildings. Most people live in houses. But, Jordan likes it up here. I prefer being closer to the ground myself. I keep telling him this is too far up for the fireman to reach."

"Did he always live here?" Kalina wanted to know more about the man she was about to meet. Billy had been busy asking her all the questions on the way over here. She had told him everything, how her parents died, and how she had a scholarship to the University of Pennsylvania. She had left no stone unturned. She had even told him about the hateful people she had left behind. Billy had seemed really interested, and she hadn't talked about everything like that before, not even with Mazetta. Her story had been buried in her so deep that once she started talking, her need to say it out loud just erupted. She had even shared her two-week stay in the hospital that she thought she had barely remembered, but realized she remembered every detail.

The elevator door opened into a large foyer made of beige and brown marble. There were huge plants on both sides of the ivory double doors with large gold ornaments for handles and knockers. He opened the doors with a key, and she stepped into a world she could not have imagined no matter how hard she had dreamed. The living room itself was bigger than her whole house in South Carolina. She stood in the middle of it and drank in every nook and cranny. It was huge, but not overly furnished. There were a few pieces here and a couple of pieces huddled together there. What impressed her the most was the floor to ceiling windows that overlooked the city. She walked to the windows and stared out over the landscape. The world truly looked round from that vantage point.

She turned to see an older gentleman walking spryly down the spiral staircase. He was tall and thin, but stood straighter than some of the boys in her school. He was dressed in a black pin-stripe suit, with a white shirt and red tie. His skin was almost as dark as his suit and his hair almost whiter than his shirt. His hair was in a short afro that framed his face nicely. He walked over to his son and they hugged. The contrast was extremely noticeable. Billy was pale with gray eyes and loose wavy hair sprinkled with bits of gray. If this was his father, she wondered what Billy's mother looked like. Her parents were different shades of Black, too. But the contrast was not as stark as these two.

"Daddy, this is Kalina Denise Harris," Billy stood back and let his father gaze at her gradually.

Jordan started at her feet that were still in the white socks and slide on shoes. Then, he slowly viewed her until he reached her face.

"Doc did this?" he said, shaking his head.

"Doc's wife," Billy answered with a smirk on his face.

"You know Mazetta and Doc?" Kalina was instantly confused.

"Mazetta used to be one of my girls," Jordan rubbed his chin, "'til she fell for that drunken Doc. He used to work for me, too. I had to let them both go."

"You didn't tell me you knew my aunt and uncle," she said looking at Billy, who was heading for the door.

"Philadelphia is a small town," Jordan said as he sat down on a white leather sofa. "Come, sit and talk to me."

Kalina hesitantly sat down on the sofa putting a safe distance between them. Though Jordan sat tall and comfortable on the one end, the soft, buttery leather seemed to swallow her up.

"It's nice, isn't it," Jordan patted the sofa. "I brought it all the way from Italy. They have the best leather there, absolutely the best."

"You are really rich?" Kalina blurted it out before thinking that was not the right thing to say.

"I'm not wanting of anything," Jordan leaned back into the corner of the sofa so he could get a good look at her.

"You are not going to send me back to them, are you?" Kalina didn't know what to expect. She really hadn't expected there to be any connection between Mazetta and her new benefactors.

"No, you are too lovely to be living down in that chaos. You did good to get out in one piece from what I can tell. Your face is a mess," he crossed his legs.

"Well, you are not as old as I expected," Kalina was embarrassed that the words actually came out of her mouth, but she wasn't lying. Billy and Elle had told her Jordan needed to be cared for because he was up in age. She had expected to find an old man in a wheel chair or something in a little house in a decent neighborhood. She certainly did not expect to see a well-dressed businessman with a fresh manicure and able enough to run down a flight of stairs.

"Hmm," Jordan answered. "Do you always say what's on your mind?"

"Not always. I guess I'm a little unnerved. I didn't expect you to know Mazetta. Did you know my mother, too?" Again, she didn't know why she was saying things off the cuff. Just because he knew Mazetta didn't mean he knew her mother, too.

"Yes," Jordan clasped his hands around his knee. "I knew Charlotte, too. Your mother and your aunt were beautiful young girls, but neither of them as pretty as you."

Kalina reached up to hide the bad side of her face again.

"Leave it alone. It will heal all right. I'll have one of my grandsons come and look at it, but I think it's just a bruise. You seem pretty alert, so I doubt there is any other damage," Jordan leaned closer for a better look at her face.

"Now, I hear you are looking for a job," he was still looking at her face closely.

"Yes, sir, I can cook," using a recipe book, she kept that fact to herself, "and I can clean."

"I have a housekeeper who keeps the place pretty tidy. That's not hard with just me. The only thing she has to keep up with is the dust, the bathrooms, and the kitchen. She works different rooms each day to keep the dust down. But, the bathrooms that we regularly use and the kitchen are her main focus. She cooks my meals in bulk."

"How many rooms are in this place?" Kalina noticed a hallway with doors in one direction, two doors behind her, and then the stairs.

"There's about twenty-two. We have six bedrooms. Four of them are suites with their own dressing rooms or sitting rooms or both. Everybody has their own bathroom."

"Wow, who else lives here?" Kalina wanted to get up and explore.

"Just me," Jordan said as he stood up and waved her toward the stairs. She followed him. "My son and my grandsons stayed with me for awhile. But, as they grew up and went away to school, they left me by myself. Billy never really stayed here that much though. He would leave the boys here to be with his woman of the month or whatever. I loved having the boys here. They kept me company."

"What would I be doing if I came to work for you? Would I be doing what Mother and Mazetta did for you?" Kalina asked, she had heard her father call her mother a whore and implied it was her line of work before he married her.

"No, your aunt and your mother worked for me in the clubs I owned. You are too young to be working in a club. I have a little something different in mind for you."

"Like what?" Kalina asked, not too sure she really wanted to know.

"Like keeping an old man from dying a lonely old man. I want somebody else in this apartment besides me. I had another young lady working for me – Ruby. Ruby stayed with me for about seven years. She got her bachelors degree and eventually a doctorate while working for me. Now she's marrying one of my grandsons, Micah. He moved her out of here about three weeks ago. That's why when Billy found out you were homeless, he thought of me. Thought we might be able to help each other out."

"I'm good at keeping people company. I love to talk," Kalina volunteered. She touched the gold banisters gently as they ascended the stairs.

"I bet you are. You might just work out. But, I have certain rules, and those rules can't be broken by no means. Break them, and you are gone."

"What rules are those?" she asked.

"Well, as long as you live under my roof, you won't bring any men or any strangers, period, into my home."

"I can do that. I mean I wouldn't do that," Kalina was confident of that rule since she didn't know anyone in Philadelphia besides Mazetta, Doc, and their kids.

"And, I can be very demanding, so when I say jump, I mean jump. Not tomorrow or in a minute or give me a second or two. I mean instantaneously."

Kalina thought about that. She had always had a way of doing things her own way, but she didn't have much choice. She could learn to respond instantly.

"Is that it?" Kalina asked, feeling like she could easily pass the Jordan test.

"No. Since my employment doesn't have anything specific, your terms will be pretty much: Do what I say do when I say do it, no matter what I tell you to do or where or how. No questions asked. Especially, why? Like I said, when I say jump, I mean jump. No bargaining, no questions, no nothing. Just do."

"Like what?" Kalina was curious why he would hire someone on those terms.

"Like call the car for me to take me the airport. Like go to the store and buy me seven packs of cigarettes. I don't know. I don't have a clue. I will introduce you to Ruby one day and she can tell you the type of things I might ask you to do.

"What do you think? Is this the type of job you can handle?" Jordan stopped at the top of the steps. Kalina was one step behind him and one step from the landing to the second floor.

"Would I live here?" Kalina looked up at Jordan and noticed his diamond earring for the first time.

"Yes. So, is that a yes to taking the job?" they stood in the same position. She had a feeling if she answered no she would never see the rest of his home.

"That's a yes," she said eagerly.

"Good, let me show you to your room." Jordan led her down the hall.

"What about the rest of the place?" Kalina was anxious to nose around.

"You will have plenty of time to find everything. I have to go to one of my clubs this evening, so your assignment will be to learn where everything is."

"Like what?" Kalina asked.

"Like that was a question after a command," Jordan teased her.

"Okay, I'll get it right. I promise. I'll find out where all the important rooms are, and where everything in the kitchen belongs, and where all the linens and stuff are," Kalina answered quickly.

"That's exactly what you will do. You will be in here most of the night by yourself. I'll lock up when I leave. I don't expect any of the kids tonight. But, don't worry, we have all day to talk and eat. I'm hungry. Are you?" Jordan opened a door to one of the suites.

"This used to be Ashton's room. It's the one closest to mine, just in case I need you for something in the middle of the night. This has a large dressing room, a sitting area off the side of the bedroom, its own bath with a fitness area for workouts and massages. Oh, and its own washer and dryer. So when you start to buy yourself some clothes, you can wash them."

Kalina stuck her head in and was thrilled to see more floor to ceiling windows plus patio doors.

"Oh, yeah, you have a little ledge out there they call a patio. It's very small, just big enough to stand and stare off into space. The view is perfect, though, for the fireworks during the holidays."

"Great. Would you like me to fix you something to eat?" she asked, even though he had told her there was the housekeeper who did that.

"No, why don't you and I go out to lunch?" he smiled.

She put her hand to her face. He gently pulled it down.

"You have nothing to be ashamed of. Besides, we are going to the Beggars House and nobody in there pays anybody any attention. Trust me," he said and walked back down the hallway. Though Kalina was pretty tall, his long legs had a faster stride, leaving her lagging behind. Some old man, she observed thoughtfully. He seemed almost the same age as Billy.

"How old are you?" she asked, as she took a few quick steps to catch up to him.

"I'm seventy-four. I'll be seventy-five in February. I hope you will be here to help me celebrate. How is that?"

"I'd like that," Kalina went through the same question and answer session as she had with Billy while they walked to the Beggars House a few blocks away on Walnut Street.

"You really don't look like you are seventy-four, though. You look a lot younger. For a minute, I thought you were closer to Mr. Billy's age."

Jordan laughed. "I've heard that before. Billy isn't aging very well. I keep telling him that. He needs to do something except pour over those law cases and drink, I'm afraid."

"Mr. Billy is a lawyer?" Kalina was impressed. She wondered about Mandy and all those other folks in Roebuck. What would they say now? She was going to be living in a penthouse and be making friends with lawyers.

"That explains his suit on a Saturday. What about you? Why are you so dressed up? I mean, we're just walking around, and it's hot out here. You can't be comfortable," Kalina looked up at him concerned.

"Suits are my trademark. Though you are right, today is a bit warm for one. We are not going to be walking around all day, either," Jordan was starting to warm up to the young girl. It was something about her earnestness, he thought.

"How are those feet by the way? I heard you ran through a bunch of glass and cut your feet up some."

Kalina looked down at her feet. The thick white socks hid the band-aids. And now that he had mentioned it, her feet were feeling sore again. She was so excited at the prospect of having her own room again that she had forgotten about the pain, even forgotten about how she looked.

Jordan saw that Kalina was in pain, and he decided to distract her.

"Would you look at that? It must be getting late. The stores are already opened," he said glancing at his big gold watch.

"It's after twelve o'clock," Kalina observed. "Wouldn't the stores be open? What time do they usually open here?"

"Well, I really couldn't tell you. I'm not usually out shopping before twelve," Jordan laughed again.

Kalina liked his laugh. She liked his voice and how it put her at ease. Somehow, he made her feel safe, not uneasy the way Doc did with his fidgetiness and filthiness.

"My boys love this store. Jordan pointed at an Urban Clothiers. They come in here and buy jeans and Docksiders and hats. You name it. They sell girl things, too. If you are interested, that is," Jordan stopped in front of the door.

"I'm interested, just don't have any money," Kalina turned to look in the window. The clothes looked sort of plain to her, but they did have some comfortable looking shoes. Right now, she only owned a few pair of shoes and they were all at Mazetta's.

"Do you think she will throw out my things? My clothes," Kalina's voice trailed off, a bit defeated. In less than two months, she had lost two families and two homes and everything she owned. Sadly reflecting, she didn't even own the clothes she had on her back. Ms. Elle had said she could borrow them. Except, she didn't know why anyone would want a bra and panties back, but she would give them back or buy replacements as soon as she got her first paycheck.

"Jordan, this is like a real job, right?" Kalina asked sheepishly.

"Yes, of course." Jordan led her into the store.

"How much will I get paid and how often?" Kalina thought those were fair questions.

"You will get paid $200 a week," Jordan checked her out to see her reaction.

"When will I get my first paycheck?" she persisted and stopped in front of the shoes. She wasn't thrilled with the look of the chunky sandals or the Docksiders' loafers. She picked up a pair of blue sneakers and examined them closely.

"What size do you wear?" Jordan was looking for the name of the shoe on the boxes stacked on the shelf.

"Seven," she said, still waiting for his answer.

"You are about to get it," Jordan pulled out the box and pointed her to the chair. She sat down and he pulled up a stool and sat in front of her. He unlaced the shoe and gingerly picked up one of her feet and slid it into the shoe.

The tenderness made her eyes tear up.

"It's okay," Jordan said, noticing the tears. "You have been through a lot. We're going to buy you some clothes today. Once you're settled, we'll worry about you paying me back."

He put the other shoe on her, then dropped the slippers in the box and tucked it under his arm. Kalina kept wiping away tears. The shoes made her feel human again. The two of them roamed Chestnut Street, Walnut Street and ended up at John Wanamaker's where Kalina fell in love with everything she touched. Jordan bought her so many things that there were too many packages to carry. A sales representative who seemed to know Jordan called them a cab.

The doorman was surprised to see her getting out of the cab as he opened the car door for her once again.

"Good afternoon, Miss," he tipped his hat.

"Gordy, we need help with all these packages. The lady went crazy in the stores," Jordan said while handing the cabbie some cash. The man had eagerly jumped out of his car and was helping the doorman take all the bags inside. The doorman followed the cabbie back out and was shocked when the cabbie opened his trunk producing more bags. Kalina was grinning like a princess. Every bag was hers. Jordan had spent way more than $200. She was going to have to work weeks without seeing a paycheck, but she didn't care. She was going to have to find that Social Security office and get in school. School, she wasn't sure if she had mentioned school to Jordan. She hoped he wouldn't mind if she took a class here or there.

Kalina made several trips getting the bags up to her room. When she opened a drawer to start putting her new things away, she realized each drawer was already full with Jordan's grandson's clothes. She opened her closet door, and neatly hanging were lines of men's clothes and shoes. Reality set in. This was someone else's elegantly furnished room. Jordan walked in as she walked out of the dressing room.

"No room?" he inquired.

She shook her head.

"That can be easily remedied you know. It's called storage. I'll have Reggie rearrange things for you Monday morning. In the meantime, just put the bags in the dressing room and take out what you need."

"Okay," Kalina sighed with relief. Now all she had to do was decide what she needed before Monday morning.

"Do you go to church on Sundays?" Kalina asked. She had noticed a big older looking church just a few blocks away.

"No, I'm usually cleaning up one of my clubs on Sundays. I go from club to club auditing the cash flow and the records. Sundays are the best days for that since most of our income is made on Saturday nights."

"Oh," Kalina answered, wondering if anyone in Philadelphia

went to church.

"You are welcomed to go. Let me guess, you are Baptist?" Jordan pulled at the rogue curl that had made its debut between her eyes.

"Yes, sir, born and raised." Kalina pushed the curl back and tried to wrap it up in her other curls.

"Yes, sir. Your drawl is only kind of cute, you know. As you grow older, people will be less inclined to take you seriously. Here's a job edict for you. Work on losing the drawl. Watch your words closely. Don't sing them."

"What?" Kalina looked puzzled. "Sing them? I don't sing my words."

"Wha aat," Jordan mocked her. "You don't si ing your wo erds."

"Oh," Kalina was surprised by how her voice was perceived.

"I have a cassette tape recorder in my study. Use it and lose the drawl. See how many people will ask you if you are from the south, when you lose it."

"None?"

"Right, none. Today, I bet if I introduce you to anyone, they will say something either about your accent or where you are from."

"You think they would call me a country hick?" Kalina remembered Jamal's reference to her.

"Yes, that is what that accent portrays. Here at least. You are a smart girl, let people hear your intelligence, not your accent." Jordan walked out of the room and Kalina plopped on the bed. She looked over at the mirror and mouthed the word accent. Her first assignment in her new job was to lose her accent.

Two weeks flew by and Kalina learned something new every day. She learned one morning that Reggie didn't just look mannish, she was. Kalina had run down the stairs to answer the doorbell.

She was expecting the doorman to bring up a package for Jordan. When she opened it, she found Reggie kissing another woman. They were in a long passionate kiss. The woman was leaning on the doorbell.

"Whoa!" Kalina's eyes were popping out of her head. "Excuse me!"

She closed the door back quickly. Reggie opened the door and the two women followed her in through the foyer. Kalina was really uncomfortable, and tried not to look back at the two.

"Kalina, this is my girlfriend Erin. She's going to help me clean out Ashton's things today. I know I've been delinquent. Jordan's been fussing at me about it, so what we are going to do is get it packed up and out of your way, pronto. Is that okay with you?"

"That's fine," Kalina answered. "But, does Jordan know Erin? He's not too thrilled about strangers in his home."

"I think I know Jordan better than you," Reggie said, putting her hands on her hips. "Do you want Ashton's things out of your room or not?"

"I want them out." Kalina turned and went back up the stairs. She knew there had been a reason Reggie made her feel uneasy. Reggie looked at her the same way all those nasty men in the Badlands had looked at her.

Kalina picked up a magazine and tried to read it, but she couldn't shake the fact that a stranger was in the penthouse. She went back downstairs and looked in the study for Jordan. He was buried in paperwork as usual and gave her that "do not disturb me" look she had become accustomed to while living there.

"Jordan, I hate to bother you. But, do you know Erin?" Kalina folded her arms.

"Do I know who? Get to the point, Kalina. I need to concentrate," Jordan leaned over the papers on his desk. "I am leaving town for a couple of days. You will need to keep a close eye on this place."

"Okay. Her name is Erin. Reggie just brought her in to help her move Ashton's things out of my room."

"The hell she didn't!" Jordan jumped up from his desk and almost staggered. Kalina ran to him and he brushed her off. He regained his composure, started out of the room and then stopped.

"Go get them," he said firmly. "I'll be at the bottom of the stairs."

Kalina happily ran up the stairs to her room. The woman, Erin, had on one of Ashton's jackets. Kalina cleared her throat. Reggie and Erin looked at her for a second and continued talking as if she weren't in the room.

"Reggie," Kalina made an effort to call the name without singing it. "Jordan would like to see you and Erin. He's at the bottom of the stairs waiting."

Reggie helped Erin out of the jacket and hung it back up while Kalina watched. She put her arm around Erin and led her out of the room. She turned and sneered at Kalina.

Kalina followed them down the stairs where Jordan stood angrily.

"Did I give you permission to bring a stranger into my home?" Jordan's voice was hard and his eyes were so cold they made Reggie stand at attention.

"I like you Reggie. I have entrusted you into my home to take care of it. I take it this is not the first time you have brought strangers into my home. I just spoke with Ruby, so don't lie."

"Erin is not a stranger, Jordan. We live together," Reggie answered. "I would never bring anybody off the street in here. I trust Erin."

"I don't," Jordan said. "And if this happens again, I won't be trusting you either. Get her out of here. You work here, not your friends or family. This is not a museum or showplace. I don't want anyone I don't know in this house. You understand?"

"Yes, sir, I'll walk her out. It's just that you have been on me to move the things out of that girl's room and, and…" Reggie tried to find the words.

"And, you haven't done what I've asked you to do. If you needed help, all you had to do was ask. Kalina can help. So can Kenny. Hell, call Ruby. Don't bring uninvited guests into my home. Now this is the only time I am going to say this. You know my creed. You have got this one time," Jordan walked away.

The two women turned and stared angrily at Kalina. Kalina tilted her head triumphantly and saluted. She had done what Jordan had asked her to do. An hour later, Reggie came back into Ashton's room. Kalina had already packed everything from the drawers into the containers Reggie had brought in earlier. Reggie began picking them up and taking them out into the hallway.

"You could have just told me his policy," Reggie said.

"I tried," Kalina said.

"You didn't have to go snitch on me," Reggie came back.

"I wasn't snitching. I was doing what I am hired to do."

"No, you ain't doing that yet," Reggie sucked her teeth and made a clicking sound. There had been a woman in church that used to do that. It annoyed Kalina then, and the sound still annoyed her.

"What does that mean?" Kalina asked as Reggie turned her back and went into the dressing room.

She followed Reggie into the dressing room.

"What are you talking about, Reggie?" Kalina asked. "What am I not doing yet?"

"Oh, nothing, girl. I was just playing," Reggie started putting Ashton's suits in suit bags. "You have already almost cost me my job once today. We ain't going that route again."

"Tell me, please, if I am not doing something I'm supposed to be doing," Kalina said.

Reggie laughed and shook her head.

"Trust me, Jordan will let you know. As you can see, he don't have a problem with that. No problem at all.

"Now, get out of here and let me do what I'm paid to do."

Kalina walked out of the dressing room and into the bathroom. She sat on the side of the big hot tub and leaned on her hands. She was bored. She liked living there, but she didn't really have anything to do. She turned and looked into the mirrored tile surrounding the tub. Her face had cleared up just fine. The swelling and blackness was gone with just a few traces of where the bruises had been left, but no pain. She saw a few splashes on the tiles and got up to get the Windex from under the sink. She began to spray.

"What are you doing?" Reggie stood in the doorway with her hands on her big hips.

"I'm cleaning the tile."

"Would you put that down and go somewhere? Seriously, all you're going to do is make a mess. Now, go bother Jordan or something. He seems to like it when you bother him."

"What are you doing with his clothes?" Kalina walked back into the dressing room and looked at the stack of suits.

"Don't worry about it."

"Well, yeah. If the man comes looking for his clothes, I need to be able to tell him where to find them."

"He knows, trust me. We wouldn't be touching his things if he didn't know."

"So where are you putting them?" Kalina pressed.

"In the little room next to the music room. There's nothing in there but space, so that's where they're going."

Kalina's face lit up, the music room. She had forgotten all about it. She almost ran out of the bathroom to go down the hall. She could play the piano. It had been a long time since she had felt the smooth ivory keys beneath her fingers. She entered the room, walked along the bookshelves, and stopped at the mantelpiece with the fake fireplace. She was still in awe of the real Grammy Award that held the center spot. Jordan Banks was a renowned saxophonist. He had won all kinds of awards and plaques. She picked up one of his album covers, one she had seen lying in her own house a million times. Her parents loved listening to jazz. She wished her father had been alive to meet Jordan. Though he no longer had the youth of the man on the album, he was still the same. She sat at the keyboard and softly played one of her mother's favorite hymns.

"You play piano!" Jordan walked into the room. "You play it well. You have to accompany me one day."

Kalina looked up at him and smiled. "Are you feeling better?" she asked. "I was planning to come back to check up on you. But, I didn't want to disturb you again."

"I'm fine. I stood up too fast. Don't be telling no one about it. You hear?" Jordan sat next to her on the piano bench and his long dark fingers jazzed up the tune she had just played.

"Wow," Kalina exclaimed. "That was real cool."

"Groovy," Jordan grinned back.

"Ashton is going to be a little pissed when he comes in tonight. I just asked Reggie to leave a few of his things in your room for him to get his hands on quickly. If I had known he was coming this soon, I would have had the rooms changed. He rarely comes home anymore. I'm hoping everything is alright."

"Where is he going to sleep?" Kalina realized she was occupying his bed.

"There are plenty of rooms and beds for him to lay his head.

You don't have to worry about that. I'm just worried about him coming home. Like I said, he doesn't come here often, maybe once or twice a year, and he's already been here twice."

"Where does he live?"

"New York City. He married one of those supermodels, and that's where she wanted him to live, so that's where they live. Except, she travels a lot. So he is alone a lot. I thought that would make him visit more often, but he is always busy. He's a lawyer, too, like his daddy. I got three lawyers, two doctors and a photographer in the family," Jordan stated proudly.

"Really, who's who?" Kalina had heard it all before, but she didn't mind when Jordan told her the same stories over and over. She liked hearing his voice, it was soothing.

"Well, Micah and Ashton became lawyers like their dad. Ashton went straight through school to become one. Micah broke his time up with the military. For a minute there, I thought he was going to become a career soldier and then…Well, he got the smell of Ruby in his nose. And that was that. He came home, went to law school. And he's been practicing criminal law with his dad.

"Now my two doctors, I am so proud of those little boys. Ricky, the youngest little boy, will be finishing his residency in June. He's gone into surgery. Talking about performing plastic surgery. He's got the hands for it. I used to think he was going to follow in my footsteps and become a musician. But, I ain't mad at him.

"Chico is into taking care of women. He delivers babies. I can't believe he's somebody's gynecologist. I am sure he is good at it though, he has a soft touch."

"And you have a photographer," Kalina edged him on.

"Yeah, that's my lost boy. He's good at it though. He is very artistic. He paints, too. That painting at the top of the stairs, the one that has me watching over the place."

"That huge painting," Kalina added before Jordan did and he smiled sheepishly.

"Yes, that huge painting was done by Asa. Most of the things on the wall are done by Asa. He inherited my artistic genes."

"Did any of them play an instrument?"

"Are you kidding?" Jordan waved his hand at the display of instruments all around. "I had my own private family band. We created some beautiful music in this room, in every room. That's why it was so nice to hear your music as I walked down the hallway. The penthouse didn't seem like such a mausoleum. You bring life in here, my dear. You bring life." He ran his fingers across the keyboard and Kalina tried to follow him. They both giggled playfully.

"I told you I have to leave for a few days. I've delayed it a day to see what's up with Ashton. I would take you with me, but I am going to be tied up with a lot of business deals and business meetings. My label is trying to convince me to go back on the road for a few tours. I have to see if it's going to be worth my while. Have to see if I can pull together the right people.

"You'll be alright, just don't bug Reggie too much. She's a little pissed at you right now. She had won over Ruby, so Ruby didn't keep her in check. I like that about you, you have no fear. You will keep her in check just by being here. She knows you follow orders, so she will, too."

"I'm the big boss," Kalina lifted her shoulders and swayed.

"Aye, aye, ma'am," Jordan's fingers kept moving across the keys unassumingly. "Ashton can be a handful. You think I'm demanding. He's more. Billy says I spoiled him rotten. Billy likes to remind me that Ashton was my favorite, and my favorite was the one that abandoned me."

"He didn't abandon you, Jordan. He got married."

"That strange disease, marriage, it gets everybody from time to time."

"How long has he been married?"

"About seven years now, I guess."

"What's she like?" Kalina had seen pictures of the tall, thin white woman with the fire red hair and extremely pale skin.

"She's a bitch," Jordan said. "Don't tell Ashton I said that. Problem is, I think she married the wrong twin. She was dating Asa when she met Ashton who was home on a spring break. Claims she fell for Ashton. I know Ashton fell for her. I think she married Ashton for the money potential and knew she would still have Asa to toy with."

"I don't understand," Kalina had never heard this story before.

"Asa is now Redd's personal manager. Wherever she goes, he goes. Ashton is left holding the candy jar taking care of home, while wifey and his twin brother get to play footsies in exotic places. If you get my drift."

"Oh," Kalina tried to sound worldly.

"How does Ashton feel about that?" she asked.

"Hurt, of course. But, he hides it very well. He leads such a sophisticated life these days. It scares me what could come out of this. I tried to talk him out of marrying her. They could just keep the threesome going forever. Marriage changes things. Ownership becomes an investment and not everybody is willing to share their assets so freely. Asa and Ashton were never really close as most twins go. Asa looked up to Ashton and Ashton looked down on Asa.

"Ashton was disappointed when Asa chose not to go to the same college as he did, but there were rifts long before that. Reason being, Asa liked playing Ashton. He would make trouble for Ashton and then laugh about it. Ashton was creative though, he would get himself out of whatever Asa would get him into. But, that made him resent his brother. I don't like the dynamics of their relationship. I was hoping it would get better as they aged. Now, I'm told, Redd and Asa are going to be gone to Europe for a six-month tour. How do you think that makes Ashton feel?"

Kalina shook her head.

"It makes him resent his brother even more. He had gotten used to three weeks here, two weeks there, at the most a month of her absence at a time. He'd become accustomed to her demanding to have Asa as her personal photographer on most of her shoots. Now this, this twist, this 'in your face I'm with him, not you.' I don't like it."

"Is that why he's coming home?"

"I think it may have a little something to do with it. What do you think?"

"I think he is hurt and lonely."

"And a mean drunk. If he starts drinking, lock up the liquor. Then lock up yourself," Jordan warned.

"You won't have to tell me twice," Kalina reached up and touched her face where her aunt's fist had caressed it.

"How long is he staying?" she asked Jordan, not wanting to deal with another drunk alone.

"Don't get me wrong. He is not a perpetual drunk like Doc. It's just that if he gets in the mood, he can drink himself into a stupor. He's a big boy, though. Takes a lot to get him drunk first.

"Remind him that I don't want cigar smoke all over the penthouse either. I don't mind a good cigar myself, but I try to keep it down to the study, the dining room, and the rec room. Don't want that smell in my furniture in the other rooms, including the bedrooms. Keep him straight, now. That's your job."

"And if he doesn't listen?"

"Preface everything with what Jordan expects, wants, says. You get it."

"Yep. Everybody's going to know I'm the snitch," Kalina leaned toward Jordan and he put his arm around her.

"You are a good woman," he smiled at her. "And your drawl. I can barely hear it anymore. You have done a real good job, little lady."

"Thank you," she smiled back at him. She liked his arm around her. It was warm and strong.

"Now I have got to get back to work. When Ashton comes, I won't be able to get anything done. You will see." He hit a few notes before he got up and winked at her. He left her in the room running her fingers over the keys thinking about home.

CHAPTER FOUR

"Big boy," Kalina said under her breath as he walked into the room.

"What?" his hazel eyes met hers.

"Nothing," she shook her head. "Your grandfather's in the study."

"You mean, Jordan," he walked past her as if he barely knew she was there. She started to answer him, but his long strides had taken him way down the hall. He was as tall as Jordan, if not taller. She had seen his pictures, but had not expected him to be so big.

Ashton knocked on the door and opened it simultaneously. Jordan turned and sized him up.

"You're looking good, son," said Jordan. Ashton crossed the room and grabbed Jordan with a bear hug.

"Down boy, down." Jordan gathered himself and stood up from behind the desk. "Now, give Jordan a hug." Ashton hugged him a little too long. Kalina walked in and witnessed Ashton's head on his grandfather's shoulder. Jordan smoothed his hair and whispered something in his ear. Ashton stood back.

"It's good to see you, Jordan." Ashton took a few steps back and plopped on the chocolate leather sofa near the bookshelves.

"It's good to see you, boy. Kalina, pour him a drink. Looks like he needs one," Jordan saw the hesitation in Kalina's eyes. "It's okay. One drink."

"Make it a Scotch, straight," Ashton said, without looking in her direction. He was preoccupied. The last thing on his mind right now was a little girl trying to act like a big girl. He sized her up the minute his eyes met hers. He needed a woman tonight. She wasn't it.

Kalina poured the drink neat the way Jordan had taught her and handed him the large crystal tumbler. His hand wrapped around it touching hers. She was surprised how soft his hand was. She had poured two and carried the second one to Jordan.

"Should you be drinking?" Ashton leaned forward, his arms propped on his tall knees.

"One every once in awhile is okay," Jordan looked over at Kalina who was perched in the corner. "It's okay, Kalina. You can go now. I'll call you if I need you."

Kalina wasn't sure why, but she didn't want to leave Jordan alone with Ashton. She looked at the man whose hair was long and slightly curly. His hair was dark, and his eyes, his eyes were just like hers. He had to be at least six feet, if not six feet something. He had on a white suit. Who wore white suits? That was so early seventies. She walked slowly out of the room hoping Jordan would say something – ask her something – to give her an excuse to stay, or just give her an opportunity to look at this Ashton even longer. She backed out of the door and closed it.

"What the hell was that all about?" Ashton asked.

"She's very protective," Jordan lifted his glass. "She's a winner, Ashton. She's a winner. Trains real well."

Ashton sat up. Maybe she would make for an interesting night.

"Yeah," Jordan nodded as if reading his mind. "I asked you here for that very reason."

"I don't know, Jordan." Ashton stood up and took off his jacket. "She looks like a baby."

"Technically, she is. She won't turn eighteen until October. I plan to get her in school. She has already been accepted at the University of Pennsylvania."

"Another smart one," Ashton thought about Ruby. Ruby was one of Jordan's biggest moneymakers. "Another psychologist in the making?"

"No, and this one isn't a market item. This is personal stock," Jordan twirled the glass. "I'm too old to be sharing with the world anymore."

"For your eyes only?" Ashton was surprised. "Then what am I doing here?"

"You are opening the door for me, son. And you get the fringe benefits."

"What does Billy have to say about that? Did he know when he brought her here she was going to be restricted?"

"No, I just decided it this morning. I really like this one. I mean genuinely. She's sweet. She's caring. She's smart and she's a tiger. She's got Reggie running scared."

Both men laughed.

"I'll be back in October then," Ashton sat back down and crossed his legs.

"No, I don't want to wait that long. I don't know how much longer I got on this good earth. I want to enjoy it all," Jordan put his glass down and pulled a checkbook from his drawer.

"You still looking for that seeder?"

Ashton leaned forward and focused on the checkbook.

"Are you trying to buy my services?"

"You are the one who has been bellyaching about getting out of law and into the real world. What kind of business you and Micah want to start again?"

"A security business for corporations, but more personal defense and high tech stuff." Ashton got up from the sofa and took a seat in the chair across from Jordan.

"I don't want you to hurt her. It can't be rape. It has to be seduction, and I want it to be addictive," he said as he wrote the check – a very large check – and handed it to Ashton.

Ashton stared at the check a long time.

"When?" Ashton asked.

"Right now is good for me," Jordan picked up his glass. "She's staying in your room and she thinks you are a mean drunk."

"But, not rape you said," Ashton reminded him.

"Definitely not. The girl has a very tragic history. Rape could send her over the edge."

"Then it's seduction. I can't do that with you here. Especially since she's protecting you all the time."

"I'm actually leaving for a tour tonight. She thinks I'm going away for a couple of days. I'm actually gone for four weeks. I want to slide right in when I come home, you understand?" Jordan patted the hand holding the check. Ashton couldn't believe Jordan had just hired him to have sex with a girl.

"Catch me up," Jordan said, leaning back in his chair.

The two men stayed in the study a long time. Kalina walked toward the door three or four times. She didn't know why she was obsessing. She scolded herself and ran upstairs to her room to lie across the bed. She kept thinking about Ashton. She wondered how old he was. Jordan hadn't told her how old any of the boys, as he called them, were. All she knew was there was something about Ashton and his dismissive hazel eyes that had her spellbound.

She was startled by the door as it opened. She turned quickly to see who it was because both Jordan and Reggie usually knocked. As she suspected, it was the cad in the white suit.

"Hell, I know it's your room, but I was coming to get a few of my things."

"Your things have been moved down the hall," she said haughtily, rolling out of the bed and straightening her clothes.

"Don't get up on my account." He opened the dressing room door and went inside opening drawers and pushing things aside.

Kalina followed him and stopped short. He was stripping down. She turned quickly and walked away.

"What are you doing?" she asked.

"I'm changing clothes. Want to see," he walked out of the dressing room shirtless.

Kalina had seen buff men in the Cosmo and Playgirl magazines on the newsstands. But, she wasn't really prepared for it up close and personal. Ashton's arms and chest were all tight muscles. They were large. There wasn't any fat anywhere. She didn't know whether she wanted to run from him or run to him. He had her all confused.

"Why are you doing that here?" she protested. Her eyes still glued to his chest.

"Are you looking at my tits?" He stuck his chest out proudly.

She gasped and turned her head humiliated by being caught. She had never seen a shirtless man before. Sure, there had been boys at the pool and always someone on television. If there had been any shirtless men in her real world, she hadn't noticed. And her dad was always wearing one of those sleeveless white shirts, so a male breast was kind of new, especially one so taut and beautifully carved.

She heard him unzipping his pants.

"No you are not taking your pants off in my room."

"No, I'm not. I'm in my room, and I am changing my clothes. My jeans and t-shirts are still in here."

Kalina turned around to see him shimmy into a pair of neatly pressed whitewashed jeans. He then pulled a red t-shirt over his head. When he turned around Kalina thought his butt was built pretty well, too.

"I hope you're going to throw away that hideous white suit," Kalina covered her mouth as soon as she said it.

"Okay, let me guess. You are an expert on fashion. Oops, let me see, I'm married to one of the top models in the world. She picked out the suit for me and has a lot of good taste in clothes."

"No, she doesn't," Kalina rolled her eyes. "People dress her. She wouldn't know how to dress herself if her life depended on it. Not if she is dressing you like that."

Ashton couldn't help but smile. He had hated that suit, but he wore it to see her and his own brother off at the airport. Redd had seemed pleased to see him in it.

Redd was half way cross the ocean by now, and he missed her. Not that it mattered. He always missed her, but she never seemed to miss him. How could she, he thought, she saw him everyday when she was with Asa. He hated being an identical twin. To him, that was the greatest curse anyone could have: someone who looked exactly like you. That's why he was always doing things to set himself apart. He became a lawyer, not because he had wanted to, but because Asa didn't have the stamina to catch up to him once he had gotten out of undergraduate school. He wanted to put the biggest divide between their knowledge base as possible. And now, weightlifting was making him appear thinner and more attractive than Asa. Even Redd was taking special notice. And he looked back at Kalina and saw that she was attracted to him. She didn't even know it yet.

Kalina went over to her bed and sat down. She was claiming her territory. She had gotten used to this room, loved this room. This was her new home and no big thug was going to take it from her. She kicked off her sandals and swayed her feet. He walked over to her and dropped on his knees.

"What?" She swung her feet up away from him and onto the bed. He reached up, grabbed her foot, and then went to the floor. She kicked as his hand kept a singular firm grasp on her foot. She managed to swing her body around to see him. He was looking under her bed. He let go of her foot. She crawled to the other side of the bed and off it.

"What is your problem?" she yelled.

"I just needed some leverage to get me down there."

"Using my foot?" She was shaking her hands and walking toward the bedroom door.

"It was there. You were in my way," Ashton said, standing up with a small box in his hands.

"You have been protecting precious cargo, my dear." He waved the little box in her direction.

"I know that is not a box of cigars!" Kalina let go of the doorknob.

"Not just cigars, baby. Cuban cigars," Ashton plopped on her bed and began to open the sealed box.

"Jordan said no smoking cigars in any of the bedrooms or..." Kalina was cut off by the door opening behind her. She had to move fast to keep from getting hit. What had happened to knocking? She was starting to get angry. This time it was Reggie.

"Boy, come here," the hefty black woman with the crew cut ran right past her. Ashton hugged her and picked her up. He even swung her a little bit.

"Look at you. The older you get, the cuter you get. You know you are my favorite Sperling, now don't you?" Reggie playfully slapped his face.

"And you are my favorite Reggie," he laughed. He sat back down and pried the box open.

"You gon' give me one?" Reggie smiled and twisted like a two year old.

"Maybe," Ashton said as he held one of the cigars up to his nose and breathed it in. "If you keep Miss Snitch here from telling on me."

"I guess I won't be getting one. This one here's got a mouth the size of the Grand Canyon," Reggie rolled her eyes at Kalina.

"I do not. I just do my job well." Kalina was a little upset her room had become a gathering place. She decided she was going to leave it.

"Not yet," Reggie said and then winked an eye at Ashton. He looked away from her.

"Reggie, why don't you fix me one of your famous hoagies, and I might – just might – be willing to give you a cigar."

"A Cuban cigar?" she asked. "'Cause I know you have cigars hidden all over this place. I want a Cuban cigar."

"I'll think about it."

"Well then, I'll think about making you that sandwich," Reggie snickered and skipped out the door.

"Give me fifteen," Reggie yelled back. Then she came back to the door to find out if Kalina wanted one, too.

"Ka Lean A," Ashton broke Kalina's name down in syllables. "Man, that's hard to say. You need a nickname."

"No, I don't. I like my name," Kalina was ready for him to leave. But, he was too big to force out, and she was afraid to touch him to guide him out.

"Ka is such a hard syllable. You need something soft, like your head." Ashton took another sniff of his cigar.

Kalina's eyes widened, and her mouth dropped open.

"K A L E N A?" he asked, spelling it out.

"No," she replied. "I. K A L I N A."

"Good, shorten it," he said. "Two syllables are all you need. I don't like letter names like Kay and Jay and Dee and Bee. I like two syllable names like Ashton."

You want to change a woman, change her name. Jordan had once told him that when he had first gone on the prowl for him earning extra money through school. Jordan had been looking for high-class whores, someone he could train to interact with his high-end customers. Jordan thought college girls were perfect for that role, and Ashton was smack dab in the middle of a bunch of elite college girls at Columbia. He had brought home some of Jordan's top sellers.

"Kali, that's good. I'm good. You look more like a California girl anyway. You have that exotic curly hair thing going, and the smooth, pretty, almost yellow skin, and the eyes. You've got hazel eyes. You look bronze and beautiful." He lay back on the bed and put his hands under his head. "Kali, it sort of rolls off your tongue, doesn't it?"

"My name is Kalina." She walked over to him and snatched the box of cigars off his lap and ran. She would get him out of her room one way or another. She ran straight into Jordan. She handed him the cigar box and stood behind him.

"Little girl, don't play with my cigars." Ashton walked slowly into the hallway.

"Stay out of my room!" she yelled from behind Jordan. She didn't dare stick her head out. She was afraid he would chop it off.

"The hoagies are ready," Reggie called from downstairs.

"Well, let's go eat," Jordan walked around Kalina and she followed closely behind him. He held onto the cigar box and Ashton followed them down the stairs, slightly pouting. He wasn't sure what Jordan was going to do with his cigars. Jordan's moods changed like the weather. He hadn't expected Kalina to be this crazy. He kind of liked it though.

"Jordan," Ashton was eyeing his box of cigars, "can I have them back, please?"

"Yes, of course," Jordan slid the box of cigars across the table. "Whatever makes you happy."

Ashton snatched the box of cigars up and put them under his chair. He looked up at Reggie who raised her eyebrow and nodded her head toward Kalina. Kalina was trying to hide a smile. Ashton resolved he would get her back for that. Reggie was right, she was Jordan's little snitch.

Jordan watched Ashton's body language. There was something different about it. He looked at Kalina, and she was looking really pleased with herself. He hoped this wasn't a real dance going on between these two. This one was his. Ashton had a job to do, and he needed to get focused on that job, not toying with the girl's emotions.

"Kali," Ashton said loudly, "pass me the oregano."

Kalina looked at her food and picked the onions off the sandwich.

"Kali," Ashton said again, "I want the oregano."

Kalina continued to ignore him. Jordan smiled and pushed the oregano in his direction and continued to observe. This girl was stubborn. That was Ashton's problem. She wasn't falling all over herself because he had shown her his muscles.

"Her name is Kalina," Jordan decided to play along.

"I don't like it," Ashton said. "I like Kali. She looks like a Cali girl, don't she? She should be on Soul Train or something."

Kalina tried not to look up. She had always wanted to be on Soul Train. Some of those girls were exotic looking. She was pleased that he thought that's where she belonged.

"Well, you just don't walk in and change somebody's name," Jordan said.

"It's all I'm gonna call her," Ashton said stubbornly. "Damn name's too long."

"And who are you to decide my nickname? Who says I want one?" Kalina threw the onions on her plate.

"I told you she was a testy little thing," Reggie piped in. "And why didn't you tell me you didn't want onions?"

Ashton reached over, took the onions from her plate, and began to put them on his sandwich.

"Are your hands clean? I don't recall seeing you take the time to go wash your hands. Keep them off my plate, thank you very much." Kalina picked up a fork as if she dared Ashton to reach back onto her plate.

"Whoa," Jordan exclaimed. "Truce! Truce! Why are the two of you acting like a couple of kindergartners? How am I suppose to trust the two of you to take care of this place while I'm gone if you're fighting? Now stop it! Right now. Now shut up and let me finish my food in peace."

Jordan was having a small sandwich and a bowl of soup, while Ashton was eating a foot long or more. The rest of the lunch proceeded quietly.

Jordan stood up and held his hand out toward Ashton.

"What?" Ashton said.

Jordan's hand stayed extended. Ashton reached under his chair and produced the cigars.

"They will be in the study. I want you two to make up before I leave. No fighting, no biting, no forking," he turned to Kalina. "I didn't know you had it in you.

"Ashton, take her to the post office. Get my mail for me," said Jordan as he threw Ashton a set of keys.

"Yes, sir."

"Don't walk. Take the train. Show her how to take the trains." Jordan left the two of them sitting quietly at the table. Reggie went back to cleaning the kitchen. She kept her mouth shut, too.

The two of them followed Jordan's instructions and went out onto the street. There was a nice breeze, it wasn't too hot.

"I'd rather walk. It's really not that far," Ashton said. "I can show you how to catch the train coming back."

She shrugged her shoulders and followed him.

"How tall are you?" she asked.

"I'm six one," he said, looking down at her. "Am I walking too fast?"

"Yes," she said and he slowed down his pace.

"Your legs are just so long compared to mine. Your stride is longer," she tried to sound civil and northern.

"I'll adjust to your tiny stride," he teased. "How tall are you?"

"Five, six. Maybe a quarter inch shorter," she said, trying to stand as tall as she could. She knew from her mother's observation that she had a tendency to slouch on occasion.

"You are pretty tall for a woman. You could be a super model. You are beautiful and all."

"You are just saying that 'cause you want me to fall for your nickname," Kalina smiled.

"No, well yes," Ashton laughed. "I think you…Well, I know it doesn't matter what I think. Even though I am responsible for my wife's modeling career. I started out as her manager, but then I had to make a decision, my career or her career. I chose mine, which was the wrong career choice, but I'm correcting that now."

"You're going back to being her manager again?" Kalina asked.

"No," he shook his head vehemently. "Don't like the slime in that profession nor my profession. My brother and I are going to capitalize on some new security innovations. As a matter of fact, I just got the funding to move ahead. It's going to blow up big. We're going to be so filthy rich it will make Jordan seem like a peasant farmer."

"Wow, you dream big," Kalina said, now walking comfortably next to him.

"It's the only way to dream, Kali," he blew at the curl in her face as they waited for the light to change.

She hit him. "Eew, you! Onions."

They both smiled as he covered his mouth.

"I'll stop at a store and buy some mints."

"Good idea."

Jordan left them right after dinner that evening. They had all eaten out at a neighborhood restaurant. They had made peace with each other during the walk. They actually began to have real conversations about real things. Ashton could see why Jordan had tagged this one as special and exclusive. She was smart and fearless. He liked that.

Kalina was getting used to being called Kali. It made her feel sophisticated. She was actually surprised when Jordan kissed her cheek and said goodbye, that he had called her Kali. That night when she went to bed, she went to sleep repeating Kali and imagined famous people calling her that. No one down south would know her by the name. But, when her face would appear on television, they would realize it was her and that she had moved up in the world. They would be taken aback that she had shed the Kalina they knew and had become Kali.

She awakened the next morning with Ashton standing over her. He startled her.

"I was trying to see if you were breathing," he said. "You weren't moving. Do you always sleep like that?"

"Do you always sneak in people's rooms while they're sleeping?" she pulled the covers up to her neck.

"I knocked and I called you. You kind of scared me when you didn't answer." Ashton stuffed his hands in his pockets.

"I guess I was tired after that long walk yesterday," said Kalina, still holding the covers up tightly even though she had on a big shirt that covered everything.

"I was... I was just checking." Ashton backed out of the door into the hallway.

Kalina jumped up and got dressed. She went downstairs as fast as she could. He was sitting in the study, his bare feet propped up on Jordan's desk. He was smoking a cigar. He looked like James Bond or somebody from a movie. He was gorgeous with the blue smoke curling around him. His facial hair was sticking out of his face this morning and his unruly hair hadn't been combed. She liked this morning look of his. He looked like a wild savage.

She walked over and sat in the chair across from him.

"What are you doing today?" she asked.

"Nothing. What are you doing today?" He kept smoking the cigar. He was blowing circles and trying to stick his tongue through them. That made her squirm uncomfortably in her chair. He looked at her and stuck his tongue out at her.

She giggled.

"Anything will make you laugh, huh?" His eyes were sparkling.

"You make me laugh," she said, "you are funny."

"Yeah, I am," he grinned. "My brothers don't always appreciate my humor, though. Nor does my wife." The grin faded away and his eyes darkened.

"Let's take another walk…in the opposite direction. You can show me how to catch the train back."

"How about backwards?" Ashton said. "Since I didn't show you how to catch the train out of here yesterday, let's take public transportation somewhere and walk back."

"Okay, where?" Kalina asked.

"South Street," Ashton thought it was the perfect place to start the seduction.

Kalina thought the trains were neat, but she wasn't a big fan of the buses, especially when she had to stand and hold onto a pole. On the train she was less likely to be thrown around holding onto the pole. Ashton watched her get her bearings and was amused by her open gaze at the strange people around her. He was going to have to talk to her about that.

They made it down to his favorite hoagie shop on South Street. They sat down in an open-air cafe to eat it. He remembered not to order onions, and he kept the new mints in his pocket. Kalina watched how animated some people were and how timid others looked. They all looked mad about something. She sipped her orange Frank's soda that she had to come to love, and she savored every bite of her cheesesteak. *You and Reggie are going to make me fat. I was eating whatever Jordan was eating until you got here.*

"I hate health food. I like real food," he lifted his bare arm and flexed. He saw the amusement in her eyes. He could tell she liked his raw muscles.

"Rehearsing for a TV commercial?" She flexed her own slender little arm. "I can do that, too."

"Ha," he said, "ha, ha. You wish."

"What's it like?" Kalina asked. "Being married to a supermodel?"

"It's not like anything most of the time. Sometimes my picture is in magazines, newspapers, and such. My brother makes sure I get paid for the ones I can get paid for. I get to read all kinds of garbage like I'm Spanish or something or Armenian. Nobody wants to believe I'm a Black man married to a White supermodel, but it makes no difference to me. It's her publicity machine. Whatever it takes to make her happy and successful. 'Successful' is the key word. Gotta keep that money flowing in."

"Is she funding your business?" Kalina was curious about their relationship.

"No, I have asked her for nada. She helps pay the expensive rent, and I pay all the utilities 'cause she's never there. I am funding my business venture the good, old-fashioned way. I'm borrowing the money."

"Oh." Kalina was confused. "Why don't you just borrow from your wife?"

"Why don't you just mind your business?" He picked her up and carried her across the street.

"What are you doing?" she scolded him as they reached the other side. His arms were wrapped around her just below her butt. Then he let her slide through them, keeping her close to him. He smelled like cologne and cheesesteak. It was an intoxicating blend, coupled with the fact that she could feel his chest muscles and then a muscle somewhere down below that poked her.

"Don't do that," she walked away from him. He grabbed her hand.

"I just wanted to make sure we had time to get across the street with your short legs and all," he walked past her.

"Where are we going?" she asked, as he put some distance between them.

"I'm going to the skating rink," he sped up. He could hear her almost running to catch him.

"It says "Ice" skating rink," said Kalina as she looked at the empty pond below. The place was deserted.

"Sometimes people come over here and skateboard or roller skate. I guess everybody's busy getting ready for school."

"I wish I was getting ready for school." Kalina walked around one of the columns and stared out over the river. She hadn't noticed it before, but there were huge ships slowly making their way in both directions.

"Wow," she said. "I have never seen a ship in person before. I never imagined they were that big. Look at those things."

Kalina walked toward the edge of the river. Ashton sat down on a concrete wall and watched her. He remembered coming down there all the time with his family – Jordan, Billy and all four of his brothers. There were never any women around. "No women allowed," Jordan used to say when Micah would cry for his mother. The rest of them didn't have the luxury of a mother.

"Do you miss her?" he walked up behind her and put his arm around her.

"My mother?" Kalina stood still, surprised by the arm on her shoulder.

"Yes, your mother," he was really interested. He had been thinking about babies lately. He wanted to know what it was like to have a mother.

"Yes, I miss her and a lot more than I would have expected. I would have thought that it was my father that I would have been missing the most, but it's my mom that I can't fathom losing. I guess 'cause I wasn't very nice to her."

"I can't imagine you not being nice to anyone," Ashton pulled her closer to him.

"You know what they say, familiarity breeds contempt." Kalina started to pull away, but he pulled her even closer.

"What's it like?" he asked. "What's it really like to have a mother? Mine died when I was born. I was six or seven when Daddy brought Micah and Miss Elle home. She tried to be our mother, but by then I really didn't need one as much, I had Jordan. I used to get jealous though when Micah used to call her and refer to her, 'You know my mom this and my mom that.'"

"Yeah, I can imagine. My mom was there for me all the time whether I wanted her to or expected her to at all. She taught me how to play piano. She taught me how to braid my hair. Things like that."

He pulled her close enough that their bodies almost meshed. She could feel him rising against her stomach. She thought about its hardness as she looked into his eyes. They stood there staring at each other.

"She changed your diapers. Picked you up when you cried," he said, with a melancholy sadness in his voice. "Did she breast feed you?"

Kalina looked shocked and pushed him away.

"She taught me boys only want one thing." She started walking down the side of the concrete wall separating them from the riverbank.

He grabbed her and put her up on the wall.

"Let me down," she squirmed away from him, jumped off the wall and kept walking.

"Are you afraid of the wall?" he asked, walking behind her.

"You might push me over into the water and drown me," she yelled back.

"Why would I do that?" he asked, following close on her heels.

"You might be jealous," she said. "You might not like the fact that Jordan likes me better than you. I know you are his favorite," she taunted.

"You are scared," he said and grabbed her again just before the bridge column. He pulled her to him again and kissed her.

Her hands automatically went up to his head, and her fingers ran through his silky hair. She liked it. He kissed her deeper, and her body began to arch toward his and his hardness.

She pulled away again.

"You don't know how to kiss, do you?" Ashton smiled. "You ever been kissed before?"

"Plenty of times," she lied. Her only kiss had been a closed mouth one, if you didn't count the time Doc tried to stick his tongue in her mouth.

"Yeah, right! I think the girl needs a kissing lesson or two." Ashton stopped her and leaned in for another kiss. She turned her head. He turned it back and kissed her again. This time she opened her mouth and let him in.

They walked back most of the way home holding hands, stopping in shops along the way. Her feet were tired by the time she saw their building. She wanted to collapse. Sensing her exhaustion, he picked her up and carried her into the building. She didn't fight it.

It was raining a little as they entered the building. The doorman ran for the elevator and inserted the key. She laid her head in the crevice of his neck. She loved the way he smelled. He carried her up the stairs and laid her on the bed. He took her shoes off and massaged her feet. Kalina laid back and enjoyed the gentle motion of his nimble fingers. He stopped and sat on the side of the bed.

"Why don't you go take a hot bath? It will relax you and help your feet. I'll go see if Jordan left any messages."

Kalina sat up and watched him walk out the door. She didn't want to move. She was tired from all the walking and exhausted from the flood of emotions that had started raging inside her. Her mind said he was a married man – an older man, and she shouldn't even let him touch her. But, her body was saying touch me again.

Later that evening the two of them were sitting on another one of Jordan's many leather sofas. This one was in the recreation room with a large television in front of them. They had their feet propped up on the coffee table in front of them. Ashton kept flipping the channels. Kalina would protest about the channel change, but that didn't stop him.

They finally settled on a rerun of 'What's Happening'. Ashton hated the show, but Kalina thought it was funny, so he left it on. He watched her as she melted into the leather becoming more and more at ease with him. He pushed her foot with his.

"Whew, stop it with the footsies and those ugly toes of yours." Kalina drew her feet away from him. He liked her attempts at humor. They were childish and cute.

"My toes? Look at yours. At least, mine have been pedicured."

"They have been what?" Kalina asked. "You had a pedicure?"

"Get them all the time."

"You mean you go get your nails done?"

"No, I mean, someone comes to my place, gives me a massage, a facial, a manicure and a pedicure once a month."

"Get out! Are you serious?" Kalina sat up on her elbows.

"Yeah, I am. You haven't had one yet? Jordan usually brings Kenny in frequently for the works. I figured you had already had the works."

"No," Kalina shook her head. "He talks about Kenny. So does Reggie. But, I haven't met him yet."

"We will have to change that, won't we?" He reached behind him and picked up the phone. He asked Kenny to come at noon the next day.

"Now, I don't want to get you too excited, but it's the baddest thing that will ever happen to you. The boy has hands that will make you liquefy." He pushed the curl out of her eyes again. She slapped his hand away. He brought the hand back to her face, grabbed her face and then kissed her.

She started to pull away, but stopped as she began to enjoy his kisses. They were sweet and succulent and exciting. They made her whole body tingle.

He looked down and saw her toes curl.

"Let me paint them," he said.

"Paint what?" she asked.

"Your toes, silly. Let me put some polish on them."

"What's the use if I'm getting a pedicure tomorrow?"

"There's nail polish remover, Kali. Think," he poked her in the forehead.

She started to respond that her name was Kalina, but she liked the way he saw her. She liked the way he called her Kali.

"Come on," he pulled her up off the couch. "Let's go upstairs. I know you have some nail polish up there."

She let him lead her upstairs to her bedroom. She waited with her legs folded on the bed while he went through her nail polish in the dressing room. He came out with cherry red.

"I like red," he whispered. "And don't you dare say it."

"Say what?" She closed her eyes.

"You know? My wife is named Redd. I don't want to think about her right now. I want to think about your toes."

He took a foot in his hand and kissed the top of it. She jumped.

"You just kissed my foot."

"I could kiss every inch of your body," he said and began to massage her foot with both his hands. He stretched out her bare leg. She had put on a pair of jean shorts and a short cotton tee after her bath. He began to massage upward. He was rubbing the calf of her leg.

"What happened to polishing my toes?" she whispered.

"I'm getting back to that. It's just your leg is so pretty, I wanted to give it a preview of what it was like to have a massage."

He took the other leg and massaged its calf.

"Your hands are real nice," she said. "They are really soft. So are your feet."

"My feet?" he raised his eyebrow.

"Yeah, when your ugly toe foot touched mine, I was surprised how soft it was," she admitted.

"It's that regular massage and pedicure."

"Wow, I guess it works." Kalina realized his hand was resting on her bare thigh.

His eyes followed her gaze down to his hand that began to massage the inside of her thigh. He rose up and over her. Then she fell on the bed beneath him as he began to kiss her again. His hand was moving up higher. She jumped when his hand moved inside the pants leg of her shorts and rested on a place no one had ever touched before. She reached down to move his hand, but he moved it before she could reach him. He kept kissing her and rocking her on the bed. His hand began to massage her back underneath her shirt. Kalina was getting dizzy from the slow but frenzied activity. She reached for his head to pry it away from hers, but his tongue and his mouth persisted. She slid her hands between their bodies and felt his heart pounding beneath his hard muscular chest. She let them stay there a minute, and let him keep kissing her.

Finally, he rolled off her. She climbed off the bed quickly and saw her own reflection in the mirror, her hair standing wildly around her face.

"Look what you did to my hair," was all she could come up with in light of what had just happened. Her mind kept telling her that she was making out with a married man, but she really wanted to climb back onto the bed and let him explore her some more.

"Where's the nail polish?" he said, hanging off the bed looking into the shag carpet.

"It must have fallen," she said, wiping the wetness from around her lips. She noticed her eyes were wide from the stimulation as she looked at herself again in the mirror trying to tame her hair.

He ran his fingers through the carpet and retrieved the small bottle.

"Ta da!" he said triumphantly. "Eureka, I have found it."

He patted the bed and started shaking the bottle. She sat down on the edge of the bed facing the door.

"Now how am I supposed to do your toes like that?"

"Like what?" she asked.

"Like your feet buried in the carpet. Turn around. Give me a foot," he patted the bed again.

"We should go downstairs. Jordan would have a fit if we got nail polish on this bedspread."

"Then we'll pull the covers back," he reached for the top of the bedding and flung the covers toward her.

"I think we should go downstairs." She stood up, and he grabbed her around the waist then pulled her back onto the sheets. She scampered to the other side, but he caught her foot and pulled her back as he rolled on top of her. He did it with such ease, it surprised her.

"You are pretty strong," she said, astonished as she lay beneath him once again. Now his hand was really busy. The button of her pants' loosened and the zipper was suddenly hanging open. She grabbed his hand and his face covered hers and found her mouth again. This time his kiss was harder and more urgent. And she kissed him back.

When he came up for air, she was astounded by the discovery she was naked from the waist down. She slid from beneath him and started reaching for her clothes. He yanked her back, kissing her again. His hand was holding onto one of her cheeks, his fingers brushing against her most delicate flesh.

"We can't do this," she said, coming up for air.

"Why not?" he asked, and slid her shirt off her in one fell swoop. Her bra had already been unclasped and was hanging loose. As she reached for the shirt, he slid off the bra. She sat on her knees and tried to cover herself. He raised himself up and removed his shirt, then dropped his pants. He had on no underwear, and the hardness she kept experiencing against her belly was no longer a mystery.

He gently placed her on her back and mounted her flesh to flesh. He was warm and moist. His tongue was enticing as he began to kiss her all over, letting his tongue flicker here and there. She began to moan with pleasure. He licked her and kissed her and sucked her into a frenzied state. Then, without fanfare, he began the great entry. She wanted to say no, but she couldn't. She wanted to know what it was like to be a woman. She wanted to know what the celebrated connection was between a man and a woman.

The next morning when she awakened, she felt moist and gooey and a little sore. She was afraid to move and wake him up. He had been on her almost all night. It was as if he was on a mission, and he was not going to stop until he succeeded. He had. He had finally made it inside of her. She had felt the hot searing tear of the intruder. She was glad no one else was in the house at the time because she had no idea she could scream so loudly.

She scooted out of the bed and ran to the bathroom. The urine burned her injured vagina. Before she could get off the toilet, he sauntered into the bathroom.

"I'm in here," she said, hoping he wouldn't try to pee on her in his sleep.

"I see you, Miss Kali," he sat on the side of the hot tub and started running water.

"Last night was your first time," he held his hand under the water. "You need to get in the hot tub and soak a little. Let me bathe you."

"I can bathe myself," she said, remembering last night's offer to paint her toes.

"I can bathe you better," he said seductively.

"That's okay," she said, trying to find a way out of what she had just done.

"You finished?" he pointed to the toilet. She wiped and was startled to see drops of blood.

"You are not dying," he laughed. "Move. I gotta go."

She stood up trying to cover her body parts as she walked by him. She turned to see him standing over the toilet. It seemed like he would never stop peeing.

"Come on. Get in the tub," he said.

She went back and stepped into the hot tub, the one she had been warned not to put any soap in. The water was hot and bubbling, but not too bad. He had gotten it just right. She sat down in it and began to relax. She let her hair get wet as she leaned back against the porcelain. She closed her eyes and tried to pretend she had not had sex with a married man. That bothered her.

The water splashed and she opened her eyes to see him getting into the tub on the opposite side. His legs sandwiched hers. He bent his knees and lay back against the porcelain on his side. They sat there until the water started to cool down.

He helped her up and walked her to the shower. He turned it on and stepped in with her. He took the bar of soap and lathered her from head to toe. He handed her the soap and she began to lather him. She hadn't touched him like that before. She soaped his back and his buttocks, his legs, his arms, his feet, his hands. She tried to avoid the most obvious part of his body. She tried to put the soap down, but he grabbed her hands cupping the soap and brought them to his outstanding member. He helped her lather it and rub it. She looked up at him and his eyes were half-closed and dreamy. This was pleasing him. He knelt down to her and kissed her while the hot water rinsed the soap from their bodies and their hair. She kissed him back, not knowing why she wanted to because she was still sore from last night. She tried not to think. He lifted her and tried to slide inside of her. Her body jolted with the pain, but she didn't run. She adapted to him and him to her. She lost track of time.

That morning they sat quietly at the breakfast table while Reggie complained about this and that. She cracked jokes, but no one laughed. Ashton read the newspaper and ate slowly. Kalina picked at her food. Reggie finally took the dishes from them and went away to clean whatever room was on her schedule for the day. Ashton reached beneath the kitchen table and let his hand find his way up to her crotch. He rubbed her gently.

"Thank you," he said. "Thank you."

"Why are you thanking me?"

"Because I really, really needed you last night." His eyes were sincere. "I haven't made love like that in years."

"You're welcome," she said and began to toy with her coffee cup.

"What do you want to do today?" he asked.

She shrugged.

"Can I show you something?" he asked.

"I think you have already showed me enough," her eyes gleamed over the cup as she took a sip of the coffee.

"Well, maybe I should say, teach you something," his hand was beginning to probe her, pulling her panties back so he could touch her flesh. Her legs clamped shut. He pulled his hand back.

"Never mind," he said and began to fold up the newspaper.

"Show me what?" she said.

"How to really do the nasty," he said, grinning.

"You are nasty."

"You are horny," he picked up the paper and threw it on the counter. He began to go back up stairs.

"I thought that was what you did last night," she stood up and her robe fell open.

"Don't be showing a horny man tits," he walked back to her and picked her up high enough to let one of her breasts fall into his mouth. She opened her legs and she locked them around him. He sat her down on the kitchen table and began to rock her beneath him.

"What's your name?" he said.

"Kalina Denise Harris," she said.

"No, your name is Kali," he said roughly. "Your pussy's name is Niecy. I'm your lover boy, Ashton, and my dick is Taylor. When Niecy wants Taylor to come out to play, just call him. He will always be there for you, no matter what," he plunged harder and deeper than he had previously. She screamed.

"What's your name, girl?" he plunged again. He had her pinned so she couldn't wiggle away.

"Kalina," she yelled.

He plunged again with greater force. She feared he was trying to rip her apart.

"What's your name?" he lifted her up and grabbed her hips so firmly he frightened her. She was afraid the next plunge would do some serious damage.

"What's your name?" Kalina knew he had a really good grip on her and was in a real good position to make her scream even louder. She remembered Reggie was somewhere in the house. And she knew how much pleasure Reggie would have telling Jordan what she had done.

"Kali," she whispered.

"What's that?" his rhythm was steady and even as he eased in and out.

"My name is Kali," she buried her head into his neck and closed her eyes.

"Now, that's what I'm talking about, Kali. Now let Taylor take Niecy out to play."

CHAPTER FIVE

Kalina awakened another morning with Ashton snuggled closely. He would fall asleep spooning her as if she were a big teddy bear. She was always surprised at how they would fall asleep in that position and wake up in that same position. She was beginning to depend on that early morning cuddle. Sometimes she would lay there holding her urine to the last minute, not wanting to break out of that warm cocoon. There was something about the intimacy, the smell, the safety of his arms in the slightly darkened room that made her feel like a real woman, made her feel like she really belonged there.

She slid from beneath his heavy arm and eased herself out of bed, then ran to the bathroom. She had been playing out this same scene for almost two weeks. She was wondering when it was going to end. She didn't want it to end. But, she knew Jordan would be coming back or Ashton's wife would be calling him home. Something was going to tear them apart and the thought made her extremely sad. She stepped into the shower and let the hot water flush away the sadness and the emptiness whenever his body wasn't close to hers.

"Kali," she heard his voice as she reached for the big terrycloth robe on the back of the door.

"I'm in here, Ashton." She strode out of the bathroom seductively. She knew he had an early morning appointment. That's why she had beaten him to the shower. She didn't want to be left behind in the bed without the warmth of his body, the smell of his body, and his weight that would crush her so divinely.

She sat on the bed next to him and pushed his hair away from his face.

"You need a shave, son," she teased, using his favorite name for everybody and everything.

"Taylor wants to come out to play." His eyes twinkled and his body stretched like an alley cat pleased to be alive and awake to battle another day.

"Niecy will play later. Taylor's got to take Ashton on an appointment," she nodded toward the clock.

Ashton sat up quickly and looked at the clock again.

"Good girl," he swung his long legs out of the bed.

She grabbed him for a second and kissed his forehead. He grabbed her and threw her down on the bed.

"I've got five to ten minutes," he gathered her into his arms and worked his way between her soft thighs and enjoyed her girlish moans as he began slow and gentle morning thrusts.

Kali waited at the breakfast table picking over her food. She didn't know why she was waiting. She knew he would have to run to his meeting. His business was getting started. Every day there was a meeting here and meeting there. And every day, she was getting more and more anxious when he left her. When he entered the room, she stood up excitedly, hoping he was going to say it was cancelled, and he was going to stay home with her. Instead, he grabbed her toast and a sausage then stuffed them in a napkin. He kissed her on the forehead and squeezed her butt with his free hand. Then he was gone.

"Somebody's got it bad," Reggie walked into the dining room just as Ashton had left.

"That boy must be hitting it in all the right places," Reggie said as she took her plate.

"I'm not finished," Kalina protested.

"Oh, me thinks you are madam," Reggie walked out with the plate. "And here, Jordan thought you were such an innocent, virginal little angel. Wait 'til he hears Ashton's been knocking them boots all night long every night since he left."

"Not every night," Kalina remembered the first night she had slept alone, still a virgin.

"Oh, that's right, not the first night," Reggie laughed.

"How would you know?" Kalina screamed.

"I know everything that goes on in this house. So, you better be nice to me or your gig is up, little girl."

"Mind your own business, Reggie," Kalina stormed out of the kitchen.

"You are my business. You spy on me and I spy on you," Reggie yelled after her.

Kalina ran up to her room. She was afraid. Jordan had taken her in and given her a place to live, and now she had betrayed him. What was he going to think of her? Kalina jumped into the bed and pulled Ashton's pillow up to her face. She could still smell him. She bit the pillow and tried to muffle her scream. Was this how her mother had ended up murdered? She thought about the man her mother was with when she died and wondered if that had been their first time together. Kalina sat up and cried. "I'm a whore," she whispered. "Just like my mother." Tears began to flow freely.

Ashton was home in the early afternoon pouring over some paperwork in Jordan's study. Kalina stuck her head in the door hesitantly. He had come home and hadn't come looking for her. He looked engrossed in his work.

"Hi," she said, hoping he would beckon her to come and jump into his lap. Instead, he looked up briefly and then back at the papers.

"Not now, Kali. I've got something terribly important to attend to." He sat back in his chair and rocked a little.

"Okay," she couldn't hide the disappointment in her voice. "See you at dinner?"

"Not tonight," he said. "I have a business dinner. I will ask Reggie to fix you something special. Okay?"

"That's okay. I can fix something to eat for myself. So, I am going to be here by myself tonight?" she asked a little worried. She had never slept anywhere alone before, especially not in a place so big.

"Oh, I'll be in your bed tonight. You are a big girl. You can find something to keep you occupied for a few hours. Right?"

"Sure," she said as she backed out of the door.

"Oh, Kali," Ashton called after her, and she eagerly entered back into the room.

"Jordan's pulled some strings, and you can register for school tomorrow at Penn. I'll take you down there. We need to get there early so you can get some good classes, okay," he tapped the pencil he held on the papers.

"Sure," she said excitedly. "I'll leave you alone to your work."

Kalina walked out into the hallway and jumped up and down gleefully. Her dreams were coming true. She was going to enroll in an Ivy League school. She was already living in a luxury home with men who were wealthy. And then, her joy meter dropped a few notches. What was Jordan going to say about her affair with Ashton, his married grandson? She sauntered back to her room bouncing from happiness to fear.

She began to think about God. It had been a few weeks since she had gotten on her knees and prayed. Now it was time. She knew without a doubt, she wasn't going to share the bed with Ashton tonight. She was going to end it before the affair ended her dreams.

Kalina fell asleep alone in her bed hugging Ashton's pillow. She said a prayer to keep him from coming to her in the middle of the night. She said another prayer asking God to forgive her for falling for a married man. But, when morning came and the heavy arm lay across her, and his deep, even breaths tickled her hair, she smiled. She forgot her prayers. She sank back into him and he instinctively pulled her closer.

"Good morning," she whispered.

"Good morning," he whispered back.

She turned to him and he lay there smiling at her.

"You missed me," he asked, blowing the rogue curl from her face.

"Yes, I missed you" She kissed him.

"Why don't you show me how much you missed me?" he said, grinning.

"In a minute," she said, pulling away. "Where are my clothes?"

She realized as she got up that the nightshirt she had fallen asleep in now lay on the floor.

"You didn't look comfortable," he said as he caressed her breast. "So I remedied that."

"You are so bad." Kalina laughed and turned to run to the bathroom, but the door opened and she froze.

"Good morning," Jordan said. He was standing in the door with a large bouquet of yellow roses. "What do we have here?"

Kalina turned and snatched a pillow off the bed to hide her

nakedness. She stepped back quickly into the end table and almost knocked over the lamp. Ashton's hand reached up and steadied her.

"Jordan, Jordan…" Kalina looked at Ashton who was rising from the covers naked and then back to Jordan who was still holding the roses and staring at her.

"I'm sorry, Jordan." Kalina thought about her mother and how she must have reacted when her father had opened the door.

"What are you sorry for?" Jordan was smiling at Kalina. He walked toward her and she moved away from him, still holding the pillow in front of her body.

"We are all adults here, aren't we?" Jordan reached out for her. She wanted to pull away, but she had cornered herself and had no place to move.

"I don't know what to say," she said and began to cry. She turned to look at Ashton for help, but he had lain back on the bed staring at the ceiling. He was stroking Taylor.

"Drop the pillow, Kali. He just wants to see what you are hiding," Ashton said nonchalantly.

"Satisfy my imagination." Jordan reached for the pillow and gently tugged it from her hand. "You are even more beautiful than I had imagined."

Kali sat in the student center reading the same paragraph over and over. She just wasn't getting it. She hated to track down her professor to have him explain it, but that was the only way she was going to understand this theory. The author must have either been high when he wrote this or purposely perpetrating a weird joke. She took another sip from her milk carton and began to pull a cracker from the plastic wrap.

"Is that lunch?" said a boy with a round brown face who was standing over her. He had a couple of spiral notebooks in his hand and a brown paper bag.

"No, it's a snack. I snack all day long. Nervousness, I guess," she answered, not sure if she wanted the company or not.

"Mind if I sit down? The place is sort of packed today." He looked around the busy center. There were students everywhere.

"Midterms," Kali said, sipping her milk again.

"Are you finished yours?" he asked, pulling a sandwich from the paper bag.

"No, I still have one left. Advanced Economics. It's killing me. You are in that class, aren't you?" she asked.

"No, I'm in your Stat class and in your Management class." He smiled at her. "Want some?" He offered his sandwich toward her.

"No, thank you," she shook her head and smiled back at him. "I knew you looked familiar."

"Oh, is that all? Just familiar," he said and grinned. "I don't look like the guy who is always staring at you. I speak to you in every class. Haven't you even noticed? I'm hurt." He put his hand over his heart.

"You have a kind face," Kali said quietly. "But, I still don't know your name."

"I'm Thaddeus," he said, extending his hand. She took it. It wasn't as soft as Ashton's. It was a little more like Jordan's whose padded fingers had played the saxophone so long, they were hardened.

"I'm Kali Harris." She noticed eagerness in his eyes.

"My friend and I have a bet going on," he said then took a bite out of his sandwich.

"A bet?" Kali remembered her mother's words about what boys wanted. She figured that was the source of the bet and she didn't have time for that. She sipped the last of her milk and made a gurgling sound. She crumpled up the crackers package. She needed to leave.

"Yeah, I say you are sophomore taking big classes, and he says you are senior. He thinks you are one of those super geniuses. I just think you look like a baby in makeup."

Kali stopped for a second and sized him up a bit. She smiled.

"So, sophomore or senior?" He popped open his soda and it sprayed her a little.

"Boy, you better be careful," she said, jumping back from the spray. They both laughed.

"You are both wrong," she said, "so neither of you win the bet."

"Don't tell me you are a freshman" The boy leaned toward her.

"Try last semester junior. I'll be a senior in the spring. And if I have my way, I'll be out by the end of summer."

"Really, did you start school early or something? You can't be more than sixteen."

"So how old are you?" she asked.

"I'll be 21 in December. And, I'm a senior who will be out in May," he answered.

"Good for you. I started Penn two years ago. I have taken classes at every semester or mini-semester offered. I have a dual major, accounting and marketing. And I intend to graduate magna cum laude," said Kali as she flipped her hair behind her shoulder and smiled. She could see in his eyes that he was impressed.

"How old are you?" he asked.

"I'll be 20 on the 18th of October," she said proudly.

"Wow, you look so young," he grinned.

"You thought I was jailbait," Kali said as she closed her book and wished she hadn't used that word.

"Well, like I said, I thought you were a bit young, Miss Harris."

Kali looked at her watch as a hint, not because she had to be anywhere soon.

"I have to leave soon, Thaddeus," she said. "The table is yours."

She dropped her book in her book bag and slid her arms through the loops.

"You know you are in college now. You don't have to carry book bags," he teased.

"You do if that's what you want to do. And I'm used to doing what I want to do," she lied. She stood up and waved him good-bye. She walked across campus toward her next class and thought about her home life in South Carolina. She had always wished and wanted to be far, far away doing anything else other than what she was doing at the time. Though she was content where she was now, she missed those days when it was just her and her parents and no-body from the outside world.

Kali woke up alone on her birthday, but her room was covered in rose petals of all colors. There were red, yellow, blue, purple, white, pink, and colors that looked like they had been mixed as hy-brids. The white ones led a trail to the dressing room. There were big boxes and small boxes with large bows stacked in the middle of the floor. She went wild opening them. She found silk dresses, cashmere sweaters, a leather jacket, and leather knee-high boots. Everything was in black, Jordan's favorite color. She turned to run down the hall and there stood Kenny with a big smile on his face and a curling iron in his hand.

"We know you have school, but Jordan won't let you leave

without the works, girlfriend," he said, twisting her around like a little girl being pointed in the right direction. "Happy Birthday, My Queen."

She turned, ran into his arms, and hugged him. She loved Kenny. He was the only man that touched her without sex on his mind and she loved the way he touched her.

"Come on. Let me bathe you and do your hair," he grinned. Of all the women he was hired to dress, Kali was his favorite. She never made fun of his desire to be a woman. More than anything or anyone, she made him feel more womanly. He knew without a doubt that he was her best friend. The two of them talked and gossiped whenever they were together. They had secret signals and words that meant certain things only to them. Kali would call him every day as soon as she got home from school, and they would talk about their dreams and their love lives or lack there of.

Kali succumbed to Kenny's magic fingers as they massaged her back.

"What are you going to do, today?" Kenny asked as she became one with the universe and lost touch with the real world. His touch was so divine, so righteous.

"School," Kali murmured. She had a fleeting thought of her father opening her bedroom door with a rose lying across a tray laden with her favorite foods. She had always dismissed the fact that her mother had cooked and prepared the food he had brought to her. Now, this was her third birthday without her, without them.

"Heard from Ashton?" Kenny could feel tension returning to her muscles when he mentioned the name. He patted the muscles back down.

"No, I haven't heard from him in weeks. When he calls, he just talks to Jordan. I don't think he even asks about me anymore." She sighed.

Ashton had been her lover, her hero, her protector, and now he was missing in action. She knew he had a wife, and Redd would always come first, but he had her, too. He would always have her. No one would ever come as close to her heart as Ashton had.

"Well, you know how men are," Kenny said, patting the muscles a little too hard.

"Ouch, that hurt." Kali turned over, her bare breasts pointing up at him.

"It got your mind off Ashton," he giggled.

"You brought him up." She snatched a towel from the rack behind her and scooted off the table. "We've got to hurry up. I cannot afford to miss this class. I have another big test next week."

Kali went downstairs to eat. Reggie had fixed all her favorite foods and set them on the tall kitchen table. She hadn't eaten in the dining room in a long time. There was no one to keep her company at the long formal table. She tried to talk Kenny into staying, but he had another client to dress, so he was on his way. She sat there sampling all the different dishes while Reggie hustled busily in the kitchen.

"Everything is delicious, Reggie," Kali was savoring every bite. There were no doubts that Reggie was an excellent cook. "I wish I could eat it all."

Kali looked at the little white birth control pill next to her orange juice. She popped it into her mouth and washed it down with the juice. Gone were the days when Reggie was crushing it up and hiding it in her food, which was something Reggie had been instructed to do on day one of her arrival. It took Kali a few weeks after Jordan stepped into the picture with his sexual demands to realize that her situation had been his intent all along. Kali had grown up a lot in the past two years, and now she applauded herself on recognizing situations a lot sooner. She was no longer that naïve little cheerleader from down south.

"Jordan is still asleep," she said after taking another swallow of orange juice. "He scared me this morning."

"Have you called Ashton?" Reggie asked sincerely.

"No, but he spoke to Jordan last night." Kali knew that was an excuse. "But, I know I need to call him. Jordan sleeps all the time."

"Has he even...?" Reggie thrust her hips a couple of times with a sadistic grin on her face, "lately?"

Kali shook her head. Occasionally he would go down on her and have her go down on him, but even that was becoming extremely rare.

"You think he's getting ready to croak?" Reggie asked.

"Will you call, Billy?" Kali asked. "He doesn't like me for some reason. And I don't like talking to him. He's lewd."

"Billy is more lewd than the others? I thought all of them were pretty lewd."

"No," Kali shook her head. "Only Billy and Asa. I'll call Ashton. I'm going upstairs to check on Jordan. Then I'm leaving. Thank you for a wonderful breakfast."

"You are welcome, My Queen," Reggie's said, her eyes glinting with humor.

Kali bowed toward her and smiled. It had been Billy who had called her a Queen and it had become a running joke ever since. However, his reference to her royalty was not meant in a favorable light.

Kali knocked lightly on Jordan's bedroom door for the second time that morning. This time his eyes were open as she entered the room. She ran to him and jumped on the bed.

"Good morning, sleepy head," she said and scooted down beside him and kissed him on the lips.

He smiled.

"You need something before I go to school?" She looked at him naughtily.

He shook his head.

"You are going to wish me happy birthday?" she asked.

"Happy Birthday," he said and his thin spidery hand brushed her hair from her face.

"I plan to have dinner with you in a very special place this evening. So don't dilly dally your time away at school."

"I won't Jordan. Are you getting up?" Kali sat on the side of the bed watching him closely.

"I don't have to rush anywhere, woman. Now you go on, so you don't miss class." He patted her arm.

"I would miss it if you need me, Jordan. Don't ever doubt that." She leaned over and hugged him tight. Her life with him was anything but perfect, but she knew she was safe with him. She knew he would always take care of her and she would always take care of him, not because she had to, but because she really wanted to care for him. He was all the family she had anymore, him and Kenny.

Kali went to class, but her mind kept wandering. She was going to have to call Ashton, and she really didn't want to talk to him at all. He was the one that had decreed silence, and he should be the one to break it. But, there was Jordan to consider. Something was wrong. No one should sleep as much as Jordan had been sleeping.

She made her way across campus and decided to stop for a pretzel. She got in line behind four or five people. A hand touched her arm. She turned to see Thaddeus and his beautiful smile.

"Hey you," he said. "You run through campus like a whirlwind.

It's hard to catch up to you."

"You're just too slow," she teased. "What are you doing with yourself these days? I haven't seen any women hanging on you like a tether lately."

"Like a what?" he asked.

"Never mind," she turned to move up in line.

"Guess what I have in my pocket," he patted his back hip.

"Well, back there," she said, grinning, "I'd never guess."

"You are a bad little girl," he shook his head. "But, I am going to tell you anyway. I have two tickets to the Earth, Wind and Fire concert at the Spectrum Friday night." He paused, waiting for her reaction.

"That's nice," she said as she moved another step closer to the vendor.

"Nice, nice? Is that all you can say? These are the hottest tickets in town. Don't you know that?"

"I do," she said, playing along, hoping he wasn't about to ask her out. That was one of the things Jordan had made her promise. No men outside of the Sperling circle.

"Well, you wouldn't happen to know anyone else with tickets, would you?" He leaned down close to her face. His eyes were locked onto hers.

"Kali," she heard the deep voice booming from behind Thaddeus. They both looked toward the voice.

"Ashton," she said, almost holding her breath at the same time.

He stepped close to the two of them and put his arm around her shoulder.

"I know you are not eating a pretzel for lunch. Not on your birthday," he said as he pulled her gently out of line.

"Well, yeah," she said as he pulled her closer to him.

"Happy Birthday." He tried to kiss her on the lips, but she turned her head and tried to pull away.

"Aren't you happy to see me?" he said, guiding her a few steps further away from Thaddeus who was now taking steps in the same direction.

"Kalina, are you alright?" Thaddeus said protectively.

"Yeah," she said and broke free from Ashton. "I'm fine."

"She's fine, son," Ashton said and put his arm around her again. This time his other hand produced a black velvet box. She took it and held it down by her side.

"Aren't you going to open it?" he asked.

"I will," she said, looking back at Thaddeus who was still standing there watching her closely.

"She's fine, son. She's just a little bit pissed." He bent down and kissed her on the top of her head.

"What are you doing here?" she tried not to sound angry, though she could feel her throat tensing up as she fought the urge to scream.

"It's your birthday." He reached behind her and slid her book bag from her shoulders. "This thing is heavy."

She reached for it, but he held it out of her reach with his long arm.

"Kali, let me take you to the Italian restaurant down the street. The food is great. And we can talk," he said, grabbing her around the waist again as if he owned her.

She took the black box and hit him with it.

"I'm not very happy with you at this moment," she said and stormed off further into campus.

"Women," Ashton said and winked at the young man. "You can't live with them and you can't live without them." Ashton caught up with her in just a few steps. He picked her up and threw her over his shoulder. She hit him a few more times with the black box. He laughed and walked faster.

"Kali, I'm sorry. I couldn't talk to you, not with her at home. You know it. You know why I couldn't talk to you."

"You could talk to Jordan," she screamed. He let her slide down his front and he kept her close with his free arm.

"Don't make a scene, okay? What would Jordan think of you sneaking off to a concert with that young man?"

"Were you eavesdropping? If you were, he hadn't asked me, and I wasn't going to accept."

"So you say." He kissed the top of her head again. "Aren't you going to open your gift?"

She pulled away again and marched over to one of the stone benches. She opened the box to find a diamond-studded bracelet. She gasped. It was beautiful and elegant.

"You like it?" He sat next to her. She nodded her head and let her fingers run across the cool metal and stones.

He kissed her and she kissed him back. As their faces parted, she saw Thaddeus standing over by a tree watching them. He looked disappointed. She wanted to tell him she was sorry, but she knew that it wouldn't matter. Ashton picked her up and carried her across the street to his car.

She ordered a light lunch because she knew Jordan would be taking her to an early dinner. Jordan did everything early these days. She told Ashton how concerned she was and how Jordan needed him to come see him more often.

"What about Billy?" Ashton called his father by his first name. "Does he come by?"

"About once a month if that often. He says he's busy. Has a case log out the wah hoo."

"That could be true. Business is hot for Billy these days. He's driving Micah crazy. Does Micah come by?" Ashton asked, toying with his pasta.

"Micah comes by once a week. But, Jordan puts on a show for him, you know. You are the only one he will come clean with." She looked at her watch.

"And you. He loves you. The sun rises and sets on you," Ashton said and looked out of the window sadly. "He's sick, Kali. You do know that, right?"

"What do you mean, sick?" Kali dropped her fork.

"Jordan's doctors told him a few months before you arrived that he would live another six months to a year. You changed all that. You gave him something to fight for, and boy, did he fight," Ashton said, remembering Kali's first Thanksgiving in the Sperling household. All the Sperling boys were there and expecting to have her for dessert. She was terrified, and Jordan had unequivocally said no. He had had to do more than slap a few hands who thought he was kidding.

"Is that why Billy hates me?" she asked, thinking of his aborted rape two years ago. Jordan had stopped him from pinning her beneath him.

"My father hates you?" Ashton feigned surprise.

"Yeah, he treats me like doggie doo doo. And so does your brother, Asa."

"How so?" Ashton reached over and stroked her hand.

"The way they talk to me. For one thing, Billy only refers to me as the Queen Bitch."

"Oh, yeah, I have heard that reference before. My father's jealous, so is Asa. Don't feel too bad, though. I am on their shit list, too."

"You? Whatever for?"

"Well, let's see. I guess that Thanksgiving when Jordan tried to pry my father off you and my father pushed him, remember?"

"Like I would ever forget that Thanksgiving."

"Well, I couldn't stand there and let Daddy push Granddaddy, now could I?" Ashton snorted. "I still can't believe he came at Jordan with such intense coldness over some pussy."

"Is that all I am to you, Ashton?" Kali was offended.

"No," he shook his head. "I care very deeply for you, but you know what I mean." He frowned and looked around their table to see if anyone was listening to their conversation.

"My grandfather is the ultimate pimp. He's the pimp for kings, presidents, mayors, police chiefs, and anybody with deep pockets. His whores are known worldwide. What my father and my brother couldn't, nor still can't as a matter of fact, understand is that you weren't just any elitist's whore. It seems you are my grandfather's last chance of having a relationship, whether it was normal or not, with a woman. He didn't want to share his last woman with anybody, definitely not the six horny boys he raised to think of women as desserts to be passed around on Thanksgiving Day while watching football games."

"A relationship?" Kali was intrigued. "That's what happened, isn't it? Jordan and I have a relationship."

"Yes, you do. Thus, me, stepping out of the picture. We couldn't be a three-way. Jordan needed a two-way. You see why I wouldn't talk to you? Jordan could see how much we cared about each other. He needed you to care about him like that. I needed you to care about him like that."

"You really are the only one that understands him, aren't you?" Kali squeezed his hand.

"And I don't know what the hell I'm going to do without him." Kali saw Ashton's eyes glaze over.

"I can skip the next class," she said, expecting him to take her to the nearest hotel.

"Good, let's go home and sit with Jordan," he waved for the check.

Jordan was ecstatic to see Ashton. He kept hugging him and kissing him. Ashton sat beside Jordan on the bed and leaned against him like he used to when he was little. Kali decided to leave the two alone. She told them she was going to her room to study and to call her for dinner.

"She looks good," Ashton said, poking Jordan who was grinning like a Cheshire cat.

"She is good," Jordan said, very pleased. "I don't know that I would have lived this long without her."

"Jordan, you are going to outlive us all," Ashton joked.

"Oh, would that be nice," Jordan smiled. "The only thing I am missing is great-grandchildren. Otherwise I will be dying a very happy man."

"Great-grandchildren? I never knew that even crossed your mind, old man."

"I just started thinking about it. I was thinking about the legacy I was leaving. Billy is only interested in anything material that I may have. You know I honestly don't know whether I have any other grands or descendants out there. You boys have planted a lot of oats that I don't know about."

"You also taught us boys about how to be extremely careful and choosy. Besides, neither Chico nor Ricky is going to give you any offspring. They are too busy banging other men."

"Damn, I didn't hear that," Jordan chuckled. "I was trying to stay in the dark on those two. And you just had to say it out loud."

"Well, it's because they are both out of the closet. That's why you haven't seen them recently. Daddy has literally disowned them."

"Now, that is a very selfish man who is leading your vulnerable twin brother down the same path," said Jordan.

"This I know. Kali tells me they are very disrespectful to her and to you," said Ashton.

"Yeah, Billy is getting worse the sicker I get. It's like he is getting impatient for me to die," said Jordan

"He's a real bastard," Ashton said angrily.

"Well, you will still have Micah. That boy's a rock. I'll be glad when your business gets off the ground so he can tell his daddy to kiss his black ass. If he hadn't jumped up and married Ruby he could have told him already."

"It's not just that, Jordan. You know how loyal Micah is to everybody. Daddy keeps playing a guilt trip on him. I keep telling him not to listen. But, Micah is Micah and Daddy did marry his mother."

"Yeah, Elle got that spell still going," Jordan looked at Ashton and patted his head.

"How are you and Redd doing?"

"We're doing. I have been trying to talk her into having a baby. I'm thirty-three years old and I am ready to procreate, if you know what I mean. I want my own flesh and blood child. I'll even settle for a daughter." The two men laughed again. Jordan used to tell Billy not to bring home any of those girl babies he made, just the boy ones. That's how they ended up in a household of five boys. Billy brought home his boy babies. He never said a word about any girl babies.

"Well, what does Redd think about that?"

"She thinks her mother's hips spread too far after giving birth and she can't afford the same spread. Not at this stage in her career."

"So, no babies," Jordan sighed.

"Well, she has agreed to adopt. But, she wants me to do all the legwork. She thinks adopting would be good publicity."

"Oh! How do you feel about that?" Jordan squeezed Ashton's hand.

"I want my own flesh and blood. I want to make some more little Banks and Sperling babies."

"That's my boy," Jordan said, smiling. "Give Jordan his legacy."

Jordan pushed himself up straight and wrapped his arm around Ashton. "Tell me, what's on Ashton's mind?"

Ashton looked in his grandfather's eyes that were weary and defeated only a few minutes ago. Now they were bright and defiant. He knew why. From birth, his grandfather had coddled and cared for him, had talked to him, and taught him; and he had grown into the man Jordan had shaped him into becoming. They thought alike.

"She's got the perfect hips to carry a baby, don't you think, son?" Ashton laid his head on Jordan's shoulders.

"I think, son," said Jordan, his eyes were filled with joy. He had one more thing to live for, a great-grandchild.

CHAPTER SIX

"You made it down for breakfast," Kali said, so happy to see Jordan that she kissed him. "Your visit with Ashton must have gone well." She wasn't angry that Ashton had left without telling her goodbye. She understood his distance now. Besides, they had found a way to steal some time together over the weekend. Micah had kept Jordan occupied for them.

"It did. It did. It always does. I love seeing that boy. I wish he could have stayed longer than a few days though. He promised to come back soon. He's thinking about moving his office down here. Said it would be cheaper," Reggie poured Jordan a cup of coffee. He held his hand for her to stop at half.

"Thank you, Reggie," said Kali as she watched her pour a cup for her. Reggie winked at her. She was happy to see Jordan, too. Kali knew Reggie was concerned about finding another job that easy if Jordan died.

"Did I detect civility?" Jordan looked from one woman to the next. "Are you two getting ready to gang up on me or something?"

"No, we've just been concerned about you sleeping all the time," Reggie said, stopping to put her signature hand on her hip. "Now, you are here. And we are happy."

"Very happy," Kali added. "Would you like me to stay home today?"

"No, Sweetheart. That school's important to you. You go on now. I'll be here when you get back." Jordan sipped his coffee and waited until he heard the door. He pulled a new pack of birth control pills out of his jacket pocket.

"Reggie, I need you to do me a favor. Chico says these are better pills than the others. I need you to toss the other ones and start giving Kali these, please."

"Yes, sir," Reggie turned the container of pills over and over. There wasn't a label anywhere, but she agreed to do it.

Kali was standing on campus in front of one of the buildings' bulletin boards. She wanted to find out the dates of the winter mini-semester and see what classes were available. They were usually posted early. She had studied her roster and the catalog the night before. It was entirely possible for her to finish all her requirements by the last summer mini-semester if all the right classes were available. Then she would be finished. She could get a real job if she found herself alone. She was starting to think about that a lot lately. It had been almost three years since she had lost her parents, and now it looked as if she were going to lose Jordan. Even though his recent burst of energy did give her hope, she knew it was inevitable that she was going to be left alone once again.

"Oh, my God! You're her!" a young woman's voice said from behind her and squealed.

Kali turned to the young girl, confused.

"I've seen you, like, several times," the girl continued.

Kali touched her chest and looked at the girl questioningly.

"It's her," the girl turned to Thaddeus who had just walked up beside the girl.

"Yeah, that's her," Thaddeus looked on disapprovingly.

"Hi Thaddeus, is this your girlfriend?" Kali asked. She wasn't sure why the girl was so excited to be near her.

"My younger sister. She is graduating from high school in the spring. I brought her here to show her the campus," Thaddeus responded.

"I'm Kali," she extended her hand. The young girl took it and screamed. Thaddeus punched her in the arm.

"Stop it," she and Kali whined in unison.

"Why did you do that?" Kali reached over and rubbed the young girl's arm. "And who do you think I am?"

"I don't know, but my brother and I saw you with Earth, Wind and Fire after the concert. I saw you with Prince. And my friend who was with us at the concert last Friday said she saw you with the Isley Brothers. You must be somebody special. You know a lot of people."

"I just met all of them at their concerts," said Kali, unsure she liked being spied on by a school mate and his sister. "And I was just as excited as you are now, but I didn't show it. If I showed it, I wouldn't get to meet anybody."

"No, why not?" the young girl asked.

"Well, people hyperventilating over you would make anybody nervous. Can you imagine? Everybody you meet is looking at you like you are some sort of freak of nature. I mean, let's face it. Prince is a man just like other men. He just wears more makeup."

"Wow!" The excited girl didn't take the hint to calm down. She was making Kali nervous.

"Who else have you met?"

"I honestly can't tell you that. I would be breaking my friend's trust and his friends' trust. He just happens to be in the type of business that crosses these people's paths, that's all. And I'm lucky enough to just tag along."

"Oh, I wish I could tag along," the girl said, turning back to Thaddeus who was staring at the bulletin board. "Thaddeus, you need to ask this girl's friend for a job."

"I don't believe we are in the same league," he said, still looking at the bulletin board. "Her friends are old people."

"Good to see you, Thaddeus," Kali walked away. He was right. He was out of her league, and her friends were old people. She realized at that moment why she had never fit in back in high school. Her mind was out of their league. Everybody there was like Thaddeus. They could not fathom the type of life she was living now. She could. It was all she had dreamed about, and here she was walking across the campus of an Ivy League school in a pair of classic black wool slacks that cost as much as some people's rent, along with soft leather boots, and a hot-ass black cashmere sweater. She looked rich. She knew that was what Thaddeus was thinking. She figured he had toyed with the idea of asking her out, but he was shot down by an older brother in a business suit with a little black velvet box. Yeah, Thaddeus, she noticed his eyes were still on her as she turned to leave. She was way, way out of his league, no matter who he was.

Kali caught a cab back to the penthouse that day. She was suddenly feeling quite okay with her entire life. Ashton was back in it. The two of them would keep Jordan happy as long as they could. She tried not to think beyond that. She tried to keep only happy thoughts of Ashton sneaking into her bed as soon as Jordan was asleep. Or the two of them in a hidden rendezvous while Micah kept Jordan occupied. Kali thought about the ongoing flirtation she had had with Thaddeus and realized even if she had been free to see him, it never would have worked out.

Kali and Ashton hooked up even more intensely. They were

sneaking into different rooms all over the house whenever Jordan took a nap. Kali couldn't get enough of Ashton, and it seemed he couldn't get enough of her.

"Meet me at the Embassy Suites tomorrow, down by the airport. Wear something professional," Ashton was holding her hand.

"Professional?"

"Yeah, I need to hire an assistant. I don't have an office yet, so I'm interviewing in the front part of the suite. I think if you are with me, the women who are applying won't feel so awkward. But, you have to wear something business like."

Kali walked into the dressing room and came out with a black dress.

"Does it come with a jacket?" he sized the dress up.

"No, but I can buy one tomorrow," Kali thought about the interviewing process. She was going to be listening carefully. Sometime soon, she would be looking for a job. She wondered where she would live when Jordan died. She knew Billy wasn't about to let her continue living at the penthouse. She shook the thought of Jordan's death from her head and ran into Ashton's arms.

"What does Niecy want?" he teased.

"I want Taylor to come out and play," she whispered in his ear.

The next day Kali showed up at the Embassy Suites in a brand new suit. It was black with a white silk shirt beneath it. She had even bought the classic pair of pumps to top it off. Ashton was sincerely impressed. For a minute, he thought about hiring her. But, that wouldn't work if she were pregnant he reminded himself. He had been wearing protection lately to let her body adapt from not taking the pill. His brother had warned him to wait a few months, but he was getting impatient. He wanted to start seeing a baby grow in her belly.

When she walked into the room, he told her what to do during each interview. What to say, what to ask, and how to present herself. She listened attentively and followed his instructions to the letter until the fourth woman arrived.

Her name was Tawny Elliott. He liked her right away. She was oddly familiar to him. He noticed Kali had become strangely quiet. Ashton sat across from her at the small table in the living room area and talked frankly about the skill sets he needed to get his office opened in Philadelphia. She answered everything right, even offering him advice on how to set things up. He soon ran out of the questions he had planned to ask. When he looked to Kali so that she could interject the scenarios they had discussed, she said nothing. She just stared at the woman.

"Miss Harris, do you have any questions?" Ashton tried to snap her out of her fixation.

"Yes," Kali said hesitantly. "Do you have any? No, I mean. Are you related to a woman named Mazetta Duchess?"

Ms. Elliott seemed to think about it a moment, and shook her head.

"No, I can't think of any Mazetta's. Nor Duchess as a family name."

"I was just wondering," Kali said with a touch of nostalgia in her voice. "You look a lot like my mother's family," her voice trailed, "a lot like my mother. Her name was Charlotte Duchess Harris."

"No, sweetheart, I don't believe I know them," Ms. Elliot instinctively got up and sat next to Kali.

"Where are they from?"

"Here, my mother was from here," Kali's voice broke. Ashton was shocked to see tears welling up in her eyes.

"Are you alright?" the woman took her hand.

"Yes," Kali lied. The familiarity and resemblance had struck a chord in her heart. Maybe it had been her recent birthday with no family. Maybe it was the woman's voice and mannerisms that re-minded her of her mother. Maybe it was the realization that Jordan would only be in her life for a short time and she was going to have to find another life somewhere else. She looked from Ms. Elliott to Ashton. Maybe it was the fact that life with a married man wasn't long term either. Kali was feeling isolated, and the fear she had been fighting off for almost four years was starting to creep up on her.

"Where is your mother now?" the woman asked.

"Dead," Kali began to openly sob. Ms. Elliott took her in her arms and rocked her.

She looked back at Ashton whose head was down. Kali had never broken down before. She had always been filled with fight and defiance. He couldn't bear to witness it. He looked at his watch. He had two more interviews scheduled. One of them was due any minute.

"Kali," he whispered. "The fifth interview is due."

Kali's head was buried on the woman's shoulder. Her body was heaving from the constant and violent flow of tears.

"We can go into the bedroom," Ms. Elliott offered. "I'm sure she will be fine."

Ashton jumped up and opened the bedroom door. He then lifted Kali into his arms and carried her to the bed. Ms. Elliott gathered her things and followed him.

"Water, do you have any water?" Ms. Elliott asked.

Ashton left the room and came back with glasses, an ice bucket, and two bottles of Perrier. He sat them on the desk in the bed-room and walked back out into the living room area.

Ms. Elliott followed him to the door.

"Mr. Sperling," she offered. "Maybe you should open the cur-tains to make the next lady feel more comfortable."

Ashton looked at the heavy curtains and nodded. He hadn't thought about that, but at least Kali had been there through all the other interviews. He pulled the curtains back and looked out at the huge atrium overshadowing the multiple walkways with rooms lined up as far as you could see. He watched the next woman walk up and knock on the door.

Ashton hurried through the next two interviews. His mind was no longer focused on finding an assistant. He had already found her. He had watched Ms. Elliott take charge and comfort Kali without any hesitation. He had watched Kali melt in her arms. He realized that was the one thing that was missing. During the pregnancy, Kali was going to need an experienced woman to come to for advice. He certainly didn't know anything about pregnant women. He had never even lived in the same house with one. He would have no idea what to expect, and he knew Kali would be clueless.

He informed the last candidate that he would be making a decision by the end of the week and that he would contact her if she were chosen. The young woman backed out of the door, obviously wanting to say more. But, he didn't give her the chance. He closed the door. His long legs took him to the bedroom door in two steps. He knocked lightly before entering. The two women were sitting in the middle of the bed with the wild fall-colored spread. They were both dressed in black. He wanted to ask them if they were practicing witchcraft for Halloween, but decided he had better hold his jokes. He walked in to find Ms. Elliott showing Kali pictures out of her wallet. Kali was holding the pictures with reverence and awe. Her tears had dried up and there was a smile on her face.

Ms. Elliott had taken off her shoes and was on her knees on the bed. When she looked up and saw Ashton, she got down quickly and slid back into her shoes. Ashton watched her transform from a soft motherly woman back into a professional take-charge woman. She was the one.

He pulled the desk chair out toward them and sat down.

"Can you breathe now?" he asked Kali.

She nodded her head.

"Good. I'm so sorry, Ms. Elliott. I want to thank you, though, for staying with Kali. I hope we haven't delayed you too long."

"No, of course not. I've actually enjoyed the company." She smiled at Kali. Kali was gathering the pictures and putting the wallet back together. She handed them to Ms. Elliott.

"Ms. Elliott," Ashton leaned forward and folded his hands under his chin. He looked at the woman intently.

"This position requires someone who can be extremely discreet. This business caters to clients who prefer that no one knows our services are required. So, we don't talk about them to anyone. Our transactions, our actions, our services are all highly confidential. We are anything but a typical security firm. Do you understand?"

"Yes, sir," Ms. Elliott answered clearly.

"Not only will my professional life require discretion and tact, so will my personal life," he said, looking at Kali. So did Ms. Elliott.

"I know who you are, sir," Ms. Elliott answered. "Your personal life is your personal life. I don't have any room or reason to judge. Nor will I share anything that I become privy to."

"Who am I?" Ashton was curious.

"You are Ashton Sperling. Your wife is Redd, the supermodel. Your grandfather is Jordan Banks, the great saxophonist by day, and well…I am aware of what his part-time profession is related to by night. I used to work for him many, many years ago."

Ashton sat up straight and grinned. He couldn't believe it. Was that why she was familiar to him, too? He had probably seen her when his grandfather used to bring him into the club as a kid and drop him on a bar stool.

"You used to work for my grandfather?"

"Yes, I worked in one of his after hours clubs. But, I got sick and he fired me, sent me on my way. The next time you see him. Thank him for me. I never should have been there. I'll never forget. He said, "You got a family?" I said, "Yes, but I don't want to go home." He said, "They want you home. Ask some of these girls who don't have families. They don't want to be here. Go home to your family.""

"My grandfather actually sent you home?" Ashton was stunned.

"Yes, he did. No one else believed it either. Your father even tried to stop me, but your grandfather said, let her go. He said I didn't belong there. I went home and my parents welcomed me with open arms. I got over my illness, got back in school and got my life together."

Ashton opened his briefcase and pulled out some paperwork. He handed it to Ms. Elliott.

"I have a lot of sales meetings and account meetings with clients. I am usually on the run between here and New York. I want to open an office here in Philadelphia soon, real soon. It's more central. I am expanding my clients as far south as Washington, D. C. Plus, my family is here. My wife is gone most of the time, so New York doesn't feel like home. Here is home. You know, this is where I grew up.

"Here are the specs for the office suite I will need. I would prefer to walk to work from the penthouse, so I want something in Center City. Not too far from City Hall."

He reached over and touched the papers.

"That's the budget. You can go over if it's not more than five to ten percent. The money is coming in, slowly. Also, on the budget is your salary that started when your interview ended. I want you to go to the next room and memorize it. You can't take it with you. Everything stays with me or locked up in my office."

"Can I make a few notes? There won't be any connotation as to what they mean. I'll know," Ms. Elliott asked, as she looked closely at the papers in her hand.

"Discretion and good decisions," Ashton said as he looked over at Kali who was pulling herself back together. "That's all I expect."

"That's what you will get," Ms. Elliott said frankly. She strode out of the room and closed the door behind her.

Ashton walked over to the bed and pulled Kali close to him.

"What the hell was that all about?" he pulled her down onto the bed.

"I don't know. She looks and acts and sounds like my momma. And, I just couldn't keep it in anymore," Kali tried to look away. She was ashamed she had cried in front of a stranger, and she was angry with herself for letting Ashton see her weakness. Until now, she had stood her ground with the Sperling men. They had hurt her, but they hadn't broken her.

Ashton gently turned her head back to his face. They stared at each other.

"It's okay," he whispered. "At least you have a real mother to mourn. I never knew my mother. I've heard so many different stories that I don't know which one is true. For all I know, my mother could be alive out there somewhere, at least according to one tale. Or, she died giving birth to me and my brother.

"You know what's funny? I don't even know her real name. The only mother figure I encountered was Elle. And frankly, she was only a concerned mother for Micah. The rest of us, well, she could have been a housekeeper as far as we were concerned. She never kissed our boo boos or did anything special. She yelled at us when we did stupid stuff. She fed us. She was in the house with us, but she was also a key sexual object employed by my grandfather, and we knew that. So a mom, she wasn't."

"I'm sorry," Kali said, rubbing his face. They kissed deeply. Ashton was getting anxious about starting his family.

Ashton went back into the room and found Ms. Elliott dubiously making notes in a small, leather notebook. She looked up at him and smiled.

"Check your hair," she said.

He turned to look in the mirror and saw that it was sticking out where Kali had run her fingers. He fixed it and looked back at Ms. Elliott smiling.

"I have another assignment in addition to that" He pointed at the papers. "Kali needs a house, preferably in an upscale neighborhood. Close to town. I will need quick access."

"A budget, price range for that?" Ms. Elliott poised her pen over the paper.

"Unlimited. It will only be her, so it doesn't have to be big. But, it has to be really, really nice in a really, really nice area. I will pay anything. That's not company budget. That's personal financing."

Ashton was pleased with his choice. He walked Ms. Elliott to the elevator. He explained the logistics of how they would work together until they moved into the office. She was fine with the arrangements. As she got into the elevator, he held it a moment.

"The house," he said firmly, "takes precedence over everything else. Get me the house," he said, letting the elevator door go so it could close. He saw Ms. Elliott nod.

Two weeks later, Kali was watching Jordan eat lunch at the restaurant downstairs in their building.

"Boy, what's come over you, Jordan?" she was grinning from

ear to ear. "You have just like made this big change overnight."

"Really?" he said, smiling at her. "What kind of change?"

"You went from sleeping all day to barely walking to holding onto walls and stuff to this straight and tall man I met when I first came here. On top of that, you're eating me under the table. What gives?"

"I am feeling better. Thanks to you. I am feeling better."

"Thanks to me or thanks to Ashton? I think you started perking up when Ashton moved back in."

"I think somebody else has perked up since Ashton moved back in," he winked.

She froze. She was afraid to breathe. She and Ashton had been sneaking around, but they thought they had been undercover. The first person she thought of was Reggie. She was going to have to have a word with Reggie.

"It's quite alright, precious," he held her hand. "I'm an old man. He's a young virile stud. I can't compete with that. Heck, I don't want to compete with that anymore. I'm a happy man. You come to me when you want to, I won't turn you away, but I'm not sweating your relationship with Ashton. You have changed, too, you know? You were moping around before he got back."

"I was not," Kali protested.

"You were, too."

"You knew about us?" she said, still trying to figure out how.

"Ashton told me last night. He doesn't want to sneak around anymore. It takes up too much time. He would rather just come home and be with you, he says."

"Oh, well, he could have told me."

"He will. He had to get back up to New York this morning, and you were asleep."

Kali took a sip of tea and looked at Jordan, whose dark skin was glowing with health.

"I'll come to you tonight, then," she said, feeling like she owed him that much.

"No, not tonight," Jordan shook his head. "I'm going to the club tonight. You can come, too, if you like."

"No," Kali thought about the all the nude women walking around and the men there paying to touch them. "I think I'll pass."

⟫⟨◍⟩⟪

"That was a short trip," Kali said to Ashton. She was sitting on Jordan's desk in the study. She was holding one of his leather-bound philosophy books. She loved being able to go into his library to do research for some of her classes. Jordan owned all the classics, and they lined the cavernous study with oversized furniture to accommodate all the long-legged men that grew up there.

"Redd was on her way to LA from Europe. She had a one-night layover. I thought it was my duty to go see her."

"Of course," Kali agreed, although there was a pang of jealousy and hurt that she had to make every effort to hide. She wondered if he knew that every time he mentioned his wife, it was like putting a knife to her throat. Every time she heard the name Redd, she knew that she was in the wrong place doing the wrong thing.

"You okay?" he brushed the untamed curl from her face.

"Yeah, I'm fine," she lied, thinking that she is just an adulteress that fears that God is going to punish her yet.

"You look sad," he said as if reading her thoughts.

"What would I have to be sad about?" She smiled, grabbed his hand, and kissed it. "I'm just trying to make sense of Greek myths and Socrates."

"I have something to cheer you up," Ashton said, lifting her off the desk. He was always picking her up and placing her around wherever he wanted like she was a china doll. She never protested or hardly ever resisted. She liked the feel of his strength as he lifted her in the air. She also loved his touch, he was so gentle.

"I can't do any shows or plays tonight, son," she said, prying his hands away. "I've got a paper to write."

"No, nothing like that. Have you got an hour or two now? I'd like to show you something."

"I've seen Taylor on many occasions," she teased.

"No, not that." His eyes were serious. "Something special."

"Taylor's special," she joked, wanting to change that serious look he had just given her. It frightened her.

"Come on. I'll drive," he said as he took the book from her hand and placed it on the desk.

"I have to put that back. Jordan, if not Reggie, will have a fit if it's not in its proper place." She started back for it, but his arms wrapped around her and guided her toward the door.

"Okay. I guess I'm outvoted. But, I'm going to tell on you if I get yelled at," she said. She looked up at him, hoping he would at least return a smile. Instead, he was looking straight ahead. She decided to be quiet and let the bad news come out. She wondered if his wife was in town. She had always thought it was odd that his wife had never visited the penthouse the entire time she had been there.

Ashton drove the little black Porsche madly through the streets of Center City until they reached a small tree-lined avenue with exquisite older homes. He slowed down and backed into a parking space in front of one of the red-bricked row homes with a flower box on the right side of a huge gleaming black door. The flower box was filled with purple pansies. Kali wondered who lived there. He got out of the car and opened the door for her. She got out of the car shivering from the November chill. She had forgotten to bring a jacket, and the air was cold and brisk. She followed him up the gleaming marble steps that were shaped in semi-circles. He pulled out a set of keys from his pocket and opened the door.

Kali followed him into a freshly painted living room with brand new chocolate brown leather furniture. Everything shined, including the huge mirror over the fireplace. She stood in awe at the intricate woodwork throughout the room on the many built-in bookshelves, on the mantle of the fireplace, and bordering the ceiling. He walked her through a dining room that was small and crowded with a dining room set that had never been used, not once.

"Who lives here or lived here? Everything is new, isn't it? I mean, it smells and looks brand new."

"You like it?" he asked, still not looking in her direction. His eyes were looking at every inch of the place as if he were seeing it for the first time. They walked into the kitchen together to see black counter tops and black appliances. It was small, but big enough for a black kitchenette set that sat in the middle. Kali looked down at white-tiled floor.

"This place is really cool."

"Let's go upstairs. No, downstairs. Let's go downstairs first," he said, opening a door that led to the basement. The stairs were narrow with a single steel banister leading down to the bottom step.

It was brighter than she had expected. There was a washer and dryer and a washtub. Facing them was a long counter with cabinets above and below it. Kali opened a cabinet door and found laundry detergent and other sundries stored there. None of them had been opened.

"I bet there's food in the kitchen," Ashton said, almost cheerfully as he took a few long steps back upstairs. Kali almost had to run behind him to catch up. As he suspected, there was, as they opened the refrigerator and the cabinets, food. Anything they could have asked for was already there.

"Upstairs," Ashton was moving faster and with more excitement now. Kali was beginning to feed off his excitement. Was this his new place? She was afraid to think of the possibilities. She didn't want to think. She didn't want to conceive life after Jordan. Not yet. But, maybe, here, just maybe she could live with Ashton in this cute little place. It wasn't the penthouse, but she really liked it.

Upstairs were only two bedrooms, but there were two baths. The large bedroom had a bathroom connected to it. It was small, but it was private. The hall bathroom was larger and across from the second bedroom. Both of which had the same black and white motif as the kitchen. Kali smiled at all the possibilities, but she had to keep her mouth shut. She kept looking at Ashton trying to read his face, his mood even. He was different today.

The small bedroom across the hall had a bed and a dresser in it. Like downstairs, it was lined with ornate built-in bookshelves that were extremely neat, since she loved books. Even better, these shelves were already lined with some of her favorites.

She followed Ashton back into the larger bedroom with a king-sized bed that took up the whole room, which was okay since its best feature was a huge ornate wardrobe that covered the entire side of one wall. The other side had extra long double windows that overlooked the trees on the front side of the house. Ashton sat on the bed and then lay back.

"Come here," he said as he patted the quilt on the bed.

She obediently sat next to him waiting for him to tell her something.

"Merry Early Christmas," he said and pulled her on top of him.

"What?" she said.

"I couldn't bear to think of you without a home when Jordan goes. So I bought you this."

Tears ran down her face as she kissed him. She didn't care that he was married. That was only a piece of paper anyway. She would do anything for this man. They spent the rest of the afternoon wrapped in each other's arms celebrating their privacy and their lust for each other.

Kali had never experienced lovemaking like that before. She was more uninhibited than she had ever been before. She was more accepting. She wanted to please him. She wanted to devour him, and it was as if he were devouring her. They didn't come up for air. Their bodies meshed like the ocean ebbing and flowing to the shore and back. Kali lifted when he descended, making music that she never knew existed before. When darkness fell and the room darkened, they were too exhausted to turn on the lights. They lay there in the cool dampness without anything but their body heat. Kali began to shiver, and he pulled her close and warmed her with his intensity. He worked his way back between her thighs that were sore from the friction and plunged. A spark ignited deep within her soul and they both screamed with pleasure and once all their energy had been released, they lie spent staring at the ceiling peacefully and fulfilled.

"Have you been to Ashton's office yet?" Jordan was walking her down Chestnut Street for a cup of coffee. He had started taking walks again.

"No, I haven't received an invitation, yet," Kali tried not to walk into anyone while she window shopped. She loved the little stores on Chestnut Street.

"See something you like?" Jordan stuffed his gloved hand into his pocket.

"Are you cold?" She watched him like a hawk. Even though she owned her own place now, she didn't live there. It was where she and Ashton would rendezvous for sex, great sex.

"I'm fine, Kali. Stop babying me," Jordan protested.

"I just don't want you to catch cold. That's all."

"Are you my lover or my mother?" Jordan retorted.

"I'll be both if I have, too," she said and stopped in front of a shop that was known for its high-fashioned clothing. Jordan was friends with the owner.

"What do you see?" he asked, absent-mindedly. He was wondering what was taking Ashton so long to get her pregnant.

"I really like that coat. You can get me something like that for Christmas." She pointed to a red-belted coat with its collar standing straight up.

"If I'm here," Jordan said, knowing that would get under her skin. He loved the fact that she hovered over him with everything she had. He looked down at her and thought he loved her. There had been only one woman he had ever come close to thinking about that way, and that was Eva Sperling, the bitch that got pregnant and ran away with his child. He still couldn't believe that she thought she could run to Europe and hide with his child.

"You are not fit to be a father," she had yelled, as he pried Billy out of her arms.

"I'll kill you, bitch. Now, let him go," said Jordan as he took the child and promised he would kill her on sight if she ever set foot near Billy.

Both of them knew that he would. He had certainly proved he was capable of murder. That's why she had run. She had taken her little pale white skinny behind and run to Ireland. He had found her. She should have known he had connections – underworld connections – all around the world. No woman was going to separate him from his son.

It was the only child that he knew for sure was his, and he wasn't going to let a woman raise him. Jordan was adamant about that. A boy had to be raised by a man. He was proud that he had raised Billy Banks into the man he was. Billy Banks was his son's real name. Whenever Jordan thought about it, it hurt that Billy took his mother's name to sever his ties from the Banks' heritage. He had come home from college and informed Jordan that he couldn't be affiliated with prostitution and extortion because he was planning to become a lawyer, so he was changing his name.

Jordan had gone through great lengths to keep him in the dark about his mother, but Eva had found him and told him the truth. Jordan had to make her pay for that. Billy was still holding it against him for taking him away from his mother, but he did the same damn thing. He pried his boys away from their mothers' arms to raise them in a real man's household. Then he turned around and married the woman that ran Jordan's stables. So how dare he judge Jordan?

Jordan had raised Billy to be a man's man. That was his culture, his heritage. Jordan's father had made sure he was a man's man by beating it into him. But, Jordan didn't beat Billy nor did he beat his grandsons, but he taught them. He taught them right. He taught them a man's place in this world. That's why he knew Ashton was doing the right thing by making his own baby.

"Why do you say stuff like that, Jordan?" Kali had her hand on the door to the store.

"Not today, Kali," he took her hand and they kept walking down the street. "Let's go see Ashton."

There was a glass door at the street level. Once you entered, there was only a stairway that led to the second floor. The office building was clean, but old. They walked to the right and down to the end of the hallway. There was a sign next to the dark, blue door that said "SPERLING ENTERPRISES."

"This is it," Jordan said, opening the door. Ms. Elliott was in a beige suit and blue blouse. She looked up from her desk with a fancy typewriter and looked genuinely pleased to see Kali.

"How are you?" she asked as she stood up. Kali walked into her open arms and hugged her. She even smelled like her mother.

"I'm fine," Kali said, grinning from ear to ear. "I believe you know Jordan. This is Ashton's grandfather."

"Yes, we have met a long time ago. I don't know if you even remember me, but I remember you well," Ms. Elliott said and held out her hand.

"Yes, sweetheart, I do. I never forget a beautiful woman." Jordan took her hand and kissed the back of it.

"I'm happy to see you went on in life and did well for yourself. And I am equally happy you are working for Ashton. He needs someone who understands him. I think you do, from what I have heard." Jordan looked at Kali who was quietly trying to decipher what they were talking about. He liked her for that. She knew when not to ask questions. She would just smile and wait patiently.

"Well, it is really good seeing you," she said, looking from Jordan to Kali. "He's in. I'll see if he can break a moment. Why don't you have a seat?" She pointed to the black loveseat against the wall with a very tasteful and sedate picture hanging over it.

Kali went over and sat down. Jordan walked around the small waiting area.

"Papa," Ashton walked out of his office behind Ms. Elliott.

"Boy, you haven't called me that in years," said Jordan, smiling.

"No, but it sounds good, doesn't it?" Ashton had a twinkle in his eyes. He was definitely happy about something.

"Come on in. It's small now, but we are taking over the suite next door in a couple of months. The tenant next door is letting go of their lease when it ends, so we're taking it over. Then I'll have an office for Micah and for Brady."

"Brady?" Jordan shook his head. "What are you hiring Brady for? You know I don't trust that boy. Never have. He's a hanger on. What about Troy?"

"Troy is in the police business. You know he did some time in the military, came out, and went into law enforcement."

"Same field, hire his ass," Jordan sat down in a chair across from the desk.

"Brady is going to do the marketing and public relations. That's what he's good at. I need someone to make us visible to the right people, help me get the right contracts."

"And what's Micah going to do?" Jordan still seemed a bit uncomfortable talking about Brady.

"Micah's the brains. He's pulling together the services, the products. He's my operations officer and top security officer.

"I think you're bringing Brady in too soon. He will try to get a part of this company."

"He is going to be paid well, and he will be given bonuses appropriately. I got it all in a contract."

"Well, watch him. I don't like anything about that boy. Never did," Jordan remembered the short freckled-faced boy with the nappy red hair. "There's something sneaky about him. He kisses up too easily."

"I will keep that in mind," Ashton sat on the edge of his desk and held his arms open for Kali to walk into. She enjoyed all the hugs. His hands dropped and began to tug on her long skirt.

"What are you doing?" she pushed his hands away.

"I just thought we might christen the office," he said and winked at Jordan.

"Why don't the two of you have some fun? I'm gone." Jordan got up to leave.

"He's just kidding." Kali pulled away from Ashton to help Jordan out of his chair.

"No, no. Stop babying me, Kali." Jordan was standing freely. He and Ashton were looking at each other as if they were communicating without letting her in on something.

"I'm going home with you," said Kali. She didn't like the idea of having sex in the small office with Ms. Elliott sitting right outside.

"She's getting ready to take lunch," Ashton said. Kali turned quickly not expecting to hear him address what she was thinking. He was always doing that.

"And I'm taking myself home," Jordan said and walked out of the door. Ashton followed him and locked it. He returned and began to help her undress. For three weeks, Kali met Ashton at the same time in his office every day dressed for the occasion. One day she showed up with nothing on but a fur coat and a pair of pumps. Another day she wore a dress with no underwear. She was getting good at coming up with different outfits and scenarios, and each day when she came to his office, Ms. Elliott would stop what she was doing to accommodate their afternoon fling. Then one day Kali didn't show.

"Ms. Elliott, I'm going to run home a minute. Nobody is answering the phone and I know Kali has only morning classes this semester. I'll be back." Ashton put on his heavy coat and gloves then ran into the snowy wintry day down the street to the penthouse.

He rushed past the doorman with a slight nod and to the elevator for the penthouse. He pushed the key in roughly, trying to hasten the elevator down. The only thing he could think that would have kept her from coming was that something was wrong with Jordan. His heart was beating faster and faster as the slow antiquated elevator crept down the shaft to pick him up. He got on and pushed the P several times before the light came on. He stuck the key in and turned. The elevator ascended at a snail's pace before opening onto the private foyer. The front door to the penthouse was slightly ajar. He heard Jordan's raised voice, but he couldn't understand what he was saying. Jordan was in the side room where he entertained mostly his older friends. The room was furnished with a mixture of old and new flavors, 1930s furniture mixed with contemporary glass tables and etageres where he was shocked to see Kali pinned under his brother Asa.

"I said get the hell off of her! You hear me? She don't want you touching her!" Jordan had grabbed Asa's shoulder.

Asa pushed his grandfather's hand away and shoved him. He grabbed a handful of Kali's hair and made her shriek in pain. He smiled as if he were taking pleasure in hurting her.

"Get off of me!" she said, trying to fight him off.

"What the hell is going on in here?" Ashton's voice boomed through the chaos.

"Get him off of her, Ashton!" Jordan sounded like a helpless child. "I told him not to touch her."

Ashton could see his brother was half-clothed and Kali's clothes had been ripped from her body.

"Asa, get off of her," Ashton said calmly, walking decisively toward the two bodies draped awkwardly over the red velvet sofa.

"Why? You hitting it! Why can't I get some? Oh, let me guess. Because you're Papa's favorite son. Is that right?" he plunged into Kali still holding her by the hair. She cried out in pain.

"I said," Ashton gently moved his grandfather out of the way

— 145 —

by holding onto his shoulders. For a moment, he stopped to look at the old man and wondered if he had hurt him. He felt like a feather being brushed out of his way.

"He won't listen!" Jordan pleaded. His voice was frail and defeated.

Ashton reached his brother and grabbed him around his neck and yanked him off Kali. She scrambled over the high back of the old stuffed sofa trying to pull her clothes back together. She was aching from the blows she had received while trying to fight him off. Ashton made the mistake of letting him go. Asa lunged at him and they began to fight earnestly.

Kali was trapped in a corner afraid to move because the huge giants were destroying the room, but it all came to a halt when they both went crashing through the large glass coffee table that had been custom made for Jordan with all sorts of colored crystal beneath it. The room fell silent.

"Oh, oh! Oh, my God!" Jordan stumbled over to the twins as they lay on the floor, blood spreading beneath them.

"Ashton! Oh, my God, Ashton!" Jordan reached for Ashton who wasn't moving. Neither was Asa.

Kali climbed back over the sofa and ran to catch Jordan as he began to crumble. She held his weight as best she could and helped him down on the sofa.

"It's okay, Jordan. It's okay," she went over to Ashton and hit him on the shoulder. He jumped. He turned, startled to see her standing there half naked with a bruised face and a bloodied lip.

"Are you all right?" she asked, shaking. She looked back to see Jordan holding his heart, gasping for breath.

"Oh, my God, Jordan!" she shrieked.

Ashton lifted himself up. His hands were bleeding, but that was all. He looked down and saw his brother lying still in the blood. He turned to hear what Kali was screaming about and saw his grandfather taking his last breaths. He stood there motionless. Tears flooded his face, not knowing which way to turn, what to do.

He looked down at his brother's blood and then looked back into his grandfather's blank eyes. He knelt down and turned Asa over. It was his face. His face was letting out all the blood. He stood there and counted to ten.

"Kali," he said calmly. "Go get dressed. Take the keys to the car and go to the house. Don't come back here until I tell you it's safe. He's gone."

Kali kissed Jordan on the cheek and rubbed his head. She knew he was gone. She knew she had to run, just like Ashton said. And she did. She went upstairs and packed as many things as she could between pulling on anything she could find. She took the two bags she could carry, her book bag, and the keys. She didn't look back. Her life in the penthouse as she knew it was over.

CHAPTER SEVEN

Kali paced the floor from the kitchen through the dining room to the living room and back again. She couldn't be still. She looked out the front window of the pristine street and saw no one. She stopped her pacing near the phone, tempted to pick it up and call the penthouse, but she knew better. She couldn't do anything until she heard from Ashton. Billy was probably out for blood – her blood – though she had nothing to do with Jordan's death and nothing to do with Asa's act of violating her.

She stopped in the middle of the floor and physically tried to erase the memory of his touch from her. She cringed. He had raped her. He had come at her so abruptly and so violently. There was nothing she could do to stop him. She went to the fireplace and looked in the mirror. She had bruises around her neck and her face looked as bad as when she had had to run from her aunt's house. Her hands were still shaking. To make matters worse, Jordan had died because of that man's brutality. No wonder Ashton hated his brother. She did, too.

Suddenly, Kali's stomach began churning. She was feeling queasy, so queasy that she ran up the steps as fast as she could. She just made it to the hallway bathroom before throwing up. She hung over the porcelain seat, her whole body heaving and shivering. She didn't think she would ever stop. When she finally stopped, she slid across the cold tile and leaned against the bathroom door. She cried. She cried so hard her entire body ached.

She had been violated and frightened more than she had ever been. Even when Mazetta had come at her with a flurry of fists, even when Billy and Asa had grabbed her on that first Thanksgiving Day with the Sperlings, this type of fear had not ever coursed through her veins. With Mazetta, she had run. She fled and got away. On that Thanksgiving, Ashton and Jordan had come to her aid and protected her. She thought she knew how to maneuver among those men as long as Jordan and Ashton said they could not touch her. But, Asa was drunk. She could still smell the stench of liquor, stale smoke, and his sour breath. He had come to the penthouse looking for her. She was his primary focus. He had thrown Jordan out of the way as if he were a baby being thrown from a crib. He was angry and mean and vicious.

She pulled herself together and cleaned up her mess. She got up and staggered into her bathroom. She took a hot shower and tried to scrub any remnants of Asa from her body. She wrapped herself in the large terry cloth robe that belonged to Ashton and made her way back down the stairs. She was suddenly hungry, immensely hungry. She went into the kitchen and grabbed the peanut butter. She made a thick sandwich and sat on the edge of one of the kitchen chairs eating it hurriedly. Tears began to flow down her face once again. She wanted to hear from Ashton.

The day passed and the house was darkening as night began to fall. She turned on the television just in time to see a newscast about Jordan. The anchor was saying that a legendary jazz musician had died at his home of a heart attack, and Philadelphia would mourn one of its greatest artists. They showed pictures of him with his Grammy awards, in the company of the Queen of England, with Presidents of the United States and other celebrities. They had pictures of him with Billy, Ashton, and Micah standing in the background. Then, they showed his picture with the dates of his life beneath him. They mentioned nothing about Asa's bloodied body lying in the midst of the shattered glass coffee table. There was no mention that she had been savagely raped while Jordan stood by helplessly. No mention of Asa's cruelty contributing to his heart attack and her having to witness Jordan's last desperate heart-breaking breaths.

Another day went by and the telephone did not ring. Kali's body continually played games with her swinging from queasiness to hunger to uncontrollable shivers. She was scared and began to wonder if she needed to go to a doctor.

Three days later as she lie across the king-sized bed half asleep, she felt the bed lower on one side. She turned to see Ashton looking down on her sadly. She sat up and wrapped her arms around his neck. He laid his large head on her shoulders. They just sat there silently.

"He's really gone. Isn't he?" she finally said.

Ashton nodded.

"And Asa, is he?" she didn't really want to know.

"He's got a cut on his face. Ricky says he can fix it when it's healed. Plastic surgery," Ashton's voice trailed off.

"Why did he want to hurt me?" Kali asked while fighting back tears again.

"He thought that was the best way to hurt Jordan or me, I guess," Ashton took a deep breath. "The funeral is tomorrow. I think its best you stay away. Redd is in town."

"Oh," Kali hated the thought that she couldn't say goodbye.

"What if I sit in the back of the church?" Kali asked. She

wanted to see Jordan at least one more time. Her parents' caskets had been closed. She had been whisked into the funeral and out of town as soon as they had been lowered into the ground. Was she doomed again to another unfulfilled closure?

"No, not a good idea. Daddy wants to take everything out on you. And he would, even in public. You have to stay here. Don't go out," Ashton said adamantly.

"I've already missed two days of school," Kali protested.

"Then just go to school. Jordan would want you to do that." Ashton removed himself from her arms and stood up.

"I've got to go. I just wanted to make sure you were okay. Reggie has already packed up your things. I'll send over as much as I can by Kenny. He's the only one I trust to know where you are. Ms. Elliott knows, but she won't tell anyone."

"When will you be back?" Kali was already feeling abandoned.

"I don't know. You're okay, right?" he asked, with his back to her.

"I've been feeling sick to my stomach one minute and starving the next. And I keep dreaming about Jordan and Asa, and then you and Asa fighting. I'm scared, Ashton. Can't you stay just a little longer?" Kali pleaded.

He turned to her and knelt down next to the bed where she sat.

"You've been feeling queasy?" his voice changed, but his eyes were still flat.

"Yes," Kali answered. She reached and brushed his hair with her hand. His face was cold. She knew he was hurting and she wanted to help him. She also wanted to ask him if Redd was in her bed, but she thought better of it. Redd was his wife, and she was probably trying to help him get through this, too. Kali let her hand drop to her lap, the queasiness was back. She jumped up and ran to the bathroom. This time nothing came up, but her body was wracked with shivers.

Ashton picked her up and put her in the bed.

"What can I get you?" he pulled the covers up over her.

"A peanut butter sandwich," she said.

A week later as she sat at the dining room table trying to study, Ashton walked in the door with one of his brothers behind him.

"You remember Chico, right?" he said pointing to the shorter brother with tan skin and straight black hair.

"Yes. Hello," she stood up and buckled her pants. Everything had been fitting awkwardly. Kali thought she was going to have to leave peanut butter alone.

"Chico is a doctor. I'm sorry it has taken me so long to get back, but I thought you needed a checkup," he walked over to her and dismissed the curl from her eyes.

"Where's the bed?" Chico asked, swinging his bag.

"Bed?" Kali asked suspiciously.

"Yeah, I need you to lie down so I can examine you," Chico peeled off his coat and threw it over the sofa.

Ashton kissed her, but not with the passion that he had on the morning of Jordan's death. She wanted him to hold her, but there was a coolness emanating from him that concerned her. She tried not to think about him. She let her mind wander to whether she were going to be able to afford to get through summer school. It was obvious life with the Sperlings was almost over.

She let Ashton lead her up to the bedroom. She sat on the bed and he began to unbutton her oxford shirt. It was bulging. She slid out of the shirt because it was Ashton who was undressing her. When he finished unbuttoning, unfastening, and unzipping, she was completely nude. He motioned for her to lie down. She did and tried not to think about anything. Chico walked into her bathroom and lathered his hands with soap, then rinsed. The room was quiet.

She waited patiently as she replayed a conversation she had once had with Ashton. He had had a little too much to drink and they were talking about mothers. He said something like, "women have a way of disappearing permanently in the Sperling household." He had alluded they had died, never to be seen again. Now, the two of them were acting so aloof. Maybe that was the plan. Jordan was dead, and now she was next. She lay in the bed resigned to her fate.

Chico sat next to her and began to examine her breasts. He lifted them and then pressed them gently with two of his fingers. He pressed on her stomach gently, but firmly. Then he began to spread her legs.

"I'm an obstetrician and gynecologist," he said, still guiding her legs and bending her knees. "I would prefer an examining table," he said, looking over at Ashton, pointing to the pillows.

Ashton lifted her and shoved pillows beneath her and then he climbed behind her on the bed supporting her. Chico slid his fingers into her vagina and continued to press on her stomach.

"Who's the father?" he asked. "Is this Jordan's baby?"

"No," Ashton answered quietly. "Jordan hadn't slept with her in months. The only thing he was up for was a few nibbles here and there. He was losing interest in sex."

"A john? You?" Chico asked with a big grin on his small bird-like face.

"Mine," Ashton said proudly. "This baby is mine."

"Baby?" Kali looked from one to the other. She was lying there exposed with the man's fingers still inside her as they chatted as if she didn't exist.

"I need a couple of more things," Chico was talking directly to Ashton, with his fingers still inside her. Now they were moving in a circular motion. He was enjoying being inside her. "I need some blood to see how far along she really is. And I need some urine to validate my diagnosis."

She snapped her legs shut, and he removed his hand.

"Sorry," he said, still grinning. He opened his bag and brought out a syringe. He loaded it with a tube and laid it next to her. He pulled out a strip of latex and tied it around her arm.

"Make a fist," said Chico. She did and turned her head. She hated needles. However, he was an expert. She barely felt the pinch, unlike when she had had her physical for school and the woman had to make several attempts to get her blood. He placed the tube of blood in his bag and pulled out a plastic cup wrapped in plastic.

"I bet you have to pee. Go pee in this," he instructed.

She gladly got off the bed and ran into the bathroom. She left the door open so she could hear if they talked. They said nothing. As she was finishing, Chico entered the small bathroom and held the cup over the sink. He stuck a strip of paper in it and winked at her.

"Congratulations, Mommy," he said as he smiled and poured out the pee in the toilet, then washed his hands. She waited for him to leave so she could wash hers. She stared in the mirror praying that this was a nightmare and that she would wake up in her bed in the penthouse with Jordan's or Ashton's arms wrapped around her. She went back into the room and picked up her bra from the floor. She flung it around her and began to clasp it shut when Ashton's hands stopped her. He shook his head. She stood there, a chill running down her spine, not from the cold air, but from his manner. He grabbed her hand and she followed him and Chico down the stairs.

"Okay, little Mommy. I hear you have been experiencing morning sickness. When you do, eat some crackers. Saltines, without the salt, are the best. Also, don't over eat, but don't go without eating. You don't want to gain too much weight. You will have a hell of a time shedding the pounds if you do. Just eat healthy. Stay away from cat litter, smoke, alcohol, and bluefish. You will be fine. I will be back in about four weeks to check on you. I'll call Ashton and let him know your due date after I get the blood test back."

"Chico," said Ashton. He let go of her hand and hugged his brother. "This needs to stay between you and me. No records of any kind. None. You understand?"

Chico looked around him at Kali and nodded wholeheartedly.

"I hope it's a boy," Chico said, laughing and patted Ashton on the shoulder. "Right, Jordan Junior."

The reference made Kali uneasy. She knew there were five boys raised in that household with only one mother accounted for and the way Ashton was acting she wondered if history was about to repeat itself.

"Don't even play, Chico," Ashton said. "Redd can't find out about this baby. Neither can Billy nor Asa. No one for that matter. Keep it to your chest. I am counting on you."

Ashton pulled Chico close to him and whispered something in his ear. Chico pulled away, the smile wiped from his face.

"I got it. Trust me, I got it," he said fumbling with the knob to the front door. He opened the door and left abruptly, not stopping to put his coat on before hitting the cold winter wind.

"What did you say to him?" Kali stood naked with her arms hugging her body to ward off the cold air from the front door.

"Nothing. Nothing that matters," he said and sat on the back of the sofa and let out a heavy sigh.

"Wow," he said. "I've been through so much over the last couple of weeks. I don't know if I'm coming or going."

He looked at her belly. He could see the thickening of her waist. She was still standing there shaking from the cold blast of winter.

"I'm going to be a father." His eyes began to glaze over with tears. He motioned her to come to him, and he kissed her. There was the passion that she had missed. She felt the tension fade from his body as he picked her up and carried her up the stairs. He stayed with her the entire night. Though Kali wanted to believe she was safe again, there was still something missing. His body was the same, his breathing had the same rhythm to it, and his touch was still soft and gentle. His lips still made her body arch, but his eyes looked at her differently. She wanted to believe he was mourning Jordan, but that wasn't it. Even with the circumstances of Jordan's death, they both had known his life was limited, and Jordan was living on borrowed time.

The phone rang waking them up. It was an odd sound since no one ever called there. He grabbed the phone quickly.

"It's Ms. Elliott," he said, holding the phone out to her. "She says you have some mail."

"Mail?" Kali took the phone.

"Hi, Ms. Elliott. How are you?" Kali eagerly spoke into the phone. It had been a long time since she had had a phone conversation.

"Hi, Sweetheart. How are you doing?" Ms. Elliott answered. "I have some mail for you. Reggie dropped it off this morning. Would you like me to bring it to you?"

"I would love that," Kali perked up. She looked back at Ashton who was staring at her again, but not the way he used to stare at her. "When can you come? I have one class this afternoon, but I'll be home by four. Is that too late?"

Kali and Ms. Elliott chitchatted some more and then hung up. Kali wanted to get up and get dressed, but she didn't want to chase Ashton out of her bed. It had been so lonely without him, even if he did seem different.

"It's okay," he said, reading her mind was still something he could do. "I have to get in to work myself. And then, this afternoon is the reading of the will. I have to go to that."

"Jordan's will reading is today?" Kali wondered if Jordan had mentioned her in it and then thought if he had, she would have received some sort of notice. At least, that is what they had taught her in school.

"I hope he left you everything," Kali leaned back and put her head on his chest. He sat up with her on it, bouncing her back a little. It was a rejection, the little push. She shrugged it off and got up and went into the bathroom.

Ashton sat on the edge of the bed listening to the water run. He cared for Kali. Maybe he cared too much. He knew Redd was at the penthouse waking up in his bed, probably with his brother since he didn't go home last night. But, he couldn't leave Kali alone another night, she was getting fidgety, and she was pregnant. That was supposed to be good news, but it scared the hell out of him.

"Be patient," he whispered to himself. "You have got to be patient. You have got to get it right, son."

"What?" Kali was coming out of the bathroom wrapped in a towel. "Do you want me to fix you breakfast."

"And have you throwing up all over the place," he teased. "No, thank you."

"How much do you think Jordan left?" she sat on the edge of the bed applying lotion to her body. He sat there and watched, his eyes settling on her waistline. He had lost track of time. How long ago had Jordan taken her off the pill?

"A lot. Millions. He had money overseas, his dirty money. And he had money here, somewhere. I guess we will account for all of it. He was pretty thrifty and detailed enough to keep up with every dime."

"Then I'm sure he left you most of it. I really hope he didn't leave Asa a dime," Kali said angrily. "You know what I don't understand?" Kali was talking fast. She knew once he left she was not assured she would see him again anytime soon.

"What?"

"How did I get pregnant? You, yourself said that Jordan put me on the pill as soon as I walked in the door. And when I knew I was taking them, I took one everyday without fail. I even took the little green ones."

"Did you have sex with that boy?" Ashton was suddenly suspicious. He couldn't believe she was really pregnant. He was looking at how thick her waistline was and he knew he had been careful for a while. For how long, he started trying to count back in his head.

"What boy?" Kali was stunned by the question.

"The concert ticket boy," Ashton said gruffly.

"You and Jordan are the only men I have had sex with. At least until…" the bottle of lotion dropped from her hand. Ashton got off the bed and on his knees. He picked up the bottle and handed it to her. He wiped the spilled lotion off the carpet. He looked in her eyes and saw the pain. His brother had raped her, and he was sitting here accusing her of cheating on him, the greatest cheater in the world.

"I'm sorry," he said, patting her hand. "I'm not myself."

He got up and went into the bathroom, closing the door behind him. He never closes the door, she thought. He used to say that small bathroom made him claustrophobic. She got dressed quickly and went downstairs. She ate a peanut butter sandwich for break-fast. She couldn't get enough of peanut butter.

He came down dressed and didn't bother to kiss her goodbye.

"I'll call you," he said and left her in the house alone again. This time she didn't mind so much. She had known life would change when Jordan was gone. She had sort of expected to eventually lose touch with Ashton. After all, he was still married and had not once told her that he would leave his wife for her. He had never mentioned any future for either of them. Now she was pregnant, and he was probably feeling trapped. She wondered if they should discuss abortion.

She made it through the afternoon class and came home to find Ms. Elliott parked in front of her door. The two women hugged, and she led Ms. Elliott into the house.

"I'd show you around, but I know now that you found it and furnished it. I don't know if I ever thanked you for that. I don't know where I would be living either now that Jordan is gone," Kali led her to the dining room table.

Ms. Elliott pulled out a stack of mail. It was mostly junk mail and school mail, but there was an important looking letter from a lawyer's office.

"You really need to go to the post office and have your mail forwarded. I don't know how much longer Reggie will be needed at the penthouse. She is awfully worried about her job. She said that if I ever came across you to say hi and that she misses you."

"Oddly enough, I miss her, too," Kali sorted the mail. "She and I used to fight all the time. But, it was good fighting, just verbal sparring."

"She said that no one knew where you were, but that everybody believed Ashton knew where you were. I didn't tell her any differ-ent. I told her that I would ask Ashton if he knew where I could forward it."

"So, they are asking about me," Kali sighed. "Probably not in a good way."

Kali toyed with the mail and looked closely at the envelope from the attorney. She opened it. It was a notice. She had been invited to attend the reading of the will. Ashton and his family had been copied on it. Ashton hadn't said a word.

Ashton walked into the door just as Ms. Elliott was leaving. He could have sworn she had just given him a disapproving look. Kali didn't bother to speak to him. She went back to the dining room table and gathered the mail together. She wasn't sure what she was going to do other than finish school. That was the only thing she could focus on now. And she thought about maybe, just maybe, getting rid of the baby.

"Two months," he said, following her as she put the mail away and then walked into the kitchen. There were the two glasses and a plate in the sink that she washed while he leaned against the kitchen door.

"You look and feel like you are three he says. Two months is about right," he said as if talking to himself. He had stopped using the condoms about two months ago.

"Maybe we shouldn't have this baby," she said, putting the glasses up in the cabinet.

"What?" Ashton asked as his eyes flashed darts across the kitchen right into her heart.

"I said, maybe we shouldn't have this baby. Let's face it Ashton, you are married, and I am still in school." She knew from the darkening of his hazel eyes she was treading on dangerous terrain.

"I will keep the baby. You can finish school," his voice was low, but she heard him clearly.

"Like Billy did? Like Jordan did? Are you cutting me out?" She wished she hadn't started this conversation.

"If you want to be cut out," Ashton was hoping that was what she wanted. He didn't know if he had the heart to hurt her.

"I don't know. I don't know what I want," she slammed the plate on top of the others and stormed out of the kitchen.

"You got the letter, didn't you?" he asked. "The mail had that letter in it. Didn't it?"

"You could have stopped it, I'm sure," Kali sat in the chair in the living room. She didn't want him attempting to sit near her on the sofa. Then it hit her, she still hadn't seen the deed to this house. She could still be homeless because she had never signed anything. Her heart sank.

"It's been rescheduled for next Tuesday at 1:00 pm. I didn't say anything because I knew they couldn't hold it today, anyway."

"But, you said," Kali hid her face in her hands. She was on her own now. There was no doubt about it. She was going to have to put some of Jordan's training and some of Penn's to use.

"I know, I said I was going today, but I was banking on it not happening. And it didn't. So I need you to be there, Tuesday."

"You guys tried to have it, but it couldn't happen 'cause I wasn't there!" Kali shouted. "I'm not stupid! Just because I am female and pregnant doesn't mean I'm unable to comprehend what happened. Why didn't you want me there?"

"That's not what happened, I promise. They are trying to get their hands on the accounts from overseas. I didn't want you in that fight."

"Did they find it?"

"No, but I did," Ashton plopped down on the sofa. "I followed the instructions Jordan had given me before he died."

Ashton reached into his pocket and pulled out an index card. He handed it to her.

"Other than what's in my safe deposit box, this is the only record. So don't lose it. It's your account number and your password. It's the location and contact of your offshore account."

"What are you saying?" Kali looked at Ashton's scribble on the card, but she could read it clearly.

"Either memorize or wear it. Don't lose it, whatever you do. You lose it and you lose three million dollars," he stared at the ceiling and shook his head.

"You're giving me Jordan's money?" Kali was shocked at the revelation.

"No, Jordan left implicit instructions on how to deal with the offshore cash. He left you three million dollars. He left me more and Micah some. He didn't leave the other ones any of it. Tuesday, no matter what is in that estate has nothing to do with this estate. This is separate from anything else that will be revealed. So keep your mouth shut and keep away from me during the whole preceding. My wife is going to be there. And Kali," he looked at her from the side of his eyes, "don't you ever let me hear you say anything about terminating this baby again."

Tuesday arrived quickly. Kali made arrangements to get her school assignments so she would be prepared on Wednesday. It was an overwhelmingly cold February day, the wind felt like slivers of ice chips slicing across her skin. She arrived at the lawyer's office ten minutes before the meeting, and all the Sperlings were already there. She was dressed in a black suit with a black silk shirt beneath it. She wore the diamond necklace and earrings Jordan had given her on her 20th birthday. She sported rubies and diamonds on her fingers that he had gifted her. She wore a tasteful black-rimmed hat that kept her rogue curl from creeping. She let the rest of her hair hang loose from beneath. She knew when she walked in the room that she would be the most beautiful woman they had ever seen. She wanted them to see what Jordan saw, and she wanted them to know that she didn't need them or want them in her life, not even Ashton.

The lawyer, Mr. Atkins, jumped up right away and showed her to her seat. His secretary, who had followed her into the room, asked if she could get her anything. Kali had been given top-notch treatment from the moment she walked into the building. The security guard had held the elevator door for her. The first receptionist had personally walked her to the appropriate suite. Everyone was eyeing her with admiration. She was poised and self-assured the way Jordan had taught her to be. She missed him and she was going to make him proud. Today she didn't care what his family thought of her.

She looked across the table and saw a very jealous green-eyed Redd who had on way too much make-up trying to cover puffy dark circles. Kali showed no expression as she met the eyes of each Sperling: Billy, Chico, Ricky, Micah, Micah's wife Ruby, Redd, Ashton and then Asa. She stared into Asa's eyes until he diverted them. She wanted them to know, she was not afraid.

"Now that we are all here, we can proceed," the lawyer kept looking in her direction. They were all obviously well heeled, but Jordan had uplifted her higher than the rest. She could feel it.

The lawyer began to outline how the will was created and Jordan's intent to divide his assets. He then read a very touching letter to the family as a whole. A portion of the letter was to Kali and Kali only.

My loving Kali,
You have shown me more love in the last few years than I have ever known in my entire life. And I thank you for that. Had you not come into my life when you did, I would have died an

empty man. You have taught me more about love and family than everything else I have learned in my seventy-something years on this earth. I know I won't be around to watch you graduate, but I know you will with top honors. You are a smart and intelligent woman, a strong woman, a formidable match for anyone. I believe right now you are probably mourning me more than anyone else on this planet and I love you for that. Take care, my sweet. If I had known a woman like you in my earlier days, things might have been different for me and my boys. Go on your way now. Make a good life for yourself. You owe no one anything. Remember that.

Kali sat stoically as the letter was read, but her heart was dissolving beneath her steel woman exterior. She was mourning him, maybe more than she had mourned her own parents. Jordan had lifted her up in so many ways. Her eyes met with Ashton's momentarily and for that second she saw them soften.

"Now for the reading of the will," the attorney said. The room was so quiet a mouse could have caused an uproar that out-thundered the trains moving beneath them.

"To William Marshall Banks, aka Billy Sperling. I leave my love and a sum total of $200,000. You are a man of means with a thriving business. You no longer need anything I could give you, especially the Banks name.

"To Ricardo Enrique Sperling, aka Ricky. I know your practice as a plastic surgeon will thrive, but I am going to give you the gift of $200,000 to get your practice off the ground wherever you want. You were a good grandson. Though we were never close, I still loved you. So, I am giving you my club in San Francisco, which is where I believe you really want to be.

"To Charles Anderson Sperling, aka Chico. You were the smallest in stature, but the biggest in heart. That's why you are out there delivering babies. You get $200,000 and my club in Los Angeles. Sell it. Keep it. Whatever makes you happy is all I want for you. You brought me lots of laughter and sunshine, and may you keep sharing that side of you with the world.

"To Asa Thomas Sperling, the photographer and keeper of another man's wife. I had to think this one through, because there were days when I thought you hated me more than you loved me. But, I am leaving you $200,000 and your daddy. Oh, and I guess I'll throw in all those wonderful pictures you created that are hanging on the wall in the penthouse, with the exception of me. I want that picture to remain where it is. And yes, I will leave you most of the paintings since you're an artist, a cruel artist with no heart. I will leave it at that.

"Now, for the women in your lives I leave you a few trinkets to remember me by. To Mrs. Ashton Sperling, aka Redd, I leave you a diamond necklace that once belonged to Ashton's mother. It's worth about $25,000, in case you are wondering.

"And to Mrs. Micah Sperling, aka Ruby, you were good to me so I am leaving you the Bentley. Just do me a favor and let Micah drive it every once in awhile.

"Micah Jordan Sperling, the man with the plan. Micah you are smarter than the whole bunch and the military made you far more dangerous than any of these fools can imagine. That's the Jordan in you. I own twelve nightclubs around the world and two of them I just gave to your brothers who didn't get to know me as well as you. So, I am giving you the remaining ten, plus $1,000,000. I hope you and Ruby can live with that.

"Now, I leave my love and my heart to the man who stood by me in every hour of need, the man who would come to check on me and rub my head, the man who lifted me and carried me to the bathroom when I couldn't carry myself. To my Ashton Taylor Sperling, aka Jordan Junior. I know that's what you are called behind your back and in front of your face when they are trying to be mean to you. You couldn't help it. You stole my heart the moment Billy put you into my arms, and I have never hidden that from anyone. So Ashton, for you, son, I leave $10,000,000, and the building that houses the penthouse. Yes, to those of you who are stunned, I owned the whole building. Bought it in 1976 when the owner was about to lose it. So now, it belongs to Ashton, with one exception.

"To Kalina Denise Harris, my sweet Kali, the exotic one, the Queen Bitch, the little girl from down south with the big heart, I leave the penthouse and everything that's in it, except the pictures and paintings that are on the wall, minus the picture of me on the stairway. And since you will need money to take care of it, I leave you $500,000 in expense money until you start earning your way. All I ask is that you never sell it and you never let any of my things walk out of it.

"Billy, I know you are sitting at the table ready to explode. You couldn't wait for me to die. Well, I am gone. And the things you coveted are gone. Now go on with your life and let everyone else go on with theirs."

The lawyer put down the paper and started passing out packages for each person to sign. Everyone was still silent. Kali noticed that Redd was giving her the once over. Kali accepted her package and began to read it.

"Like you know what the fuck it says," Billy shouted across the table at her.

"Excuse me," the lawyer said. "Please refrain from any outbursts. Your father also added a stipulation that should anyone decide to fight this will, they will forfeit everything that was willed to them.

Asa hastily signed his papers and got up from the table. He

handed them to the lawyer and then leaned so close to Kali that she could feel his breath blowing fiercely in her ear.

"I'm on my way over to pick up my paintings and anything else I want," he hissed and stood up and smiled at Ashton and Redd. Redd was holding onto Ashton's arm tightly. Kali noticed the veins in Ashton's neck bulging. He said nothing, but his eyes followed Asa to the door leading out of the room.

"That won't be possible, Mr. Sperling," the lawyer called across the table.

"Why not? I still have my keys to the place," Asa triumphantly patted his pocket.

"No sir, the locks were changed last evening. The staff has already been made aware that a change in ownership was taking place today. As noted in the paperwork you just signed, sir, you will have to contact my office to gain access and a supervisor will assist you in removing the paintings and pictures. Also, in your paperwork is a list of those paintings and pictures that are on the wall. Any others in Mr. Banks' ownership defaults with the penthouse."

"How, the hell, will I know if she doesn't switch them before I get there?" Asa asked.

"That's why there is list in your package, sir. If you would like to stay, I will gladly go over the package with you. Or if you like, you can schedule an appointment on your way out," said the lawyer, pointing toward the door. Asa stormed out the door and slammed it behind him.

"I'll let that go," the lawyer said, looking at Billy. "Would you like to review yours, sir?" Billy shook his head and began thumbing through the lengthy paperwork. He was looking for the loophole that would let him fight it. First, he was upset that he had only gotten $200,000 and was even more upset that Ashton had received $10,000,000 and the building, but what got him really boiling was the fact that the Queen Bitch was going to remain in the penthouse. He stood up and put his copy in his briefcase.

"I'll be in touch," he said to the lawyer. "Good day, boys."

"Bye, Daddy," Chico said cheerfully. He and Ricky spoke quietly. They were both smiling.

"What's the bottom line, sir? For me," Chico asked leaning back and rocking in the chair.

"The club is worth about $1,000,000 in real estate. You can sell it or keep it. You will have to look closely at the books to see what the business is worth. I am guessing at least that much."

"Is that it?" asked Chico.

"Yes, and make sure the lady at the front desk has your address. We will make sure you receive the $200,000 once it is liquidated."

"And mine," Ricky asked, he bounced happily out of his chair. "How much?"

"About $1.5 million in real estate, maybe more depending on the current market. Your area is a little hotter than Charles'."

The two high-fived each other and chuckled.

"Thanks, old man," Ricky said, kissing the document before he signed it. He walked past Ashton and patted him on the shoulder. "Man, I feel sorry for you."

Ashton sat stone-faced with the untouched paperwork in front of him.

"Aren't you going to read it?" Redd asked, her green eyes watching Kali as she sat carefully reading her paperwork.

"I will," he said, pulling away from her clutch. "Give me a little space," he whispered. She sat back in her chair and smoothed out her clothes looking at Ruby who was looking bored and uninterested as Micah read through his package.

"Ladies and gentlemen, I will be in my office next door. Should you have any questions, I am at your disposal." The lawyer stacked up his papers and left the room.

"I really need to get back to the office," Ruby said as she kissed Micah on his bald head. She left the room quietly.

"How long are we going to be here, darling?" Redd said as if she were announcing it to the world.

"As long as it takes," Ashton answered, still letting the paperwork lay in front of him.

"Well, you should start reading it, don't you think?" She was pushing him and he was pushing back.

"Darling," he said, "why don't you go across the street to Wanamaker's and spend some of the millions I just inherited?"

"What a wonderful idea!" she said loudly. She got up and made a big production of kissing Ashton draping herself over him. "I'm leaving now," she announced again. Micah kept reading his paperwork line item by line item and so did Kali. They both heard her as she fumbled with the door making as much noise as she could. Neither of them acknowledged her.

"You already know what's in it, don't you?" Micah leaned back and folded his hands behind his head.

Ashton nodded, then reached into his pocket and slid an index card to Micah.

Micah looked down at Kali and then at the index card.

"It's okay. She knows what it is," Ashton answered. "It's six million."

Micah looked knowingly at the card. "Who else?"

"You, me, her," Ashton said. "Only copy. Six, six, three, and that's it."

"Sweet," Micah stared at the card. "I loved that old man."

"We were the only ones that did," Ashton said.

"What else is in these things?" Micah hit the paperwork on the table.

"The real estate where the undeclared clubs and whore houses were. Fifty-fifty, you and me," Ashton said.

"How much?" Micah's face was as blank as Ashton's.

"Twenty…Million." Ashton folded his arms.

"What's in mine?" Kali decided to ask.

"Me," he smirked.

"Ha. Ha," said Kali.

"Seriously, I am your guardian and executor, until you reach the age of 25. You can't get rid of me before that."

"I don't think I like the sound of that," Kali said. She didn't care to have him in her life that much longer. She had imagined severing ties with Ashton quickly and cleanly. Especially if she had a girl, the break would be easy. He wouldn't try to take a girl baby from her, not if he followed the Sperling pattern. She looked at the index card in Micah's hand.

"I'll know every penny you spend," Ashton said as he opened the paperwork and signed it. He picked up his copy and put it in a briefcase.

"Don't you have school or something, preggers?" he joked.

"Preggers!" Micah sat up at attention.

"She is pregnant with my baby," Ashton said proudly. "Jordan is probably up in heaven shouting with the best of them. He is going to have a great-grandchild by a woman that he loved."

"Wish he could have been here to hold it," Micah said grinning. "I'll never forget when Daddy brought me home to Jordan. I must have been about five. Jordan picked me up and said, "Finally, a little brown boy. I was beginning to think my family was going to be completely washed out." I had no clue what he was talking about. But, I liked him. He took me everywhere, to the zoo, to the museums. I think he spent almost as much time with me as he did with you until I went into the Air Force."

"He did. You and me. We were his family. It hurt him when Ruby came between the two of you, and he hated Daddy for making you work for him," said Ashton.

"Well, I hated Daddy for that. But, I don't regret Ruby. She is everything I want and I need. I'm happy. How about you?"

"I will be," he looked down at Kali.

"She's having my baby," he sang sweetly. She dropped her head and started reading the package again. Ashton had become an unsolvable puzzle. His mood swings and his game playing were taxing her. She didn't know if she could trust his smiles, his playfulness, or him at all.

"When do I move back?" she asked, tired of reading all the fine print. There appeared to be a stipulation behind everything. She wanted to get to the point.

"You don't," Ashton said quickly. "Not until after the baby. We have to keep the baby quiet. I don't want anybody trying to hurt either of you."

"There's a clause in here about the baby?" Kali asked, but not really expecting an answer as she read the clause herself.

"Yeah, there is. All it says is that the two of you will be taken care of for the rest of your lives. No questions asked."

"Hmmm," said Kali. She didn't want to sign the papers too soon. She looked at both men sitting at the table on the other end of the long conference room. They were both trained lawyers, and she was still getting her education, but she smelled a rat. And his name was Ashton.

"Why?" she asked. The two of them looked her way expectantly. "Why wouldn't Jordan leave a million or two million to Billy? Something more than 200K and I love you, you ungrateful son of a bitch."

"Because, he had already given Billy five million dollars. Billy won't tell anybody that, but he got his inheritance last year. The screwed up part is that he has probably already spent it. And don't feel sorry for Asa. Those paintings and pictures are worth millions. Some of them are classics. That's why he is so anxious to get them," Ashton said and stood up from the table.

"Let's get back to the office," he said to Micah. "I just got an interesting contract offer this morning."

"I'd offer you a ride," Ashton said to Kali while straightening his tie, "but we are not supposed to be seen together. I'll see you tomorrow, though.

"Redd is getting ready for another long stint in Europe. I'll take care of the penthouse. Don't worry. I got you covered." He winked at her. The wink gave her the creeps.

"Always use your instincts," she heard Jordan's voice in her head. Her instincts were on high alert these days.

"I can get home just fine," she continued to read her paperwork while the men walked out of the room. She was disappointed to find that Ashton was right. Jordan had assigned him as her executor. The money wasn't hers to do with what she pleased until she was 25. That is, if she made it to 25. There was also a clause that everything would go to Ashton should anything happen to her. What was going to happen to her after the baby?

CHAPTER EIGHT

The first two months after Jordan's will was read became a whirlwind. School had kept Kali occupied on the nights that Ashton wasn't there. At first, they had spent their days together as if they were hiding out from the world, and then suddenly Ashton wanted to go everywhere. He took her dancing. Something he knew she loved to do. She was beginning to feel off balanced as her waistline continued to thicken quickly. He paid her compliments. Bought her anything she desired, fixed her dinner, and pampered her to no end. Then he received a call. Redd was coming back to the States.

Spring was budding in the United States, and she was in demand here. Their time turned into short phone calls that became even shorter as the time went by. He stopped by twice to see her and spent all of his time talking to her stomach. She was getting jealous and annoyed by the fact that the rest of her could not hold his attention. He was no longer interested in her conversations, just her condition. Then there was the silence, a totally deafening silence that frightened her a little.

The more she thought about it, the more she realized there was a side of Ashton that she didn't know. He was thirteen years older than she was. He had experiences in life that she could not even imagine, especially since he was a man – a married man. She chastised herself for her predicament, but couldn't come up with a way she could have prevented it. After all, Jordan had had complete control of her life, and they had probably planned her pregnancy long before his death. She smoothed the soft material covering her belly and sighed. Maybe it wasn't a curse. She had $500,000 that she had access to immediately. She had a roof over her head and her education was almost complete, at least the first half. She had planned to get her MBA in maybe a year or two, after she had gotten used to being a mother. A mother, she smiled at the thought. Maybe this was Jordan's way of ensuring she would continue to have family.

Maybe he knew Ashton would soon abandon her when sex was no longer a major factor in their relationship. That thought made her sad. She had a deep longing for Ashton. She wasn't sure if what she was experiencing could be associated with the word "love." But, even though she hated him one minute, the next minute she didn't know what her life would be like without him in it. He made her laugh. He made her cry. Heck, he was the first man to be intimate with her at so many levels. She could talk to him. She told him everything about her life. She thought he told her everything about his, except when it came to his wife. She understood why he couldn't share that part. She was the woman outside of his marriage. She was the woman who couldn't be his wife. She wasn't about to kid herself about being in that role one day. Ashton had never given her any hope for that. She was his sex kitten, his confidante, his intimate link with Jordan. Now she was carrying his baby, creating a bond that would last a lifetime.

It had been weeks since she had heard from Ashton. Her days had been pretty much the same over and over. And her stomach was getting bigger and bigger. Her only human contact had been Kenny who came over every day and massaged her feet, fed her, and talked to her to keep her from going absolutely insane. After he would leave, she would study. She couldn't bear turning on the television.

One day, she had turned it on to see both Ashton and Asa draped over Redd in a photo shoot. The reporter had asked her about the gorgeous bronze twins who seemed to worship her. She had answered in her thick South Philly accent that it was like heaven.

Kali thought it was obvious that Redd had never been brutalized by either of the twins, and what Jordan used to say about Redd was on point. That woman had the best of both worlds. She had the twin that she loved with her all year round, and the twin that was in love with her always there to support her with his millions, and always willing to accept any crumb she threw his way. Redd had nothing to worry about. She didn't have to fall asleep alone in a big king-sized bed in a small two-bedroom house surrounded by strangers outside her door.

Kali had to face it. Everybody in her world was a stranger, except Kenny. Kenny was her whole world, and her ever-growing stomach was her universe. The baby sometimes felt like it was fighting a war inside of her, and she had no one to talk to about it. She was afraid to call Ms. Elliott. She knew she would have to follow whatever script Ashton would give her.

Kali almost stumbled into her door that evening. The day had been long and filled with final exams. She was glad the semester was over. The weather wasn't hot yet. People were still wearing jackets in the May sunshine, but she was burning up from the extra weight. She shoved the door open with her heavy book bag and threw it on the chair next to the door. She began to peel out of her jean jacket and as she closed the door, she noticed the petals. Rose petals were everywhere just like on her 20th birthday, except these were all red. The petals covered the furniture, the floors, the stairs and even the dining room table where the table was set with two tall candles burning in the late afternoon light.

"Kenny," she called, hearing someone moving around in the kitchen just beyond her sight.

"Surprise!" Ashton quickly filled the doorway. He held two plates in his hands.

"What are you doing here?" she said defensively. She wasn't feeling well at all, and he was waving food in her direction. She was immediately sorry for the tone of her voice, because although irritated, she didn't want to chase him away. She was dreading being alone all the way home.

"Oh, look at the little mommy. Kenny told me you were huge. I just never imagined this big." He put the plates at their settings and walked toward her with open arms. Her head immediately fell against his chest and tears ran freely down her face. She couldn't explain it, but his arms made her want to crumble into them. His warmth and his smell made her cry.

"Oh, baby. What's the matter?" he picked her up and gently sat her on the sofa. "You have a bad day?"

"Yes," she said, between sobs. She couldn't believe how hard she was crying. He got on his knees and removed her sneakers. She didn't have on any socks. She could barely get the shoes on her feet.

"Oh, Ashton's here. I'm going to make it better," he said as if talking to a child and that made her cry even harder.

"Kali, Kali." He smoothed her hair from her face, "You want to lie down?"

She nodded as the tears flowed like an ocean, and her body hiccupped with sobs.

"Okay," he said, sweetly. "Let me take you upstairs."

Ashton carried her upstairs to their bed and pulled back the covers. She buried her head in the pillow and turned away from him. He sat next to her quietly, gently stroking her hair.

"Do you want me to rub your back?" he asked.

She shook her head. She wasn't sure if she wanted him to touch her or leave. All she knew was that she couldn't stop crying.

The next morning she awakened nude with a nude Ashton lying next to her.

"Good morning," he said, "you must have been really tired yesterday. You cried yourself to sleep."

"I was," she said, wiping her face and wondering if there were streaks of tears dried on her face.

"I'll run you a bath." He got up quickly and helped her sit up.

"I can't get out of the bath tub," she said. "I only take showers."

"I'll put you in and take you out," he said trying to acquiesce to whatever she wanted.

"You really grew these last two months."

"Three," she corrected him.

"I'm here now," he said eagerly. "I'll be here until the baby is born. I swear."

"Wifey is out of the country again?" she asked defiantly.

"Yes," he said and left for the bathroom.

"I've got to go," she said awkwardly, hoping he wasn't going to make her walk all the way to the hallway bathroom to pee.

"I was just going," he stopped, realizing there was only a shower in that bathroom. "I'll go out here and run your bath. Can you make it?" he looked concerned.

"Yes, I can go to the bathroom by myself," she said arrogantly.

"Okay." He didn't argue with her. But, he stood and watched

her waddle toward the bathroom. She hated him seeing her like that.

After he had put her into the tub and bathed her, he massaged her back and her feet.

"Are you extremely uncomfortable?" he asked.

"Now, that's a silly question. Don't you think?" she said, not sure why she was feeling so evil and irritable. She should have been happy to see the father of her child. She had imagined him coming home to her a million times. Now he was here, and she wanted to do nothing but fight with him, and he wouldn't fight back. He hovered over her at a loss of what to do or say. Then the doorbell rang.

Kali lay there thinking it was Kenny, so she didn't move. Right now, she did prefer Kenny's company over Ashton's. She heard him go down the stairs and she closed her eyes shut tight. This is not happening to me, she thought. I am not grossly huge and pregnant.

She opened her eyes to see Chico standing over her.

"Playing hide and seek?" Chico asked, his smile unnerved her. She still hadn't decided whether she liked him or not. He was always joking, and she was never sure if it was at her expense.

"You are overdue," she said, turning on her back waiting for the uncomfortable probe and his lewd little swipes during the exam.

"Wow," he said. "We have got to get another ultrasound. She is way too big."

He sat on the bed beside her and began to gently prod her belly.

"Folks, I think we got a set of twins or something here," he looked up at Ashton who looked as if he were going to lift off into space.

"What?" Ashton asked excitedly.

"I think I just felt more than one little hiney," Chico chuckled.

"Are there any twins in your family, like your mother or something?" Chico asked her "You know twins usually skip a generation unless your mother or grandmother is a twin."

"I don't know," Kali answered honestly. "My dad was adopted. And I never knew anything about my mother's family except for Aunt Mazie."

"You gotta bring her down to the office," Chico insisted. "We can do it after hours. I need to confirm this, plus I need to give her a real physical. Tonight?"

Ashton nodded and climbed up on the bed beside her.

"Two, two. Two mints in one," he and Chico laughed. Kali buried her head in the pillow. She was really cursed, she thought.

The ultrasound showed twins. One of them was definitely a boy, but the other had his back turned. The two acted as if they had hit the jackpot and were eagerly swapping stories about their childhood. Kali was too stunned to even think. Chico gave her more vitamins and insisted that she spend the rest of her pregnancy in bed. He was afraid she wasn't carrying the babies well, and needed bed rest. All she could think about was that all that hard work to finish school by the end of summer, and she couldn't even make it to class.

The time dragged on like molasses. Ashton was with her almost everyday with the exception of a day or two when he had to leave on business. On those days, Kenny moved into the house with her. She was always happy to see Kenny. At least he would watch the soaps with her or play cards with her, do something to keep her occupied. All Ashton would do is gaze at her as if she were going to explode at any minute. When she was mean and nasty, he countered her with kind and soothing words.

When she would reach for him in the night, he would be there.

That did comfort her, but she wanted more. He was treating her like the Rosetta stone. Look, but don't touch, until she had finished reading a book about preparing for childbirth. The author had advised to roughen your nipples in order to breast feed comfortably. She got a washcloth and was rubbing her nipples like instructed. He took the washcloth from her and began sucking them. She was excited by this and wanted to have sex. He stopped immediately and left the room. He spent that night in the guest bedroom. She was furious. She had gone from being a sex toy to a Madonna in just a few months. She couldn't believe how angry that made her. Everything was making her angry. She hated looking at her body in the mirror. She didn't recognize herself anymore. Whenever she would read how some women thought this was the happiest time in their lives, she accused them of lying.

Then it happened. Ashton was on one of his business trips, and Kenny was supposed to be keeping watch. The problem with that day, he was overbooked. Ashton had funded Kenny's salon, and business was booming. He had garnered clients that wanted his services, and his services only. This was a day when three of his biggest patrons were booked, along with too many others. He had promised to call her every hour to see if she needed anything. She had encouraged him to go ahead. She wasn't due for another week to ten days, so she was alone when the pain hit her.

It hit her so hard it took her a few minutes to realize she was screaming from the contractions. It was so devastatingly painful that she panicked. She tried to dial Ashton, and then dropped the phone as another pain rolled through her back and abdomen. She reached over to pick it up and remembered that Ashton was not in the office or in the penthouse. She sank to the floor breathing hard and panting like they told her to in the book, except she didn't think it could be right, because the pains kept coming. For some crazy reason she thought the breathing would stop the pain.

She was finally able to reach the phone as she crawled around the bed. She dialed Kenny and all he could do on the other end of the phone was to scream and cry with her. Kali sat in the floor and realized it was wet beneath her, so she screamed some more.

"Call me an ambulance!" she demanded and dropped the phone. She crawled up on the bed and tried to think of what she should do. She realized she should have called an ambulance herself and tried to roll back over to pick up the phone. Another pain hit her and she lay there screaming. Kali forgot about the phone and began crying.

About an hour later she heard footsteps on the stairs and thought it was Kenny. But, it was Ashton and Chico.

"Get me...get me to the hospital!" she yelled between the agonizing and tortuous pain of the babies trying to escape her womb.

"It's going to be fine," Chico said calmly. "Everybody is going to be fine."

"I thought you were out of town," she accused Ashton who was letting her squeeze his hand.

"I just got back this morning. I was planning to come home tonight," he kept trying to keep her calm.

"Is it ready?" she asked. He didn't answer her.

"The nursery? You said you were setting up a nursery in the penthouse. Is it ready?" she tried to think beyond the pain to when this would be all over and she could go back to the penthouse.

"Yeah, everything's ready," he said and tried to help her breathe.

Kali gave birth to the boy first. Chico put the damp squirming little thing on her chest and told her to push some more. Ashton reached for the baby, but Chico told him to wait.

"Get behind her. Steady her and support her so she can push.

The baby's okay. We don't have anything to put him in," Chico said.

"Yes, we do," Ashton countered. "The bassinets are in the guest bedroom."

Kali remembered the day he had brought home two white bassinets, one trimmed in blue and the other in yellow since the one baby was always hiding during the ultrasounds.

"Then get it, quick," Chico commanded. Ashton let go of her and ran out of the room returning with the blue one. He moved the angry screaming baby carefully to the bassinet.

"We gotta clean him up," Ashton's voice sounded as if he were going to choke.

"We've got time. I cleaned his mouth. He's okay. Can't you tell? He's hurting my fucking ears."

"Yeah," Ashton climbed behind her and propped the tired Kali up, and she shoved out a baby girl.

"Okay, Junior has a little sister," he told Ashton.

"And what's her name?" he handed the girl to Ashton.

"Katie," Kali and Ashton said in unison. "Katie."

The two of them had discussed names and had decided a boy would be named Ashton Jr., and if the second were a girl, they would name her Katie after his mother.

"Kathryn Charlotte Sperling," Kali said weakly. She saw the needle glisten in the late afternoon light from the bedroom window.

"What's that for?" she asked as Chico injected her.

"To keep down the risk of infection," Chico said and rubbed her arm.

"You did good, Kali. You did real good," Ashton said as he walked over to her and kissed her on the forehead.

Kali was startled by the darkness, but more so by the silence. She reached for the lamp. It lit the room that had been cleaned of the crazy sight that she had last seen. She was dressed in a pair of pink satin pajamas. She slid her feet into her fuzzy slippers as she balanced herself on the edge of the bed.

"Ashton," she called. "Ashton."

She flung her hair back away from her face and stood up. She was surprised how easy it was considering how she had had to struggle over the past few months. She went to the bathroom. The urine stung her a little and she realized she had on panties with a pad. She walked back into the room that looked as if it had been thoroughly cleaned from top to bottom. There was no sign of bloodied sheets or towels or anything that might signify babies had been born in that room.

"Ashton," she called again and went into the dark hallway. She flipped on the switch and went to the guest bedroom expecting to see the sleeping father and infants. The door was closed. She opened it as quietly as she could and could see nothing. She turned on the light to find nothing more than the bedroom set that was always there. The bassinets were gone. A chill crawled up her spine and into the back of her head like a brain freeze, it ached. She rubbed her temples and stepped into the room as if she didn't want to disturb anything that was in the room.

She opened the drawers to see if the tiny clothes, the baby wipes, and sheets and things she had bought were still there. They were all gone. She opened the closet to see if the bottles, warmers, and diapers she had bought were there. They, too, were gone. There was no sign of anyone expecting a baby in that room.

"Ashton!" she called loudly, not caring if they were somewhere in the house and she would wake them.

She turned on all the lights as she went down the stairs. The house was empty. She even went to the laundry room in the basement and found nothing, no one. She went back into the living room and reached for the phone. There was an envelope beneath the phone. The envelope wasn't addressed to anyone, but she had never seen it before.

She tore it open and a typed note said only: THIS NEVER HAPPENED.

"What?" she said, her hands shaking with anger. "What the hell does this mean?"

She picked up the phone and dialed the penthouse. Someone picked up the phone and hung up. She heard a baby crying in the background.

"Oh, no, he did not steal my children," she said, gaining strength as she went up the stairs. She dressed quickly and headed toward the door. There was another note taped to the door, it said: YOUR LIFE DEPENDS ON IT.

Kali stopped cold. She dropped the note and backed away from the door.

This had to be some kind of sick joke. Ashton was cold, but not that cold, not to her. She didn't want to believe history was repeating itself in the Sperling family. Ashton had said his values were different. He had talked about wanting the perfect family, the one that he had never had. Sure, she had had moments of doubt, but none that imagined this.

She headed out the door. Ashton would not have left those messages. She was sure it was a mistake. She was surprised that it was waning daylight when she hit the street. She finally looked at her watch and realized she had been sleeping for almost 24 hours.

That was plenty of time for someone to clean out her house and take the new infants. She walked over to South Street and hailed a cab. Rush hour traffic was ending, but the pace was still slow, so she sat anxiously in the cab bouncing from one rough street terrain to the next.

She jumped out of the cab at Rittenhouse Square and ran across the park to the building. The doorman recognized her and tipped his hat. She nodded and went through the double doors. The concierge greeted her cheerfully. She waved and went straight for the elevator in the rear on the right. She pulled out her key, stuck it in, and twisted it hastily. The door opened to the mirrored and red velvet car that sluggishly took her up the 14 floors. The elevator doors opened onto the lavish foyer, she ran to the double ivory doors and tried the knob. It was unlocked. She walked into the living room area. It was the same. The tall painting of Jordan was still at the top of the landing of the curved stairway. She looked to her right, and his same all white living room remained in tact.

Kali took two steps up and Ashton appeared suddenly at the top of the stairs. He was coming down fast and she moved to meet him. He had her by her shoulders before she knew what hit her. He carried her as she struggled back to the entryway.

"What are you doing here?" his face contorted and angry.

"I came to be with my children," Kali answered as she was being brutishly carried to the door.

"Didn't you get the message?" he held her up so that her face was level with his, eye to eye.

"What message?" She started kicking and swinging her feet. He dropped her. She landed heavily on her feet. She wasn't expecting gravity to pull her downward so quickly, and she hadn't realized how high she was off the ground. Her shins ached from the impact.

"Don't play with me," Ashton shoved her against the door and grabbed her by the neck. He lifted her again with both of his hands wrapped tightly around her neck. Her feet fought for the ground below, and her lungs fought for air as he squeezed her throat blocking its flow of oxygen.

"It's over, Kali." He looked behind him as if he were expecting someone. "I don't want to ever lay eyes on you again. You come within a thousand feet of me and the children and you won't live to regret it. You understand?"

He shook her while holding her by the neck with both his hands. Her body swayed under the momentum. She thought she was about to lose consciousness. She coughed and gasped for breath as he let her go, and she sank down to the floor. He used his foot to move her away from the door. He opened it and she crawled desperately out of the door.

"Don't regret it," he said in a low voice.

Kali sat in the foyer and heard the tumblers drop on the locks of the door. She shook uncontrollably. She tried to stand up, but she couldn't get her balance. She wanted to throw up. She must have sat there about ten minutes when she realized she would have to move before he found her there. She held onto the wall to pull her body upright and went back into the elevator. She had to try several times to get the key back into its slot on the elevator. She saw her horrified reflection in the mirror and tried to clean herself up. She lifted the collar of her shirt to hide the big, bluish bruises around her neck. She shuddered as she realized one of them was a fingerprint. She nervously ran her fingers through her hair to stop it from standing out all over the place. She dug in her purse and pulled out a pair of sunglasses. She took a deep breath and walked out of the building as quickly as she could pass the men she used to see every day and who used to wish her a good day. All she could think was that she didn't want or need anymore of these good days.

———◦◉◦———

Kali finally finished her last class in December. She had spent the last four months in a small apartment off campus. She saw no one other than anyone she had to nor did she talk to anyone. Not even Kenny. She hadn't called him to let him know where she was and he hadn't called to leave a message on her old phone. She knew anyway that his allegiance would be to Ashton. His livelihood depended on it. Once again, she had been ostracized and left to fend for herself. But, at least this time, money was the least of her worries. She had only the amount she needed transferred, and now she was trying to determine how much she was going to need to get out of Philadelphia. She never wanted to see that town again.

She never wanted to watch television or pick up a magazine. All the entertainment news was about the noble Redd and her wealthy husband adopting twins. Kali would turn on the television to see the happy family crossing a street in Manhattan or taking a walk in Central Park. Or she would be at the checkout counter in the grocery store and there would be Redd staring at her holding her babies. The loneliness was unbearable, but she did whatever it was she had to do to make it through the day. Goal number one had been completed.

Kali sifted through the recruiters' literature on a daily basis. She had even gone on a few interviews. One of them was a financial brokerage firm whose main office was on Wall Street. That really interested her. She wanted to learn how to manage the money Jordan had left her, and she couldn't think of a better place to start. When she got the call, she jumped up and clapped her hands. She ran to the mirror and smiled at herself. There was hope she could have her life back.

"Everything is going to be all right, Kalina Denise Harris. You are going to get this job, meet some new people, get married and have children that you can keep. Everything is going to be just fine," she stepped back from the mirror and sized herself up. She looked good. She hadn't retained any of the baby fat, and she didn't have one stretch mark to show for all that stretched skin. She had taken good care of herself. She knew she always would, regardless of how other people wanted her to end up.

Kali was excited about her trip to New York. She used to love her excursions there with either Ashton or Jordan. She especially loved the World Trade Center. She decided she would venture to the top after her interview where she would either celebrate or look out beyond to the future. The interview went well. She strode into the manager's office with confidence and knowledge, plus a highly coveted credential – a bachelor's degree in accounting from the University of Pennsylvania's Wharton School of Business. Kali knew she had the job when she walked out the door. She had spent three hours meeting potential teammates and looking at potential office space. She could hardly wait to get the definitive answer and the start date.

Kali walked to the Plaza where the twin towers stood and looked up at the impressive buildings. Unlike other times, she was going to the top alone, and she was going eat up there alone. She walked focusing on the buildings, happily and contentedly. It had been months since her future had seemed so promising, no…years, she thought. She had not felt like this since near the last few months of high school. She had so much to look forward to and she was getting ready to put her hands on it. Her new life was finally within her grasp.

Someone bumped into Kali, and she lost the grip on her bag. She stopped to pick it up. She was checking to make sure it was secure and that she hadn't lost anything when she looked up and saw them coming across the plaza. Ashton was pushing the double carriage, the babies were bundled up in hats and coats and mittens. Redd was sporting a white fur with a matching hat, and Ashton was dressed completely in black.

Their eyes met. Kali took a few steps backwards and suddenly heard a yell just as she felt a shove and the swoosh of a passing car. She turned to the passerby who had caught her to thank him, but he was gone just as quickly. She looked up to see Ashton's gaze still on her. She turned to see which way the crowd was crossing the street. She crossed with them nervously, afraid to look back. That night back in Philadelphia, Kali poured through more recruiting materials. She looked for jobs in places away from the east coast.

CHAPTER NINE

"Asa, we really need to cancel this photo shoot. AJ is running a fever. Katie's been up all night with a stomach virus. I'm not taking them out for a photo shoot in this weather. It's too cold." Ashton said, sitting half dressed on the sofa in his New York apartment.

"Okay, don't take them out. I don't want them out in the cold and getting sick. Or sicker either. But, this publicity is really great for Redd. Until the babies, things were getting a little slow. She was beginning to think she was getting too old for the game, or at least the designers were thinking that. Now everybody wants a picture. And everybody's paying. Just this one last time. I swear, after this shoot, we will go back to Europe. And the kids get a break," Asa explained while fumbling with a new camera he had just gotten. He snapped pictures of Ashton who was now slumped to one side.

"You look like shit, big brother," Asa said as he smiled and took another shot.

"You stay up all night with a sick kid and tell me you look great. Not only that, I have a contract I need to be working on," Ashton said, scratching his head. He had never been so tired in his entire life.

"Couldn't the nanny stay up, man?" Asa crossed his leg and leaned back in his chair. "Isn't that what you are paying her for?"

"A nanny is not a parent," Ashton answered.

"How the hell would you know what a parent is?" Asa laughed. "We had screwy Daddy and Jordan who pushed us off on women they were banging and selling for profit."

Ashton frowned. "Watch your mouth."

"They are six months old, son. They don't know what I'm saying. Besides, they aren't even in the room," said Asa.

"Let's get this over. Do I have to be in it?" asked Ashton.

"No, just stay here and supervise."

"I can do that." Ashton went to check on the babies while Asa moved the furniture around on the stone patio. He thought it would be perfect.

Redd entered the room and saw him moving the table.

"Darling, what are you doing?" She walked in wearing a white satin pantsuit.

"You look, fabulous," Asa teased, mocking her voice. He stopped as she walked to him and put her arms around his neck. They kissed. He pulled back swiftly hoping his brother wouldn't walk in on them.

"How is mommy duty coming along?" Asa said, giving her a cursory peck on her neck. She purred.

"Boringly, darling. Boringly. All he thinks and talks about are those messy, smelly little creatures. I'm bored to death. Did you get me a gig somewhere?"

"After the shoot, I have to make a couple of calls. I believe we will be on our way back to Europe by the end of the month," said Asa.

"Yippee. Get me out of this domestic bliss. He is worse than he was before the babies. Now, instead of doting on me trying to keep up with my every move, he dotes on them and me. Like I said, boring." She admired her new nails and went to the mirror to check her hair.

Both of them turned as they heard one of the babies crying, Ashton had them both in his arms. They were both dressed like Easter Bunnies, the theme for the magazine for the *Good Housekeeping* magazine cover due out in March. They both looked sick.

"Can't you perk them up?" Redd groaned when she saw their sleepy eyes and their lethargic manner.

"They're sick, Redd. They have caught a cold or virus or something. I'm taking them to the doctor this afternoon, so be happy with what you get," Ashton said.

"Oh, all right." She strode out onto the enclosed patio. Asa had been busy pulling together as many green plants as he could and anything pastel he could throw in the picture. They were supposed to be shooting at the studio with all the Easter props. But, he respected his brother's concern for his children. He actually admired him for it.

"Okay, the three of you can sit here on the settee. I think it will be perfect. No one will know the difference. Absolutely, this is perfect," he viewed the scene from his lenses. "Perfect. Ashton, give her the babies."

Ashton handed AJ to Redd first. She begrudgingly took the child and then held him up. There was something odd about his face. She was getting ready to mention it when a mucus-filled explosion escaped from his mouth, hitting her in the face and getting on her white suit. She instinctively tossed him toward the floor. Ashton caught him with one hand, still holding Katie in the other. He was horrified. He gathered the screaming child into his free arm and stormed out of the room.

"Oh, this is so gross. I can't stand it," Redd stormed out of the room in the other direction.

"Goodbye, *Good Housekeeping*," Asa whispered to himself and began to pack up his camera.

That was the last straw among the thousands that she kept heaping upon him everyday that the four of them were together. Redd had been all talk. If a camera wasn't in the vicinity, she wanted nothing to do with the little creatures as she called them. Ashton had been both hurt and disappointed by her reaction. She had kept her promise and stayed home with them the first six months, though she didn't stop working. Whenever he wasn't around, she was calling Asa to get her some work. He knew that. He heard it from Micah and sometimes even Asa himself. But, this was it. Had AJ hit that stone floor, he may have suffered brain damage or broken bones or something devastating to a baby. That moment of selfishness proved to him that she didn't love him or the children, and he had given her all the love he knew how to give. Worst of all, he had crushed a heart that had been given to him just to be with his Almighty Redd.

Ashton carried the sick babies into the nursery and started to pack a few things. He was going back to Philadelphia. He hated New York. He was going to take his babies back to the penthouse.

⎯⎯⎯◆⎯⎯⎯

Settling in was easier now that he was back where he belonged. He rehired Reggie, hired a new nanny named Carol, and started having Kenny come in on a regular basis for his massages, pedicures, and manicures. It was comforting to be back in his old room surrounded by his old life. The only thing that was missing was companionship. He had none. He went to work, came home and played with the children, then went to bed.

The children grew fast. They quickly began to walk and pronounce words. One day, he was playing with Katie, and she slapped him playfully in the face and said, "Mama." She said it clearly.

He put her on his hip and tracked down Carol who was watching television in the recreation room with a sleeping AJ in her lap.

"Who taught her that?" he asked.

Carol shook her head confused.

"The word *mama*? She called me mama. Usually they say dada first. But, she said mama," said Ashton. He wasn't angry, he just insisted on knowing.

"Books, I guess," Carol hunched her shoulders. "I read them two or three books a day. Should I skip the ones that have a mother?" she asked.

"No, no, of course not. I was just surprised, that's all." Ashton carried the squirming child back upstairs and tried to tuck her into bed. But, this night she wasn't having any of it. It didn't matter that her brother was already out for the count, Katie was full of energy. He sat in the gliding chair and pulled a book out of the pocket, it was *The Berenstain Bears*. There was a mama and a papa. Ashton read it three times before she finally fell asleep. As he tried to sleep that night, he wondered if a one-year-old child could comprehended not having a mother. He thought about Kali touching the air pretending to push her curl from between her eyes. Then he remembered the terror in her eyes the last time he saw her.

The next day he left the office early and drove down to Society Hill. He was hoping she would be home. If not, he would wait for her. He parked the car in front of the house and walked up to the door. He started to knock, but the mail drop was slightly open. He used his keys to get in and had to shove the door to get past the mail that was piling up in the floor. The house was dark and smelled musty. He turned on the light and noticed the cobwebs hanging from the corners in the ceiling. He bent down and gathered the mail. He filled his arms with it and walked into the dining room. He turned on the light in the darkened, cramped room and dropped the mail on the table. Everything was in its place, but it was obvious nobody lived there.

Ashton wandered from room to room expecting to find a sign of her somewhere, but there was none. He went back and went through the mail. The gas and the electric had been paid in advance. All the bills showed credits. By his calculations, there were enough credits for about a year. He wondered how long she had been gone. He went upstairs and fell across the bed where she had given birth to the twins, where possibly they had even been conceived. He was trying to get close to her. He wanted to know where *mama* was. He knew he would be restless until he found her.

He sat up quickly, thinking she went back to South Carolina. Where else would she go? She was afraid. She didn't know anyone else in this entire world except those people. He ran back downstairs to the kitchen and found the latest yellow pages. He looked up the airlines and a rental car company. He made arrangements to go there the next day.

Ashton was getting tired of driving when he finally came across the two-lane highway on the trip ticket he had gotten from AAA. He followed the directions carefully until he came across a small brick split-level up on a hill with a long driveway. It was just like Kali had said it would be. There was neatly trimmed grass as far as you could see that was bordered by trees in the background. It was beautiful. As he pulled into the driveway, he saw the swing set that sat between the apple trees. It was freshly painted blue. Somebody lives here, he thought hopefully. He got out of the car and walked up to the front door, a door that was rarely entered if you used the spiders and spider webs as a gauge. He rang the doorbell anyway.

A short brown skin woman with large brown eyes answered the door.

"Can I help you?" she asked with a deep southern drawl.

"I'm looking for Kalina Harris," Ashton was straightforward.

"Kalina don't live here," the woman said. "Kalina ain't lived here in years."

"Do you know where I can find her?" he asked, trying to stick his head inside the door.

"No, I ain't seen or heard from her since she left," the woman said.

"So you know her?" Ashton asked, hoping the woman would let him in to see the house.

"We went to school together," she answered as a small child walked up to her and hugged her leg.

"Girl?" Ashton asked, assuming so since the child was wearing red pants.

"Yes," the woman rubbed the child's short wild hair. "What do you want with Kalina?"

"I just want to make sure she's okay. She left Philadelphia without a word, and I was worried. I considered myself a close friend," he lied. "But, she left."

"Oh," the young woman said, still blocking the door.

"Who are you?" she asked. "You look real familiar."

"Ashton Taylor Sperling," he said, extending his hand. He saw the smile slide across her face as she recognized the name.

"My name is Mandy," she said eagerly, thinking no one was going to believe somebody this famous was darkening her door.

"Mandy. You were Kalina's best friend?" he said, his eyes looking beyond Mandy.

"Come on in," she said, picking up her daughter and leading him into the living room.

"So, this is it," he said, walking around the room. "She described it perfectly, every nuance. You wouldn't happen to know what happened to her personal things. Would you?"

"The church people put most of it in boxes and stored it in the attic. They thought she might come back for it one day. I guess they were feeling a little guilty," Mandy sat down in Preach's favorite leather chair. Ashton had the desire to touch it for some reason.

"You kept the furniture," he said and moved off the sofa and ran his hand over the arm of the chair.

"Well, after the tragedy, no one would buy it or rent it, except for my husband and me. We needed a place bigger than my room in my mama's house, so we got a good deal on the rent," Mandy patted her stomach. "Especially since I'm pregnant again."

"I see," Ashton started thinking about the stuff in the attic. "What if she never comes back for it? What then?"

"She will be back one day. Once she hits it big. She will come back and rub our little town faces in it," Mandy smiled thinking about Kalina's grandiose goals.

"She did that already," Ashton said absent-mindedly. He was thinking about how foolish it was to think she would come back here.

"You want to see her stuff, don't you?" Mandy asked.

He nodded.

"You will have to reach it. I ain't going up in that hot attic. It's creepy up there," she faked a shiver.

"Creepier than sleeping in the bedroom where her father killed her mother?" he said crossly and then caught himself. "I mean, that had to be a little unnerving at first," he tried to knock his tone down.

"It was. But, they cleaned and painted everything and aired the house out good. People even talked like Kalina was going to show back up and move right back in. But, she didn't."

"Why would she?" he said aloud, but was really asking himself.

"Well, it's a long story. Reverend Harris killed his wife and all, but he was also accused of stealing the church's money to put Kalina into one of those fancy colleges." She led the way to the attic entry in the upstairs hallway.

"He didn't, did he?" Ashton pulled the stairs down easily.

"No, it turned out to be the church treasurer's doing. He's serving time now."

"Did anyone try to tell Kalina she could come back?" he asked.

"Ms. Rosemarie wrote her a letter, but it came back in the mail," Mandy offered.

"It's a wonder it came back. Mazetta must have missed it." Ashton shook his head.

"You really know her, huh?" Mandy watched him climb up the stairs and turn on the light switch.

"Yeah, I really know her." He thought about that as he said it, but not anymore he wanted to add. How could he know her now after what he had done? He had no idea how she was handling it.

He sat on the beams and went through a few boxes. He took one and condensed all the things he thought she would want. He brought the box down with him. He was covered in sweat.

"Some sweet tea?" she offered him a glass of tea filled with ice. He drank it down in one gulp then started walking toward the door.

"She might want this," Mandy walked over to the worn wooden desk by the door overlooking the front porch. "It's his sermon Bible. Everybody was afraid to touch it. But, I read it every once in awhile. He has a lot of notes for his sermons in it. It's real cool. He was a really smart man. I really liked him."

Ashton took the Bible and put it on the top of the box.

"Did you really like her?" Ashton was curious. Kali had left the town feeling hated and abhorred.

"Yes," Mandy's eyes watered. "I'm really sorry I turned my back on her. I will always regret that. So if you see her, you tell her. You hear?"

Ashton nodded his head and was out the door on the front porch.

"You want to meet my mama?" Mandy asked as she followed him to the porch.

"Excuse me?" Ashton wasn't sure why he should meet her mother.

"My mama and her mama were best friends. Mama took some of their things, some pictures and stuff home with her. Maybe you will find something else she might want if she comes back to Philadelphia."

"Okay." Ashton stood awkwardly at the door.

"You have to give us a ride over there. Don't worry, I can get a ride home," Mandy was already closing the door behind her. Ashton noticed she only had a set of keys, no pocket book or looking in the mirror. She just walked out on the porch and followed him to the car.

"This is a nice car. It's a rental one, huh?" she asked, strapping the baby in the seat belt with her.

"Is that wise?" he said, concerned should the airbag go off.

"It's just a short piece down the road. We'll be okay," she assured him.

Ashton sat in the small kitchen and nibbled on the piece of pound cake and cup of coffee that Mandy's mother Glynda had eagerly placed in front of him. She was as excited as Mandy to meet him.

"Why did she leave Philadelphia? Is she running from something or someone?" Glynda tilted her head so that her eyes almost seemed cross.

"She used to work for my grandfather. He died, and I got a little tied up with my family and lost touch. When I went back to check on her, she was gone. I didn't expect it. I mean, she did graduate from the University of Pennsylvania and it makes sense that she took a job somewhere. It's just that I expected her to at least leave me some type of word, or at least someone in the family. We knew she was alone, no family. I guess I just feel like I dropped the ball," Ashton said and took a sip of coffee.

"Hmmm," Glynda said knowingly. "I guess you are not going to tell me the real story, but I ain't going to judge you. I let her down, too. She was my best friend's child, and I let her get railroaded out of this town. I was too busy basking in my own hurt and disappointment like a lot of us here. Trust me, we've paid for it.

"God knows, I hope she does come back and put some peace and prosperity back in this place. 'Cause ain't nothing but bad is been happening these last few years. The church even had a prayer meeting to try to lift the curse, but it just keeps perpetuating.

"You looking at me like I'm crazy, but I ain't. Six months after they put her on that train, my husband died. Then I lost my job. And then my daughter's husband lost his job.

"And that was just us. People been coming down with cancer and dying all over the place."

"And you think...?" Ashton stifled his amusement.

"Laugh if you want. What goes around do comes around. What all of us did to that child will haunt us for the rest of our lives. What have you done, mister, that's got you feeling so guilty?" she took his cup and plate away from the table.

"I didn't keep a promise," he said, barely audible. His eyes met the woman's eyes and she nodded her head knowingly.

Ashton went back to Philadelphia and put the things in the spare bedroom at Kali's. He sent Reggie over to the house to clean it up. He was going to keep it ready for her whenever she was ready to return. He knew it was going to take a whole lot of work to get her back into the penthouse. "Baby steps," he said to himself, "baby steps."

"I don't believe you, Ashton," Micah was sitting across from him in the study. "You think that after coming within seconds of taking her life, stealing her children, and almost causing her to step in front of dangerous traffic that she would willingly come home to you and the kids?"

"Yeah," Ashton was twisting one of his cigars between his fingers. His eyes lit up when he thought about her. He could make it right. He knew he could. She loved him. He knew that would never change. "He was her first," he thought proudly.

"Let me see. I just want to get this straight," Micah said, leaning forward. "When you had her all wrapped up in you, carrying your babies, you had your ideal family of four just waiting to happen. Right?

"Now during this phase in your life where everything was perfect, all you could fantasize about was your perfect family of four with Redd. And now that Redd can't or won't live up to this fantasy, you are now fantasizing about this perfect family of four with Kali? Did I get it right this time? I mean, Ashton, you are about as sick as Jordan ever was. You did exactly what he would have done. Hell, at least he never would have tried to reverse it."

"Micah, I was wrong. I did a horrible thing. I have a hard time living with it everyday. I look at my children, and I think I ruined their lives because of passion for a woman who doesn't love me. It's clear to me. It took a long time. Oh, and I know, I know you told me, Jordan told me. She never loved me. But, I loved her. I loved her beyond anything you could imagine. And there was Kali, there was Kali…" his voice trailed off.

"The one who gave you everything." Micah sat back and folded his hands. "I can't do it Ashton. Not for you, not for the children. If I do it – bring her back – and you kill her, I'll never forgive myself."

"I couldn't do that," Ashton said and dropped the cigar, then picked it up and dusted away the ashes. "I could never hurt her. Not ever again. I swear, Micah. I swear."

"Say tonight, tomorrow, Redd walks in this door and says I'm sorry I was such a selfish bitch. I'm sorry I have been sleeping with your brother more than I sleep with you. I just realized I can't live without you. I want to be the mother and wife you expect me to be. Then what? A noose around Kali's neck and a cement block at the bottom of the Schuykill? I don't want to be a part of that. I have walked away from Daddy and his shenanigans. God rest his soul. Jordan is gone, and I can try to forget all the wrongs he inflicted on women. I'm not going to continue the cycle of unlawfulness and evil with you. Do you understand?" Micah stood up.

"I understand, Micah," Ashton ran from behind the desk and grabbed his brother. "I know what I did. I am not excusing what I did. I don't expect her to come running back into my arms. I just want the chance to fix it, Micah. I can fix it. You know, Jordan was changing. Kali brought about that change. And guess what, I did things I didn't know I was capable of, and it frightened me. I don't want to be Daddy. I don't want to follow in Jordan's footsteps. All I want is to bring my family back together. It might take baby steps, little baby steps, but as long as they are bringing us toward each other. That's all I want. Yeah, the fantasy is the four of us. But, I can live with her just being in their lives. It's more about the kids, I swear. Micah, they need their mother."

"If I bring her back, I am going to do everything in my power to protect her. I'll hurt you if you hurt her. You hear me?" Micah's tone was so deadly Ashton took a step backwards.

"I got it," Ashton stood in the middle of the floor and watched Micah.

"You don't have to worry, little brother," he said to himself, "I'm going to do everything in my power to make her happy again. I'd die before I put that fear back into her eyes." Every day was a day closer to Kali, he told himself. He started telling the babies about their mother.

"She's a feisty one. She won't let you get away with half the things I do. So you better get it all out of your system before she comes home," he said, liking the sound of that.

"She's in Chicago," said Micah, walking in on Ashton bathing the twins.

"She took a job as a junior accountant with Ernst and Young," he said and waved a piece of paper in the air.

"Wow, I am impressed," Ashton answered, covered in bubbles.

"Yeah, you should be. After all she went through, she graduated magna cum laude. She can write her own ticket anywhere. Apparently, she had been offered a job on Wall Street. That was probably why she was in New York that day. I guess she had thought New York was big enough for the four of you. Yet, it turned out to be smaller than she had imagined."

"Yeah." He splashed the twins with water and they giggled, splashing back.

"What's her address?" Ashton asked.

"Don't you go," Micah warned. "She will run. And next time she will change her name, so you can't find her. Let me go, or Elliott. You are the last person that needs to show up at her door. You are still probably causing her nightmares."

"I can fix this, son," Ashton said, self-assured. "I can fix this."

"What? With a bouquet of roses and a roll in the hay. A bunch of I'm sorrys, and it's fixed. Wake up, Ashton. She will run."

"She won't leave everything she has worked so hard to accomplish. I know her, she will fight me," Ashton said.

"You have already proven you are stronger than she is. She will run."

Ashton arrived in Chicago and rented a car. He went straight to her place, but it was too early. He sat in the car and watched people come and go from her apartment building. Again, he was impressed. The place looked really nice from the outside, and it was just beyond the lake. He wondered if her apartment had a lakeside view. About five o'clock, she strolled down the street with a grocery bag in one arm, and the other arm was swinging in satisfactory form. She looked content. Her rogue curl was hanging across her eyes that were fixed ahead. She turned into the building, and a man held the door open for her. She smiled at him. Ashton wanted to see that smile up close and in his direction. He knew it was going to take time, but he could convince her to come home. He knew he could. She understood him better than anybody, and she would know instinctively how sorry he was. He sat there for a few more minutes going over in his head what he was going to say.

He walked up to the second landing, instead of taking the elevator, buying time to get composed. He wanted to say, and planned to say, words that were sincere and from his heart. He stopped at her door and stood there taking several deep breaths as if he were emerging on stage in front of thousands of people. Then he knocked on the door.

Kali had curled up on the sofa and was flipping through her new benefits book. She averted her eyes from the family plan. She was in no need for that. She went down the line of items on the menu and started making notes. She was healthy, but did need to go to the dentist. Then she heard the light knock on the door. She sat up at attention. No one, not even the landlord ever knocked on her door. She didn't know anyone. At first, she thought it would be better if she didn't answer it, but then she decided to put her shoes on and go to the peep hole.

She walked quietly to the door and squinted through the peephole. She gasped. She covered her mouth quickly hoping it hadn't been loud enough for him to hear. She looked again and he stood there, oblivious to her watching him. She stepped back as inaudibly as she could. She was thankful for the carpeted floors. She ran into her bedroom, took the smaller pocketbook she had carried that day and dropped it into a larger one. She went into the bathroom and grabbed her toothbrush, some toothpaste, and deodorant.

She heard the knock again. It was louder. She grabbed her duffle bag and dumped whatever she could put her hands on into it. She walked quickly back through the living room and out onto her iron patio that overlooked the lake. She dropped the duffle bag the two stories and she climbed over the side of the patio reaching the next landing. Then she climbed down there. Thank God, she thought she was still agile from her cheerleading and tree climbing days, and she was not afraid of heights.

Ashton didn't know why he was waiting so long for her to answer the door. Maybe because she was nervous and scared, so he knocked again and began to call her.

"Kali, Kali. Please open the door. I know you are in there. I saw you come in. I just need to talk to you. Please, we need to discuss the twins. That's all. Kali, let me in," he called. His voice began to get urgent because he began to think there was probably another entrance. She may have taken one look outside and ran, just like Micah said she would. He became frantic, calling her louder and louder and banging harder and harder on the door. When she didn't come, he kicked the door in. Every fiber of him telling him it was the wrong thing to do, but he had to see her. He couldn't control the need to see her. He stumbled into the door and looked around. It was a very nice place, and as he suspected, there was a grand view of the lake. He ran through the two-bedroom apartment looking for her behind curtains, in closets, and in the shower. She wasn't there, but he didn't see another entrance and then he went to the patio doors and sighed. He walked out on the patio expecting to see a set of stairs going down, but there were none. He leaned over the patio and realized she would have had to climb down. Then he saw her jumping into a cab.

"Kali," he screamed. "Don't run, Kali!"

He ran back down to the street to try to follow the cab, but they were gone. In which direction, he couldn't tell. Micah had been right, and he had been so pigheaded and conceited he wouldn't listen. Now he had lost her. He was crushed when he arrived home. Micah held him while he actually sobbed heavily over the loss.

"I'll find her," Micah promised. "I won't give up. You don't give up."

Like Micah had suspected, Kali was a very clever young lady. It took him another five months to track her down. Her name was Patty now and she worked for a Black couple that owned an insurance agency in Madison, Wisconsin. She lived in a garage apartment near downtown Madison. She drove a little blue 280Z. Micah's only saving grace was that she had needed to withdraw money from her Swiss account, and it had been wired to Madison. He followed her trail from there. The insurance company wasn't paying her bills, he thought. He talked to Ashton and convinced him not to go Madison. He hired a detective to keep an eye on her until he could get there. He was in the middle of a big security setup, and his attention couldn't be diverted. As long as someone was keeping an eye on her, she could wait two to three more days.

That Saturday morning as Kali manned the phones and typed contracts for the Martins, a man positioned himself down the street. It was like any other Saturday at the agency. It was a half day.

"What are you doing after work, Patty?" Mr. Martin asked. He was a tall man with a bulging beer belly.

"Nothing that matters," Kali answered, thinking he was going to ask her to work longer hours today.

"Then it's settled. Mrs. Martin insists and I insist that you join us around four o'clock for a cookout. She's at home busy buying and preparing side dishes. I'm going home and I'm going to strike up the grill," he said proudly. "What about it?" he arched his thick black eyebrows.

"Okay," she was happy to receive an invitation. She was getting tired of going home alone and staring at the blank walls. She had moved into the place with a duffel bag and a cot, and that was all she needed. Heaven knows when Ashton was going to rear his murderous head again.

Kali arrived at the Martins to find their home crawling with people. Mrs. Martin introduced her to everybody. Everyone there was in a cheerful barbecue mode. The music that filled the air was rhythm and blues. A young man pulled her on to the grass that was the dance floor. Kali danced freely, feeling happy in that moment. All she had to live for she had concluded was the very moment she was living in. By the end of the evening, Kali had made several new friends. They had exchanged telephone numbers and had begun to make plans to meet again. She liked Madison. She was beginning to feel at home. The Martins walked her to her car that was parked almost a block from their house. She hugged them goodbye and drove off. Mr. Martin noticed a black sedan moments later racing down the street. He shook his head.

"People should respect the speed limit," he said to his wife.

Kali was pacing the floor of her apartment, thinking that maybe she should take some of the money and buy a few pieces of furniture. She wouldn't buy as much as she did in Chicago, in case she had to leave again. Oh, God, she pleaded silently, she hoped she didn't have to leave again.

Monday morning she drove to work the same way she always had, listening to the public radio station. The woman who told the news had a soothing accent, letting her know what was going on in the world without causing more paranoia than was already a part of her being. She turned into the small parking lot of the insurance agency and noticed a black sedan slow down as she was getting out of the car. The hairs on the back of her neck stood at attention. She had noticed that car before, but she didn't know where.

Later that day, she went to the fax machine. It was near the large pane window that looked out onto the street. She saw it again sitting in the parking lot across the street at the Burger King and thought it could have been a coincidence. There were so many black cars like that in the world. However, her instincts said it had something to do with her. She started thinking about leaving.

"Patty, Patty," Mr. Martin said. He was standing next to her desk. "Patty," he spoke a little louder than normal.

She jumped.

"Are you alright?" he asked.

"Yes, sir," she said in a slow southern drawl. She caught herself. That sound hadn't escaped her lips in a long time. Jordan wouldn't allow it.

"That's cute," Mr. Martin said and smiled.

She looked at him questioningly.

"The accent," he said.

"Oh, it just came out like that. I'm sorry," she said, looking toward the window.

"Nothing to be sorry about." He was still standing there.

"Can I help you with something?" she asked, wondering if she were acting funny. The last thing she wanted to do is have to field a lot of questions that she couldn't answer.

"No, Mrs. Martin was very pleased you could make it to the barbecue. I think she is trying to hook you up with some young men. One in particular, I might add."

"I think so, too," Kali smiled sadly. She had a date scheduled with the young man, but it wasn't going to happen.

"She was wondering if you would like to come over for dinner this evening. To help us eat the leftovers," he added.

"I don't know, Mr. Martin," she tried to think of a good excuse.

"My wife wants you to come over, and we are not taking no for an answer." He patted her on the shoulder.

"As a matter of fact, I was thinking," he paused and looked out the window in the direction she was looking. "Why don't you stop at home and pick up a few things? Spend the night."

She was surprised by the offer, but she liked it. She wasn't going to sleep well on that cot tonight.

"Okay," she said.

"I tell you what. It's kind of slow in here today. Why don't I follow you home? I'll wait outside while you pack a few things," he emphasized the word pack. She nodded.

At four o'clock, the two cars left the parking lot and went to the garage apartment. Kali went in, packed her cash in her large pocketbook, and packed her one duffel bag with as many clothes as it would hold. Though it was heavy, she acted as if it was light as feather. She walked over to Mr. Martin's car and got in.

The two of them drove quietly the twenty minutes it took to get back to his neighborhood. He kept his eye on the traffic behind them in the rear view mirror. She was doing the same with the side view. As they went down the hill to his home, he caught sight of the black sedan cresting the hill.

Mrs. Martin was waiting in the doorway as they came in through the garage. She gave Kali a big hug holding onto her for a while. It was the most comforting hug Kali had had in a long time. "Dinner's ready," she whispered.

Kali and Mr. Martin washed their hands and sat down at the table. They joked and talked quietly until it was time to clear the dishes. Kali was the first to get up. She grabbed their plates.

"Put those down, dear," Mrs. Martin said politely. "Sit down and talk to us. What kind of trouble are you in, child?"

"What?" Kali looked from one expectant face to the next.

"Someone's following you. I noticed him Saturday when you left, but I didn't put it together until last night. I had to drop a friend off that lives down the street from you. There was a man sitting in the car as I passed. Over an hour later, I passed him again. And both times, he was looking at your place so intently he didn't even notice me.

"We are only asking this because we want to help you," Mr. Martin paused, waiting for her response.

"There isn't anything you can do," Kali said. She was surprised at how calm her voice was.

"You would be surprised," Mr. Martin smiled.

"What does he want?" Mrs. Martin asked.

"He wants me dead," she started scraping and stacking the plates, as if she hadn't said those odd words.

"Why would someone want you dead?" Mrs. Martin's voice trembled.

"Because I know something he doesn't want anyone else to

know," Kali said, thinking of Ashton's perfect family, the one without the real mother. She wanted to tell the Martins about how she became an incubator to help him get what he wanted. Then when he got it, how crudely he had discarded her. But, she couldn't. It would put them in danger.

"My husband sensed you were in grave danger." Mrs. Martin reached across the table and squeezed her hand. "We are going to help you."

"Do you have everything you need from the apartment?" he asked. She nodded her head.

"I don't know where to go, though," Kali wiped a tear beading up in the corner of her eye.

"How does San Francisco sound?"

"I have never been there before," she answered.

"It's a wonderful city of mazes to get lost in, to hide in, especially if you have the right tools." Mr. Martin said as he dropped an envelope on the table.

She was about to turn it down. She thought it was stuffed with cash, hard-earned cash that she knew they had struggled to obtain. But, something else fell out.

"It's a new identity. And it's the name of a friend of mine. He is good at taking people underground. I called him this morning, and he already has a place for you and a job."

"I don't know what to say." Kali struggled not to break down. She wasn't sure why the Martins had gone through so much trouble nor could she believe how fast they had deduced she was in danger.

"How can I thank you?" she said, wiping her face as fast she could, but the torrent of tears were faster.

"Survive," Mrs. Martin said. "I did. I was an abused wife once. Not my baby here," she grinned at her husband. "He's been my champion. But, before him. You sort of recognize the signs after awhile. I knew you were running from someone the day I met you, Patty. I know that's not your real name. You don't respond to it half the time. You have got to work on that."

"Yes, ma'am," it was all Kali could say from one battered woman to another. She had never thought of herself in those terms before. But, that's what Ashton had done. The thought of her hanging by her neck with his large hands wrapped around it made her shudder. She hadn't believed she would ever feel her feet touching the ground again, and when they finally touched down, all they wanted to do was run. Her feet had the urge to keep running no matter how hard she tried to convince herself to stay put.

She had had six wonderful months in Chicago and now only four good ones in Madison. She was in love with Madison and the Martins, but her feet were limbering up at the next starting line. She was getting ready to run again.

Mr. Martin went to the door and opened it. He stretched as if he were just waking up from a nap. He walked out on the porch and picked up the evening newspaper. He stood there opening it in the dusk. Then he stooped and picked a leaf off a bush. As he turned to go in, he noticed the car near the end of the block sitting. He went back in.

"Tonight," he said to Kali. "Give her one of your wigs, baby. Get ready to drive her to the airport. Her flight leaves in less than two hours."

Mr. Martin backed his car out first and drove it around the block. Mrs. Martin drove her car out after he had cleared the corner. She pulled into the street and sat there. Mr. Martin's car came barreling around the corner and she pulled off. He turned the car fast and did a 180. The black car ran up on the sidewalk narrowly missing him and blew a tire. Mrs. Martin gunned the car and soon they were on the expressway headed for the airport.

Mrs. Martin hugged Kali and kissed her on the cheek as she let her out on the curbside of the airport.

"You know where to find me, Lena," she winked her eye, sending Kali on her way with a new persona.

Kali ran into the airport as fast she could. In little or no time, she was taking the first leg of her journey to San Francisco.

The next morning, the Martins were getting dressed for work when the doorbell rang.

"Good morning." Mr. Martin faced a tall brown skin man with a bald head. "What can I do for you?"

"You can help me," Micah said. "You can help me put a family back together."

"Me, how can I do that?" Mr. Martin asked.

"By telling me where she is," he held a picture of Kali in his hand.

"What are you doing with a picture of Patty?" Mr. Martin asked.

"Good morning," Mrs. Martin said, walking up behind her husband. "Oh, what a lovely picture of Patty! Do you know her?"

"Yes, ma'am. I was hoping you would help me find her," he said.

"Why would I do that?" Mrs. Martin asked. "I don't believe I know anything about you. Who are you?"

Micah pulled a card out of his pocket. He handed it to Mr. Martin.

"My name is Micah Sperling. I need to find Kali. It's urgent. I need to get her back home," he said, earnestly.

"What's urgent?" Mr. Martin asked. He looked out down the street. "Haven't you been following her for the last few days?"

"No, however, I was the one who hired the man to follow her

until I could get here and convince her to come home."

"Why follow her?" Mr. Martin was frank.

"To keep her safe," Micah lied.

"Safe from what?" Mr. Martin asked, arching his big black eyebrows.

"May I come in?" Micah asked.

"She's not here," Mrs. Martin said, moving away from the doorway.

"You are concerned. I can see that, but I promise you I am not here in anyway to harm her," Micah stepped inside the modest, but very neat, home.

"Marines?" Mr. Martin asked, and took a step toward Micah with a glare that held a message.

"Air Force. Special Forces?" Micah asked.

"Yes," the two men shook hands again and smiled.

"Trained to observe," Micah said and didn't go any further into the room. The man was ready to fight, and he wasn't.

"Yes," Mr. Martin answered.

Micah reached into his pocket and pulled out another card and handed it to Mrs. Martin.

"My only intent is to protect her," he said and started back out of the door.

"She's in good hands." Mr. Martin held the door open and closed it gently behind Micah who was dreading his next conversation with his brother.

CHAPTER TEN

S an Francisco was good. It was big enough to get lost in and small enough to meet new people. Kali didn't have a hard time fitting in. Everybody was friendly and relaxed about everything. She didn't even worry about running into Ricky. She doubted he even remembered what she looked like, and it was a plus that he wasn't really close to Ashton at all.

She found a little walk-up apartment that had a fantastic view of the Golden Gate Bridge. She was finally letting go of her past. She still had a hard time looking at magazines with Redd's face staring at her, and she still flipped channels when an entertainment report showed the happy family. She had convinced herself that she had not gone through that horrible ordeal in Philadelphia. She had built for herself a whole new façade. No one knew who she really was, and the images of her past were beginning to fade even in her own mind. She had been Lena for almost a year and there was no sign of anything wrong. She was a brand new woman without a past, only a future.

Kali enjoyed her new job. The Martins' friend had gotten her an interview at Macy's and she was now the head of the jewelry department. All of the diamonds and rubies that the Sperlings had bestowed upon her had come in handy. Kali could recognize fakes as well as brand names. She easily impressed her customers.

She had kept in touch with the Martins and was looking forward to a visit. She had promised Mrs. Martin something special if she would meet her for lunch at Macy's. Kali was excited that morning. She arrived early and made sure the jewelry section was shiny and inviting. She was on the floor today, something she truly enjoyed. Standing behind that counter made her feel visible and important. She was looking at her watch for the hundredth time when she heard her voice.

"Am I late?" Mrs. Martin asked. Kali walked around the counter with open arms and hugged her tightly. The Martins were her family now.

"No, I was just anxious to see you. I missed you," Kali was still hugging her.

"Oh my, we missed you too, sweetheart. Jason is in an uproar. He can't find anyone to replace you at the office for one. And, for two, he had so many plans for you. They can still happen, you know."

"Oh, I would love that," Kali thought nostalgically. She missed the cold wind off the lake in Madison, and she missed the fact that she could ride a bike anywhere. Here, there were so many hills she was afraid to buy a bike.

"So, this is where you are working?" Mrs. Martin walked over to the counter and looked down at the sparkling gems under the glass.

"Yes," Kali ran behind the counter and used the key that was dangling from her wrist to open it.

"Pick one," she smiled at Mrs. Martin.

"Pick one?" Mrs. Martin laughed. "Sweetie, some of these probably cost more than you and I make in a week or a month even. Oh, huh," she looked closer, "a year."

"It doesn't matter. I have set aside some money to give you the perfect gift. I remember you said that you always wanted diamonds, but they were always out of your reach. So reach for one," Kali smiled.

"You can't be serious," Mrs. Martin protested as she looked closely at the diamonds.

"Pick one," Kali opened the counter and pulled out a pair of large studs. Then she pulled out a pair of tear drops.

"Do you like these?" Kali took her hand and placed the tear-drops in it.

"Oh, I don't know what to say," Mrs. Martin flipped them over and saw that they were over a $1000. "I can't, sweetheart."

"You can. I get a discount remember," Kali took the earrings out and exchanged the earrings out of Mrs. Martin's ears. She boxed the old earrings and took them to the cash register. Mrs. Martin waited patiently while Kali went to another associate and had them rung up. Mrs. Martin stood in the mirror admiring her new earrings.

Kali came back around the counter smiling and happy that she could put such a look of pleasure on Mrs. Martin's face. To do that, she had taken a lump sum out of her account again. Mrs. Martin had been right. She couldn't live off the money she was earning. But, that was something Jordan had made sure she would never have to worry about.

"Let's go to lunch," Kali waved to the girl on the other side of the counter and the two women walked out of the doors onto Market Street.

Ashton was tired. He had been traveling all week, and San Francisco was his last stop. He couldn't wait to get home to the kids. His business was growing fast, too fast for him and Micah to handle. Brady was marketing the company well. He had hired some new people and was trying to coax his close friend Troy into joining him to help run the business. It had grown already from the original four, Micah, Ms. Elliott, Brady and himself to 50 employees. Now he had an offer on the table to grab up a similar company on the West Coast. That would mean he would have to hire at least 40 more employees on the East Coast, because he was not going to have bi-coastal offices.

He thought about the proposal carefully as he walked up Market Street. He saw the Macy's sign and remembered the kids' birthday was coming up. He decided to stop to see what he could buy to save himself some time when he got back to Philadelphia. He walked in and asked for directions to the children's department. He searched the racks for cute outfits. Every time he went shopping for them, he was surprised that he was always looking for a larger size. They were growing so fast. Katie was growing faster than A.J. They both were looking more and more like their mother every day. Katie had even inherited her mother's wild curls. He was glad that his nanny knew how to tame them, because he just couldn't get a handle on combing out the tangles. Otherwise, the child would look like one of those children found in the wild. He smiled thinking about Katie's Medusa look most mornings.

Ashton took an armload of clothes and stuffed animals to the counter. He was always buying toys and clothes. He looked around trying to think of something special. As he leaned forward to help straighten and fold the clothes on the counter, he felt the gold chain he wore cool against his chest. Jewelry, he thought. Katie had pierced ears. She was due for a pair of studs, and maybe he could buy them both watches. He asked the girl at the register if he could leave the boxes with her while he shopped some more. She eagerly agreed. Ashton had noticed her deference to him. He tried not to feed in to it. These days, he was never sure if women liked him for his looks or because they recognized him. Either way, he was too busy being and thinking about being a father to care. He thanked her and went toward the jewelry department.

Kali had eaten too much while she was talking non-stop. She loved talking to Mrs. Martin. She imagined that was what it could have been like with her own mother. The two women strolled back into the store and to the jewelry counter. Kali stood closely to Mrs. Martin talking, telling her some more of her favorite customer stories.

"Oh, I wish I could see you more often," Mrs. Martin sighed. "You know I am surrounded by men at home. They don't talk about anything except sports, cars, and money."

"Well, the money part is not a bad thing to discuss," Kali leaned her elbows on the counter and looked at the large clock over the door. It was getting late and she had a manager's meeting to attend that afternoon.

Noticing the time herself, Mrs. Martin hugged her one last time.

"You know where to find me if you need anything, dear," said Mrs. Martin and pushed Kali's curl from her face.

"Thank you." Kali's eyes glistened with a little sadness. "Thank you and Mr. Martin for everything."

Kali turned to grab a tissue from under the register when she saw him. It was unmistakably him. She gasped and put her hand over her mouth. She backed up, stumbled, and knocked over the trash can.

"What's wrong, dear?" Mrs. Martin asked, recognizing fear in the young woman's eyes.

"It's him," Kali answered hoarsely. She hurriedly moved from behind the counter, grabbing her purse.

"The man you are running from?"

"Yes," Kali nodded as she kept walking. There was a group of people coming toward her. She tried to step away from them and as she did, her eyes met his. She panicked. She pushed someone aside and ran.

Ashton began running through the store to try to catch her. He was so glad to see her. He wanted to catch her and tell her he was sorry.

"Kali," he called across the store as she disappeared behind a column. "Kali," he yelled again as loud as he could. He knew people were staring at him, but he didn't care. The store was crowded and people kept getting in his way. He caught a glimpse of her going through a door marked 'Employees Only'. As he made headway to that door, the fire alarm went off and the shoppers went into a panic mode. Everyone was moving his way, pushing him further and further away from that door.

Kali lived in walking distance. She kept looking to make sure she wasn't being followed. She was sorry she had lost track of Mrs. Martin, but she had to get out of there. She packed lightly and made sure she put the last of her cash in the bag. She had counted it twice to see how much she had left. It was a little under 15 thousand, and she realized as she counted it that she would never have access to her account again. This was how they found her. She had made a withdrawal in Madison and then again in San Francisco. Ashton must be tracing the money, she thought. She jumped in her car and sped south. She was going to Los Angeles. She was hoping it would be big enough to get lost in and become invisible once more.

There was a big difference between Los Angeles and San Francisco. People up north were genuinely friendly. People down there were suspect and cold. Everybody either had big plans or was envious of other people's big plans. In some form, shape or another, they were all there to become movie stars. Kali found she was alone once again. It was more expensive to live there and she was spending money way too fast. She could no longer settle for a small time job. She was going to have to use her degree to get something she could live on. Kali sat up one night staring at her degree. She was going to have to use her own name. By doing that, he would surely find her. She thought about altering her degree, but she didn't have the heart to deface it.

"Kalina Denise Harris, who are you? A skinny little girl from the south with a degree in Accounting from the University of Pennsylvania, magna cum laude, and you can't strut your stuff. What's a girl to do?" She walked over to the mirror.

"I liked being Lena," she spoke to the mirror. "At least it was close to my name. I just need to adjust the last name or something and get a job in an accounting department. That way, I can work my way up and no one will care who I am. Right?" she pointed at herself in the mirror.

"Right," she answered herself.

She went back to the bed and sat on it, picking up a notepad.

"Lena," she said, while thinking of her father. He had wanted to name her Lena after Lena Horne. He used to call her his baby Lena.

"Lena Harrison," she wrote it down.

"No, too close to Harris," she scratched it out. "They are detectives. They specialize in security and surveillance. How do I hide from them?"

"In plain sight," she answered. "In plain sight!"

"Lena Denison," she wrote it out. And then wrote it out again. She got back up and stood in front of the mirror again. She extended her hand to herself in the mirror.

"Good morning, I'm Lena Denison. I am a graduate of the University of Pennsylvania. My degree says Kalina Denise Harris, which is who I am, but my married name is Denison and my nickname is Lena. It kind of grew out of my father's pet name for me, Lena. He said I looked like a baby Lena Horne."

Kali went out that morning and bought herself a wedding ring, and stopped at every employment agency in town, and then went home and doctored her latest social security card. By the same time the next week, she received a job offer as a junior accountant in a large firm in downtown LA.

Kali went to work, ate, shopped, and slept. She hadn't met anyone she could relate to no matter how much effort she put into it. No one had the same interests. She was definitely not interested in the entertainment industry and she didn't want to hear anything about Redd who was still popping up all over the place. She was guest starring on television shows and appearing on all types of magazine covers. She was even making a movie in town. Kali was absolutely not interested.

The other accountants were standoffish. She could never connect with them either. She was alone again. But, at least she thought, she was self-sufficient. She called Mrs. Martin once a week from a different pay phone outside of Los Angeles, just in case he was still trying to find her. She couldn't help thinking about his eyes in Macy's. They actually looked tired and beat down.

"Now, don't you feel sorry for him," she whispered to herself as she sat up one night doing her toe nails. "He was going to kill you, Kali."

She put her feet on the carpeted floor of the little apartment and messed up the polish on her big toe.

"Damn," she said aloud. "You are talking to yourself and spending your evenings polishing your own toes. This is a really big city. There is someone here that can be your friend. Right, God? Everybody is not a fake, just the people I have met so far. There are so many other people out there that I haven't even met."

Kali took the time to remove the polish from her toes using a wand. She showered and dressed. Then she drove to a section of Los Angeles that had a couple of little live theatres. There were people at the box office for one of them. She headed straight for that one. She had no idea what type of play she was going to see, but at least she was out of her apartment.

Kali sat in the play bored to tears. She had never heard of it before and couldn't wait to forget she had ever heard of it now. She started shifting around in the hard auditorium seat and as she did, she caught the eye of a beautiful chocolate man who was smiling at her. She smiled back, caught by his date who grabbed the man's hand and leaned closer to him. Kali nodded to the woman acknowledging her territory, but the woman turned her head. The chocolate god noticed, and his eyes continued to meet Kali's over the woman's head. Kali leaned back into her seat satisfied that she was still attractive. Suddenly, she was horny. She hadn't had sex in years. She wondered if everything still worked. She looked back to see if Mr. Chocolate was still watching her, and he was. She wondered what he was like in bed.

Kali wasn't really comfortable in the area. It was a cross between the hood and the re-gentrified, a weird aspect of Los Angeles. She saw a restaurant that appeared to be nice, so she wandered in. The place was packed. The waitress asked if she wouldn't mind waiting for a seat at the bar. Kali slid onto the red stool and saw the happy couple from the play seated in a booth behind her. The great chocolate one noticed her immediately, looking at her reflection in the mirror as she looked at his. They had made a connection. Kali didn't know how it was going to play out, but she was going to stay right there on that stool until she found out. She ordered a drink.

Ms. Possessive got up from the booth, probably to go to the ladies' room. Mr. Chocolate watched her disappear and he suddenly appeared next to Kali. She could smell the sweet musk of his cologne. She turned and carefully examined his beautiful blemish-free brown face and his large supple lips. They were topped off with the most gorgeous dark brown eyes she had ever seen.

"My name is Marcus Roberson," he said, with a slight southern accent. Kali was intrigued.

"I'm Lena," she extended her hand. He took it and held onto it.

"She's not my girlfriend," he said. "It's actually a blind date."

"You better be careful, then," Kali teased, "I think she has found the love of her life."

"I'm afraid I have to agree with you," he grinned. "What are you doing after dinner?" He was still holding her hand.

"What does it matter to you?" she asked, her eyes twinkling.

"I am taking the young lady home after dinner. After that, I am going to be a very lonely man."

"Nope. Can't have that," Kali said and tried to tug her hand back, but he was still holding onto it.

"Nope, you're right. Would you like to go to a movie? Or, let me buy you dinner?" he finally let go of her hand.

"I tell you what. Where do you work?" Kali asked.

"Not too far from here," he answered suspiciously.

"Let's do lunch. On Monday. Can you do that?" She didn't want him rushing to dump the girl, and she wasn't sure if he were lying or not. Even though she could have followed him home right that minute and ravaged him, she thought about how predatory the Sperlings were, and she didn't want to be like them.

"Wow, a girl with her own agenda," Marcus took her hand and kissed the back of it. He pulled out his business card and handed it to her. "Call me Monday morning. Just say when and where, and I'll be there two hours early waiting for you."

She took the card and saw the girl returning to their booth. She glanced in that direction. Marcus asked for a couple of beers and walked confidently back to the booth. Kali wanted to jump up and yell "touchdown." She had something to look forward to other than work in less than 48 hours.

Marcus and Kali quickly became an item. He was originally from Texas and had a heart as big as the state that spawned him. He pampered her with love and attention in ways no man ever had, and she loved his family. His parents had fallen in love with her, too. His younger sister, Sheila, worshipped her. Kali had found a home again, but to them she was Lena. She didn't want to endanger them by being her old self. The only parts left of her past were hidden in a file in the human resources department of her company and in a locked safety deposit box at the local bank. Life was good.

In less than six months of their first date, they had a small wedding in the Roberson's family church near the beach in a town below Los Angeles. They took a small apartment in a new gated community about three miles from his parents. They drove into the city behind each other every morning. They couldn't drive in together, because their jobs were so demanding. Time flew and the frenzy of the holidays was upon them.

"So what is Marcus's secret?" Sheila asked as she chopped the celery into little pieces.

"Secret?" Kali drawled the question. Her southern accent was making a revival since living amongst the Texans.

"Yeah, I overheard him tell Daddy he had an announcement to make over dinner," Sheila said and grabbed another stalk.

"What are you talking about?" Margaret walked up behind the two young women. She had washed more vegetables for them to chop and placed them on the table.

"I heard him, Mommy. As clear as day," Sheila said and started shifting things around to make room.

"He said he had an announcement to make," she insisted.

"I don't know anything about an announcement." Kali got up to run water over the onion she was getting ready to chop.

"That's enough celery, Sheila." Margaret grabbed the rest and began to package it for the refrigerator. "That should be the last onion, too."

"Come, on Lena. He is your husband. You have to know something," Sheila pressed.

"No," Kali shook her head. She couldn't imagine what it was. All she knew is lately he had been asking her about having a baby. He wanted her to become a housewife and mother. Kali didn't have the heart to tell him she wanted no parts of either. She would go stir crazy being at home, and she never wanted to be pregnant again, ever in her life.

As the fates would have it, the kitchen television was on and there they were, the four of them. The announcer said what a beautiful family they were. Ashton, Redd and the twins were on a float in Philadelphia's Thanksgiving Day parade. Her instinct was to jump up and turn it off the way she normally would, but instead her eyes were glued to them as long as they were on the screen. The twins were beautiful, and Ashton's eyes were as sad as the day she had seen him at Macy's. What was wrong, she wondered.

About four o'clock, dinner was finally spread across the table in the greatest fanfare. Marcus and his father made a big to do over whose turn it was to cut the turkey. The women fussed and everyone made fake disgruntled noises. Finally, Mr. Roberson said a beautiful grace that was reminiscent of her father's short beautiful moments at the head of many dinner tables on Thanksgiving. Every Thanksgiving they had eaten with a different family, bringing good- ies home for the rest of the weekend. Her mother never cooked Thanksgiving dinner. Then a fleeting memory of Thanksgiving with Jordan and his lewd boys washed over her. Remembering Ashton and his family enjoying Thanksgiving brought back bad memories.

Half way through dinner, Marcus tapped his glass of iced tea.

"Lena," he held up the glass, "Dad, Mom, and whoever you are," he grinned at Sheila as she crossed her eyes and made an ugly face at him. "I have an announcement to make."

Marcus stood up and placed his arm around Kali's shoulder.

"I have a new job," he grinned, as everyone looked at him blankly.

"A new job?" Kali asked. "I thought you liked working for Mr. Papadopolous."

"I love working for him. I have learned so much. But, he has decided to sell the business. He wants to retire and enjoy his grandkids. So, he has sold the business to a company on the east coast."

"Wow, that's a long commute," Mr. Roberson grinned. "So, where's this new job? Out east?" he joked.

"Yes, Philadelphia," Marcus looked down at Kali for her reaction.

"No, not Philadelphia," Kali leaned away from him in disbelief.

"Yes, Philadelphia. It is a fantastic opportunity. The new CEO is looking for someone to groom to run some of his subsidiaries. His company is growing rapidly, so he needs to train someone quickly, and Mr. Papadopolous convinced him I was the right man for the job. Isn't that incredible?"

"No, I hate Philadelphia!" Kali protested. "It's cold, dirty, and filthy!"

"Oh, I am sure not all of it is like that. Trust me, before I move you there, I will find a perfect place for us to live. It will definitely not be dirty or filthy."

"He couldn't promise you not cold," Mr. Roberson added.

"Marcus, I don't know whether to be happy for you or angry with you," Margaret said, throwing her napkin on the table.

"Be happy for me mother," Marcus ran to her and kissed her.

"How can I? You don't just make an announcement like this without consulting your wife," she looked a Kali who was still sitting there stunned by the news.

"I'm going to make you very happy there, Lena. I promise. We can start a family there. I'll be making more than enough money to support us, so you won't have to worry about another job. All we have to worry about is starting a family. It's going to be wonderful, you'll see."

Kali was so devastated that she couldn't catch her breath. She got up, got her purse, and walked out of the door. She needed air. Marcus had removed all the oxygen in the room. She couldn't possibly go back to Philadelphia. If she did, she would be planning her own funeral.

Margaret called to check on her everyday, and everyday Kali begged Margaret to talk Marcus out of going to Philadelphia. At one point, Kali considered going on the run again, but that would mean she would lose another family. She realized she was going to have to make a decision whether that family was worth the fight ahead of her if she went back. Everyday Marcus came home more hyped up than the previous day, and this day he came home hurriedly to pack. He needed her to take him to the airport. He was going to Philadelphia to meet his new boss.

Kali walked Marcus to his gate and kissed him goodbye. The flight was delayed, but she had to get back home before dark. Kali hated driving the expressways in the dark. She decided to stop at the restroom, in case there was a lot of traffic. As she stood at the sink washing her hands, she noticed a pregnant woman splashing water on her face. The woman's hand reached out for the paper towel. Kali reached over, grabbed a few, and put them in the woman's hands. The woman patted her eyes then looked straight into Kali's, it was Ruby.

"Oh, my God!" Kali stumbled backwards.

"Wait," Ruby reached out for her, but Kali's hands fought her off.

"Wait, let me talk to you," Ruby tried to follow her out of the bathroom, but several other women were coming in off a recent flight.

"Kali, I just want to talk to you!" Ruby yelled as she pushed her big belly away from the crowd. She stepped out into the terminal and Kali was nowhere to be seen.

One week later, Kali was being led by her husband to their room at the Embassy Suites near the airport in Philadelphia. She didn't have much choice. After her encounter with Ruby, she had decided no matter where she ran the Sperlings would always haunt her. She decided to take the fight back to Philadelphia. Her feet were tired of running, and she loved her new family enough to not to turn over and take it any more.

Marcus's new boss had wanted them to move out there before his Christmas party, and an eager Marcus had convinced her to pack as many things as she could to follow him. This was their first Christmas and he refused to be apart from her. Their life had been a whirlwind – a short courtship, a quick marriage, and now a series of firsts. She came to Philadelphia, begrudgingly, thinking it was her fate. She wanted to tell Marcus about her life. But, he was so wrapped up in his new job that she didn't want to distract him.

After he had deposited her in the hotel, he spent very little time with her. He would leave early and come home late. She sat in the hotel watching television and walking around the atrium so bored she wanted to just stand in the middle of it and scream. The day of the Christmas party, there was a knock on the door. Kali opened it to find a man with a large bouquet of winter flowers, a garment bag, and a box. Kali welcomed the excitement. She tipped the man heavily and ran back into the bedroom with the garment bag.

She had already been anxious about going to the party. All she had was a simple black dress and the well earned fear of going into Center City to buy something new. She unzipped the bag and found a beautiful blue cocktail dress. She checked the size and it was perfect. She scooted out of her sweat suit and tried it on. It hugged every curve and accentuated her long legs. She smiled. She threw open the box and found a pair blue heels trimmed in gold that matched the dress perfectly. Then there was a bag, a cute little gold and blue cloth bag trimmed in sequins. Kali squealed with delight as she strutted around in the high heels. They were comfortable.

She ran to the phone to call Marcus at his office and a woman named Rita answered the phone. She informed Kali in a soft breathy voice that her husband was in a meeting, and then she asked if Kali liked the dress and the flowers. They talked for a few minutes and Kali tried to picture her. She guessed she was large and fat, overcompensating with the voice for her lack of appearance.

Kali was going to ask Marcus about his new assistant. She was going to comment that her voice was way too sexy to be answering an office phone. Instead, her voice was perfect for one of those 800 numbers advertised on late night television. Kali thanked the woman for helping her get a new outfit after she had described how many places she had to shop to find it. At least, she had good taste. Kali was still trying to imagine her, and hoping she wasn't a sex kitten that matched her voice and her sensual sense of fashion. The outfit was hot.

As she hung up the phone, it occurred to her that Marcus must be making a decent salary. Ever since he had taken the job, he had been protective of the bills and the finances. She was supposed to be the little woman who just accepted her allowance with gratitude and adoration for her man. She smiled. Marcus still had a lot to learn about her. She could do pretty well with her own finances. After all, she was the accountant in the family.

Another thing Marcus had to learn was to let loose of his own inhibitions. Given the chance, she could show him how to heat up their life in bed. That was the main thing that was missing between them. Marcus had passion, but she found it wanting and nothing close to the passion that Ashton stirred in her. She missed the look in Ashton's eyes when she would walk in a room. Marcus looked at her with desire, but not the kind that filled up a whole room. She could literally feel Ashton several rooms away. She knew what he wanted and when he wanted it. With Marcus, she was the one who initiated most of their lovemaking. She blamed it on being a Baptist. Marcus was all fire and brimstone. She had grown up Baptist, too, but she lost the dedication to it when her Baptist father killed her Baptist mother.

Why am I thinking about Ashton? She got up and touched the dress then looked at its seams and the label. The dress wasn't cheap at all nor the shoes. She put them away and began to attend to the gorgeous bouquet. Kali hummed as she arranged the flowers. She was beginning to look forward to meeting everyone at PDSI. She had heard so much about Mr. Papadopolous when Marcus worked for him. She rarely saw Marcus now and couldn't even remember if he had ever mentioned his new boss's name. She could only remember him referring to him as The Boss. Whoever he was, he had impressed Marcus beyond words.

Kali watched the city lights appear as they rode in the back of a cab. It looked the same as it had as they went around the City Hall Circle to go up Market Street. Marcus was working in one of the new buildings being built when Kali had left the city. She was eager to see the inside of the new Penn Center. The cab dropped them off in front of the tall impressive looking building whose lobby was festive with Christmas decorations. They took an elevator up a few floors to an area that had an open loft overlooking a lower floor.

"They just moved in here about two months ago," Marcus whispered. "It's elegant as hell, isn't it?"

Kali had to nod in agreement as she looked around the open space, tastefully furnished for small conferences among employees and visitors, with a reception area in the center rear. Behind the reception area was a spiral staircase that led to the suite of executive offices. Marcus proudly pointed out that his office was up there.

"Why are they having the party here?" Kali whispered. "I thought a Christmas Party would be in a restaurant or banquet hall or something."

"We are also having our first board meeting in the brand new boardroom. PDSI is going public in January. There is so much going on. Besides, this is his way of showcasing his offices and his services and how successful he is, all in one shot. Most of the people here tonight are clients, board members, and employees, of course. Everyone. And I mean everyone," he looked around the room with the look of man who had just been given power, "will be on their best behavior."

A tall slender woman with a mole on the left side of her mouth walked up to the couple with her hand extended to Kali.

"You must be Mrs. Roberson," she said then stood back and looked at Kali up and down. "Your husband knew the exact sizes. Can you believe that? I was so sure you were going to be having a fit. That something would be wrong."

"Are you Rita?" Kali asked. "You have excellent taste," and not fat or ugly at all, she wanted to add.

"I am. Thank you. He gave me the sizes and said something blue. He said you hated red," she shook Kali's hand.

"I'm afraid I'm the woman in his life here at work. He's a hard man to pin down. Is he like that at home?"

"Without a doubt," Kali said knowingly. The two women giggled and Marcus shook his head defeated and began to look around for a diversion.

"Excuse me," he said, "Mr. Papadopolous is here. I want to make sure I hook him up with the Boss."

Kali and Rita continued to chat until a tall gray-eyed man with red hair waved in their direction. Kali watched him as he led Rita toward one of the side offices. He looked familiar to her, but she didn't know why. She walked over to the Christmas tree trying to shake the feeling of déjà vu. It was understandable, she reasoned with herself. She was back in Philadelphia. The town was familiar to her. She had been there, done that, and seen that before.

Kali loved Christmas trees. Ever since she was a little girl scouring the woods with her dad to find the perfect live tree for their living room and decorating it to perfection with everything but the kitchen sink. It was the one other thing she had shared with her mother, a love for decorating the tree. They would spend hours making things to put on the tree, most of which had to do with musical instruments. They would sing Christmas carols. Kali closed her eyes and listened to the soft Christmas music in the background. It had been a long time since she had a sung a Christmas carol or hummed one. She walked over to the tree and touched some of the sparkling ornaments. They were from all over the world. She found one that said PDSI, Personal Defense Systems Incorporated. She was surprised. Mr. Papadopolous had sold alarm systems for companies. This said personal. She was going to have to ask Marcus about that. She knew very little about his new company. He hadn't pulled out any materials or brochures or anything for her to review. He had just told her that his salary was higher and that their benefits were fantastic. She was feeling a little left out.

Micah was the first one to spot her. He was looking toward the Christmas tree as he was coming down the spiral staircase. He froze. He watched her at the Christmas tree. She was touching the ornaments, and the lights from the tree reflected off her hazel eyes. It was definitely her. She had cut her curly hair to hang just beneath the nape of her neck, but it was the same. He backed up the stairs and hastily found Ashton who was talking to a group of investors at the top of the landing. He grabbed his brother's arm.

"I need to talk to you," Micah said, trying to lead his brother away.

"Of course." Ashton looked at him a bit annoyed, but turned to the investors with a smile. "Excuse me, please. Enjoy yourselves. We will talk more later."

The gentlemen acquiesced and moved further into the suite looking around.

"This had better be good," Ashton turned to Micah in an low

angry voice.

"She's here," Micah whispered.

Ashton immediately thought of Redd, but she was on a flight to Europe yet again with Asa.

"Who's here?" he said, taking a sip from his champagne flute.

"Kali," Micah pulled him in the direction of the stairs.

Ashton's heart skipped a beat and he stood there with both relief and a reluctance to believe she was actually there. His head moved side to side trying to spy her.

"The Christmas tree! Look at the Christmas tree."

Ashton freed himself from his brother's grip and worked his way around several people coming up the stairs. He nodded and smiled at them. He took a few seconds to shake a few hands while his eyes searched downwardly toward the Christmas tree. Micah was right. There she was. He started taking several steps at a time, working his way to her and was stopped a few feet short by Marcus.

"Mr. Sperling," Marcus grabbed him. "This is Mr. Papadopolous from Los Angeles."

Ashton was torn with shaking the man's hand and running for the tree. He had just bought the man's company and couldn't ignore him. There was so much to learn about his security system. Ashton stopped and chatted with the man for a few minutes asking him if he could spend more time with him before he left Philadelphia. He turned to Micah for help, who stepped in to schedule a time. Marcus noticed Ashton's focus was on the tree and then noticed his wife reaching inside the branches for an ornament.

"Oh, gentlemen! Let me introduce you to my wife," he said proudly as the three men followed him to the tree.

Kali saw something that had startled her. It was a glass ornament with a gold saxophone inside it. She reached for it hoping she wouldn't find an engraved Merry Christmas along the bar that it sat on. She had given Jordan the exact same ornament at their first Christmas. She had just put her hand on it to take it off the tree when Marcus surprised her.

"Lena, I want you to meet my old boss and my new one. Lena, this is Mr. Papadopolous and Mr. Sperling," Kali's knees went weak as she turned and found herself within breathing distance of Ashton. Their eyes met and she crumpled. Ashton caught her and swept her up in his arms. He whisked her through the startled party goers with the other three men close behind. He took two, three steps at a time as he carried her up the spiral staircase and straight to his office. He laid her gently on the large sofa against the wall.

"Lena, Lena," Marcus called her, trying to get close to her, but Ashton was blocking him.

"Lena," Marcus squeezed in beside Ashton and grabbed her hand. Ashton was sitting on the sofa next to her smoothing the curls from her face.

She woke up with a gasp, looking from Ashton to Marcus.

"Are you all right?" Marcus asked. Ashton moved away from her and stood behind Marcus. He discreetly shook his head.

"I'm fine," she lied, fearful of what she should or should not say.

"No, you are not fine. You just fainted," Marcus was still hold-ing her hand looking worried.

"I just. I just forgot to eat," she said, trying to sit up. She wanted to get out of there.

"Women," Mr. Papadopolous said, jokingly. "They forget ev-erything." The men chuckled at Kali's expense.

"I wanted to make sure my dress fit," she said weakly.

"It fits perfectly," Marcus said, embarrassed that the men he wanted to impress the most was watching his wife act silly.

Ashton put his hand on Marcus's shoulder.

"There's plenty of food downstairs, son. You know what she'll eat. Go get her a plate," he urged and then he turned to Micah and Mr. Papadopolous.

"Why don't you show Mr. Papadopolous around and make that appointment," he squeezed his brother's arm. Micah nodded.

The two men started to leave the room while Marcus still stood there.

"Look, she will be fine here," Ashton assured Marcus. "I just have to get some notes for tonight's meeting.

He looked at his watch. "We are meeting in ten minutes and I want to introduce you to the Board. Get her a plate. Pronto," he added. Marcus left the room behind the other two men.

Kali and Ashton watched the door close. She tried to sit up again, but a wave of dizziness overtook her.

"Calm down. I'm not going to hurt you. I swear. I swear on our babies' lives. I won't hurt you," he sat on the coffee table and restrained himself from touching her again. Her hair and her skin had felt so soft and she had smelled heavenly.

"I'll leave," she said.

"And cause suspicion. You obviously haven't said anything to your husband about us. If you keep it a secret, I'll keep it a secret," he offered, not knowing what else to say. All he knew was that he didn't want her to run.

She lay still thinking, but all her thoughts jumbled together.

"There is no longer a need for you to run," he said slowly, hoping she was paying him attention. She was still distressed.

"Kali, listen to me," he leaned closer to her.

"You are safe. Safe," he repeated. He knew she didn't believe him. He hoped she would one day.

"I want to go back to the hotel," she sat up and let the dizziness pass.

"After you eat, and after your husband meets the board," he got up and went to his desk. He really did have some notes that he was taking to the meeting. He gathered his things and put them in his portfolio.

"Why did you hire him?" she asked accusingly.

"I didn't. Micah did. And it turns out, he made the right decision for everybody," Ashton walked toward the door. He realized he couldn't overwhelm her. He had to let it sink in that she was home. He wanted to skip out the door with joy, but he couldn't let her see how happy he was. She would think he was only trying to get to her in another way. He had a lot of work ahead of him.

"Oh," he stopped with his hand on the doorknob. "What's with Lena?"

"Leave me alone," she protested.

"Good enough." He opened the door and then looked out to see if Marcus was nearby. "We can do this, Lena. It's not like we will be seeing each other every day, right?"

Tears began to flow down her face and she shivered, folding her arms across her chest defensively. He wanted to go back and soothe the tears away, but instead he walked out the door. This was going to be a great Christmas.

Christmas morning, Kali and Marcus were awakened by a knock on the hotel door. Marcus pulled on his robe and walked through the suite to the door. It was a courier with a small package.

Kali joined Marcus at the table as he emptied the package onto the table. There were three sets of keys and some documents as well as a cover note.

"Oh, My God!" exclaimed Marcus. "This man is just awesome!"

He picked up the keys and looked at the labels.

"Merry First Christmas, baby! I have gifts for you, but my gifts pale in comparison to these."

"What gifts?" Kali noticed two sets of the keys belonged to cars.

"Check this out. This," Marcus held up a set of blue keys, "these belong to a house in Society Hill that we can live in rent free for a whole year. Imagine that? I have never been down there, but I hear it is really nice. No dirt, no filth," Marcus added remembering Kali's objections to living in Philadelphia.

"And this," he picked up another set, "is a key to a White Mercedes and this is a key to a Blue BMW. I think you get the blue and I get the white. According to this paperwork, they both have two year leases, fully paid."

Kali toyed with the keys. She looked at the address on the tag and immediately hated Ashton. He was sending her back to their love nest. Why would he do that? She wanted to throw the keys back at him and tell him to shove it. Her husband was busy dancing around singing with ear-splitting delight.

"Aren't you happy?" He grabbed her face and kissed her on the forehead. "This is the most awesome thing, besides marrying you, that has ever happened to me. You are without a doubt my good luck charm. I thank God for you daily, every minute of the day. Come on," he pulled her out of her chair. "Let's get dressed. We're going home for Christmas."

Kali let him lead her to the shower. He had no idea that she really was going home.

CHAPTER ELEVEN

"You are sure this is what you want?" Micah threw a clipped set of documents in front of Ashton as he sat behind his desk smoking a cigar and blowing circles.

"Yep," Ashton said, smiling. "I think I have waited long enough. Don't you?" he flipped through the documents.

"She is going to shit in her pants. This is going to be really big publicly. And beware, Asa and Daddy are going to support her at every step." Micah warned.

"My shit's in order. I'm so glad I started earlier. I never knew I would actually do it, but I'm ready," Ashton rocked in his chair.

"What about her?" Micah nodded toward the office down the hall.

"I have kept clear. She has no reason to think about anything. Hubby talks a good game. Claims she is happy being the little trying-to-get-pregnant housewife. You and I both know he's in fantasy land."

"He seems to think she can't," Micah grinned, "get pregnant."

"I love eager young hapless husbands," Ashton rocked even faster. "He doesn't have a clue. She hasn't told him a thing."

"She's trying to stay out of your reach," said Micah and picked up the papers again.

"Like that could really happen," Ashton dragged on his cigar and winked at Micah.

"Invite hubby over tonight for the card game. Let's see what kind of man he really is," Ashton held his hand out for the papers and then started signing them.

"Airport tomorrow?" Micah took the signed documents and checked all the signatures.

"Yes, sir," Ashton saluted. He was in a great mood. He had been in a great mood since the Christmas party. People were even commenting on it. Even Redd had seen the difference when he and the kids had flown to Paris for New Year's. She had comment-ed she thought he was different somehow. He told her it was the holidays and the great memories that came with them. She had ac-cepted that. Why wouldn't she? She was all wrapped up in herself anyway. There was something not being said, and of course, Asa was in on it. Ashton didn't care anymore. He had considered the trip time served and returned to Philadelphia as soon as he could.

Five months or so had come and gone, and Kali was still in Philadelphia. She had even connected with Kenny who was still running his salon, funded by a new infusion from Ashton to help keep an eye on her now that she was back. Once a week, he was now stopping at the salon to learn about Kali and her relationship with her husband. To Kali, Kenny had always been like talking to another woman and was without a doubt her best friend and only friend, even if they had parted ways after the babies.

Kali had never asked why she had never seen Kenny again. But, then she couldn't remember if she had even let him know that she had moved out of the house. What Ashton had learned on his vis-its to get his hair cut or nails manicured was that Kali was anything but happy, especially about living in their old house. There were so many things in the house that reminded her of him. Ashton took that as a sign in his favor. He was still under her skin.

The other thing she hated was the confinement. Hubby didn't want her to work. He wanted her barefoot and pregnant. He had to smile because that was the same thing he wanted. He wanted another baby and he wanted it with Kali. This time he was going to do it the right way.

He went to the airport to meet Redd and Asa on a sweet beautiful day in May. He hadn't seen Redd since the first week in January, and he had rarely talked to her this trip. When he had first got back, he tried to call her, but she wouldn't come to the phone. She was too busy and was going to call back later. But, she would never call. He hadn't even heard from Asa. He called his father, who bragged that he heard from them almost everyday. So what Ashton was about to do came without guilt, without remorse. It was just the right thing to do. It was time for a new chapter in his life.

Redd walked off the plane into the gate area wearing a huge pair of sunglasses. They were so huge they almost covered her sallow face that was smeared with makeup too pale for such a bright day. A tired and red-eyed Asa followed her close behind.

"Darling," she ran to Ashton and hugged him. "It is so good to see you. I have never been so happy to see you and this country in my entire life. We just had a horrid run over there. I didn't think I was ever going to get home." Redd continued to jabber holding onto Ashton as they walked away from the gate.

"What's this?" she tugged at the bag hanging over his shoulder.

"Oh, it's my carry-on. I'm actually on my way to Toronto for a few days. I tried to time it so I could at least keep my promise to meet you at the airport," Ashton said and gently removed her hands that were clutching him tightly.

"Well, get me a ticket," she demanded. "Or, do you already have one for me?"

"No, this is business. I'm going to be tied up day and night. Why don't you just go home and get some rest? You both look like you could use it.

"What happened? Getting too old to party all night and then do a cross-Atlantic? You should have slept coming over here," Ashton stopped and hugged his brother briefly.

"Daddy didn't tell you, did he?" Asa asked.

"Tell me, what?" Ashton asked then looked at his watch.

"Like Redd said. This was a hell of a trip. We'll talk about it when you get back," Asa noticed Ashton was in a hurry. "Go on."

Ashton kissed Redd on the forehead and tapped his brother's shoulder. He was off.

Redd was the first to notice the guy in a suit with a sign that read PDSI. She strode over to him hoping he would just take her bag.

"Mrs. Sperling?" the man asked.

"Yes," she said.

"Mrs. Elizabeth O'Reilly Sperling?" he asked.

"Yes, you have done your research," she said, her voice hoarse with tiredness.

He handed her a brown envelope. She took it and looked at how it was addressed.

"You have been served, Mrs. Sperling," he walked away and handed the sign off to another man standing nearby. The man with the sign approached and picked up the bag she had dropped as she realized the papers were from Micah's law firm. She took the papers from the envelope and realized it was a document for a divorce and a date with the court. She shrieked a loud agonizing howl that made the airport grow quiet with the exception of the gate announcements. Everyone watched as the great Redd melted down in the airport. An ingenious onlooker recorded it and sent it to all the news stations. While Ashton talked business in Toronto, America talked about his impending divorce.

Ashton wouldn't take his father's calls. Billy had made it clear in his voice messages that he was not only representing Redd, he was going to take Ashton to the cleaners in the process. He had never heard his father sound so happy before. Billy thought he was finally going to get the chance to get even for Jordan's inheritance and Ashton knew Billy had planned to split the winnings with Asa and Redd.

Asa sat back quietly and let Billy take charge. Asa had no fight in him. All he wanted to do was see Redd through this turmoil. The reporters and paparazzi that shadowed them would always get confused. They would report sightings of Redd and Ashton when it was actually Redd and Asa. As many times as Asa had escorted Redd around the world, no one had ever mistaken the two before. Now, the media was grasping for straws.

It took three months for the proceedings to come to a head. Redd and Billy sat on one side of the judge's chamber as Micah and Ashton sat on the other side. The judge sat before them rifling through the latest documents Ashton had to produce.

"So, you placed everything in your children's names over two years ago?" The judge looked at Ashton over his glasses.

"Sir, life is short. I work in security. I see and I hear it every day. I work for my children, so I give everything to my children."

"According to all your accounts and brokers, you personally are worth about three million dollars, and your company is a public company."

"Yes sir, I only own a portion of it," Ashton answered.

"And, this." The judge pulled up another document, "is a prenup signed by both you and Mrs. Sperling?"

"Yes, sir," Ashton nodded.

Redd and Billy sat up quickly. Billy tried to snatch the document from the judge's hand. The judge looked at him reproachfully.

"I'm sorry, Your Honor. I wasn't aware of any pre-nuptial agreement," Billy stuttered apologetically.

"Is this your handwriting and signature, Mrs. Sperling?" the judge handed the copy of a handwritten note to Redd. Her face went pale.

"Yes," she said, her lips began to tremble with anger. "I wrote this when I was very young, sir. It was a joke. I wrote it as a joke."

"But, you wrote it, nonetheless. And it looks like Mr. Ashton Sperling signed it, with Mr. Asa Sperling witnessing it," the judge looked at the document again.

"Yes, but it was a joke. We were all drinking and talking about how rich we were going to be one day and I said..." she stopped and remembered that evening. Ashton had almost caught her in bed with Asa. She and Asa were angry that night over the fact they thought Ashton's management was ruining her fledgling career. She wanted to make sure he didn't keep a dime of her money when she finally left him for Asa. She had hurt Ashton that night and she had done it purposefully. She knew she should have apologized, but she never did. Ashton was the one that had given her the career in the first place. Ashton had been the strong man in her life that she had taken for granted and now he had had enough, but for all the wrong reasons. She wanted to talk to him and tell him about her last trip, but he wouldn't come to the phone and he wouldn't meet her anywhere. She had thought about writing it, but was afraid it would get into the wrong hands. She wanted to crawl across Billy and Micah and fall into his arms. She wanted to tell him she had come home that day to really make a home. That was all she had thought about in Europe that season. She wanted to come home and build a home. She was even ready to be a mother. She wanted to tell him how sorry she was that she hadn't even tried.

"I want joint custody of the children," she blurted out.

Ashton started laughing. He shrugged as he told the judge, "this from a woman who literally tried to throw a baby to a marble floor because he spit up on her. This from a woman who has spent literally about four months out of almost three years with the children. And this, from a woman who refers to them as the little creatures! Your Honor, I moved my children to Philadelphia when they were six months old. This woman has never sat foot in our happy abode since. Trust me. If she saw them, it was because they just happened to be with me. Or, or better yet, if she wanted us to make a public appearance together as a family. Publicity, Your Honor, to keep her career on track!"

"Okay, I'm tired of this case. This is how it's going down," the judge said.

"They are my children, too. I signed their adoption papers," Redd drowned out the judge.

"No, you never signed crap," Ashton sat back in his chair. "Remember."

"Sit down, Mrs. Sperling, before I toss you out of my chamber," the judge used his gavel to get her attention.

"Since the children have never been in your custody and since that was not part of this filing, we will not consider it. I will decree that Mr. Sperling will give you $1.5 million dollars and a monthly stipend of $10,000 until you remarry. At that time, he will no longer have to provide you with anything," the judge sat back in his chair. "Now get out. All of you."

As the four of them left the chamber, Redd was busy trying to get to Ashton, and he was literally running out of the huge court-house. He couldn't wait to feel the summer heat on his face.

"You will regret this Ashton. All you had to do was talk to me. We could have worked this out. I was coming home to you. To you!" she screamed. "I was ready. I was ready to be your wife. I was ready to take care of the children. I still am. I am going to file for custody of those children. They are mine, too."

Ashton walked calmly back to where she stood and leaned over to her.

"No," he said low enough for her ears only. "They are mine. Remember when you said, you heard they were mine biologically, and I denied it. Well, I am not denying it anymore. You wouldn't give me my own blood, so I went out and got them. You come near them, and you will be the one to regret it."

The blood ran from her face and she collapsed into Billy's arms. Micah followed Ashton onto the elevator and they left the building working their way through the frenzy of nosey reporters. Word had gotten out fast. Reporters were begging for comments, but he ignored them and continued walking down the courthouse stairs. The motion of running down the stairs caused his jacket to flap and the appearance of wind coursing through his hair. It was like oxygen being pumped back into his being. All he could think about was sweeping Kali back into his arms.

Kali watched the evening news and of all things, there was Ashton descending the courthouse steps in New York City. His face was blank, but his eyes were smiling. He was divorced. Redd was a thing of the past. She wondered what was in his and their children's future. She turned off the television just as Marcus walked in the door.

"You're home early." She ran to him and tried to hug him.

"Poker game tonight," he said, rushing past her. "They were

supposed to play a few months ago, but it got called at the last minute. But, tonight we're on.

"I guess he's ready to celebrate."

"Celebrate what?" Kali acted dumb.

"His divorce, didn't I tell you? He was married to that big time model, the one that has recently fallen from grace. Can't get a job no matter how hard she tries. Rumor has it that she looked so bad last year none of the designers would use her. They said she went all over Europe begging for work and ended up in Germany, stuck. Had something to do with her passport. Anyway, she came home to a divorce proceeding and got literally nothing," Marcus laughed. "It's the only thing anybody at PDSI is talking about. I had heard the man was cutthroat and coldblooded. Now, I believe. I believe."

"Wow," Kali followed Marcus into the bedroom. She wanted to tell him not to go to the poker game. She had a feeling that he was the one about to get his throat cut.

"So, when did you start playing poker?" she asked.

"Oh, I've been reading up on it for the last two days. Ms. Elliott even played me a few hands. I'm sure I'll be fine. Besides, I am invited to the Boss's penthouse with his friends. This is going to be unreal. You don't mind, do you? I promise to take you out this weekend. Just pick something."

"Can I come?" Kali asked, suddenly wanting to protect her husband from Ashton.

"Don't be silly. It's the guys' night. Why don't you call Kenny and see if he can come over?" Marcus flapped his hands in the air. Kali hit him.

"Don't be making fun of my friend," she teased. Then she flopped on the bed and watched him carefully select what he was wearing tonight. She thought he was worse than Kenny in some respects. But, she didn't say anything. He went out of the door eagerly without even a kiss. She was bored. She went downstairs to find something to read. She saw his Mercedes go down the street. She really did want to go back to the penthouse, if nothing more than to see whether it had changed at all.

Marcus was feeling really important walking into the large marble lobby of the Banks Building. He had heard so much about the apartment tower off Rittenhouse Square. Now, he was finally there. Marcus loved his job, and he loved being around people with money. He knew that meant that he would have money one day.

He walked onto the elevator with the concierge who escorted him to the door of the penthouse. A huge Black woman with a crew cut answered the door.

"Come on in," she said gently. "The boys are down the hall. I hope you brought a pocketful of change. They are ready to celebrate."

"Yes, ma'am," Marcus said and followed her down the hall to a large room that had a poker table in the middle of it and a large screen television with a football game glaring across it. He walked in just in time to see the men jumping and yelling about a touch down.

"Y'all have seen that game how many times?" Reggie put her hands on her hips.

"It's get better every time I see it," Ashton yelled. "Come on in, Marcus. Don't be scared. We won't bite you too hard."

Micah stood up and pointed to a chair.

"I hope you brought cash. We don't take checks around here."

"No credit cards."

"No jewelry," everybody chimed in cheerfully.

"First born children, we take," Ashton laughed. Marcus walked over to him and shook his hand.

"Thank you for inviting me," Marcus said formally.

"Yes, sir, Boss, thank you, thank you," Brady said and bowed at the waist. Marcus looked back at the gray-eyed man. He never really liked him very much, and that comment made him like him less.

"Give him a break, Brady. At least he's polite. Something your mama didn't know nothing about," Ashton came to Marcus's defense. The other two men in the room snickered as Brady turned beet red.

"Son, you know big mouth here and my brother. This dude right here is my bestest friend from college. We went to Columbia together. He just moved back to the city to be a detective," the two of them howled some sort of fraternity howl. Marcus used to watch the camaraderie of the frats on his campus and wished he could have fit in like that.

"Let me guess, Q dogs," Marcus took a seat.

"Naw, Kappas," three of them yelled. Apparently, Micah was a Kappa, too.

"What about you, Brady?" Marcus asked to include him and to try to make friends.

"I didn't have time for fraternities. I had to work my way through school," he said, lighting his cigar.

"I had to work my way through, too," Troy said, as if he were offended. "Hell, if it weren't for the Kappas, I wouldn't have gotten a decent enough job to help me survive those long lean years."

"What about you?" Troy asked. He cut his cigar before lighting it and handed the cutter to Ashton who passed it to Micah. Micah handed his cut cigar to Marcus who looked at it strangely. Then he cut another one.

"I was busy," Marcus said. "I belonged to a lot of clubs, just not a fraternity."

"Nothing wrong with that," Micah said.

"Not a thing," Troy said. "Let's play some cards, boys."

"Let's make some noise, boys," Ashton got up and turned the volume of the television down and pushed in a tape of the Ohio Players. The music started blaring and Ashton started dancing and singing to the music. Troy was dealing the cards and Micah was rocking his head.

"What you know, boy?" Troy asked, as Ashton eased himself back into the chair next to him.

"I know I'm going to kick some ass tonight, son," he picked up his hand and studied it.

"How about you, Texas? You gone try to kick my ass," Ashton drawled a fake southern accent.

Marcus looked into Ashton's eyes and saw that they were already a little red. He reasoned he had gotten a head start on the liquor. The maid, or whoever she was, pushed a cart into the room. There was a tin tub of ice that fit the cart filled with bottles of beer. The men attacked it.

"You sure you're in the right place?" she asked.

"Ma'am?" He looked at her questioningly.

"You look too young to be hanging with these old cougars. They are dangerous" She picked up a beer and handed it to him. "Plus, they've had a good head start on the liquor.

"I'll be upstairs with the kids if you need some help down here. Don't let them scare you," she gathered up the empty bottles and tumblers and left the room.

Marcus played well. He even won a couple of hands and took the ribbing from the other guys, but he noticed Ashton was becoming more intense with every hand. Ashton got up from the table and poured a fresh Scotch.

"You want one, son," Ashton held up the bottle.

"No, thank you, sir," Marcus wanted to bite his lip after he said, sir. No one else in the room called Ashton sir, but he was calling everybody son. Besides, he was only about eight to ten years older than he was. Marcus didn't know why, but Ashton could make him want to shrink into hiding with one word or one look.

"How's that pretty little pussy, at home? Boy, she's hot. Ain't she boys?" Ashton dropped into one of the over stuffed chairs near the television.

"Damn, Ashton," Micah started laughing. "You getting horny or something?"

"I have been horny for damn near two years," they all started laughing. "Now I bet this boy right here ain't horny. I bet he is eating pussy every night. Every night. I know I would."

Marcus rubbed his face and tried to hold his smile. The Boss was definitely drunk.

"Come on, Marcus. Give us a blow by blow. Does she blow?"

"Oooh!" the men yelled in unison.

"Ashton, I think its time for you to go to bed," Troy said, grinning. "And not, with his wife!"

The men oohed with laughter again.

"I would love to. Go to bed that is. If there was somebody in it besides my kids and the pillows," Ashton took a long swig.

"Come on, Marcus. Tell us, does it taste good? She smelled good. God, she smelled so good," Ashton leaned his head on the glass to cool his forehead and to get a look at Marcus's face without intimidating him any further.

"I don't think I need to discuss that," Marcus tried to sound as respectful as he could.

"Oh, shit," Brady exclaimed. "That means he ain't eating it."

"That's exactly what it means," Troy chimed in.

"Boy, if it was good. You would say it was good. I mean, I'd be bragging like it was all that and a bag of chips. Man, I saw your woman at the Christmas party. She is so fine. I bet she tastes like butter," Brady wiped his mouth lewdly. Marcus looked away.

"Son, do you really? I mean, don't you? Have you ever?" Ashton was back into the conversation. "She looks like the type that would bury your head, you know."

Marcus shook his head.

"It's not my thing, man," he said, awkwardly, not knowing why he was sharing.

"You really don't eat it?" Micah grinned.

"You better hope somebody else don't come along and taste it for you," Ashton said, leaning back into his chair. "She might like it."

Marcus looked at his watch. It was later than he had anticipated. He tried to think of a kind way to get up and leave.

"Don't be looking at your watch, son. You don't have to go to work tomorrow. You can stay home and make your baby. Or did you make it already?" Ashton stood up unsteadily and walked back to the poker table. He relit his cigar and propped his feet up on the cards.

"I guess we ain't playing cards no more," Micah threw the rest of the deck in the middle of the table.

"We're not pregnant, yet," Marcus answered. "But, I will be happy to stay home and make a good effort." The men laughed again.

Micah patted Marcus on the back.

"Did you ever get your physical, man?" He bewildered Marcus with the question.

"Excuse me?" Marcus thought Ashton wasn't the only one who was drunk. Micah just held his liquor better.

"We have this physical. You get tested for everything. It creates this panel of vulnerabilities and shits, you know like diseases you may be pre-disposed to and stuff. You need to get that done. Especially if you're talking about babies. You want to know if you gon' be around to raise 'em. Ya know?" Micah nodded his head and Marcus nodded it with him. He hadn't thought about that. That would be very important.

Micah walked Marcus all the way to his car.

"I hope you won't hold anything my brother said tonight against him. He is in a low place right now. The divorce has been coming a long time, but it's here and it hurts."

"I can understand that. I'm happy that I was included in the card party. I hope I will get another invite," Marcus shook Micah's hand.

"I'm sure you will," Micah closed the door of the Mercedes and waved him goodbye.

Kali sat up waiting for Marcus. He reeked of liquor and smoke as he crawled into the bed and went straight to sleep. He awakened the next morning, barely brushed her lips with a kiss, and headed straight to work. He was eager to talk to Micah about getting that physical.

Kali walked through the house dusting every little thing, finding absolutely no dust. She was going crazy. How many times could she clean that little house? She pulled back the drapes and thought about changing them. While looking out of the window she saw a huge bouquet of roses going past her window. They were roses of all colors. She was thrilled when she saw the feet and the roses coming up her steps. She opened the door before the man could ring the doorbell.

"Wow, I hope you have the right address," the roses stepped into her door way and they were placed on the table next to the stairs. She was digging in her purse to tip the delivery man until she looked up. She dropped the purse.

Ashton knelt down and picked up the items and her purse, putting them back together. Then he closed the door.

"What are you doing here?" she took a few side steps to the door.

"I bring apologies and roses," he said, as he put her purse under his arm and turned his attention back to the roses. He was breaking them down.

"Get the vases. They'll die like this."

Kali didn't move.

"Kali, I kept my distance. Didn't I?" he pulled a few more roses out and started to bunch them.

"Okay, I'll get them," he walked into the kitchen and came back with four large vases. They were the same ones she had picked out when they were together.

"How about some water?" he asked. She was still standing in the same place.

"Kali, you have got to let your guard down just a little. I don't know how many ways or how many times I can tell you, I'm sorry. 'Cause I am. I am so sorry. I regret what I did to you every day of my life." He tried to take a step toward her, and she jumped. He stepped backwards and went back to work on the flowers. He went into the kitchen, filled the vases with water, and placed them on the kitchen table. He carried the roses to the vases, and then he put a vase filled with the roses on the dining room table and then one on the coffee table. He handed her one.

"Bedrooms? One for your room and one for the guest bedroom?"

She took the vase and set it next to the one on the coffee table. She thought she might need it to hit him over the head if he tried to attack her. She looked at her purse still tucked tightly under his arm.

"You want this?" He took the purse from under his arm and held it out, but not too far from him.

"Put it down," she said, her breathing getting faster.

"Don't pass out on me, Kali." Ashton saw her chest moving fast as she began to gasp for air. "Calm down. I promise I won't hurt you. I won't even touch you. I just want to talk to you. I want to talk to you about our children."

"I don't have any children," she began to gasp for air.

"Don't do this, Kali," Ashton looked around the room quickly. He ran back into the kitchen and found a little brown paper bag in the drawer. He walked toward her gingerly and handed her the bag. She snatched it and began to breathe into it.

"Okay, when you settle down and when you are ready, I want to talk to you about my children," he said. "But, I can't leave now until I know you are all right." He moved to the door and she moved to the other side of the room and leaned on a chair. She sat down, keeping her eyes on him. He put his hand on the doorknob. When he noticed her chest was moving more rhythmically, he let himself out.

Kali had nightmares for a week. She couldn't remember any of them upon waking, but she knew they all had to do with Ashton. Marcus would try to comfort her some mornings, but other mornings he lectured her on eating too much junk and told her he couldn't stick around. He left her hanging. Left her wishing that the man she married so hastily was a little more affectionate. But, it really didn't matter. Kali anguished over the fact that she wasn't being honest with her husband. Maybe somehow, he could sense it. Maybe that was why she felt farther and farther apart from him every day. She wanted to talk to somebody.

She called Kenny who talked her into coming to the salon for a spa makeover. She went down there and spent all day. Kenny made her feel like a pampered queen. She had missed his skilled hands and was happy to have those back in her life. Having Kenny to talk to comforted her enough to go home, and on the way, she started planning a romantic evening. She was going to re-engage Marcus with some good food and good loving.

Feeling better than she had, at least since Ashton's visit, Kali almost floated up the stairs to her house. As she opened her front door, she was surprised by the sound of children. Ashton was sitting in the chair facing the door, and the twins were busy climbing over him. Marcus was sitting opposite him smiling and trying to coax a knickknack out of one of the twins' hands.

"Hi, Lena," said Marcus. He got up and took her hand. "Look who stopped by to see if everything was going well with the house. I told him we love it. Don't we?" He gently squeezed Kali's hand. She was too astounded by Ashton's audacity to respond. She was watching the two curly- haired children roam in the little space they called a living room. They weren't motionless for one second.

Ashton stood up and picked up both the children.

"This is Katie and this is Ashton Jr. We call him AJ," he kissed each one as he introduced them. They giggled. One of them reached for her. She wasn't sure what to do.

"It's okay. He might be a little heavy, but he doesn't bite," Ashton relinquished AJ to Kali who took her son in her arms for the first time. She turned away from Marcus. She could feel her eyes watering up.

"Want some juice?" she asked the little boy who smelled like cotton candy and baby powder. The boy shook his head.

"No juice?" she said, trying to keep her voice from quivering.

"His yes's sometimes means no, and his no's sometimes mean yes. I think they will both take some juice." Ashton put the little girl down on her feet and she took Kali's hand. Kali knelt down and kissed her, shocking Marcus. He looked as if he wanted to apologize. Ashton stood there watching Kali as she and the children awkwardly worked their way around the large dining room set to get to the kitchen.

"Anyway," Ashton said, sitting back down. "I was thinking that I don't use this house, and I haven't rented it out in years. If you want to put roots down here another year, feel free."

"You have to, at least, let us pay rent," Marcus couldn't believe how kind Ashton was to him. He was thinking he would do anything not to let him down.

"Well, I am going to be working you pretty hard. You might think of the rent as extra compensation. I want you to start taking some of my business trips. I don't like leaving the kids for very long. I just had to hire another new nanny. We seem to go through them like water," Ashton was telling the truth. Most of the nannies wanted the job to try to get next to him, and when they realized he had no interest, not even sexually, they were ready to leave.

"I'm sorry to hear that," he said, looking back at Kali who was setting the kids up at the dining room table.

"Maybe Lena can help you out some time. They seem to like her." Marcus noticed her kissing the little boy again.

Ashton noticed it, too. He was hoping she would finally be ready to talk.

"Well, I might just do that," Ashton said. He leaned forward and started talking to Marcus about a possible itinerary. Marcus grabbed a notepad and the two men talked for a good half hour or more. Kali sat there taking in every inch and every nuance of the children. She held and examined their little hands. She smiled down into their wide eyes and full moist lips. She was overwhelmed. She had tried to imagine how they would feel or smell, but nothing had prepared her for this. She couldn't stop hugging and kissing them.

They were so soft and sweet.

"Time to go home," she heard Ashton call. She looked away from him still trying to hide her tears.

"It's okay," he whispered. "I cry sometimes, and I see them everyday." He reached over her and picked up Katie. AJ climbed over her lap into his daddy's arms. Ashton's scent and the warmth of his body that close to hers made Kali tremble. He noticed and stepped away quickly.

"I'll see you Monday," he said to Marcus. "We'll work out that schedule."

Kali didn't give Marcus a chance to look her in the face, she ran up the stairs and straight into the shower. She didn't know why, but she slept through the night without a nightmare.

It was the Fourth of July, and she had to take Marcus to the airport. She had been looking forward to walking down to Penn's Landing to see the fireworks. She called Kenny when she got home, but he was already leaving for Atlantic City. She was going to be alone, the story of her life, she thought. She was born alone, she lived alone, and more than likely, she would die alone.

She walked over to South Street anyway to get something to eat from the health food store. Then she saw them; the three of them were walking aimlessly down the street. Ashton held their hands tightly as they pressed their little noses to the storefront windows. She approached him, keeping her distance. She craved another hug or two.

"Hello," he said. "Did Marcus get off okay?"

She nodded. "Why on a holiday?"

"It's not a holiday in England. We had to go by their schedule."

"Oh," she said and held her hand out to be touched by AJ. He grabbed it. She fell into step with Ashton who reached down and picked up Katie.

"Are you and Kenny going to see the fireworks?"

"Kenny's going to AC with his new boyfriend," she said, sounding disappointed.

"Well, if it makes you feel better. I don't have any plans either," he reached around her to pick up AJ and she didn't shiver from his slight touch. He noticed.

They walked her back to her house and she fixed dinner while the twins ran around her legs. The four of them sat at the table and Ashton actually said grace. She was impressed.

"How long have you been saying grace?" she asked.

"It was the one thing I thought you would want them to do, that and say their prayers at night. Reggie taught us 'now I lay me down to sleep' and they say it every night. It gets a little funny sometimes. They get the words mixed up. But, we do it most nights when I can tuck them in. Other nights, they just crash." He helped Katie with her mashed potatoes.

"You're a good father," Kali took a bite of AJ's potatoes and he squealed with delight.

"You're going to make a very good mother," he said as he got up to start clearing the table.

She sat at the table still trying to eat her dinner. Ashton reached around her and took the plate.

"I'm eating," she slapped his hand.

"We've got to get a good spot for the fireworks. I'll buy you some ice cream. Help me clean the kids up." He pulled her chair back.

"Got to move fast if you're going to be somebody's mother."

She got up and started cleaning the kitchen, while he cleaned up the kids. "Forget the kitchen. Let's go."

"Okay, one minute," she said, not used to all the commotion, but she ran up the stairs and changed into a pair of jeans and sneak-ers. When she came down, they were waiting at the door. They had to walk back to his car and drive down to the Landing to find a good spot. They were going to watch the fireworks from the car. Ashton let the roof down and the kids climbed back and forth over the seats playing. He turned the radio up loud enough to hear the music that was being simulcast with the fireworks. The night was fantastic. Kali enjoyed the fireworks, but even more, enjoyed see-ing them through her children's eyes. By eleven o'clock, the show was over and the kids were out cold. Ashton dropped her off and watched her go into her house. She stood at the window and watched them drive away. She slid down to the floor and hugged herself. She could smell the kids all over her.

Marcus was gone for seven days, and for seven straight days, she held the kids in her arms. The day after the Fourth, Ashton called her and asked if she would stop by the penthouse to take care of the kids. Their nanny had a family emergency. Kali walked into the lobby and was greeted cheerfully by the concierge who ran to get the elevator for her. She stepped off the elevator and walked right into the penthouse. It was the same. Before she could get through the living room, a frazzled young White woman entered the room holding the twins by their hands.

"I'm sorry," she said, sitting both kids on the sofa. "I'm so sorry for the short notice, but I have to catch a flight. Please tell Mr. Sperling how sorry I am."

With that the woman was gone, and Kali stood there smiling at the twins.

"So, who wants to play ring around the rosies?" Both pairs of hands shot up. The kids wore Kali out. She played with them, fed them, and tried to get them to take naps that they failed to take. She called Ashton to ask him what to do next, and he was never any help. So she winged it. He didn't get home until around eight that evening. Both kids were asleep in her lap.

"I'm sorry," he said, picking them up from her lap. "I know I kind of threw you into the mix. I just didn't want to rely on Reggie. I think she's mean to them. Plus, I'm not ready to let her know you are back in their lives yet. Daddy and Asa, you know?"

"No problem," Kali helped with Katie. They took the children upstairs to their room.

"You did a good job on the nursery," she said, looking at the murals on the wall.

"I had a decorator come in. She wasn't as good as you, but she did okay," he said pulling off shoes and shirts. She reached over and took clothes off, too. She couldn't believe how soundly they slept.

"I hate to ask," he said, wiping his eyes. "But, I have got a lot going on this week. Can you fill in and take care of them? You can stay if you want. Just pick a bedroom. I won't bother you, I promise."

"I can't stay." She looked around as if someone was watching her. "But, I'll help. What time should I be here in the morning?"

"How about six-thirty, seven at the latest?"

"I can do that." And she did. Kali was there about eleven hours every day. She got into a routine with the kids. She loved every minute of it. But, in a flash, it was time for Marcus to come home.

"When is the nanny coming back?" Kali asked.

"Tonight," Ashton answered. "But, you can still come. The kids love you as much as you love them."

"I don't think I'd better come that often. We will all get too attached. Besides, my husband is coming home."

"About that," Ashton started to say something, but thought

better of it.

"About what?" she asked.

"Never mind. You know, he offered your services."

"I don't think he meant every day."

"Can you live with that?" Ashton sat in the rocker.

"What do you mean?"

"You have free access, Kali. Anytime you want, here or at the house, it doesn't matter. They need you." He wanted to add I need you, but he knew she wasn't ready for that yet. She was just now getting used to being in his presence without fearing him. He was sure she still didn't trust him.

"Thank you," she said, heading for the door. "I'll come over for a visit tomorrow. Maybe give the nanny some time to relax while I watch them. I'll call her."

"Okay," he said and laid his head back in the chair. He fell asleep.

Marcus was growing more distant every time he took a business trip. It was as if he were beginning to outgrow her. He touched her less and talked to her less. When she asked him about it, he would just say he had a lot on his mind. Ashton was sending him out in the field at least every other week. Now he was leaving again for two whole weeks. This time Ashton was sending him to Japan.

Ashton had asked her several times why she didn't tell him about the children, about her past. He said he wouldn't be upset if she told him the whole story. It was after all, the truth. Kali was afraid she would hurt Marcus, but she was more afraid of what that would mean for her. He had given her refuge when she really needed it. He had given her a family that loved her and that she loved. She didn't want to hurt them, and she wasn't sure if she had a full foundation beneath her feet. Ashton could just as easily snatch them away at three years old as he did when they were three seconds old. If she told Marcus the truth, she could lose everything and she would have to start all over again, by herself. She didn't like being alone. At least now, she could still call Mrs. Martin, hang out with Kenny, and trade recipes over the phone with Margaret. If the news hit the fan about her children, she would lose her husband, Margaret, Mr. Roberson and Sheila. And she couldn't bear to think what the Martins would say. She really wasn't worried about Kenny. He was her friend no matter what, but she knew Ashton held his purse strings and he could still disappear just as easily. She was scared. Truth be told, she was terrified. Ashton had more of Jordan in him than he wanted to admit. Kali had seen how dangerous he could be, up close and personal. She didn't want to have to fight him all alone.

CHAPTER TWELVE

Kali enjoyed spending time with the children. Together they started making tree ornaments. She was getting them excited about Christmas and telling them stories about Jesus. The nanny was around less and less, and Kali was wondering why. She was beginning to wonder if Reggie still had a job. Ashton wouldn't let her work on the days she was there, and more and more she was there hours and hours at a time.

"Ashton." She was sitting in the study when he arrived home that evening. She was looking for some ideas in Asa's art books that were still a part of the library.

"I saw your note. They're out cold," he said, falling back on the sofa.

"Yeah, where's the nanny?" she asked bluntly. "I mean, I don't mind coming over and everything. I love it. But, what happens when I can't make it. Where's the nanny? I haven't seen her in days."

"I, um, fired her," Ashton said and pulled a pillow over his head as he stretched out on the sofa.

"You did what?" She sighed as she put the book down. She had thought as much. Everyday she was getting there at seven because he really needed her at seven, and she wasn't going home before ten, eleven o'clock at night.

"Ashton." She wasn't sure what to say.

"They are your children, too," he said, before she could say anything else. "My business is requiring a lot of my attention, and I need someone with them that loves them. You understand?"

She got up and put the books back on the shelf.

"What time tomorrow?" she asked.

"You can come as late as you want. I'm not going in tomorrow. I'm taking the day off."

She started to ask why should she come and decided not to. She needed to spend as much time with them as he would allow right now. She wasn't sure when this era would end.

She opened the door to leave.

"You can still tell your husband you have children and you can put him out of his misery to have one with you. He's sterile. You know that, don't you?"

"How would you know that?" she asked incredulously.

"The company physical," he said, in a muffled voice from beneath the pillow. She wanted to snatch it and hit him with it. So that was why she hadn't gotten pregnant in all that time. She had thought having the twins under the conditions she had had them might have damaged her in some way. But, it wasn't her. And it no longer mattered. Marcus hadn't had sex with her since late September. He was always too tired or too busy or just not there.

"Tell him, Kali," Ashton yelled after her.

She considered it all night. Maybe she was being too cautious and overly afraid of being alone. Since the day she had come back, Ashton had done nothing threatening toward her. He had done everything he could to respect her and give her distance. He had even slowly insinuated the children into her life in a manner that she was able to digest. But, it was the holidays. On the one hand, she wanted to spend the holidays with her children and on the other; she was feeling guilty about lying to Marcus. She was married to Marcus, not Ashton.

After a long sleepless night, she decided she would tell him and let the cards fall where they may. If her marriage was over, so be it. They had become strangers anyway. He was more interested in his job and the new friends he had made at work. She wondered if he would keep his job at Ashton's. She thought he would probably leave without even looking back. He would be home for Thanksgiving and she would tell him over dinner like he told her about this new job just last year.

That Wednesday morning, Marcus called her around eight-thirty. His flight had landed in California, and he was planning to spend the weekend with his family.

"I'll see if I can get a flight," Kali offered. She would tell them all together.

"No, no. It's too late. It will be too expensive. Besides, I'll be home in a couple of days. Just relax. Have dinner over Kenny's or something. It's just a day. Besides I have all these reports I have to write, and I'm going to be trying to dodge my parents as much as possible."

"I can be your buffer," Kali really wanted to spend one more Thanksgiving with the Robersons before it was all over. She was already flipping through the yellow pages for the airlines.

"Kali, calm down! There's no need for you to come out. I will probably fly back Saturday, okay?" He hung up without an "I love you" or smooches or anything. Kali looked at the phone puzzled and put it down on the cradle. She got dressed and went over to the penthouse.

Ashton was pacing the floor when she got there. He was angry, she could tell from his body language, but he didn't say anything.

"I probably won't be home tonight. Can you stay?" His voice was flat and he was avoiding eye contact with her.

"Yeah, I can stay," she said. She heard him sigh with relief.

"I've got to go. They're in their room, but I wouldn't leave them there too long by themselves. They both have the sniffles, so you might have to start them on cold meds. Call Chico or their pediatrician if you need to. I have to take a trip up to Poughkeepsie. The earliest I can make it back is tomorrow morning. You got it covered?"

"You know he's not coming home, don't you?" Kali asked.

"Yeah, and I'm a bit ticked about it. I needed those damn reports today. He's screwing up, Kali. He's messing up." Ashton walked out the door and it slammed behind him.

Marcus wasn't acting like the Marcus she had fallen in love with less than two years ago. She didn't know what was going on either. She went straight upstairs to the kids. They immediately began to work on their Christmas tree projects. They spent the afternoon in the kitchen making gingerbread people to hang on the live tree that Ashton was having delivered on Friday. She made icing to glue on the jellied candies. She saw the kids sampling the candy and warned them to stop eating, but every time her back was turned, little fingers filled little mouths with as much sweets as possible.

By seven o'clock that night, they were both complaining of tummy aches. Kali walked them and bathed them. She wrongly attributed the tummy aches to the colds. About nine o'clock she was exhausted and both kids were crying. She had picked up the phone to call Chico, when the first one exploded like a volcano. Kali was covered in a soured candy and cookie mess. As she rushed to the bathroom with the first one, the second exploded on her, too. She was covered in throw-up, and so were both kids. The smell turned her stomach and she barely made it to the toilet. She threw up too, then slid and fell in the throw-up from the kids. They were all messy and icky. All three sat unhappily in the goop crying.

Finally, Kali gathered herself together and ran a tub of water. She sat the sticky kids in the water and cleaned up the mess that led from their room to the bathroom. She threw their clothes and towels in the washing machine in the laundry room section of the bathroom. She then peeled off her clothes and carried everybody into the shower. The warm running water soothed everybody as she washed chunks of food out of curls, hers and theirs. She walked naked with the two naked children in her arms into their room. She dressed them and put them in their bed. She went to kiss them good night and realized they needed to brush their teeth. She got them back up and stood them on their stools to brush their teeth. She saw her naked body in the mirror and realized she had to put something on. Every stitch of the clothing she had had to go in the wash. She went into the dressing room and saw that none of her things was there anymore, so she rifled through Ashton's shirts and found a soft blue cotton pajama top. She slid into it and rolled up the sleeves. She helped the kids finish their teeth and put them back to bed. She turned on the washing machine and walked into Ashton's room, formerly her room. She turned the television on low and lay back on the bed. The fatigue overtook her and she slipped into a deep sound sleep.

Things had gone a lot better for Ashton in Poughkeepsie than he had expected. He was able to get an earlier train home with a contract in his briefcase. He was still concerned about Marcus though. He had started out with so much energy and so much promise. That was another reason he wanted it all out on the table. He wanted to give the boy an out if he couldn't handle the work anymore. But, he knew that wasn't it. He'd seen Rita whispering to the boy a lot lately. He was going to have to ask Troy to talk to her about it. Rita was a piranha, though Troy would deny it. Who would want to call his own sister a maneater? But, that was what she was. Rita was still ticked with him for pulling away. He hadn't wanted to upset his friendship with Troy. All he had wanted from Rita was a booty call. So he gave her a job to appease her, and he assigned her to Marcus when his workload became too heavy for Elliott to handle. Maybe that was a mistake.

Ashton knew he was walking on thin ice trying to bring his family together. He understood too well why Kali was so hesitant. He had put a huge obstacle to trust in her way and she was a long way from overcoming it. If he told her that he suspected Marcus was cheating on her with Rita, she would hate him even more. He just had to wait. That was the only medicine his relationship with her needed right now, patience.

He walked into the kids' room and tucked the covers up to their necks, kissing each one. They smelled fresh and sweet. He kissed their little hands and sat a few minutes in the rocker just watching them breathe. He wondered what room Kali took. He got up and started peeling off his clothes. He still had the smell of Penn Station and the Metroliner on him. He dropped all of his clothes into the laundry basket and turned on the shower. He lingered in the shower a long time. He was tired and the wind outside had sent a serious chill through his body. He stepped out and reached for his robe, but it wasn't hanging where he normally left it. He found it between the washing machine and the dryer. He picked it up and then dropped it immediately. It was funky with vomit.

He went back to the sink and washed his hands, then brushed his teeth. He stood naked and combed the tangles out of his hair, until he got another chill. He opened the washing machine lid with the intent of adding the robe, but it was already filled with clothes.

He took each item out and shook it before throwing it into the dryer. He wasn't surprised to see the little Osh Kosh clothes, but he was shocked to pull out Kali's jeans, her bra, her panties and sweater. He smiled. Mommy had just been christened. He put everything, except Kali's underwear, in the dryer. He hung her deli-cates over the shower door. He dropped the robe and the towels he had found with the robe in the washing machine. They were all filled with gook. He turned on the washing machine and carefully washed his hands again. He couldn't afford to catch anything that the kids had.

He went into the dressing room and pulled on a pair of draw-string pants. He walked into his room and found the television on with the volume turned down real low. He saw her hanging over the bed like a drunk. They had worn her out.

He pulled back the covers, picked her up, and tucked her in. She settled in without waking up. He sat down next to her and stared at her. She was still the most beautiful woman he had ever laid eyes on. He had no idea why he had treated her so shabbily. Not only was she physically gorgeous, she had a beautiful soul. She loved and trusted everybody. But for some ungodly reason, the two men that loved her the most had betrayed her. Now, he thought sadly, a third. He wished he could talk to Marcus and explain to him that he had a chance to make it right, but he really didn't want him to do that. Not if he wanted to keep her for himself.

Her father had been the first man who screwed her over by taking his own life. Then, he had screwed her over by making her fear for her life, and now this. A man she was being loyal to and loving unconditionally was probably screwing around just to prove his manhood. He wanted to slap Marcus and tell him that he had it all wrong, that he needed to hold onto her with everything he had. Money and power would mean nothing without her. The ability to brag about his conquests in bed would mean even less. Ashton blew at a lash that was sticking in her eye. He carefully removed it, and she turned away from him in her sleep. Then she kicked off the cover, revealing her smooth, golden buns underneath the oversized shirt. He let his hand lie lightly on the soft skin. He became aroused. He removed his hand quickly as she shifted again. This time he saw her vagina. It was shaven, like in the old days when Jordan demanded it bald and clean at all times. Ashton wanted to kiss it, and before the thought was completed, his head was down there, lightly probing her with his tongue seeking the sweetness he had been craving. Her back arched and her legs fell open. He wondered if she thought she was dreaming. He pulled back the cover and climbed on the bed and then buried his head between her legs. He knew she was awake when her strong thighs tried to clamp his head. At first her hands tried to push his head away and then she began to pull his head in deeper. Ashton explored deeper and deeper. She began to moan passionately until she let out a primal scream of pleasure. When she did that, he crawled up her body and plunged inside of her. He was home. It was two o'clock in the morning when he began and daylight when he finally rolled off her. They lay in the bed spent. She rolled away from him, her back to him. He grabbed her and pulled her on top of him. She lay there listening to his heart beat steadily. It lulled her back to sleep.

Kali didn't know how long she had slept when she felt a cold and clammy little hand hitting her in the face. She awakened to find both children crawling into the bed. She tried to hold the cover up tightly, even though she had been nude in front of them just the night before. At least then they were taking a bath, but now they would have no part of it. The room had a chill in it and they wanted to be under the cover. Ashton awakened and lifted the cover. The children snuggled up to them.

"I think it's time to get up," he said, winking his eye at her. She just watched him. Kali couldn't believe she had succumbed to him so easily. She worked her away around the children and headed for the bathroom. Before she could get off the toilet, they were all in the bathroom together.

"Family shower," Ashton announced and the kids beat them to the shower.

"They just showered a few hours ago," she remembered all the cleaning she had to do once she had gotten their stomachs to settle.

"It's okay. We'll just bond." He kissed the top of her head. The four of them bathed and giggled and played with the soap. They all stood in the mirror and brushed their teeth. Ashton brought out two terry cloth robes, one for her and one for him. Kali checked the dryer. The clothes were still wet. He had helped her out, but forgot to turn on the dryer. They laughed. She reached for her underwear that was hanging on the towel rack, but he removed them from her hand.

"Let me show you where your things are." He led her down the hallway to Jordan's room. Some of Kali's things were hanging and others were folded neatly in Jordan's dressing room. "Anytime you want any of these things, you know where to find them."

Kali opened a drawer of her favorite undies and slid into them. The kids ran around her as she dressed. Ashton had put them back into their pajamas.

"They may be getting a little too old for group baths." Kali noticed AJ staring at her breasts.

"Maybe you're right, Mommy," Ashton said loud enough for the kids to hear.

AJ's ears perked up and he ran in front of Kali as she slid into a pair of pink velour sweatpants.

"Are you my mommy?" he asked.

"No, she is my mommy," Katie protested.

"No, she is your mommy and AJ's mommy," Ashton corrected.

Kali sat in the middle of the dressing room and hugged both the kids.

"I'm your mommy," she kissed AJ. "And, I'm your mommy," she said as she kissed Katie. Both kids jumped excitedly around the room. "We have a mommy," AJ told Katie.

"I know. I know," Katie answered.

"And you know what mommies do?" Ashton was now on the floor with them.

"What?" AJ and Katie both asked.

"Mommies make great pancakes," the kids got even more excited as Kali arched her eyebrows at Ashton. Both kids tried to jump in her arms and knocked her to the floor. Ashton picked up all three of them and carried them downstairs.

Kali made Ashton's favorite pancakes with whipped cream and strawberries.

"Mile high," Ashton said, showing AJ his plate.

"Mile high," AJ repeated. "I want mine mile high."

"Me, too," Katie added.

"Oh, no! Not after last night. One pancake for each of you," Kali loved the feeling of being in the kitchen with the three of them. She couldn't wait for Marcus to come back. She wasn't going to wait any longer. This was where she wanted to be for as long as she could.

The kids ate hungrily and asked her "mommy" questions in between bites. She swung between tears and laughter as Ashton instigated more questions and precipitated more jokes. She was happy. She couldn't remember being this happy before.

Ashton took the kids down the hall to the recreation room where they could watch television and play with some of their toys. Kali cleaned the table and started to wash the dishes. She was humming and swaying to the rhythm of her own little song. Her hands were in the dishwater swishing and cleaning a large knife she had just used to slice the strawberries. Ashton had teased her for using such a big knife and she had wondered why she had chosen it herself. Suddenly she felt his arm near her throat and a panicked, fear-stricken scream emerged from her mouth as she swung around wielding the knife toward him. He grabbed her hand and twisted it causing the knife to hit the floor. He kicked it away and slowly backed away from her.

"What the hell?" He backed away in slow motion. "I was just trying to hug you. I didn't mean to startle you. I wasn't trying to harm you."

Kali could see the hurt in his eyes, but her body was still shaking uncontrollably. It was almost like the dreams she used to have, the ones with him choking her. His arm coming from nowhere and touching her neck made her cringe. She touched her neck with both hands. She wanted to run. She looked both ways to see which way she could leave. She chose the door toward the dining room. She heard him following her.

"Kali, I swear," he said, gently, quietly. "I wasn't trying to hurt you. I just wanted to be close to you after last night and this morning. I won't touch you again if that's what you want. Don't leave," he pleaded.

Kali couldn't explain it, but all she wanted to do was flee. Her heart was pounding so loud it hurt her ears and made her head feel like it was going to explode. Tears poured from her eyes like a watershed. She tried to wipe them away so she could see where she was going. She saw his hand reaching out to her. She jumped backwards and crashed into the door leading to the elevators. It was the same door that had supported her back as her feet tried to find the floor beneath them. It was the same door where he held her by the throat, pressing it so hard she couldn't breathe. It was the same door whose hardness was all she felt as her world began to succumb to darkness. She slid down into the same spot where she had come crashing down when his fingers let go of her and she had hit the floor with such a force that her shins had quivered with pain. She sobbed hysterically while Ashton stood there watching helplessly.

Ashton thought about Ruby. He backed away from her and ran to the telephone. He was hoping Ruby was at home. She was a psychologist. Maybe there was something she could do to help. It hadn't been until that moment, seeing her melting down from his casual touch, did he realize the real damage he had caused.

Kali started breathing rapidly. He knew she was getting ready to hyperventilate. He dropped the phone and ran into kitchen digging for a paper bag. He found a pack of lunch bags and brought one back to the foyer only to find the door slightly ajar. He opened it to find her sitting next to elevator gasping for breath. He walked over as non-menacing as possible and put the bag in her hands. He pushed her hands and bag up to her face. She began to breathe into the bag. Her eyes watched him closely, as if she were still horrified by his presence. He backed away and stood inside the door way.

"Kali, I swear. I swear on my life, our children's lives, I will never ever hurt you again. I swear. I swear," He slid down the doorway and sat on the floor watching her. Her breathing was beginning to return to normal. The fear in her eyes was beginning to subside. The elevator door opened. Ruby and Micah stepped around her. Ruby slid down to the floor and whispered something to Kali, then started helping her up off the floor. Micah extended his hand to Ashton and pulled him up.

"Let's talk," Micah patted his brother on the back. "Where are the kids?"

"Rec room. Oblivious to what just happened," Ashton replied.

"What happened?" Micah took Ashton by the hand and led him to the study as if he were a lost child.

"I tried to hug her. From behind. She wasn't expecting it. My arm touched her throat," he began to sob.

"What made you do that? I thought you were keeping your distance so she wouldn't run again."

"We made love last night. We had pancakes. She was doing the dishes and I wanted to hug her. I wanted to tell her how much I loved her," Ashton dropped his head on the desk.

"Ashton, you have got to be patient. You don't try to take someone's life one minute and make love to her the next. I was there. Remember? I saw your hands let go of her throat just seconds before she would have succumbed to death. I mean seconds and she would have been gone, forever.

"Remember that? That's not something she is ever going to forget. And quite frankly, I don't see how she could ever forgive you for that. I wouldn't. I'm having a hard time reconciling the fact that you even did that. And that was years ago, I know. But, I can still see it so clearly. I can still see her feet running in mid-air trying to find the ground. Do you remember that?"

"Yes," Ashton answered and tried to wipe the tears from his face.

"I know what I did. And I know I would never, ever do it again. I want her, Micah. I want my family. How can I get her to forgive me? How can I win her back?"

"Ashton, all I can tell you is that you have to wait until she is ready. It's all in her court. Hell, she is back in your life. She obviously loves the kids and she is getting more comfortable with you. But, she is always, always going to fear you. You are the reason for an unthinkable, unfathomable trauma in her life. I hate to be so negative and not try to give you any hope. But, honestly I don't think you deserve it." Micah was interrupted as Ruby walked into the room.

"She's okay, now. I got her to lie down in Jordan's room. She really wants to go home, but I don't think she should be alone. I'll stick around in case she needs me," Ruby walked over to the books and started reading the titles.

"Does she know I wasn't trying to hurt her?" Ashton asked.

"Technically, yes. But, she has nightmares from time to time. Different things trigger them, and this was like one of those nightmares."

"Oh, God," Ashton pushed away from the desk. "I have got to go talk to her. You think she'll listen to me?"

"I don't recommend it. I would rather she come to you when she's ready. I think you need to just keep your distance," Ruby pulled a classic off the shelf and left the room. She decided to go read it in Jordan's sitting room so she could be close to Kali.

"Listen to us, Ashton," Micah was firm. "If you really want this, you have to be patient."

Kali spent most of the day hiding beneath the covers in Jordan's room. She knew she was being illogical, but her fear was paralyzing her. What was she to do? She turned and looked at the clock, it was getting late, and it was Thanksgiving. She thought about the children and the Thanksgiving center-piece they had made. She wondered what they were doing and if anyone was heating up the dinner Reggie had made for them. She sat up. She was a mother. She couldn't afford to lose it like that anymore. She had to get over it. He was their father and he would always be in their lives.

Kali came down the stairs dressed for dinner. She smelled the food and walked into the dining room. Ruby had taken charge. She was setting the table with a steaming hot Turkey meal. Someone had placed the homemade centerpiece out and it looked beautiful.

"How are you feeling?" Ruby asked as she stopped to help her own toddler, Artie, into a high chair.

"Better," Kali answered. She did indeed feel better.

"We were worried about you," Ruby said while finishing setting the table.

"Can I help?" Kali asked.

"No. I would say yes, but there are knives in the kitchen." Ruby smiled.

"You know me and knives." Kali smiled back at her. "Did I hurt him?"

"No, you rightfully scared the shit of him. But, that's okay. He deserved it," both women laughed, but Kali's laughter was covering more tears.

"Where are the kids?"

Ashton and Micah are upstairs getting them washed up and ready for dinner. They took them out to the parade earlier, and then they went ice skating, so all of them are tired.

"Wow, I missed a lot today."

"No, you got some rest and relaxation. I hear you have been doing all the womanly chores and babysitting these days. I think maybe you have taken on too much for a brand new mother," Ruby smiled. "He tried to bring you into the fold a little too fast. I told him to hire another nanny and back off you for a little while."

"What about the kids?" Kali was concerned. She didn't want to lose her children again.

"They are still yours. You still have right of way. You can see them all day, everyday. But, let someone else help with the leg work. Don't spend the night over here anymore, not unless it is absolutely necessary. Not just because that's what he wants," Ruby advised.

"And don't have sex with him," Kali whimpered. "I knew that was a mistake."

"Look, trust me. I know how good he is in bed. But, yeah, I recommend separating that until you have gotten everything else in your life figured out. Besides, it was the sex that made him feel comfortable with touching you outside of the bed. Neither of you could have known that that intimacy didn't translate into daylight, everyday touching." Ruby sat down next to Artie and gave him a kiss.

"He is beautiful. Looks like a miniature Micah with hair," Kali smiled and took the little boy's hand. "You carried really big."

"You remember?" Ruby said.

"Yeah, you triggered a couple of weeks of nightmares," Kali said and shrugged.

"I'm sorry. I wanted so bad to tell you that you didn't have to run anymore and that your children needed you," Ruby shifted her plate. "Where are they? The food is getting cold."

"Here we are," Ashton announced with the twins riding his feet. They were playing the friendly giant.

"You know, we have missed most of the football games," Micah winked at Ruby.

"Poor daddies, poor, poor daddies," Ruby teased as the men and children took their places at the dining room table.

"Let's hold hands and say grace," Ashton said, surprising them as he reached for Kali's hand.

She looked at it for what seemed an eternity and then she took it.

"Dear God, I know I haven't prayed much since Catholic

School, but I remember You are there. And I thank You for all my blessings this day. I thank You for my brother and his family. I thank You for my children and their mother. And I thank You for all this wonderful food. And Dear God, let's keep Kali out of the kitchen. Amen," he smiled at her and she sheepishly smiled back. Ruby and Micah groaned appreciatively.

"Amen, let's eat," Micah said, grinning. "Knives stay on this side of the table. I'll carve the turkey."

After dinner, Kali took the twins upstairs and spent some time with them singing and playing games. Micah and Ashton went down to the rec room to watch as much football as they could and Ruby went home with Artie. Kali looked out the window and saw how dark it had become. It was time for her to go home. She led the kids down to the rec room to leave them with Ashton.

"You're leaving?" he asked disappointedly. "Why?"

"I think it best," Kali answered.

"You can stay in Jordan's room. I promise I won't come near you," Ashton was tempted to move her curl from her eyes.

Her hand reached up and pushed the rogue curl behind her ear.

"I know, Ashton. I know I overreacted this morning, but I did, and it just helped me to realize I'm not quite ready for us, yet." She emphasized the yet.

He stood there wanting to touch her, wanting to hug and reach out to her. He could feel this magnet between them, and it was pulling at them fiercely, but he didn't extend his hand nor did he move close to her. Time, he thought. She needs time.

Kali kissed each of the kids and headed for the door. Ashton started to follow her, but Micah called him.

"She's a big girl. She'll drive home safely, and you'll see her again tomorrow," Micah said and patted the sofa where he had been sitting. "Sit down."

The last game ended and Micah left. Ashton carried the sleeping twins up to bed and tucked them in. He crawled into his empty bed once again and tried to sleep. He couldn't. Her smell was still there. She had left the blue pajama top lying on the pillow. He grabbed it and laid it on his face. There was no peace in that either. He wanted her. He grabbed the phone and dialed Micah.

Ashton knew the last thing he should be doing was showing up on her doorstep late at night. She had already had one breakdown today, but he couldn't tear himself away from her. He rang the doorbell. She didn't answer. He rang the doorbell again and there was still no answer. He started to panic. What if something had happened to her? What if she had decided to take her own life out of fear of living in his realm? Crazy things started running through his mind, so he leaned hard on the doorbell. Finally, the door swung open.

"What is wrong with you?" she pulled her robe closed. "It's after 10:00. You scared me half to death."

"You didn't call to tell me you made it home okay," he said, standing in the freezing rain shivering.

"Oh, I didn't," she answered. She had gotten into the habit of letting him know that she made it home safely.

"You could have called me," she turned angrily, still blocking the door as the rain pelted him.

"What are you doing here?" she asked sternly, not budging from the doorway.

He was afraid to go in past her, afraid he might touch her causing her to freak out again, but he was freezing out there.

"I have to show you something." He remembered the box that sat next to him on the step. "It's getting wet."

She saw a box sitting next to him and moved away from the

door. He picked it up and ran into the house to the nearest vent. He tried to warm his bare hands on it.

She saw him shivering, and she helped him out of his coat.

"You didn't dress very warm. You're going to catch a cold like this."

"I didn't expect to stand outside so long," he answered, rubbing his hands across his arms to create friction.

She went into the kitchen and poured milk into a saucepan.

"You want some hot chocolate?" she asked. He nodded quickly.

She ran upstairs and got a blanket. She turned on the fake fireplace and it started pushing out heat immediately. He wrapped up real tight and waited patiently as she brought out two big mugs of hot chocolate.

"Now, what are you doing here?" She watched him sip the hot chocolate, and his body begin to shiver less and less until it was warmed.

"The box," he pointed to the damp cardboard box. "Some of your things are in the box. I went to South Carolina when I started looking for you. For some idiotic reason I thought you went back there."

"You did what?" Kali sat on the floor next to the box.

"I brought back loads of stuff. They are in the storage room next to the music room. Nobody goes in there anymore. I did keep them here, hoping you would come back. But, when you came back with a husband, I had to move them again.

"This is just a few things I thought might help you a little through the night, that is," Ashton said, not knowing what else to say.

"I was getting through the night just fine," Kali lied. She had been afraid to go to sleep. She didn't want to have another nightmare. She had seen him drive up and bring the box to the door.

She had heard every ring from that doorbell, but she lie there wondering what it was he really wanted. She only answered when she realized he was not going away.

"What's in the box?" she asked, just above a whisper, almost reverently for her past life.

"Open it," he whispered back.

She opened it, and the first thing she saw was a baby picture, her baby picture. The eight by ten, black and white touched up with some color by a photographer. She smiled.

"This used to sit on the mantelpiece," she wiped away a couple of tears.

"Oh, I got your stuff back from Mazetta's too. And a little family news if you are interested…" he let it go. She didn't respond. There was no need to give her bad news, not now.

Kali found the pictures and the Bible from Mazetta's. She then found the sermon Bible. She cried. Ashton made a concerted effort not to touch her. He sat there and watched her page through the sermon Bible and read her father's notes. When she reached into the box one last time, she found a music composition by her mother. She wailed loudly and rocked back and forth holding the worn pages close to her. It was the song and music that had been written for her.

She dropped the music and jumped into Ashton's lap. He stroked her head and kissed her. He held her until she fell asleep. When the phone rang, the two of them were still cuddled on the sofa in an awkward position. Ashton's body ached, and Kali didn't look too rested herself. As they both silently stretched, she answered on the third ring. It was Marcus. Ashton left the room to go upstairs to the bathroom while a wife spoke with her husband. It hurt. Had he been smarter and paid attention to his real feelings in the first place, she could have been his wife.

When he came back downstairs, Kali was carefully packing her things in another box.

"This one is coming apart from the rain," she said.

He picked the waffling box up and peered out of the window.

"It's trash day. I'll put it out in the morning. Have anything else to go out?" he started looking around.

"There's probably something in the can downstairs. I wasn't here to put it out last week," she was feeling a little guilty. When Marcus wasn't home, neither was she.

"What did he say?"

"Sunday. His flight will be in Sunday. He was faxing some of his reports into the office this morning, but he hadn't been able to reach you to tell you. He left you a message at the office. He was also concerned that he couldn't reach me earlier. He had had Thanksgiving dinner with his parents, and they had wanted to wish me Happy Thanksgiving.

"And," Kali sighed, "He's bringing his mother and sister with him Sunday for a visit. They have never been on the east coast before, so he wants me to get the guest room ready and get some food in the house."

"Screw him," Ashton blurted out, "just tell him, Kali. Just tell him it's time for you to move on. Tell him about our babies."

"Oh, Ashton. Not now. Please not now. After everything we went through today, I don't know what to think or feel anymore. Just let me get through this, please."

"Be patient," Ashton said, staring at the box.

"What?" Kali asked.

"My brother and his wife keep reminding me I have to learn to be patient," he sighed. "I know they're right. But, I couldn't sleep. That's why I brought you the box. I was afraid you were over here alone having nightmares about me. And I couldn't be patient. I came running over here to protect you from the nightmarish me."

"You did," Kali touched his hand, sending a spiral of warmth throughout his entire body, much like an electric shock with healing powers. She watched his eyes well up again.

"What a pair we make." She reached up and touched the corner of his eye. "We sure do cry a lot."

"I love you," he said, holding her hand to his face. "I love you with all my heart. If you let me, I will spend the rest of my life protecting you and caring for you with every ounce of my life."

She eased into his lap, and they kissed passionately. She did not recoil from his touch, she melted from it.

CHAPTER THIRTEEN

Ashton could always find an excuse for them to spend the night together. She fell asleep in his arms again after making love the rest of the night.

"Don't you need to get home to the kids? I need to clean up in here. Remember, my mother-in-law is in LA packing and getting ready to come in for an inspection," Kali gently prodded him trying to get him up out of the bed. It was interesting, when she had first moved back into the house, she was feeling guilty that she was in the same bed where she had slept with Ashton, and she was occupying it with her new husband. Now, she was feeling guilty for occupying the bed with Ashton and not her husband. "There is no peace," she thought.

"Ashton," she shoved him again. "You didn't go home last night. Who is with the kids?"

"I told you, I took them down to Micah's. They're fine."

"Don't you want to call them?" she picked up the phone and laid the receiver on his ear.

"If I do that, Ruby will make me come and get them," Ashton whined and pulled a pillow over his head. "You call them."

Kali let her feet slide to the floor. She picked up the phone and put it in her lap. She dialed Ruby's number.

"Hello," a sleepy Ruby answered the phone.

"I'm sorry, did I wake you?" Kali turned to look at the clock. It was around 7:30.

"Yeah, that's okay. Micah's been trying to get me up for awhile. The twins and Artie are up. He's got them in the den playing," Ruby let out a big sigh that Kali figured was a yawn.

"Do you want me to come get them?" Kali was hoping Ruby would say yes.

"No, no. They're fine. Uncle Micah's spoiling them, and Artie is enjoying them. You can pick them up after their afternoon nap. As for me, I am going to take advantage of Micah being home playing Da Da and go back to sleep. See you," Ruby hung up the phone before Kali could say anything else. She was off the hook literally, and so was Ashton.

She lay back down next to him and wondered if she were crazy. One minute she was scared to death of this man, and the next, she couldn't get enough of him. Right now, she just wanted to kick him out of this bed, for no other reason than there were too many people in it. Now when she looked to her left in that bed, it was Marcus who usually occupied that space. She smiled. She had automatically taken her same spot in the bed that she had had with Ashton. Although, everywhere else with Marcus she had been on the opposite side. Marcus had even commented about it. She had just responded with a joke, but she automatically went back to that spot like she was conditioned.

Two hours later Ashton rolled off her. She hadn't gotten up fast enough. She had kept bouncing around trying to make up her mind where to start cleaning, and he pulled her down to him. He made wild mad love to her and she had no complaints. But, when he rolled over, she took the opportunity to jump up. She didn't want to lie around in bed all day. She had to direct her energy elsewhere.

"Let's go over to South Street," Ashton said and followed her into the small bathroom. It was barely enough room for one person, but he squeezed in somehow taking up her space.

"Ashton, how many times do I have to tell you? I have to clean the house." She slid between him and the sink to get out of the bathroom.

"Clean what?" Ashton held the palm of his hands upward twirling them around. He looked weird. She shook her head.

"The house."

"It looks clean to me. Hell, how long does it take to vacuum and dust. What is it you're so stressed about? I'm sure there aren't any dust bunnies hidden in closets waiting to attack your pseudo mother-in-law."

"My what? My pseudo mother-in-law? Last I checked I was still married to Marcus, thus I still have a real life mother-in-law," Kali shook her head again. He was trying every angle relentlessly.

"Technically no," Ashton had plopped on the bed and was stepping into his jeans.

"What do you mean, technically no?"

"I mean Mr. Strangelove married a woman who signed her name and papers as Lena Denison not Kalina Denise Harris. Lena, Lena, Lena. I hate when he calls you that."

"What are you saying, Ashton?"

"Well, you used a bogus social security number. I'm assuming the one that the Martins provided you with since that person is really dead. You used a bogus name, although you were smart enough to work your way into a great job using both names and the right social security number, but forgot the camouflage when you got married. Imagine that," he was now fully dressed with a smirk on his face.

"Spell it out, Ashton," she was sliding into a red sweater she had just bought the other day and the tags were still hanging.

Ashton walked over to her and helped remove the tags. She noticed a mischievous glint in his eye as he bit the little vinyl tag holder and tossed the tags in the trash.

"Well," she said, following him to the trash can.

"You are not married, my love. You and I could get married today and it would be legal," he grinned.

She went back to the bed and flopped hard.

"I am not legally married to Marcus," Kali said it aloud. She wasn't sure if she wanted to feel relief or disappointment. She had so much to tell Marcus. She was getting ready to cause so much pain. She was so tired of pain.

Ashton sat next to her and kissed her on the top of the head.

"We are going to get through this together. Come with me. Let's forget all the adult, grown-up stuff today. Let's walk over to South Street. Let's go play. I promise to leave Taylor at home," Aston said, shoving her gently. She knew he was assuring her that he wasn't going to try to get kinky in public like he had so many times in the past.

"Where are my boots?" she said. "It looks pretty cold out there."

The two of them walked the six or seven blocks to South Street hugged up trying to keep each other warm. They arrived just before the lunch hour crowd and took a table in a restaurant specializing in cheesesteaks. Ashton had ordered two huge cheesesteaks.

"You know, this is breakfast," Kali was having a hard time picking up one half of the sandwich. The juices from the cheese and the meat were dripping on the thin paper plate.

"It is good though, right?" Ashton took a big bite out of his without effort. She watched as he seemed to feel such pleasure chewing and swallowing the monstrosity.

"You are ridiculous," she continued to toy with the one half. They had sat at a window where they could watch people come and go. They made comments about each one trying to figure out their life stories. In the end, they laughed because they agreed that none of them had the same amount of drama in their lives as they had.

"We are the champions," he held up his last bite of sandwich and stuffed it in his mouth. She had only finished about half of the half.

"Are you going to eat that?" He picked up her other half before she could respond.

"Maybe, if I was given half the chance." She playfully took a swipe near the sandwich. But, she didn't want it back. It was too much meat. She finally finished her portion as he finished off the other.

"Now what?" she sighed. Her stomach was completely full.

"The Rocky Horror Picture Show," he grinned. She liked the grinning Ashton. It meant he was feeling good, happy. She loved a happy Ashton.

"Oh, no," she teased. "You are not going to recite the dialogue, are you? Besides they don't show that until midnight."

"It plays all day at this little theatre. And yes, ma'am, gotta do the dialogue." He grabbed her and pulled her out of the restaurant. Soon they were in line for the first showing of the day and then sitting in the dark with a bunch of other crazies who had ventured out on a cold Black Friday to catch a cult movie.

She and Ashton recited the dialogue faithfully and jumped when they were supposed to jump. That was one thing she had missed about being with him when she was on the run. He could find fun in the oddest ways. He was an adventurer. He made her jump in the Wissahickon Creek, scale the walls behind the Art Museum, and attempt to catch a fish with her bare hands in the Delaware River. He introduced her to fine dining as well as the hole in the wall pizza joints that made pizza beyond comparison anywhere else. He coaxed her into eating pretzels from the street vendors with the dirty fingernails. To her, that was a daring feat. But, most importantly, he made her laugh a lot.

The movie was over and the afternoon was getting late. He pulled her into one more store, the health food store. He was looking for pure soap and she was looking for something exotic and healthy to fix for dinner. The two of them were looking at the different types of rice and couscous when a woman's voice startled them.

"Well, hello Mr. Sperling!" a young thin brown woman whose smile was way too sensual for Kali's liking approached them. The woman had that 'I am really interested in you' body language sway.

"Clarissa," Ashton said, nodding and turned back to the rice on the shelf.

"Why, is this... Is this Mrs. Roberson?" Clarissa eyed Kali knowingly.

"What did you say?" Ashton turned his attention back to the young woman.

Clarissa reached out and touched Kali's arm.

"You're even more beautiful close up. I knew your picture looked familiar when I saw it on Mr. Roberson's desk. Isn't it a small world?" Clarissa's head moved suggestively in a semi-circle.

Kali thought she looked real catty and finally understood what the term really meant. Kali moved away from her and stood on the other side of Ashton.

"What do you want, Clarissa?" Ashton asked. Kali immediately heard the change in the tone of his voice. It made the hair on the back of her neck stand at attention. This woman was treading in the wrong waters. She wanted to warn her to back off, but thought better of it.

"Nothing." The woman still had that stupid smile on her face, like she knew more than everybody else knew.

"I was just commenting. You are very beautiful," Clarissa's head swung to the side to look around Ashton and directly at Kali.

"Mind your own business," Ashton said, his words were measured. Kali touched his arm. He pulled away and turned directly facing the woman.

"Do you understand what I am saying?" Ashton asked.

"What do you mean?" Clarissa made another mistake. She stepped inside his personal space and touched his chest still smiling and looking up at him as if she were trying to seduce him with her forbidden knowledge.

Kali took a quick step from behind him and broke the woman's touch from him. She stood between them two of them.

"You are fired," Ashton said, shocking the woman.

"If I see you in or near my company, or me or my family, or Mrs. Roberson, you will regret it," he said, venomously in a very low voice.

The woman not only heard the words, Kali could tell from her expression that she absorbed their meaning. Kali didn't have to see Ashton's face to know the look in eyes directed at the woman. The back of Kali's head was pressed against his chest and she could hear his heart thumping. She knew he was angry and getting angrier by the second.

"I think you should leave now," Kali whispered.

"I, I didn't mean anything by it, Mr. Sperling. I swear. I am so stupid. I am sorry. I just...I just." Clarissa started to become unraveled. She was mumbling and stumbling into the store's shelves.

She backed out of the aisle.

"I was just joking," Clarissa yelled back and left the store.

They took a long route home on the cold, brisk day. Ashton carried the bags and Kali held onto his arm. As soon as she saw her house, she ran up to the top step searching for her keys.

"I'm okay, Kali." He kissed her on the butt as she tried to open the door.

"I know. And I know what I have to do to prevent people from thinking they can blackmail you." Kali opened the door and breathed in deeply. "But, how am I going to explain this?" She turned to Ashton.

"Explain what?" he asked, looking around. Everything was in its proper place. The house was neat and clean as far as he could see. He walked over to the mantle. There was barely any dust up there.

"The smell," she said. "Smell it."

Ashton took a deep breath. He didn't smell anything.

"What are you talking about, son?" he teased.

"Us. I smell us, all over the place," she said.

"What?" he asked, shaking his head, confused by her logic. The place smelled fine to him. There was nothing offensive in the air.

"Our musk," she said. She leaned over and smelled the sofa. "We did it here."

She went to the stairs where he had mounted her as she tried to run up the stairs.

"And here," she said giggling, then ran up the stairs and stooped in the floor in the hallway outside of her bedroom.

"And here." She smiled and ran into her room and jumped onto the bed. "Oh, my God! And here!"

Ashton jumped on the bed with her.

"Well, we may as well make it real funky," he teased and pulled her under him again. The phone rang, making them both jump.

She answered it after wrestling her way from beneath him.

"Hello," she tried to sound normal.

"Yes, we are still here. How are my babies?" she held the phone away from her ear. Micah was yelling. She handed the phone to Ashton like a kid in trouble.

"Yeah, yeah, I know." Ashton was grinning again. Kali smoothed his hair away from his face. They were in trouble. Micah was angry.

"I'll be there in an hour, I swear," he said and then he leaned back onto the pillow.

"Micah, come Monday morning I want you to have Ms. Elliott put together a term package for one of our employees. Her name is Clarissa. Heaven knows what her last name is, but I fired her. If she comes within breathing distance of the company or the family, I want her head.

"No, I will explain when I see you this evening." He hung up the phone.

"Her head, Ashton?" Kali sat up and ran her fingers through her hair.

"Her head," he answered. "We can't let her put the word out before you tell Dumb Nuts the truth. So you are going to have to do that this weekend. Or, you will put me in a very awkward place."

"Okay," Kali agreed. Now her lie was affecting even more people.

"Come on, we have got to go home. The kids are acting out and Uncle Micah's pissed."

Saturday morning arrived fast, and Kali was getting dressed to go home to clean.

"Forget the house, I got it covered. Elliot is taking a cleaning crew down there to get rid of our musk. All you have to do today is play with the kids, and tonight go dancing."

"Dancing." She perked up at the word.

"Dancing." He stretched his long body. "But first me needs my pancakes, Mommy."

That evening, Kenny came to watch the kids and Kali ventured into Jordan's room to find the perfect outfit for the club. She squealed with excitement as she walked into the room to find boxes and bags from Saks across Jordan's bed. She went wild tearing open packages and emptying bags. Her perfect outfit was in there. It was a blue leather pantsuit with matching boots.

"Uh Uh, you are not getting dressed in that magnificent outfit without a manicure and pedicure. The kids are asleep, so let the master do his work," Kenny had followed her into the room.

"Did you buy these?" Kali asked, as she ran to him and hugged him.

"With Big Daddy's credit card, of course. But, I picked it all out. That leather suit just shouted Kali, Kali, Kali."

The club was just as she had remembered – dark, elegant and sexy. Micah had made only a few minor changes since he had taken over. Ashton led her onto the dance floor as soon as they arrived and danced her through at least ten songs before they were ready to sit down. She was enjoying every minute.

He led her up to the second floor and down the hall to Jordan's old office. Neither one of them wanted to hang out with the other partiers. Ashton knew a lot of the people down there, and he knew they were aware of who she was and their relationship.

Ashton plopped down at the desk and put his feet up. He opened the top drawer and found a cigar. He lit it and leaned back blowing rings in the air.

Kali took off her boots and reclined on the love seat watching him. "Their life together could be perfect," she thought. All that was standing in their way was her lie. She was beginning to believe that he would never hurt her again.

There was a quick knock on the door and the red-headed man that had looked familiar to her once before entered.

"Ashton, my man! How ya doing?" the man walked over to the desk and extended his hand.

"Brady." Ashton gave the man's hand a curt shake.

"You and the little lady must have danced off a few pounds out there. I guess I need to do a few rounds myself," he patted his protruding belly.

"Yeah, I don't think that would be a bad idea," Ashton said and stood up and patted his flat stomach.

Ashton sat back down and waved toward the chair facing the desk. He pulled out a cigar and tossed it to Brady.

"I don't believe the young lady and I have been formally introduced." Brady lit his cigar and looked at her lewdly over the smoke. Kali immediately found she disliked him.

"Why would you need to meet her?" Ashton waited for an answer.

"Well, maybe because she is the reason you fired my niece." Brady leaned back into the chair.

"Ah, Clarissa is your doing?" Ashton put his feet back up on the desk.

"Look, man. I explained to her that what the boss says and how the boss lives is not under discussion. She can keep her mouth shut. Just like half your staff that is down there partying."

"That's because half my staff down there knows me personally and wouldn't want anything to upset me or hurt me. Plus, they understand their livelihoods depend on it," Ashton answered.

"Yeah, but you know the bigger the company gets and the more people you hire, it's going to be hard to keep secrets like that," Brady pointed toward Kali who was immediately offended by being called 'that'.

"Well, the way I see it, we are a company built on security, keeping other people's secrets and keeping our mouths closed. Anybody that can't do that doesn't belong in my company. Now do they?" Ashton blew a couple of more circles, but Kali could see from her vantage point that his hazel eyes were turning black.

Why couldn't Brady let them have an enjoyable evening? She sat up and started putting her boots back on.

"I'm ready to go home, Ashton," she said. "I have a long day tomorrow."

"Okay," he said. "Give me a minute with Brady, will you?"

"Sure," she looked around to see where she could go. "I'll go freshen up."

Kali closed the door behind her and went to Jordan's private bathroom. She lowered the lids and sat down on the toilet waiting.

"Brady," Ashton put his feet down and put out his cigar. He leaned across the desk toward his old friend.

"Do you forget what you are out there marketing? Do you remember what kind of business this is?"

"No, Ashton. How could I forget that?" Brady was enjoying the cigar. It was smooth, definitely top of the line.

"Just wanted to make sure, Brady. 'Cause, I'm going to do you this one favor. That is, if you really, really want me to. But, you know I can find out in a matter of minutes if that woman is really your niece. And if she isn't, then you are fired, too."

"What?" Brady almost dropped his cigar. "You wouldn't do that to an old buddy. I bring you too much business."

"Oh, but I would, old buddy. I'd fire Micah if I found out he was lying to me. So the way I see it, you have a choice. Clarissa can report to work Monday morning and life will go on as it has been. Or neither of you can report to work on Monday if she is not your niece. Your choice," Ashton got up and patted Brady on the shoulders so hard, the man's body vibrated.

"I hope I see you, Monday. You better hope I see you, Monday," Ashton walked to the door and opened it.

"Let me show you the way out, old buddy," Ashton winked at a stunned Brady who knew the last thing he should ever do was show up to work on Monday.

"Tell Clarissa, should she not show up to work Monday, we will ship her things to her home address."

Brady put the lit cigar in the ash tray and walked apprehensively past Ashton.

"Goodbye, Brady," Ashton said as he closed the door.

CHAPTER FOURTEEN

"I don't think it is a good idea for you to be taking me to the airport," Kali protested as she sat in the front seat of Jordan's old limousine. Ashton had kept it, so he could give his clients the VIP treatment. Today, he was acting as the hired driver to take her to pick up Marcus and his family.

"I am not doing this for you," Ashton said, grabbing her hand. "I am doing this to get Dumb Nuts straight to the office. We've got some things to handle."

"I thought you wanted me to tell him right away, that I'm leaving him." Kali squeezed his hand, thinking how much she dreaded facing up to this, especially with Margaret and Sheila around.

"Yeah, but first I have to debrief him and get what I need out of him before he bolts. So, I guess you got a couple of days." He squeezed her hand back.

"A couple of days?" Kali shook her head. "I'm sitting here psyching myself up for this evening and now you want me to delay it a couple of days.

"Yeah, he was working on a really important contract, my first Asian one. I can't let that slip through my fingers. The time is too ripe," he turned into the airport parking lot.

"Let's play this right. We didn't come together. Don't mention or allude to it. We both came to meet them. You took a cab. You hate driving the Schuykill out this way," he told her and pulled into the parking space. "Now go on. Just in case Brady and Clarissa are ready to catch a flight out of dodge. The last thing we want is for them to see us together."

"Why would they be flying out of dodge?" Kali looked at him questioningly and suddenly felt a bit unsettled.

"Just a guess," Ashton said, remembering a phone call he had made the evening before. Clarissa was anything but a niece, at least none that Brady's mother knew. He was sure by now Brady knew about the conversation. Brady was also probably aware that Micah had dug up some improprieties with the company cash by now, and trying to get away with the last little bit in his account. If Ashton had anything to do with it, it would be very little in there by Monday morning. He wished he had listened to Jordan on that one.

Kali was standing at the gate when the family filed out of the ramp. Margaret greeted her with a big tight hug, and so did Sheila. Marcus kissed her so lightly on the cheek that she thought it was a wisp of air shooting by. He looked tired, worn, and grumpy.

"Boy, you look a hot mess," Kali grabbed him by his arm. He pulled it away.

"Not now, Lena. I am tired. All I want to do is to get these women home and to bed." Marcus walked ahead of them without looking back.

Kali helped Margaret with her carry-on bag and strolled beside her as they headed for baggage. Ashton watched from the gate next door and noticed Rita strolling confidently a few feet behind them with a smile on her face. That made him angry, but he calmed himself down when he realized it didn't matter anymore. Kali was all his now. Rita could have the little boy if she wanted him.

Ashton hurried ahead of them to catch up with Marcus. He caught up with him at the escalator.

"My dear, Mr. Roberson," he patted him on the shoulder. "How was the trip, son? I was expecting you back Tuesday, Wednesday at the latest."

Marcus turned, shocked and speechless. He looked back down the escalator and saw Lena and his mother walking far behind with Rita not too far behind them. His face went from shocked to panic trying to hide Rita from Ashton. He looked back up the escalator hoping Ashton would look in the same direction.

"My flight stopped over in Los Angeles so I thought I would say hello to my folks. I tried to reach you. I did speak with Ms. Elliott. Didn't she relay the message?"

"Yeah, son. She relayed the message, but not the reports I was expecting."

"Yeah, I'm sorry about that Ashton. It's just that," he glanced back at the women. "It's just that my father laid some heavy news on me, and I got a bit distracted."

"What news?" Ashton looked back and caught Kali's eye. He turned away instantly before anyone else would notice.

"My mother's got breast cancer, and she's refusing treatment. I convinced her to come out here so she could spend some time with Lena. She respects Lena. I hope Lena can convince her not to give up," his voice choked a bit.

"I'm sorry," Ashton removed his hand from the man's shoulder. He was sorry to hear that his mother was sick, and he was equally sorry that it seemed Kali was going to be trapped in her lie more than a couple of more days.

"What can I do?" Ashton asked.

"Give me lots of work," Marcus answered. "I need to be distracted from this."

"So, you bring your mother home to dump her on your wife?" Ashton was taken aback by Marcus's response.

"No, no. I didn't mean it that way. But, she will be more apt to listen to a woman than me. Trust me, I have been begging her. She won't even consider it. I just don't want to think about her not being here anymore."

"Do you need to move back west?" Ashton asked, his mind was working overtime. "I'd understand. I would help you if you needed it." Ashton wanted to shout hint, hint.

"No, I like it here just fine. Besides, they are staying through Christmas. My Dad's job is sending him overseas until after New Year's. He didn't want them to be alone while he was gone, especially since she's not seeking treatment.

"A whole month." Ashton's hopes were diminishing by the minute. He knew Kali was going to feel responsible for everybody and everything. He looked back down at her again. Their eyes just would not stop capturing each other's. This time she turned her head to look at Sheila, but she was wondering what was wrong.

Kali led the way into the house. Ashton and Marcus were bringing in the bags. They both carried them all the way to the guest bedroom. Marcus followed Ashton back out the door without so much as a 'see you later'. Kali noticed that he still hadn't really touched her. Ashton noticed, too.

"Lena, this is a beautiful little house. Boy, have my children got it made," Margaret was walking through the house and touching everything. "And so spotless, I have never seen a house so clean. Is that all you do everyday, clean? I know that boy probably works all the time. I know he is away a lot. You handling that okay?"

"Dag, Ma. Slow down. How many questions are you going to ask the girl in one breath?" Sheila complained and found a spot on the sofa facing the fireplace.

"This is nice. I always wanted a house with a fireplace. Does it work?"

"Yes, it does," Kali walked over and turned on the fake fireplace and the electric generated flames roared.

"Oh, way cool," Margaret said, taking a seat next to Sheila. "Sit down, Lena and tell us how you are doing. I know how my selfish son is doing. How are you doing with your pretty little self?"

"I'm fine," Kali sat in one of the chairs and leaned forward on her hands. She was wondering how she was going to make it through the next couple of days. "Are you hungry? I can fix a nice lunch."

"In a minute or two," Margaret turned, still looking at the house. "You know, before you started that thing, I couldn't smell nothing in this house. It's almost as if nobody lives here."

"This is it," Kali squirmed a little. "This is our address. Would you like to see your room?"

"In a minute or two," Margaret stared at the wisps of fire. "You must have cleaned all day yesterday. You weren't trying to get the wrong kind of smell out of here, were you?"

"Mama," Sheila gasped. "What are you talking about?"

"Oh, nothing," Margaret shook her head. "Where is something that makes this house, your house?"

"Like what?" Kali was puzzled.

"Pictures, personal items. Stuff. This place looks like a museum," Margaret stood up and stretched. "Anyway, you decorate the way you want to decorate. Show me the little girl's room and show Sheila our room on your way.

Kali led the way up the stairs thinking that this really hadn't been a home for her and Marcus. But, what Margaret didn't know was a lot of the stuff she thought were just show pieces belonged to her and Ashton in a former life. As for pictures, the only ones that she treasured were back at the penthouse. She made a mental note to give Marcus all of their wedding pictures and honeymoon pictures. They were pretty much the only pictures they had to show that they actually knew each other. Unlike the volumes of pictures in the penthouse of her, Ashton and the kids, even her, Ashton and Jordan, and in a very special place, pictures of her and her parents. No, Marcus really had been a dream, a false vision. They, as a couple, really didn't exist.

Kali kept the women occupied until late into the evening when Marcus finally stumbled in the door, more tired than he was before. He went straight upstairs and showered.

"Does he do that all the time?" Margaret asked.

"Work late?" Kali nodded. "Yes, all the time."

"And what do you do?" Sheila asked.

"I keep house. I go get my hair done. I shop and cook," Kali shrugged. She wanted to say, "I take care of my children. I hang out with Ashton. We take long walks, go biking and swimming in Jordan's rooftop pool." But, she couldn't and besides most of that had occurred in the distant past.

"You poor thing! I'm going to have to have a talk with that boy. I am so sorry I convinced you to let him drag you out here to sit and vegetate. It's not fair," Margaret said, starting up the stairs.

"Maybe tomorrow," Kali said, smiling as she put her arm around her. "I think we all need to just go to bed right now. You look a little tired, Margaret."

"I am a little bit," Margaret looked over at Sheila who had dropped her head. "I'm okay. I just need to get ready for bed like you said. It's been a long day."

Kali climbed into bed on her side, she had long ago put on her pajamas trying to get the ladies to do the same, but they were too excited about being in Philadelphia. She had put on a pair of flannels to keep Marcus from making advances, but she realized when he had walked into the door, she didn't have to worry. She lay there thinking there was no reason she should expect him to even touch her, it had been so long.

Just as she suspected, he climbed into bed and lay on his side facing away from her. They lay there back to back in the dark without touching. Finally, she turned on her back and stared at the light from the street hitting the wall across from her.

"It was nice of you to bring your mom and sis out here. They're really excited," she said, trying to make conversation.

"Did she tell you?" Marcus asked, still lying with his back to her.

"Tell me what?" Kali asked.

"She was diagnosed with breast cancer. They want to treat it, but she's refusing treatment. Says she wants to die peacefully," Marcus's voice was flat and unemotional, as if he were reading about a stranger in a textbook.

"Is it that far along?" Kali sat up and tried to peer over his shoulder.

"No, the doctors say she still has a chance to survive, but since she has never known anyone that has survived, she's already given up."

"You are trying to convince her she's wrong, right?" Kali grabbed his shoulder and he pulled away as if her touch was toxic.

"She won't listen to me. That's why I brought her to you." He finally turned and spoke to her face to face. Kali could see tears welled in his eyes in the dimness of the street light.

"It's okay," she kissed his eyes and felt him soften in her hands. "I'll talk to her. I'll get her to go to another doctor, okay?"

Marcus nodded and he kissed her for the first time in a long time, a long passionate kiss. Her heart went out to him as he pulled her underneath him and began to make love to her. Kali awakened the next morning and saw her flannel pajamas on the floor. She hit herself in the forehead. Why now?

"Did you change beds or something?" Marcus stepped out of the bathroom pulling a sleeveless t-shirt over his head.

"No," she said, rubbing her eyes. "Why?"

"It's just that I've never slept so well in that bed before. It's like its different or something," Marcus continued to get dressed.

"Your mother mentioned she wanted to see your office. Can I bring her up there today?" Kali began to wonder about the bed. She hadn't been in the house since Friday, and Ms. Elliot had overseen the cleaning crew in the house on Saturday.

"Maybe later this week, but not today. I have a lot to make up for last week. Ashton was pretty ticked yesterday, but he understood once I told him about my mother. You know, he really isn't a bad guy. When I told him about my mother, he seemed genuinely concerned. He said his brothers might know someone who they could refer her to," Marcus actually walked over to her and kissed her on the lips. He smiled. "Seems like I have a lot to make up to you, too," he went to the door. "I'll call you later."

Kali grabbed the pillow next to her and started beating herself in the face with it. Now was not the time for him to be turning back to her. She never should have kissed his tears.

Ashton's day started going downhill the moment he woke up. There was no one to watch the twins. Reggie was out of town stuck in a snowstorm and couldn't get home. Kenny was booked and could only provide a couple of hours in the morning. Ruby was out of the question after Friday, and Kali was busy playing house with the in-laws.

He packed the twins some toys and some snacks in their backpacks, dressed them and drove them to work. He had to go to work today. He had important meetings, the Brady mess to check out, and a clueless boy to debrief for contract negotiations. The twins followed him unwillingly. They wanted to stay in their pajamas and play with Mommy.

"Why can't Mommy come over?" AJ kept asking.

"I want Mommy," Katie kept protesting.

Ashton kept promising that he would make it up to them, but he wasn't exactly sure how. Now that the kids were calling her Mommy, he couldn't just show up with them at the rowhouse and drop them off. Ms. Elliott was startled to see the disheveled looking four year olds trailing behind their father as he sped quickly through the office barking orders.

"I need your help," he stopped, after he thought she had written everything else down. "I need a nanny for a few days, possibly a month," he said as he watched Marcus speed into his office looking too happy.

"Good morning," Marcus greeted the four of them with a smile.

"What's so good about it?" Ashton could smell Kali on him a mile away. He wanted to ask him if he did her this morning.

"It's just good to be home and back to my own desk. And my own bed," Marcus stretched. "I slept so good last night. It was unbelievable."

"Good for you." Ashton looked at Ms. Elliott.

"What time are we meeting?" Marcus asked Ashton.

"Ten," Ms. Elliott answered and Marcus backed out to go to his own office.

"Did you flip the bed or something?" Ashton asked curiously.

"I replaced it," Ms. Elliott answered. "Well, you said she wanted to get rid of your smell."

Ashton worked as best he could while trying to occupy the twins, then he had an impromptu meeting with the Assistant Marketing Director who was going to need to replace Brady at least on an interim basis. He ushered the twins into the little conference room off Elliott's office and asked her to keep an eye on them. She be-grudgingly agreed as she was trying to pull together contracts and business meetings at the same time. An hour later, she had had to push back two other meetings and was typing furiously when the phone rang. It was the clerical pool that supported Marketing. Ashton was furious, the materials were put together all wrong, an-other Brady oversight. He had put way too much trust in that man.

Elliott looked back at the kids who were looking too bored to be left alone, not even for a minute. She walked in the conference room, picked up their things and marched them to Marcus's office. He had a small conference table in the corner of his office.

"What are you doing?" he protested.

"It takes a village," she said. "I have to go down to Marketing to fix something. You just keep them out of trouble for 15 min-utes, please," she closed the door behind her to keep the twins from trying to follow her.

"I want my daddy," Katie said defiantly.

"Me, too." AJ followed suit and his eyes began to tear up. "I gotta go to the bathroom."

Marcus realized he couldn't let him go by himself, so he grabbed both children by their hands and led them into their father's private bathroom. They took turns going to the bathroom. He was proud of himself. The trip to the bathroom went pretty smoothly. He didn't even have to remind them to wash their hands. Smart little kids, he thought as he helped them back in the chairs at his confer-ence table.

"I don't want to sit anymore," AJ slithered out of the chair under the table. Katie followed him.

"Okay, sit under the table," Marcus smiled then returned to his desk to finish his work. He sat there becoming engrossed in the statistics for the next contract when he realized they were crawling around his feet.

"Hello down there," he said. "You have to get up. I don't want to accidentally roll over any fingers or toes. He reached down and picked up the little boy. He was much heavier than he looked. Katie climbed into his lap next to AJ and was the first one to see Kali's picture.

"Kali," Katie pointed at the picture. AJ looked and his eyes widened cheerfully. "Mommy!" he screamed.

"Mommy," Katie sang.

"No," Marcus chuckled, "Lena."

AJ twisted out of Marcus lap and wailed at the top of his lungs. "I want my mommy!"

Both kids ran to the door and started banging on it, both crying, "I want my mommy!"

Ms. Elliott gently pushed the door open and the little ones ran past her to Ashton's office.

"Mommy! Mommy!" they both screamed, and when they reached their father's empty office, they collapsed to the floor.

It took Ms. Elliott almost an hour to calm them down and get them to take a nap. She halted everything else she was doing and started looking for a nanny. By three o'clock in the afternoon Ashton couldn't do anything with them, so he took them home. As he was leaving, she handed him a note with a name on it.

"She will be at the penthouse at 7:00 am and will stay until 7:00 pm as long as you will need her. Trust me. She is not young and pretty looking to seduce a rich man. She is a real nanny."

Kali decided to take one day at a time with Margaret who still hadn't told her about her condition. It was Tuesday, and it was still too early for them to go visit Marcus. She scheduled time with Kenny.

"This place is awesome," Sheila said, as she walked into the upscale salon with rock accented walls and waterfalls and huge fish tanks.

"This is where you come to get dolled up?" Margaret walked through the reception area looking very pleased.

"This is it," Kali said and led them through the reception area to the beauty salon. Kenny was already working his magic on someone. The shampoo girl looked up and smiled. "Kali," she waved.

Kali waved and then leaned toward Margaret. "I think she thinks I'm someone else." All three women smiled and waved.

"Girl, look at you. I just did you Saturday. You ready for another go at it," Kenny kissed her on the cheek.

"No, girl," she grinned. "I'm all good. But, I want you to meet Margaret and Sheila, Marcus's mom and sister. I want you to hook them up with the head to toe package, would you?"

"No problema." He twisted back to the shampoo girl and whispered something to her. She covered her mouth and grinned. She waved again at Kali and yelled, "Hey, Miss Lena."

The three women laughed.

Sheila whispered to Kali, "Is that a man or a woman?"

Margaret hit her.

"It don't matter as long as he makes me look like Lena."

Kenny escorted the ladies back to the spa area.

"Darling, are you going to do the works today?" he looked at Kali.

"No, I have some errands to take care of. Can I use your phone to call about these bills?" She pulled out a bunch of envelopes to make it look good.

"Go on. You know where everything is and the Robersons are in good hands, baby," Kenny blew her a kiss. She caught it in dramatic fashion, and they both squealed.

Kali called the penthouse first and spoke with the children. The new nanny had already been informed of who she was, so she was happy that she didn't have to waste time explaining.

Then she called Ashton who was not a happy camper. He missed her, but told her to do what she was felt was right. Then he told her, he wanted her in his bed and out of that new bed as soon as possible. Kali told him that was what she wanted, too. Marcus was starting to get frisky, and she was finding it hard to say no. But, she didn't dare tell Ashton that part.

Thursday rolled around, and she thought it was time for an intervention. She had been walking and driving the two around town, letting Margaret feel relaxed. But, she was ready to go home to the penthouse and her children. She planned the day out and was going to culminate the day with a doctor's visit that Margaret didn't know had been planned.

They started out in Wanamaker's shopping and listening to its world famous organ. The women fell in love with everything, but Kali spent sparingly there and bought them each a high fashion purse. They were both pleased with their pricey Coach bags. Then she took them to lunch in a nice Italian restaurant. She had already introduced them to hoagies and cheesesteaks, the Philadelphia food staples. Now she was feeding them authentic Italian food. They were exceedingly pleased. She could tell by the long pauses in the conversation and the small savory bites. Then they caught a cab to the office. Kali had tried to warn Ashton on at least two occasions. She had left a message for him on his voicemail and with Ms. Elliott, but he must have missed both.

The two women were going through their awe moments walking through the new building and then taking the elevator up to Ashton's floors.

"This boy got money, honey," Sheila said proudly. "I know someone with lots of money."

"Shut up, girl. Act like you've been somewhere outside of LA," Margaret said, smiling at herself in the gleaming stainless steel doors of the elevator.

They strode off the elevators and went up to the executive loft by the stairs. She turned to see if Margaret was taking the stairs okay. She had been looking a little strained all day, but she was fine and eager.

The receptionist wasn't at her desk, so Kali walked them straight into the suite behind the large smoked-glass window and saw Ms. Elliott on the phone. Ms. Elliott waved them absent-mindedly toward Ashton's office.

Kali opened Ashton's door. He was sitting behind the desk leaning in his chair with a handful of papers. He looked up and smiled his biggest grin.

"Kali," he said clearly and saw her stop mid-step. He suddenly realized the two women were behind her.

"Damn, you look like her. I keep telling everybody that. Hi, Mrs. Roberson, how are you?" He sat up, hoping it was a save.

"Hello Mr. Sperling. Didn't mean to interrupt you, but we thought this was Marcus's office."

"No, no, no interruption. I love being non-interrupted by beautiful women," he grinned. Margaret and Sheila grinned back at him appreciatively. Kali watched them succumb to his charms.

"Let me walk you ladies down to see Marcus. Is he expecting you?" he looked at Kali.

"He should be. We've been talking about it all week," Kali answered flippantly. Margaret tapped her on the arm.

"Don't be so nice nasty," she whispered. "The man's responsible for your husband's paycheck."

The surprise doctor visit was next and became a whirlwind that ended with Margaret scheduled for surgery the next day. Kali spent the next week sitting by her bedside and getting her ready to come home. The doctor had convinced Margaret with such ease that even Margaret was shocked to be prepped for surgery. The outcome was good and everybody was happy, the cancer was completely removed. Ricky had flown out to perform plastic surgery so the breast would still look normal. The Roberson family had bonded thick as thieves, and they were all looking at Kali as the one to hold them together. It was driving Ashton crazy as well as the kids. They hadn't seen Kali in weeks, and they were all climbing up the walls. The twins wanted their mother's hugs and kisses and so did Ashton.

On her last visit to Kenny's just before Christmas Eve she spoke with Ashton who threatened to tell the news himself. But, she convinced him to wait until January 2nd when she would be putting the Roberson women on the plane. Then she would just move out, telling Marcus the same day. Ashton wasn't going to let her out of Christmas though, and he told her so. He told her to expect the unexpected. That frightened her, but she went back into the spa and tried to relax with the ladies.

Margaret was so happy that she was on her way back to perfect health. She insisted on buying and decorating a Christmas tree. She filled the bottom of the tree with presents, mostly for Kali. Kali bought for everyone, but it was obvious that everyone was going overboard for her. She was feeling even guiltier, especially when Marcus gave her that puppy-dog look he used to give her when they first started dating. Here they were putting her high up on a pedestal, and she was about to come crashing down.

She was nervous all day Christmas Eve. She fixed a big dinner and convinced everyone to open at least one gift from each other since there were so many under the tree. They did, and everybody was excited about the presents she had bought them, and she was touched by the gifts they had bought her. At the same time, they made her sad, especially the beautiful picture frame Margaret gave her with their wedding picture in it. She put it on the mantle between the antique candle holders. It would have looked perfect had it really been the beginning of a perfect family. They played cards and sang Christmas songs with the music playing on WDAS radio. Everyone was happy except Kali, who felt like her smile was glued on like a snowman's. It was soon going to dissolve, falling off, revealing the nothing behind it. A couple of hours past midnight when they were about to turn in, the phone rang.

Marcus picked it up.

"Yeah, yeah! Are you serious?" Marcus handed her the phone. "It's Kenny."

"Kenny," Kali held her breath. "Oh, My God! Are you all right?" she said, trying to sound really concerned. "What do you want me to do? You want me to come and sit with you? Yes, I can do that. Give me a few minutes to get dressed. I'll be there."

Kali hung up the phone and tried to sound exasperated.

"His new boyfriend beat him up over the car," she looked at Margaret, hoping she would urge her to go to him.

"Where is he? Why didn't you tell him to come over here?" Margaret asked. She genuinely liked Kenny.

"He's driving himself to the emergency room down at Jeff. I told him I would meet him there and sit with him."

"We'll all go," Margaret started up the stairs as if she were going to get dressed.

"No, Momma! No, you do not need to be out there in an emergency room with all those germs. I'll go," Marcus said.

"No, he's my friend. I'll sit with him. Besides, he'll be embarrassed enough as it is. That's why he called me instead of his family," Kali said, folding her arms as if that was the final word.

"Well, I'm driving you down there and seeing that you get into emergency safely. I don't want you driving around Philadelphia this late by yourself," Marcus said. "You can call me when he's fixed up, and I'll come and get you."

"He has his car. He can drop me off or I'll drive myself home," she said. He nodded in agreement. They both dressed quickly for the weather and went straight to the hospital. Marcus pulled up in front of the emergency room and she got out of the car. He watched her go through the sliding glass doors. She turned around and waved to him just as she caught a glimpse of Ashton at the end of the corridor. She ran to meet him. He pulled her into an alcove and kissed her deeply.

"So this was your plan?" she asked. "Where's Kenny?"

"He's back there with a rag over his face, just in case the loving little family or husband tried to follow you."

"I think he pulled it off," she said.

"Well, let's not wait to find out. Come on." He led her through some hallways and out the door into the parking lot.

"Kenny's going to wait another half hour and leave. He never checked in, so it'll be okay."

Kali was happy to be home. She was excited about the big live fir standing in the living room surrounded by presents. The tree was filled with the kids' ornaments they had created. In the middle was Jordan's ornament she had given him years ago, the one that had caused her to faint a year ago at the company Holiday party.

"Where are the kids?" she asked.

"Asleep. Waiting for Santa Claus," he pulled her down in front of the tree and started helping her out of her coat and then out of some of her clothes. He slid inside of her urgently.

"You just couldn't wait," she said and grabbed a handful of hair and pulled his head closer to her.

"Why waste time?" he said, as he began to ravish her body.

They ended up in their bedroom fast asleep in each other's arms until their natural alarm went off. The kids came crashing in to their bed. They were excited to find her there and they squealed "Mommy" over and over. The four of them went down to the tree and enjoyed opening the gifts, taking pictures and eating junk. Kali didn't want it to end. After a light breakfast, Ashton told her to go upstairs and get dressed. She looked disappointed that Christmas at home was over. He followed her up the stairs and pointed her to Jordan's room. She looked at him questioningly, but when she saw the bags and boxes from Saks on the bed, she was more than delighted and ran to the bed.

"First, take a shower," he said. "Don't be long. The presents are numbered. Follow the sequence."

"She hurried out of the shower and began to open the presents. The first one was a white lace thong with pearls on the string.

"Naughty," she said, but stepped into it.

The next was a white lace push-up bra that was strapless. She grinned as she put it on and fastened the clasps. She then opened a big box and found the most stunning strapless white wedding dress. She started to cry. She knew she had had the blood tests. She knew she had signed the application for marriage while hiding in Kenny's office one day, but she didn't expect to be getting married so soon. She put on the dress and was opening the shoes when Kenny walked into the room.

"You have got to have the right hair and makeup, darling," he kissed her and held her tightly. You are going to be a beautiful Christmas bride."

That early Christmas morning, Kali descended the staircase dressed in white and was greeted by Ruby, Micah, Ricky, Chico, Kenny, and the children. There was one more person dressed in a dark robe with a Bible in his hand. She took her place next to Ashton and tried not to cry as their family witnessed their wedding vows. The two of them held out for another hour before he carried her up the stairs to consummate their marriage. They stayed there as long as they could. When Kenny drove her back to the row house, it was after eleven o'clock.

"You better take those rings off and hide them," Kenny said as he parked the car across the street. "Oh, God! We better get that makeup toned down."

Kenny reached in the backseat of his car and pulled out baby wipes. He cleaned her face with small soft strokes.

"Count down. One more week and this hide and go seek shit is over," he said as he smiled at her and reached over to open the door.

"God help us. I can't wait, Kenny," she turned around and kissed him. "Thank you. Thank you so much for being such a good friend."

"For being a crazy one," Kenny shooed her out the door.

She walked in and smelled food. She was surprised that the smell unsettled her stomach a bit. But, the greeting she received made her forget it.

"I guess he survived," Marcus greeted her with a hug and kiss.

"You smell like a baby," he teased.

"Oh, I guess I cried a little and Kenny cleaned me up with some baby wipes," the smell reminded her of her children.

"So how is he?" Margaret walked out of the kitchen with a pan of cookies.

"He'll be okay. Had a few stitches. I told him to call me when he got home. They gave him some serious pain killers, but he wouldn't let me drive his car," Kali wanted to pat herself on the back. That was a good lie she thought, and they accepted it.

The days went by but not fast enough. All Margaret and Sheila could talk about was the New Year's Eve party coming up and all Kali could think about was Ashton and the kids. She was this close, and she wasn't going to blow it. She would put them on the plane and tell Marcus goodbye. It was only a few days away.

She had put up a wall between them and wouldn't have sex with Marcus anymore. For the first time, it didn't feel like it was something she could live with, – sleeping with two men. She put on a sanitary napkin Christmas night and told him her period was on. It was then that she realized it had been a while since she had menstruated. Ashton was right. He had been teasing her whenever they talked, especially about the bed. He was upset that Ms. Elliott had gotten rid of the bed where they had made their babies. He was even more upset that Marcus was feeling frisky in the new bed. But, she had just laughed him off not wanting to confirm the newfound lust in Marcus.

She could tell Marcus noticed the change in her, and he kept asking her what was wrong. She told him she just wasn't feeling well and it would pass. Right now she just needed space. He started waiting on her hand and foot which made her feel uncomfortable. She wanted this part of her life to just be over and finalized.

New Year's Eve fell on a Thursday, and she got the ladies up early to go pick up their dresses. She kept her lies going by telling them Kenny had picked them out and all they had to do was pick them up. It was Ashton who had shopped for them. He was good at haute` couture. He knew instinctively what would look right on the right figure and picked the dresses perfectly. Margaret had a devilish red dress that hugged her slightly full figure to a tee.

Sheila's was a fun and frilly short white dress with silver stars. And Kali's was blue, her favorite color. It was deep blue, trimmed with expensive sequins that looked like fish scales and a high split up the side with easy access for wandering hands. She smiled as she imagined Ashton's soft sensual hands sliding up her bare legs. They all tried their dresses on with the matching shoes that waited for them. The evening was going to be perfect. She was starting the New Year with her new husband and only a few people knew about it.

Ashton was so excited that he tucked the kids in early against their wishes. But, he promised he would be bringing Mommy home to stay soon and they relinquished. He put on a brand new suit and stood dancing to the radio he had on low volume. He was perfecting his moves in the mirror.

Micah walked in and broke out into laughter. He thought Ashton was dancing to his own internal music.

"I haven't seen you this happy. I don't think ever." He turned Ashton around and fixed his tie.

"Is she really all that?" he asked.

"All that and a bag of chips, son," Ashton said grinning from ear to ear. "You ready, my man?"

"Yes, sir." Micah patted him on the back and motioned for him to hurry.

They rode in the back of the limo that was waiting for them outside.

"He'll be back to pick up Ruby and the boys. Then he's going to get Kali," Micah answered the question before it was asked. Ashton was still smiling.

Ashton checked out The Silver Sperling to make sure everything was in place. Micah hadn't changed the club too much since he had inherited it, but it was a little bit different. He had added a maze under an atrium out back where lovers could discreetly disappear. Ashton took a quick run through the trail. He was planning to get lost in it this evening with Kali in tow, but not too lost.

He came back just in time for the doors to open and stood there greeting the guests. The club was opened to all tonight, but his employees were getting special tickets so they could get their food and drinks for free. The DJ was already spinning the latest dance records and a band had already set up to play alternately with the DJ. Ashton was ready to dance. Troy came in with his sister Rita who licked her tongue out at him like a mischievous child.

"What was that all about?" Troy asked. He stood next to Ashton, and they both watched her walk away deeper into the club.

"She's been doing my liaison," said Ashton.

"She's been what?" Troy said.

"She's got the boy's nose wide open," Ashton chuckled.

"Oh, that's what's going on," Troy nodded knowingly. "I think he's been missing in action, though. She's been a little on the nasty side of late."

"Since Thanksgiving?" Ashton asked.

"Yeah, yeah. That's about right." Troy tried to see where she had disappeared to, but he lost her.

"She'll get back on track. Trust me," Ashton was grinning, greeting everyone as they entered the club, especially if they had a PDSI identification badge.

"Boy, I have never seen you this happy. What's up?" Troy asked.

"Well, had you been free Christmas morning you would already know," Ashton shook someone's hand and wished him Happy New Year.

"What gives?" Troy asked.

"I can't tell you right now, son. I'll be happy to clue you in later though," Ashton said. He stood there until he saw the people he really wanted to see.

"This is Margaret," he whispered. "Remember what we talked about?"

"Got it." Troy saw the woman in red. "Not bad. A little up in the years, but not bad."

"It's just one night, son. Just one night unless you want to make it longer. That will be on you," Ashton waved to Margaret.

"One night is fine," Troy leaned around Ashton for a better look and saw Kali.

"Oh, shit. She is looking too fine for words, son," Troy said with envy.

"The one in the red, son. The one in the red," Ashton said as he greeted Marcus and family with hugs. He hugged Kali a moment longer than he should have and caught Marcus's eyes when he let her go.

"I reserved some tables for my family and close friends. Micah will help you find them." He pointed to Micah who was talking to a real cute girl from the clerical pool. He reminded Ashton of Jordan in that moment, and he smiled.

Ashton looked around for Ms. Elliott, who was seated at the table smoking a cigarette leaning close to an older man who was talking incessantly. She didn't look very interested, so he waved to her. She touched the gentleman's hand and pointed to Ashton. She sauntered over and whispered thank you.

"Who's that old coot?" he teased.

"That old coot runs your janitorial service that you keep forgetting you own."

"Oh, yeah," Ashton said and waved to the gentleman.

"Do you want that?" Ashton grinned down at her.

"What?" she looked up at him puzzled.

"I thought the Christmas present you bought yourself was really cheap. Since you have done so much for me, why don't I just give you that company as a gift? You have earned it. Jordan said you would be the best thing that ever happened to me. And he was close to being right. I couldn't run any of my companies without you. I'll have the papers drawn up tomorrow."

"Are you serious?" she said.

"Yes, Elliott. What Elliott wants, Elliott gets," he joked.

"Good, then I can fire his old ass." She looked back at the man and waved.

"Take over for me," Ashton said. He kissed her on the cheek and went to find Kali.

The crowd in the club was growing rapidly. He had to work his way through groups of people who were just talking and some who had taken over the dance floor to find his tables. Ashton was pleased to see that Rita had worked her way into a chair right next to Marcus, who was sitting between her and Kali.

Ashton pulled out a chair and sat behind Kali.

"Whoa, son. I think you have the best view in the house to-night." Ashton grinned so hard Kali wanted to slap it off him.

Marcus looked at Rita uncomfortably.

"So why isn't anybody dancing?" Ashton asked and offered his hand to Sheila. She took it, and he led her onto the dance floor. They had danced one dance when a young man from the marketing department tapped his shoulder. Sheila almost didn't let him cut in, but Ashton handed her hand to the young man.

He went back to the table to find Troy sitting next to Margaret. He had already struck up a conversation. Ashton inched in closer.

"So Marcus, why don't you ask your wife to dance? She looks like a dancer to me." Ashton reached over and prodded him. Marcus swayed toward Rita, who smiled at him slyly.

"Maybe later," Marcus answered. "I'm not much of a dancer.

I'll wait for something slower."

"Do you hustle?" he asked Kali, knowing how well she danced.

"Well, yes, I do," Kali turned to Marcus who nodded his head. Ashton led her onto the floor and started the old school hustle. Other people picked up the dance steps and fell into the rhythm. The night was on.

"Excuse me one second," Margaret said to Troy. She scooted over and whispered into Marcus's ear. "I don't know what's going on between you and Lena, but you better get your butt up on that dance floor and do something."

She smiled at him and then smiled at Troy. She rolled her eyes at Rita who was just sitting there looking pretty and a little too close to Marcus for proper etiquette.

"Rita, you want a drink?" Troy said leaning across the table.

"Yeah, get me a margarita, frozen," she answered.

"Get it yourself," Troy smiled and nodded his head toward the bar. Rita ignored him.

"You tried," Margaret said, as she kept her eyes on the two.

"Is there something going on there?" she asked Troy.

"I was wondering the same thing. Do you dance?" he asked Margaret, not wanting to reveal what Ashton had just told him. Seeing the two of them together had just confirmed it.

"I do, but this old woman has to be careful. I am recovering from surgery," Margaret answered.

"I'll go easy on you," Troy held her hand and led to her to the dance floor. They did the two-step slowly. Margaret enjoyed herself. But, every chance she got she looked toward Marcus who was now whispering something to Rita.

"Those two look like they have been dancing together for years," she heard someone say and she turned to see Ashton and Kali going at it. She also saw Ashton's hand land on her daughter-in-law's bare thigh more than once. She immediately wanted to go hit her son on his hard head.

Kali finally made Ashton let her go back to the table. She promised to dance again with him later. He told her he had no doubt that they would. He went through the crowd mingling and talking with everyone he could. He was happy. Kali took her seat back at the table waving air into her face with a flurry of her hands.

"Would you like a drink?" Troy asked.

"Don't fall for that," Rita yelled to her over the music.

"What can I get you, darling?" Troy asked again.

Kali, at first, shook her head. Then she grabbed his hand as she changed her mind.

"I'll take a cranberry juice with a slice of lime in it."

"And you Margaret? Would you like a margarita?" he offered.

Margaret giggled and nodded her head. She was enjoying the attention from the younger man.

Sheila came back to the table waving, trying to cool off with the same little wave of hands. Her mother handed her a handkerchief.

"Looks like you were having fun out there." Margaret smoothed Sheila's hair away from her face.

"Yes, and, he's coming back," Sheila said giggling. "He had to go the men's room."

"Well, truth be told, I need to go myself. Where is it?" Margaret looked around.

"Find the line," Sheila said, looking around and then up.

"I'll go, too," Kali said getting up out of her seat. She led the way. They went to the back and there was a long line. She left the line and looked upwards.

"Let's try up there," the ladies followed her again. When they arrived, there was another line though not quite as long.

Margaret started shifting from side to side.

"You know, I didn't realize it. But, I really got to go. You think I can break the line?" Margaret turned to Kali.

She grabbed Margaret's hand and led her down another hall.

"There has to be another one," Kali tried to act as if she were searching aimlessly, as she led them straight to Jordan's private bath. Each of them remained on the lookout for the other while each of them used the bathroom. Then they walked past the other ladies in line nonchalantly. They went back to the table snickering about their adventure.

"Lena, you sure know how to potty," Sheila giddily joked and Margaret hit her. Troy and Marcus looked at them strangely.

"Thank you for the drinks." Margaret lifted her glass to Troy.

"You are so welcome."

"It's a slow one," Troy announced looking directly at Marcus. "I'm going to ask your mother to dance."

Kali held her hand out to Marcus. He shook his head and pointed at the drink.

"It was a little too stiff. I'm afraid to stand up," he whispered.

Margaret noticed him turning his wife down as she was led onto the floor. She saw the young man come back for Sheila.

Kali sat awkwardly next to Marcus whose eyes seemed to be rolling back in his head. She leaned forward to say something to Rita, but she too was in some sort of trance. She picked up his drink and smelled it. She turned around to see where Ashton was, the two of them sort of scared her.

Ashton walked up behind her and literally lifted her out of the chair. She turned to say something to Marcus and realized why his eyes were rolling back. Rita's hand was in his lap moving to the rhythm of the music. Kali put her hands over her mouth as Ashton flipped her around and led her back to the dance floor.

"Did you see that?" Kali was furious.

Ashton pulled her to him and started singing with the love song. She realized it was pointless to complain. It didn't matter anyway. She was leaving him and now it could look like it was his fault. She let loose. She and Ashton danced the night away.

Sheila finished dancing with the young man again and decided to get a fresh drink before going back to the table. While waiting for the drink she heard two women talking. They were talking about Ashton and his date. She turned around to see who the date was and saw him and Lena in the middle of the floor having fun. She was about to correct them, when she overheard something she wished she hadn't.

"Girl, those two have been an item since way back. I remember when his grandfather used to own this place. Every time I came here, they were tearing up the dance floor. They were the hustle king and queen. Everybody wanted to move like them. They made a great looking couple then and still do. They still got it." The woman got her drink and the two of them walked away. Sheila couldn't wait to get back to their table.

When she sat down next to her mother, she could feel the tension in the air. Margaret's right eyebrow was arched and she knew that didn't mean anything good. The Rita woman had left, and Marcus was sitting sheepishly looking at his drink, doing everything he could not to make eye contact with his mother. Sheila noticed Troy wasn't there either.

"Momma, what's wrong?" Sheila whispered.

"You don't want to know. I saw Ashton dragging Lena away from the table and it's the expression on her face that made me come back to see what happened. This fool," Margaret took a deep breath and rolled her eyes. "You don't want to know about this fool."

Margaret got up and left the table. She went back to the line upstairs.

"Momma," Sheila got in line behind her. "Momma, I think Lena knew Ashton before she came out here."

"Sheila, I don't want to hear it right now. Just let it go. I don't want to hear anything else bad tonight," Margaret put her finger to her daughter's lips. She didn't want to hear what she had already figured out.

The music and the lights changed. The DJ started counting down to midnight. The two Roberson women looked out over the floor and saw Ashton pick up Kali and head toward the atrium. Kali was laughing and draped intimately over his body. Margaret looked to see if Marcus was still at the table. He was, and he was kissing Rita.

CHAPTER FIFTEEN

K̲ali went home reluctantly with the Roberson women. When she had gotten back to the table after the midnight rendez-vous in the maze with Ashton, Marcus was nowhere to be found. Margaret looked tired and angry, and Sheila was just plain with-drawn. Kali went to the coat check and got their things. She came back and helped a sullen and quiet Margaret to put on her coat. Troy had disappeared as well. Sheila put her own coat on, but wouldn't look Kali in the eye. The limo was waiting for them when they walked out the door. The driver held the door for them and walked them to the door of the rowhouse when they arrived.

"Margaret, are you alright?" Kali asked for the hundredth time. Margaret looked dreary eyed.

"Where's your husband?" Sheila asked snidely. "You think he might have gotten tired of seeing another man's hand up your dress?"

"Sheila, shut up," Margaret said. "Come on. Let's go to bed. I'm tired. I don't want to hear nothing. I just want quiet."

Sheila shot Kali an angry glance and followed her mother upstairs. It was almost morning and Kali wanted to go home to the penthouse. Where the hell was Marcus? Then she thought about Rita.

Kali showered and went straight to bed dressed in a pair of red flannel pajamas that Margaret had given her for Christmas. She was happy not to have to share the bed with Marcus and pretend everything was normal. She fell fast asleep.

Kali didn't have to look at the clock when she awakened because she awakened in motion. She was throwing up. She jumped up and ran to the bathroom, projectiles flying. She made such a commotion that both Margaret and Sheila ran into her room.

"Lena, what is wrong?" Margaret saw her crawling out of the bathroom.

"I, I threw up," Kali struggled to get the words out. Her body was shaking so violently that she was weak. She grabbed the tissues and started to wipe her face.

"Whew," Sheila said, after peering into the bathroom. "Did you drink too much last night?"

"Don't start, Sheila." Margaret stepped over Kali and came out with a warm wet wash cloth. She helped Kali back to the bed and wiped her face down.

"I know what you saw last night. I saw it, too," Margaret cleaned little chunks of mucous from Kali's hair.

Kali started weeping again. Her body started wracking so ferociously, it hurt. She jumped and ran past Margaret.

"What did you see?" Sheila asked curiously, frowning at the sound of the heaving in the bathroom.

"Marcus is no angel," Margaret said shaking her head. "He is no angel."

"Neither is she," Sheila defended her brother.

"No, but she is not alone," Margaret shook her head. "Get her another pair of pajamas."

Margaret and Sheila helped to clean her up and get her back in bed. Margaret went into the bathroom and began to clean it.

"Call Ashton and see if he knows where we might be able to find your brother," Margaret called out of the bathroom.

"I don't know his number," Sheila looked down at her sister-in-law who was tossing and turning and holding onto her stomach.

"Lena, do you know how to get in touch with Ashton?" Sheila sat on the side of the bed next to the phone.

"I want to go home," Kali moaned. "Take me home."

"Lena, you are home," Sheila tried to steady her.

"No, home," Kali wailed.

"Do you know Ashton's number?" Sheila offered her the phone. Kali took it and dialed the number. She then dropped the phone and ran back into the bathroom.

"Oh, no," Margaret yelled, trying to help her point directly over the toilet.

"Hello," Sheila picked up the phone and heard Ashton's voice.

"Hello, who is this?" Ashton said impatiently.

"This is Sheila Roberson. I was wondering if you knew where my brother might be."

"No, I don't Sheila Roberson. Didn't he come home last night?"

"No, sir. He didn't. And Lena. Well, Lena is sick. She keeps saying she wants to go home," Sheila was stunned to hear the line go silent.

"Hello, hello. Hello." Sheila put the phone back on the hook.

"Momma, he hung up on me. And he doesn't know where Marcus is." Sheila watched as her mother guided Kali back to the bed.

"Go downstairs and see if you can find some ginger ale and crackers or something. Maybe we can get her stomach to settle. If that don't work, you might have to drive us to that hospital we keep passing downtown."

Sheila ran downstairs and was going through the cabinets when she heard the door open. It was Marcus. He was trying to enter the house quietly.

"Too late for that Dumb Head! Your wife is upstairs upchucking all over the place," Sheila said with her hands on her hips. "Do you have any ginger ale or crackers?"

Marcus walked into the kitchen and looked around.

"I'll go to the store and get some," Marcus said and ran back out the door.

"Don't you want to see her first?" Sheila was surprised that it seemed he couldn't wait to get back out of the door.

She went upstairs and told her mother. They both sat on either side of the bed and watched Kali helplessly as she whimpered.

The bedroom door flung open a few minutes later and there stood Ashton in a pair of jeans and a leather jacket. His bare feet had been stuck in a pair of brown loafers. He hadn't bothered to put on a shirt. His hair was sticking to his head like he just gotten out of the shower. He had a brown paper bag in his hand. He moved around Margaret and sat on the bed between her and Kali.

"I want to go home," Kali sat up and laid her head in his arms.

"It's okay. It's okay." He put the bag on the small chest next to the bed and pulled out a bottle of ginger ale. He opened it and put it up to her lips. She took a little sip. He pulled out a little box of saltless saltine crackers and broke off a piece of cracker. She opened her mouth and let him put the piece on her tongue. She was holding onto him for dear life, she had the leather bunched up in her fists.

He kissed her on top of her head.

"Whew. You stink."

"I want to go home," she drawled sadly.

"Eat the whole cracker. You are not messing up my car with

your throw up."

Margaret and Sheila stood up and watched as he babied her and fed her, giving her bits of crackers and small sips of ginger ale.

"What are you wearing?" he asked her, pulling back the cover to see her covered in pink pajamas. He picked her up and put her down on the comforter then wrapped her up tightly. He put the crackers and the bottle of ginger ale back in the bag and lay it on top of her. He picked her up.

"Excuse me, ladies," he walked hurriedly away from the bed.

Margaret instinctively opened the door. They followed him downstairs.

"Where are you taking her?" Margaret asked.

"Home," Ashton answered. "I'm taking her home."

Marcus came in the door minutes later with a bag in his hand. Sheila and Margaret were sitting in the living room waiting.

"I don't know what is going on, but if you really love your wife. Really, love your wife, boy. You better go and get her, 'cause your boss just walked out of here with her in his arms and looks like he knows a lot more about taking care of her than you do," Margaret was yelling.

"But, Momma," Sheila tried to interject. "That's what I have been trying to tell you. There was this girl at the club last night that said Lena and Ashton been an item for years."

"Do you love her Marcus?" Margaret asked quietly. "I don't care what's been. It is obvious that you haven't been all that faithful, especially since that Rita woman is the woman you have been traveling with all year long. Now all I am saying is, if you want your wife, go get her. Make it right."

Marcus sat on the edge of the sofa not sure what to do. He had just rolled out of Rita's bed and walked into this. He had assumed it was over when Lena saw the two of them last night in that awkward situation. Now, the unexpected had happened. She had been whisked away by another man. His mother was right. He needed to fight for her. Because when it came down to it, he didn't understand why he had gone down this path with Rita. He cherished his marriage. Marriage was forever.

"Let's go," Margaret had put on a coat and was handing Sheila hers.

"Where are you going?" Marcus asked.

"We are going to get a peak at that penthouse while you get your woman. That man promised me a visit, and I am going to get it before I leave this city tomorrow."

"Not a good idea. Taking my mother with me to get my wife," said Marcus and shook his head.

"You won't even know we are there." Sheila opened the door and they followed him out to the car.

———————

Ashton stood watching the three of them. It was finally over. She was home in her bed with her kids. Her head lay on the pillow with her freshly washed curls spread wildly. She was going to have a hell of a time detangling them. He smiled. Both kids had been so happy to see her that they cuddled up to her and went straight to sleep. He thought they looked so picturesque that he ran to get a camera from the kids' room. He had just taken a couple of pictures when the doorbell rang.

Ashton opened the door surprised that the doorman hadn't called to give him a warning of any guests. Micah or his other brothers would have just walked in.

"Marcus, she's asleep and not really up for any drama." He nodded toward Margaret and Sheila who were trying to look in past Marcus.

"Come in," he said, regretting it the minute the words fell from his lips. "I guess you and I need to talk, man to man, son."

"Ladies, you can have a seat in the living room. Marcus and I will be down the hall." He led the way into the study.

"There are some things you need to know, son." He saw Margaret walking around the room. He went back.

"She is asleep. But, she is up the stairs four doors on your left if you want to see that she is alright."

"Thank you," Margaret grabbed Sheila's hand and went toward the stairs. They stopped in awe of Jordan's huge portrait overshadowing the stairs.

"Don't you have his albums, Momma?"

"Yeah, been to a few of his concerts, too. Your daddy loved him," Margaret said as she walked by him reverently. She was tempted to peak in the other rooms, but stopped herself and stopped Sheila when she tried one of the doors.

"Stop, you don't know who is behind those doors," Margaret said, whispering. She opened one of the double doors that she thought must be Lena's room, and it was. They looked so pretty she wanted to cry. The little people looked just like her. The girl in the club had to have been right. This relationship has been going on for a long time. Sheila stuck her head in the dressing room and then in the bathroom.

"This place is the bomb," Sheila whispered.

"It's nice," Kali said. "It's my home."

She maneuvered from beneath her babies' heads and then pulled at her hair.

"Ah," she said, "I am going to have to get Kenny over here to remove these tangles."

"I'll do it," Margaret said. "You got a spray bottle with some water in it."

Kali bounded out of the bed and ran into the bathroom like a little kid. She handed Margaret a big tooth comb and the spray bottle, then she sat at the dressing table in her dressing room.

"Are all these things yours?" Sheila was looking at the beautiful clothes and shoes.

"The new stuff. My older stuff is in Jordan's room."

"Your old stuff," Margaret started spraying and detangling the curls.

"Is this why you didn't want to come to Philadelphia?" Margaret smoothed the curls down gently with both her hands.

"Yes," tears started flowing down Kali's eyes.

"Is your name?" Margaret choked back the question, "Is your name Lena or Kali?"

"My name is Kalina Denise Harris Sperling." Kali wiped the tears from her eyes with the palm of her hands.

"Ashton is my husband," Kali said and she looked back at the babies. "Those are my babies. And I am pregnant, Margaret. I am pregnant with another child. It belongs to Ashton. And," she sniffled loudly. "You can call me Kali."

Margaret looked back at the children and then at Kali's reflection. She lifted another part and began to detangle.

"I can't wait to hear this story," Sheila said. "How, when, where did this all happen?"

Ashton was downstairs with his feet up on the desk blowing smoke rings in the air. Marcus was sitting there trying to absorb the fact that he wasn't married to Lena and Lena wasn't Lena.

"She lied to me," he said, tears rolling down his eyes. "She is a good liar. Just like you, the accomplished expert liar."

"Not really. She was scared of me. She ran. She thought I was going to take her life. I threatened her. She learned how to survive on her own. She actually fell in love with you. That's why she wouldn't tell you the truth. I, on the other hand, learned your deep dark secret. You liked Rita's pussy, so I decided to bring her back home where she belonged. I'd been looking for her for so long, and she was keeping me at bay. Wouldn't let me near her at first, but I realized something. Something, it looks like you are just now realizing. I was in love with her. So I fought for her. And she's home. And son, it's too late for you. I'm not letting her go again.

"I ain't mad at you, though. Hell, I want to thank you for screwing up. I want to thank you for bringing her back to Philadelphia. Only you could have done that, because she was in love with you. She thought she could make you happy and stay clear of me. But, you, son, delivered her to my door. And like I said, all I can say is thank you and in return give you whatever you want. You want that little company in Boulder we have been checking out? It's yours. I think it would be a good match. You can go out there, take Rita with you. Start all over. Be closer to your family, too. Your mother's a nice woman. She needs you closer to her." Ashton put his feet down and leaned across the desk.

"Take my offer, Marcus. You're a good man. You screwed up. Heck, I screwed up. Looks like God is giving both of us another chance. Take it.

"I tell you what. I was planning to surprise Kali and take her and the kids to Switzerland tomorrow after we put your mom on the plane. She was going to tell you the truth, and we were going to be together again forever and ever. So I was going to surprise her. She has always wanted to go skiing in the Alps. I thought this would be the best time to clear her mind, start new on some fresh snow. Kind of cliché I know, but that was my plan.

"But, I don't think she is up to the trip now, so you take the plane. Take Rita, go check out Boulder. If you like it, stay. We will work out the logistics after you get there. What do you say?"

"I want to talk to Lena," Marcus sat up and wiped his eyes.

"Upstairs, fourth door on your left." Ashton picked up the phone and called his pilot.

Margaret braided Kali's hair as she detangled it. Kali opened up about the kids. She was telling stories about what they had done since she had been back in their lives. She even told her about the gingerbread house, but she left out the part about getting back with Ashton that night. Margaret and Sheila looked sad, but resigned. For a minute, she thought Margaret might have been happy for her.

There was a light knock on the door and Marcus walked into the room. Margaret turned and hugged him.

"I'm so sorry," she whispered.

"Me, too," Sheila said. She stopped and hugged Kali good bye. Kali stood up with her hair half braided and hugged Margaret.

"We will wait downstairs in the building lobby," Margaret hugged her son again and left.

"I'm sorry, Marcus," Kali started talking.

Marcus held his hand up. He stood in the middle of the room trying to gather his thoughts as tears poured down his face.

"I will never understand why you couldn't tell me the truth from the beginning. I don't want to hear your spoiled rich girl story of being on the run. I heard more than what I wanted to hear from Ashton. I just came up here to tell you that I'm okay with it. I'm okay with never ever having to lay eyes on your lying, whoring..." Marcus flinched when the door slammed hard.

The children, startled awake, began crying. Ashton marched in and grabbed Marcus by his arm and led him out of the room. Kali ran to her children to calm them down.

"What the hell are you doing?" Ashton almost dragged him down the stairs. "I offered you an out that you could have taken with dignity. Instead you go up and insult her."

"What do you want from me? You lied to me. Your whore lied to me," Marcus blurted out. Ashton backslapped Marcus so hard he fell over the banister. Marcus got up shakily but fast. The pain of hitting the marble was still jarring his body. He hadn't seen it coming.

"Get up, and get out." Ashton was coming toward him with his lips pinned together and fists balled.

Marcus, fearfully and fumblingly, backed out of the door. Ashton kicked it shut.

Marcus stood in the foyer by the elevator feeling his body reverberating from slamming into the hard stone. He was having a hard time moving his left arm. He wondered if it was broken. He straightened himself and took the elevator down steadying his body against the railing. He walked as best he could without alarming anyone and handed his mother the key to the house.

"Look, why don't you two take a cab home. I'll be there later," Marcus said, trying to hide the excruciating pain shooting through him.

"Are you all right?" Margaret sensed something was wrong.

"I'm fine. I'm going to be awhile. I'll be home though. Pack anything in the house you want. Anything. Ashton is giving me anything I want. So take whatever you want," he said, thinking he could lie as well as Ashton and maybe only half as good as Lena.

———— ◆ ————

Ashton was sitting in his office going through the contracts and notes from negotiations that Marcus had left behind. The year 1986 wasn't starting off too good. He still had to replace Brady and now he was going to have to replace Marcus. Kali crossed his mind. She was smart, quick and had a degree from Penn. She was no slouch. Then he dismissed the thought. She was going to have her hands full with the three kids. But, he was going to need help.

The telephone rang surprising him. It was still New Year's Day and it wasn't the private line that Kali and the family called. He answered it. It was Rita.

"Ashton, Marcus is so hurt about everything. He really wants another opportunity to talk to you. He was afraid if he called, you would hang up on him. Can he meet you? Is it possible for him to come over there right now? Please," Rita paused, "for me."

"What time does his mother leave tomorrow?" Ashton wasn't sure why it made a difference, but he did have some respect for Margaret.

"Tomorrow morning around eleven, I think," Rita answered. Ashton could hear Marcus in the background giving her the exact time.

"Then have him come to see me at seven. That will give him time to get back and get to the airport," Ashton hung up the phone and called Micah.

The next morning, Ashton was sitting at his desk smoking a cigar blowing rings into rings. His feet were propped up on the huge desk. He had thought this thing through. It was all finally going to work.

"You ready?" He saw Micah sitting over in one of the big stuffed chairs in the sitting area of his office.

"Yeah, he's not going to do shit, though," Micah said. He nodded and looked back at his newspaper.

There was a light knock on the door. Rita stuck her head in.

"Good morning, Ashton," Rita heard the newspaper and saw Micah who had started folding it.

"Good morning, where's your new sugar daddy?" Ashton

winked at her.

"Let's play nice," she said stepping in with a stiff and pained-looking Marcus behind her.

Ashton looked over at Micah who then lifted his jacket.

Micah looked down at the jacket to see if the butt of his gun was exposed. He looked up and caught both Rita and Marcus staring at it. Micah knew Ashton had meant for him to hide the gun, but just for the fun of it, he pushed his jacket back further exposing it a little more. He looked at Ashton who didn't seem bothered by the display.

"Have a seat," he pointed to the two chairs facing his desk. He noticed how awkwardly Marcus eased into the chair.

"Well, Ashton. We have decided to take your offer. Not because of any strong arming you are planning. You know Marcus could still press charges for assault," Rita started, after helping Marcus get settled comfortably. He saw Marcus frown and look at Rita from the side of his eye.

"Well, Rita. I didn't realize I had made you an offer. Besides, I believe I offered someone a business. But, if they can't speak for themselves, how can I expect them to run a business. Deal's off," he looked from Rita to Marcus.

"I can speak for myself," Marcus said something at last. "I believe I have worked hard for you and produced many contracts that will prove lucrative to you for many years to come.

"I am not going to sit here and lie and pretend I understand the games you and Lena have been playing, but I believe I was harmed mentally and physically as a result. I want compensation. I want the deal you put on the table yesterday," Marcus said firmly. He glanced over at Micah and the exposed gun.

Ashton put his feet down on the floor and slowly put out his cigar. The last of the smoke he blew in the couple's direction.

"You don't deserve it. You didn't deserve her," Ashton said bluntly. "But, I do want you gone. I don't want ever to lay eyes on you again. So here is what I am going to do. My plane is sitting at the airport, fueled up 'cause I was supposed to be using it myself. The pilot's on my dollar and he needs something to do.

"I'm keeping the company in Boulder as a subsidiary. You can run it until you can buy yourself out. I have made too big an investment to just hand it over to a weakling. In the meantime, I want you on the plane and out of Philadelphia today. When you take your momma, take your bags and your…," Ashton stopped short, as he pointed to Rita. He had to force himself to be respectful to a degree. She was still his close friend's sister.

"The two of you get on that plane, and when you land you will have instructions on where you are going to live. It damn 'sho won't be a year's lease anywhere. I will give you a month or two to get out on your own. You are on your own. You screw up and I will replace you at the drop of a hat. That's that," Ashton said and lowered his head and looked to his brother.

"He won't tolerate you anymore than I will," he nodded toward Micah, "and neither will my security staff, you understand." Ashton voice was icy cold.

Micah stood up and tilted his head toward the door.

"Let's go," Rita grabbed Marcus's arm.

"It was nice knowing you, Ashton," she said with a plastic smile on her face. Ashton could see the fear in her eyes.

Marcus limped painfully out of the office with her guiding him.

Ashton sat back and lit his cigar again. He threw one to Micah. They celebrated in brotherly silence, their eyes meeting with hopes of a new beginning.

Ashton went home. He was tired, and Kali was still puking every five minutes. He had checked in on her to find her sitting in the middle of the kids' room reading a story and pronouncing words overdramatically. She was teaching them how to read, with funny results. He shook his head as he just watched her. She had stopped dressing completely. She was now wearing that same blue pajama top that she had worn before Thanksgiving. He sat with them, occasionally admiring her long sinewy legs. He wanted to kiss them, but thought better of it. She would be using them to run and puke any minute.

After awhile, he left them alone and went downstairs to try to make some sense of this year's direction. The one thing he had no doubt about was his family. The four of them were together and soon there would be five. He was happy. He was already thinking about names and wondering which rooms he was going to put the twins in. Then again, he wasn't sure if they were ready to be separated.

Kali heard the phone ring, and she stood up too fast. She held onto the rocker for a few seconds. Then she grabbed the phone. It was Margaret.

"Hi Margaret," Kali was surprised to hear from the woman. She had thought that their relationship had ended yesterday.

"Hi Lena, I mean Kali," Margaret stumbled. "How are you feeling today?"

"Queasy, light-headed. Pretty much like I did with the twins. Chico says it's going to pass. It lasted about a month with the twins," Kali waited a few seconds. "How are you? Are you still here or have you made it back to California?"

"We're back. We're just a little worried. We haven't heard from Marcus. And, I was afraid," Margaret sounded distressed.

"We were afraid something might have happened to him or to you," Kali could hear Margaret weeping openly.

"We're fine, Margaret. Why would you think something might have happened?" Kali walked through the dressing room to her room and sat on the bed.

"Because of the plane crash," Margaret sobbed.

"Your plane crashed?"

"No, no. Kali, it's all over the news," Margaret said.

"What's on the news?" Kali got up and turned on the television and didn't see anything but a commercial.

"Try the news channel. Don't you and Ashton know?"

"Know what?" Kali was getting frightened.

"Your company plane crashed taking off at the Philadelphia airport early this afternoon your time. And I have been trying to get in touch with Marcus ever since we landed. He's not at home and he is not in the office," Margaret sniffled loudly.

"Maybe he is with that girl," Kali offered.

"She did come to the airport with us, and he said he had a surprise for us. But, he wouldn't tell us what. Kali, he brought suitcases for himself out of the house," Margaret said.

"Let me go downstairs to see if anyone has called Ashton about this. He was working in the study," Kali's mind began to race. Where was Marcus?

"I will call you back, okay." Kali hung up the phone.

She had the weirdest feeling as she was walking down the stairs. She hadn't been down them since Ashton carried her up New Year's Day morning. She was barefoot and the cold marble sent chills up her spine. As she neared the bottom of the step, she noticed one of the huge vases that sat near the curve of the banister was broken. Someone had picked up the pieces and laid them in the base of the vase.

She made it to the carpeted hallway that led to the study and walked in to find Ashton standing in the middle of the floor, one hand on his hip and the other wringing his hair. He had tears in his eyes. His desk had been wiped clean, there were papers all over the place and the phone was in two pieces in the middle of the mess.

"Where's Marcus?" Kali heard her voice crack.

She knew immediately when Ashton looked up at her that Marcus was on the plane.

She began to shake her head violently and ran from him when he tried to grab her.

"Where's Marcus?" she started to crumble, and he picked her up. She started kicking.

Micah walked into the room and saw the mess and the commotion. He took Kali from his brother and she calmed down. Ashton stood back in shock.

"You can't think?" he said to Kali as Micah was carrying her to the sofa. "I didn't have anything to do with that crash, I swear."

Kali started beating Micah with her fists.

"Call Chico," Micah said, turning to Ashton who looked back at the phone he had destroyed a few minutes earlier. He started to leave the room.

"Can you take her upstairs?" he asked Micah, realizing his touching her might make her go off again. She had stopped pounding Micah and was laying there whimpering.

Ashton called the airport trying to find the right person to talk to so he could find out what had happened. He was told the plane was ascending and had reached about a thousand feet or so when there was a loud pop and it just dropped. Ashton got off the phone and slid down to the floor against the kitchen wall. Jackie, his pilot; Rita, his best friend's sister; and Marcus, his wife's ex-ex whatever, were gone. Ashton knew that he didn't have anything to do with their deaths, but he hated how everything had played out just before this happened. Now people who wouldn't have talked before were going to start talking and what were the authorities going to think?

<hr />

Marcus had boarded the plane reluctantly. Frankly, he hadn't wanted anything else to do with the Sperlings, especially Kali-Lena and her new husband. But, Rita convinced him it was an opportunity he couldn't let go. She painted a pretty picture of money and power in the Rockies as just a beginning. He was in so much pain that the picture looked a whole lot better than how he was feeling. So he let her drag him down to that office where Micah sat with a big gun.

Marcus had heard rumors, mostly from Brady, that they were dangerous men. Brady had once likened them to just short of being hired assassins. He was never comfortable around the security force that Micah led. They were all mercenaries or ex-military hotshots. They provided personal security for the extremely wealthy, and sometimes he thought those contracts that he was not allowed to see were for the government. He knew the Sperlings were a dangerous bunch in a dangerous business. Brady had even told him a few stories of women gone missing or dead or enslaved for sex and he wondered if one of the latter women Brady talked about had been Lena. He was disappointed in himself. All he had done was walk away from her. He hadn't even talked to her to see if she were really all right. But, he was angry. He had a right to be angry, she had lied to him.

Rita helped Marcus into his seat and fastened his seat belt. He was becoming a bit annoyed that she was treating him like a baby. He was still embarrassed at how Rita had jumped in right away to try to negotiate for him. Then, he thought about his mother following him to the penthouse to get Lena. He was going to have to become a stronger man, it was time he stopped letting women lead him around by his collar. That's how Lena had gotten away with so much. Married him under a false identity and watched him struggle while she sat on millions. The worst of it, she had even married Ashton right under his nose.

He heard Rita's voice going on and on about what they were going to do when they got to Boulder. He turned his head to look out the window to try to tune her out. They were parked outside the company hangar when Marcus noticed Ashton in a pair of green coveralls walking across the floor of the hangar. He had a big white cloth hanging down as if he were hiding something.

"Let's get off this plane," Marcus said to Rita. He was reaching for his seatbelt.

"Don't be silly." Rita was wrestling with him.

"I just saw Ashton in the hangar. It didn't look right. Something is wrong," Marcus protested as the plane began to taxi out to the runway.

"Ashton, in the hangar? Honey, please. You may have seen someone that looks like him. I can promise you it wasn't Ashton," Rita wouldn't budge from her seat.

"Rita, I'm getting out of here." He started to get up, but the plane started picking up speed.

"Sit down. The pilot told us a few minutes ago that we were cleared for take off. Come on, Marcus. I am Troy's sister. Troy Lucas, Philly PD. He and Ashton have been buddies for years. Ashton would never do anything to hurt Troy's little sister, I promise. Now calm down and stop being a baby," Rita demanded as the plane was beginning to ascend.

Marcus sat down and put his seat belt back on and watched the ground race from beneath them.

CHAPTER SIXTEEN

Ashton was anxious about going to bed and everything else. Kali had had such a melt down, he wasn't sure if he should touch her. First, he sat gently on the bed and she didn't move. She was laying on her side with her back to him. He climbed under the cover and turned toward her. She flipped over and scooted right into his arms. He relaxed and kissed her lightly on her braided hair.

"I'm sorry," she said. "I know you wouldn't have had anything to do with that plane crash. It's just that I was in shock." She was still sniffling.

"It's okay," he pulled her close to him. "I talked to Margaret. She took it pretty hard."

"How are you taking it? I know you sort of liked Marcus. You used to say he was real good at his job," Kali said in a muffled voice. She was trying to hear Ashton's heart. It was beating so slowly that she was worried about him.

"I did more than sort of liked him. That's why I got so mad at him when I thought he was screwing up. I was trying to set him up in his own business. That's why he was on the plane," Ashton said, not wanting to tell her what was really worrying him. They were supposed to be on that plane. Had she not come down with morning sickness, that plane would have had his entire family on the passenger list. That unsettled him more than anything. He didn't want to say it out loud, but Jackie went over the plane tooth by tooth before he would fly it. There was no way anything was wrong with that plane.

"What's next?" she asked.

"The FAA is doing an inquiry. Trying to find out what happened to the plane or if something was wrong with Jackie. They already have the black box," Ashton didn't want to talk any longer. He just wanted to hold onto Kali and never let her go.

The next few days were a fog. He went to the office. He had meetings. He came home to two happy go lucky kids who were ecstatic to have their mother with them day and night. She looked a little sad, but she smiled for the kids and kept their days normal.

Ashton was hearing things. But, what really hurt him was that Troy wouldn't answer his calls. He had even stopped by Troy's place, but he either wasn't home or refused to answer the door. Ashton knew what that meant. It meant Troy blamed him for his sister's death. And the last thing Ashton wanted was to be blamed for those deaths.

He had developed a reputation. One that was cold and calculating. He knew how to bring people down when they threatened him, and he knew it was going to appear that Marcus was a threat. He was going to have to counter that somehow.

He got the call from the FAA as he was sitting in the study at home. It had only taken them two weeks and their decision was final. The plane had been tampered with and deliberately sabotaged. Someone intended it to go down, just as he had suspected. Ashton started doodling names, trying to come up with people who wanted him and his family dead. His father was at the top of the list.

He picked up the phone to call Micah when the door to the

study opened. It was Troy and another gentleman with a solemn look on his face.

"Troy," Ashton got up. He was going to go hug his friend and tell him how sorry he was about Rita, but Troy stepped away, backing away from the hug.

"Ashton, you know Capt. Gavronivic, don't you?" Troy nodded toward the other plain clothes cop.

Ashton looked at him for a second.

"Tony, is that you? Man, I haven't seen you since high school," Ashton held out his hand and the man shook it and held onto it.

"Ashton, you have the right to remain silent…" the man hesitated and took a deep breath. "You have the right to remain silent. Anything you say can and will be used against you in a court of law," the Captain continued his Miranda litany as Ashton tried to remove his hand.

"What the hell?" Ashton looked from Troy back to Gavronivic. "What am I being arrested for?"

Micah came running through the door.

"Ah, man, Troy. You are wrong. You know you are wrong. Let it go," Micah walked around the men and stood by Ashton.

"You killed my sister," Troy said vehemently through his teeth. His eyes were cold and hard. Gavronivic just looked sad.

"I'm sorry," Gavronivic said as he finished reciting Ashton his rights. "I think we can forego the handcuffs. Let's go take that ride down to the station."

"My wife," Ashton said as his worst dreams had come true. His instincts had told him this was coming, and he still wasn't prepared for it. "Can I tell my wife?"

"We need to get going, Ashton," Troy interjected maliciously.

"Kali is upstairs with the kids. She will need to know she is here alone," he turned to Micah who left the room running.

Gavronivic took Ashton's arm and guided him toward the door. Micah and Kali came running down the stairs. Her eyes were wide with disbelief.

"Why, Troy?" she asked, but Troy refused to look in her direction.

She ran to Ashton and hugged him.

"Come home, soon," she said with tears pouring down her face.

He bent over and kissed her before he was pulled away. She didn't like the defeatist look he had in his eyes. She had never seen that before.

"Take care of the kids, baby," Ashton yelled back.

The rest of it was a blur. Somebody had gotten through to the judge and he wouldn't grant bail. He deemed Ashton a flight risk. In preparation for the trial, there had been witnesses placing him at the airport about the same the time Ashton was walking home from work on a day when his office was closed to the rest of the staff. He hadn't stayed all day and decided to take the time walking to clear his head and run some errands. He didn't know any of his witnesses or if anyone had even noticed him enough to remember. It was a Saturday and the usuals weren't downtown on a Saturday. Ashton knew who was at the airport though. But, they were going to have to prove it. It was Asa.

Micah represented Ashton with a heavy heart. He couldn't believe Ashton could have done such a thing, but he couldn't place Asa at the scene of the crime no matter how hard he tried and no matter how many men he put on the job. Asa had witnesses placing him in New York and there was no one else that looked like Ashton, not that closely. The short circuit cameras in the hangars substantiated the witnesses' claims. The man was blurry, but still it looked a lot like Ashton.

It took three months and a lot of grief for Ashton to be brought to trial and convicted. It happened so swiftly, neither of them knew what had hit them. No one accepted the fact that it was his family that was meant for that plane, and no one believed him after hearing his history with Marcus and Kali that he was not responsible for that plane crash. Even his own employees had testified against him. It was as if the whole world wanted to see this Black man come crashing down hard and fast. He had become a criminal for having wealth, for having a beautiful woman, and a family. The press chimed in, recanting he had had the audacity to dump Redd in her time of need, whatever that was. Ashton was still unaware of what had happened in Europe and didn't really care.

Not only did the district attorney have what he called solid evidence placing him at the scene. He had even more witnesses, Margaret included, reciting why Ashton wanted Marcus dead. They built his motive on wanting another man's wife so bad he would go this far to get her. It didn't matter that she was the mother of his children and already legally married to him. Yeah, even that hit the newsstands.

Someone had even found out about Ashton knocking Marcus over the stairwell. All those well wishers and party goers, all those loyal employees and friends, all had something to say about Ashton. Everyone painted him jaded and mean. The press had a field day with that and especially the type of business he owned. They were trying to connect the dots between him and some covert operations for the government. Everybody wanted a piece of the pie. It was a modern day lynching with him at the end of the rope.

Brady even testified that Ashton had threatened his life and the life of his niece as the reason he had left the company. The press didn't bother to follow up Micah's counter that the woman was sleeping with Brady and not related.

"They did a real good job, didn't they," Ashton sat behind the thick glass in the maximum security prison he had been remanded to as soon as the trial was over. He had been there for four months. Micah and Kali had come at least twice a week. The prison was so far away from home, it was difficult to come every day. Besides, there were visiting rules they had to follow as well.

"They really did," Micah added more disappointed in himself than anything. Even when he worked for his father, he had never lost a case so badly. Everything had gone wrong. He was afraid his doubt had kept him from saving his brother from this fate. "I failed you, man."

"You did the best you could," Ashton was resigned to life in prison. "You have got to take care of the company."

"No," Micah shook his head. "I have got to walk away for a minute. I have to get this reversed. I can't do it in an office. I can't rely on anyone else to help you. I have to do it myself," Micah hit the counter with force, startling the other visitors.

"How are you going to reverse it?" Ashton leaned against the window holding the smelly phone.

"I've got to break those witnesses one by one. Everything was too tight, too good to be true. But I am working on something. I'll let you know when I figure it out completely."

"Is Kali keeping the house locked up real tight?" Ashton asked, not wanting to grasp for straws and get his hopes up, so he let Micah's comment slide.

"Yeah, she's a fighter, Ashton. I didn't know she had it in her," Micah didn't want to tell him about Billy's stunt and how Kali had handled it just a couple of days ago. Billy and Asa had taken for granted that now Ashton was away in prison with a lifetime conviction, security had lessened. And unfortunately, they were right. The men on the job had become careless.

Kali had learned after the public character assassination of her husband that she was going to have to protect herself and the kids. Ashton couldn't anymore, and the people around her weren't taking her seriously. All people had been interested in was bringing him down, hard and fast. They were like vultures trying to pick his carcass before he had succumbed to death. She would sit in the courtroom and wonder how many of these people had fallen in harm's way at Jordan's hands, and if they were making the grandson pay for the grandfather's sins. Distrust in humanity overtook her.

Kali came in early one afternoon to find that Reggie had let Billy and Asa into the penthouse. Billy startled her walking casually down the stairs holding the twins by their trusting little hands.

"Look who's home," Billy grinned. The twins let go of his hands and ran into her arms. She hugged them and put them behind her leaving the front door open.

"What are you doing here, Billy?"

"Is that any way to greet your father-in-law? I just came over to check on you to see how things were going. You know Ashton hadn't invited me over since he moved back in. Imagine my surprise to find out during the trial that you were back."

"Oh, you knew, Billy. I am sure you know everything that goes on in here," Kali realized immediately that Reggie was still tight with him and obviously had little respect for her. She knew this man was off limits.

"So how are you doing?" Billy descended the stairs and stood a couple of feet from her.

She turned back to the door and closed it. She took the kids by their hands and led them to the living room. She sat them down next to each other.

"Don't move," she whispered. Surprisingly, when she glanced back at them they were doing what they were told. They sat still watching her intently.

"I'm doing fine, Billy. You still haven't told me what you are doing here," she began to pace easing her way behind the sofa toward Jordan's old style bar in the corner of the living room.

"I just wanted to make sure you and the children were doing okay." Billy put his hands on his hips and grinned at the children. They stared at him blankly.

"Like I said, we are fine," Kali leaned against one of the bar stools for a minute. She stood up, surprised, when she saw Asa sauntering down the stairs.

"Calm down. Don't panic," Billy held up his hands. "I know you and Asa got a little history. He just wanted to see his niece and nephew. He is just as concerned as I am. We both know how important those children are to Ashton. And from the looks of it, I think you are bulging a bit around the waist. When are you due?"

Kali casually walked behind the bar and moved a glass or two. Then she pulled a .38 revolver out of its holster from one of the cubby holes that was too high for the children to reach. It was loaded. She liked the feel of the weight in her hands at that moment. She let her right hand drop to her side holding the gun firmly and she stood there watching the men smirk.

"We are fine, Billy. You can leave now. Make sure not to return," Kali said calmly.

"We can't leave you hanging like this," Billy held up his hands. "Ashton has a mighty big estate to take care of. I'm a lawyer. I can help you keep track of things. And Asa, well, Asa could help keep the children happy, protected," Billy emphasized the word protected.

"He could probably even keep you happy. It would be like having Ashton still home with you," Billy's sarcastic grin widened.

"Life is a long time in prison. I was just so shocked when I heard that verdict. I mean manslaughter is one thing, but first degree. I didn't know my son had it in him," he continued to taunt Kali.

"What's in your hand, Asa?" Kali took a few steps from behind the bar. She kept her body turned away from them so they couldn't see her right hand.

"Just something of Jordan's, I didn't think Ashton would mind since he will never use it again," Asa was swirling a watch around his forefinger.

"What did you take, Billy?" Kali leaned again against the bar stool.

"My mother's pearl earrings and one of Ashton's watches," Billy produced them from his pocket and smiled.

Kali recognized Ashton's watch. It was the one with the crazy symbols on the back. He had told her to keep it in a safe place. She had been so busy she had forgotten to put it in the safe.

She edged herself sideways in front of the children, and turned quickly taking the stance the self-defense instructor at the company had taught her. She raised the gun, like a woman who knew how to use it.

"Drop them," she said, looking Billy straight in the eye.

"What the hell?" He stumbled back into Asa, who immediately dropped Jordan's watch.

She released the safety on the gun dramatically.

"I'm a real good shot, and you are closer than most of my targets," Kali tried to keep her voice low and serious. She didn't want them to think they were messing with an airhead.

"Billy dropped the watch and the earrings," he looked back at Asa whose mouth was wide open.

"There's no call to do such a thing. We're family," Billy begged. His eyes kept looking down at the jewelry he dropped.

"You are bold. That's about all you are," Kali pointed the gun toward the door. "Since you are a lawyer and all, I am sure you know that if I find you in my house again and if I shoot you, I will not be prosecuted. That little thing called a restraining order is still in effect. So. You...And Baby You...Stay…Away…FROM…ME and MY CHILDREN! Go, or I will shoot right now!"

Asa beat Billy out of the door. Kali followed them and locked the door. She called security downstairs and told them to make sure they never entered the building again. Then she called Micah.

Kali put the gun away. Then she walked the kids to the steps.

"Mommy needs you to go upstairs to your room. And I need you to be very, very quiet." She kissed each child and watched them go up the stairs. AJ was leading the way, holding Katie's hand tightly. Katie kept looking down at her. Kali blew her a kiss. She watched them disappear down the hallway and then ran to get her purse in the foyer.

"I am armed and dangerous," she said under her breath as she pulled out a small gun that fit in the palm of her hand. She dropped it into her jacket pocket and maneuvered her way through the dining room and sitting area for the kitchen. She was in intense thought.

"Reggie," she said eagerly, "what's for lunch and dinner?"

"Oh, the usual," Reggie was at the sink running water and cutting vegetables. She had a colander on the drainer filled with fresh green beans.

"I'll snap those," Kali joined Reggie at the sink and washed her hands. She took the beans and a bowl to the kitchen table.

"You have been going to that office a lot," Reggie said smiling, thinking that Kali had probably just missed Billy and Asa.

"Yeah, I'm trying to help Micah get a handle on things while Ashton is away," Kali began to snap the beans.

"You sound like he's away on a vacation. You think you might want to sell Ashton's share to Micah or something," Reggie said, looking back at her. "Just making a suggestion. You know I don't mind watching the kids, but I don't know how you are going to manage with three."

"Well, I do appreciate you taking care of my little darlings," Kali got up and ran water into the bowl.

"I am going to make an effort, though, to find a good nanny. I don't want to continue to burden you. I'm really grateful, though, that you've been here to help us through this mess.

"Don't know what I would have done without you, Reggie."

"You're welcome," Reggie looked pleased. She sealed the vegetables up in bags and put the knife in the dishwasher.

"Reggie, do you remember the day that Marcus died?" Kali was surprised at what ease she said that. It had taken her a long time to come to terms with what had happened. It wasn't until Micah began to insist on bodyguards and self-defense classes that Kali realized what happened to Marcus and to Ashton was probably not the end of it. So she was leaving early in the morning to go to the shooting range, and from the shooting range to a class in self-defense, and from there to the office to go over the books. They were still recovering from the Brady crisis, let alone the loose contracts left by Marcus.

She had lost two nannies who didn't understand Reggie. But Kali was determined to keep some sort of familiarity around the kids by keeping Reggie employed. In the process of doing this and losing good nannies, she knew she was wearing Kenny out and was going to have to give him a break. She made a note to call Elliott to see if she could bring back that older lady who had reported that she was afraid of Reggie, now that Reggie was no longer going to be a problem.

"How could I forget?" Reggie said. Then she laughed. "I knew that boy wasn't long for this earth, though."

"Why would you say that?" Kali asked, as she turned her whole body toward Reggie questioningly.

"Oh, you probably didn't know this," Reggie chuckled. "I just happened to be coming through the dining room to the living room when I saw Ashton backslap that boy right across the banister. He hit the floor, Ka Bam! The marble floor!

"It was the funniest thing, though. That boy bounced back up quick. He was holding his arm as Ashton chased him out the door. And he was scared. You could tell he was scared. Ashton had shocked the heebeejeebies out of him. That's who broke that Egyptian vase at the bottom of the stairs. Hell, that thing might have saved his life right then."

"You think Ashton was trying to kill him?" Kali's heart started pumping fast. She had heard a reference to that in court, but as hearsay. Micah had gotten the words stricken from the record. So there was another hole in Reggie's loyalty armor.

"No, the boy was running his mouth. Called you a bad name. Pissed Ashton off so bad, he just reacted," Reggie said grinning. "You have to understand, I been around them Sperling boys a long time. Ashton is the one that snaps. I mean when he snaps, he snaps. You ought to know that."

"So, you don't think he planned to kill Marcus?" Kali asked, tilting her head to get a good look at Reggie's expressions.

"Now, I didn't say that. I said his character is the type to get into the fray while it's hot. But, he's a good thinker, though, and he will get his vengeance. Heck, Asa can tell you that from personal experience. Heck, look at his ex. I saw her on TV the other day, and she looked bad."

"You think Ashton has something to do with her looking bad?"

Kali was surprised by the theory.

"Yeah, he left her ass. He left her ass with just a few pennies in the collection box. She didn't know how to live off that. Heck, it turned out she didn't know squat about squat. Ashton was still managing her career or so I heard from the grapevine. When he took his hands off it, it was over."

"Really?" Kali wondered how true that really was, but that wasn't what she wanted to find out right now.

"So that day, though. First of all, I didn't know you were here, but what do you remember about that day?" Kali asked Reggie as she snapped the beans slowly.

"Yeah, I was here. Ashton told me you were upstairs sick, but with the kids. He said all he wanted me to do was cook some meals. Why do you ask?" Reggie was rinsing dishes and putting them in the dishwasher.

"Well, it's just that all I keep getting is more questions in my head about that day." Kali shook her head and let her voice trail.

"I don't know," Reggie said, turning off the water. "I called him…" Reggie was staring at the building across the street. "I asked him to buy some flour. Some little people had been making paper maché with the flour, so we were almost out. And, somebody else I know, I heard was craving a chocolate cake. I told him to stop on his way home to buy the flour. That was the last time I talked to him," Reggie shifted, remembering something else.

"Did you ask him to do anything else?" Kali kept her eyes on the beans.

"Oh, yeah," Reggie laughed. "The dry cleaning. He was supposed to pick up the dry cleaning. There was a note on the refrigerator for me the next time I came in to pick it up, but it was cold out there and I didn't feel like doing all that running around. He seemed happy to do it though."

"I ran some errands," Ashton had said in the courtroom. "I stopped at a few places. The dry cleaners off 19th Street. The A&P. The guy on the corner was selling roses. I bought roses for my wife. Oh, and I bought strombolis."

"How did you get to those places?" Micah had asked.

"By foot," Ashton had said. "I wanted to walk. I wanted to clear my head. I had a lot to think about."

On cross-examination, Ashton couldn't describe any of the people he had encountered. His mind had been preoccupied with family and his business. That had been so unusual for him to be so unclear that Kali could see doubt budding in Micah. Ashton usually noticed everything. And, of course, he saved no receipts.

"Why didn't you say anything?" Kali tried to maintain her composure, but was getting angrier by the minute.

"Say what?" Reggie asked, bewildered.

"That Ashton was running errands when he was supposed to have been at the airport sabotaging his own plane." Kali reached for another bean, but they were all gone.

She walked over to the sink and edged Reggie out of the way to rinse the beans.

"How was I supposed to know he didn't hire someone to run his errands? I don't keep up with Ashton. Besides, all I could think about was him backslapping that little Black boy over the banister," Reggie took the beans and shook them back through the colander before putting them in a bag.

"Aren't you going to scald those or something?" Kali was pointing to the beans.

"No, they are your dinner tomorrow. They will be just fine, madam," Reggie sighed. "Boy, I do miss him."

"What about the other ones?" Kali asked sitting back in the chair.

"What other ones?" Reggie asked.

"The other boys? The Sperlings? I still talk to Chico and Ricky. And, of course, Micah. I know you see Micah. What about the other ones?" Kali wouldn't say their names.

"Why would you ask?" Reggie gave her one of her signature none of your business looks.

"Just asking. You and I haven't really talked very much. I'm usually on my way in and you are on your way out or vice versa. God, Reggie. I really don't know what I would have done without you," Kali smiled endearingly.

"Billy and Asa?" Reggie asked grinning. She was looking back over her shoulder at Kali.

"Yeah. What is the dangerous duo up to these days?" Kali let her words settle in.

"I ain't gonna lie to you, I still hear from them now and then," Reggie said hanging up the dish towels.

"You got anything you need washed?" Reggie asked, trying to change the subject.

"No, I actually did most of the laundry last night." Kali played with the napkin holder.

"You know the strangest thing, Reggie? I thought I saw Asa and Billy leaving the building when I came in." Kali took the napkins out and neatly aligned them before putting them back in the holder.

"Oh," Reggie said. "That's odd. They know they aren't supposed to be in here. That restraining order and all."

"Yes, but I thought I overheard them say you let them in to see the kids," Kali stood up and blocked Reggie who headed toward the pantry.

"I would never do that," Reggie said.

"You know Ashton doesn't want either one of them near the

kids. Nor do I," Kali didn't move.

"Okay, I did let them in. Billy begged to see his grandbabies. I think you are being really unfair and unrealistic right now. Those kids need as much family as they can get. You can't handle all of this alone. You are still a kid yourself."

"Was this the first time, Reggie? Have they been over here before now?" Kali still wouldn't move.

Reggie reached out to move her, but Kali held her ground against the big woman. Reggie was surprised that Kali hadn't budged.

"You think you bad now, huh?" Reggie stepped around her. Kali turned to face her.

"What's up, Reggie? Don't you like me anymore?" Kali centered her hips and her protruding belly.

"Look, you little, po ass, southern trash. Ashton took you and made you, now he's gone. Now, the man who made him just wants to see his grandkids."

"And it's your prerogative to make that decision for their mother?" Kali retorted.

"Billy, Billy," Reggie tried to think of something to say.

"Did Billy know Ashton was out there wandering around running errands the day that Marcus died?" Kali asked.

"Bitch, who you talking to?" Reggie took a threatening move toward Kali and Kali pulled her gun out of her pocket.

"Bitch, I think you were just fired. Now I can really fire you up if you don't back off," Kali couldn't believe she was drawing a gun for the second time in one day, but she was in no condition to go hand to hand with Reggie.

Reggie held up her hands.

"I'm sorry. Kali, I am sorry. But, you just implied something that I wouldn't have had any part in. I love Ashton," Reggie backed up against the sink and put her hands over her face. Kali didn't buy it. She stood stoically, gun aimed and ready.

She saw Reggie's eyes dart down to the kitchen sink.

"I can shoot faster than you can move for that knife. Now get out of my house and don't come back. If you do, I will have you arrested.

"Oh, what are you going to do to Kenny?" Reggie shook her head. "Your lap dog? Your errand boy? He's still in touch with Billy, too. You think the world stopped turning cause of what you and Ashton wanted? Hell, I worked for Jordan all them damn years, held all his damn secrets and you think he left me shit? No, he left me a job working for you two spoiled bastards. You don't know how sick I am of working for you, Miss Hoity Toity. And Mr. My-Ass-Don't- Stink-My-Life-Revolves-Around-My-Twins."

"Well, you can stop being sick," Kali said, taking a step forward when the kitchen door opened. It was Micah.

He walked over to Kali and lowered her gun.

"Put it away," he said. "I need to talk to Reggie alone."

Kali put the gun in her pocket and went up the backstairs from the kitchen to check on the kids. When she returned, Micah was in the study looking for something.

"Did she leave?" Kali asked.

"Yeah, I called my office," Micah answered, looking up from the desk. "We're getting yet another restraining order in place. If I see her again though, I might kill her myself. I played the Daddy card with her and she opened up. They have been here almost every day you haven't. Do you have Ashton's watch?"

Kali touched her pocket. She had picked up the jewelry when she sent the kids upstairs.

"Lock it up. That's what they were looking for, I'm sure. Where do you keep your receipts? Do you throw them away?" Micah was going through the drawers.

"Behind you. I usually keep them for about a month if its incidentals. Longer if I think they may affect taxes or warranty or something I might want to return."

"How about Ashton's receipts for the dry cleaners, for the A&P?"

"I'll look, but he said he threw them away. If I didn't empty his pockets and keep them, he would toss them."

"But, we never looked Kali. Look," Micah commanded.

Kali ran to the file cabinet and retrieved the little accordion folder that held all the receipts. They both rifled through them. They found the dry cleaners tape marked January 2. It had a time on it and so did the A&P receipt. Micah kissed her.

Ashton had paid cash. Micah made copies and locked up the originals. Then, he went to the police station. Troy was the first person he saw when he walked into the building. Micah walked over to Troy and gave him a big bear hug.

"You owe him, you son of a bitch. You owe him. And you're going to help me get him out of prison."

Troy looked at the copy of the receipts.

"These could be anybody's receipts. You could have gone out and recruited receipts from anybody. These don't mean crap," Troy said, throwing the copies back at Micah.

"They have the time on them. Both of them. What about closed circuit tapes? You can get them. Let's see what somebody else's camera caught. Not just the airport's.

"I swear that tape from the hangar had been tampered with. If not the tape, the witnesses definitely were. You know Ashton would never have done anything to hurt Rita or Marcus. You owe him. You know that, Troy. You are responsible for him being there. You pushed for his arrest and the death penalty." Micah was leaning over Troy's desk angrily.

"You're going to sit there and tell me you honestly think Ashton killed Rita," Micah wouldn't leave.

Troy picked up the copy of the receipts. Ashton would have been picking up the dry cleaning at the same time the hangar tapes said he was there in an unbecoming jump suit. That was a detail that bothered him. Ashton dressed down for no one. He was too much like Jordan in that respect, even his bum around clothes looked great.

"I'll humor you," Troy said. He picked up his jacket and the two of them headed to Micah's little sports car.

"I thought there weren't any receipts."

"Reggie remembered removing receipts from his pocket that day and putting them on his desk. Mrs. Accountant kept them. Not having the time to destroy stuff she didn't need, she still had them."

Micah drove. His knuckles graying as he held the steering wheel with a death grip. He was angry about everything these days. He became even angrier every time they escorted Ashton in an orange jump suit to a filthy phone behind a glass wall.

Troy sat in thought staring out the window. He wanted Ashton to be guilty one minute and innocent the next. It hadn't really believed Ashton would hurt Rita at first, but he couldn't believe otherwise when they found credible witnesses to clear Asa. If he were wrong, though, it had to have been Asa and that meant Ashton was wasting his life away all because he wouldn't lift a finger to help him.

Troy flashed his badge at the dry cleaners and a little Asian woman called someone from the back to translate. A young man, about twenty, shook his head when he saw Ashton's picture and so did the woman. When asked about a closed circuit camera, the young man smiled and pointed to a camera over the door. And then to Micah's disappointment, he said they erased over the same tape daily.

As the two men were walking out of the store, the young man called them back.

"You know, we changed the tape," he said, smiling.

"We changed the tape after New Years," he said again. "I think I still have the last tape if that helps."

Micah nodded. "It will help."

The man ran in the back, his mother behind him speaking her language, as if fussing about something. The man came back with three tapes.

"I'm sorry. I don't know which one, but you can have all of these," he stopped and patted his mother's arm saying something in Chinese.

"So we have got tapes," Troy said. "It doesn't mean anything. Not yet."

"It's meaning more and more," Micah said. "I had a conversation with Reggie last night."

"And?" Troy was getting into the car.

"Ashton always uses credit cards, right?"

Troy let a slow smile cross his face. He had had to pull cash out a million times to pay for something Ashton was getting, because Ashton didn't have any cash on him.

"Yeah, he loved his damn credit cards."

"You want to know why he was using cash on that day of all days," Micah started the car and looked ahead.

"Why?" Troy took the bite.

"Kenny delivered $500 in cash to Ashton at his office that morning, just before Reggie called him and asked him to run errands. Said it was a gift for helping him open the shop. Told him he was giving him cash instead of a present because he knew he never carried it."

"So Ashton has hit Kenny up for money, too."

"Hell, Ashton has hit up everybody for cash. But, to his defense," Troy and Micah said together, "he always paid it back."

"So other than an occasional inconvenience or a 'get your damn act together, Ashton', nobody really cared. Now did we?"

"No, because he was generous to a fault," Troy was thinking about all the things he had that his friend had given him.

"Yeah, Ashton would give away the shirt on his back if he thought you needed it or even just wanted it. My brother does have a mean streak, but he has a kind streak that is unequal to it. Don't you think?"

"Yeah, yeah," Troy wiped the sweat from his face and looked at Micah who was looking at him. "Keep your eye on the road."

"A&P," Micah pulled into the parking lot.

"Why would Kenny wait to gift Ashton on January 2? Didn't he get him a Christmas present?"

"A wedding slash Christmas present. He made a big deal of it. I was there for the wedding. You were too busy, remember?" Micah and Troy were walking side by side into the A&P.

"I was getting some Christmas ass, man. How was I to know what Ashton was planning? He just said be there at 7:00 am. When I turned over, it was too late. Where is Kenny, anyway?" Troy asked. "The DA wanted him to testify. Every time we tried to reach him, he was unavailable or we couldn't find him. And then, then we just didn't need his ass."

"He's around. He's still doing Kali's hair. He watched the kids for her just this past Monday. I guess you didn't want him bad enough," Micah laughed. "You took unavailable as an answer?"

"I guess I was getting tired of Ashton's friends crucifying him," Troy said and opened the door for Micah.

Micah looked at him with a more discerning eye.

"You sound like you regret what has happened to Ashton," Micah sighed.

"There's a camera over there and one over there. What do you think the odds are that they will have the tapes? It's been six months. And don't blame me, Micah. Not for all of it. Why didn't you ask for these tapes six months ago?"

Micah couldn't answer that. He was supposed to be top in his field and on top of his game. But, he could not answer it. Maybe he had been too close to the case. He had looked up to Ashton all his life, and for the first time in his life, he didn't believe in him anymore. He actually believed he could have killed Marcus just as easily as he had almost killed Kali once. Micah had spent most of his life trying to live as cleanly as possible in their tainted family, and maybe he just wanted to wash his hands clean of his brother's dirty deeds. Like it or not, Ashton's hands were bloodied, just not in this instance.

They struck out at the A&P, but they still had the tapes from the dry cleaners. They went straight to the police station. They were going to do this one by the book. They spent three hours viewing tapes before Ashton's long stride entered the dry cleaners. It was all they needed to get a mistrial. Micah jumped into action.

Four weeks later and a two hour drive to the prison with the news that Ashton was about to be released, Troy, Kali and Micah walked into the maximum security prison hoping it was their last time. After a hard press from Micah, Troy, the press, and a friendly judge, Ashton's trial was deemed a wrongful conviction and he had been exonerated. Kali was so excited. She couldn't wait to see him. The three of them let a bodyguard drive them in Jordan's limo. Kali had packed him some brand new clothes. She knew he would be grateful to get into something besides an orange jump suit. They arrived at 8:30 a.m.

Kali paced around in the waiting room of the release area until her feet couldn't stand it anymore. Troy went to the window for what seemed like the thousandth time and all the guard could say was, "these things take time."

Micah looked at his watch, it was almost noon.

"Enough," he said. "These things don't take this much time. I want to see the warden."

"The warden is busy," the guard answered with indifference.

"Didn't I see a sign as we walked in for the warden's office?" Kali grabbed Micah's arm before he went off on the guard, she could see him seething and on edge, but she didn't want to be delayed any longer.

Troy opened the door and they went down the dreary bare hallway. They found the warden's office on the left. There was a lot of commotion going on in the warden's office. He was yelling about something. Micah walked right past the receptionist and banged on the door.

The man with a beet-red face opened it and yelled, "What? You know I am in the middle of a crisis right now. Where's the damn ambulance?"

"I don't give a crap about your crisis. Where's my brother?" Micah saw the blood drain from the man's face.

"Mr. Sperling? I'm trying to get him to the hospital," the man said. "We found him about an hour ago. He's already lost a lot of blood."

"An hour ago?" Micah grabbed the man by his collar.

"He's not here. He's still in lock-up. In the infirmary. I just found out about it a few minutes ago" They all turned to hear the ambulance pulling up.

"Shouldn't you have one of those here all the time?" Troy said, shaking his head.

"That's it. It was out this morning for repair. We haven't had anything like this happen in years, I swear. Not to this degree."

"I'll give you the directions to the hospital, in case they leave before you get to your car." He wrote the name of the hospital and the directions down hastily.

"I'm sorry. I'm so sorry."

Kali ran into the hospital room afraid of what she was going to see. They had rushed him in and took him straight to the operating room. Nobody would give them any information. They had dropped him off and walked away. Troy slid down to the floor outside of the room. He was too ashamed to go in. Ashton had told him over and over he had nothing to do with that plane crash. He had made up his mind early on not to believe him. He didn't know how Asa had pulled it off, but he was going to make him pay if it was the last thing he would do in this lifetime.

Micah stepped over him and followed Kali to his bedside. Ashton had a head injury. They had had to remove bone from his skull and reset his jaw. His face was swollen and bandaged. He was unconscious. Kali crumpled. Micah picked her up and put her in the chair next to the bed.

"We'll get through this," he said.

"But, Asa won't," Kali said quietly. "If I ever see him again, I'll kill him with my own bare hands."

"That won't be necessary," Micah answered. "I've got that covered."

⸺◦《◉》◦⸺

Weeks later, Ashton was still in a coma, but they had moved

him closer to home. His room at the hospital and his home were covered with body guards. It wasn't until one day Kali truly looked in the mirror that she thought about Kenny. She hadn't heard from him in a long time, and she had been meaning to call him. Kenny had denied what Reggie had said, stating he hadn't seen or talked to Billy and Asa in months. She believed him. She knew Kenny loved her and Ashton and would never do anything to harm them. And right now, she needed his soft touch on her head.

Kali went home and called the salon.

"Kenny hasn't been here in days," his shampoo girl said. "We've been kind of worried about him. Didn't anybody call you?"

"No, is he sick?" Kali was feeling guilty that she hadn't called Kenny because she hadn't needed anything. She had a lot to make up to him for that.

"Well," the girl lowered her voice into the receiver. "Nobody knows where he is."

"What are you saying?" Kali started feeling short of breath and she lowered herself into the chair.

"He's missing," the girl said. "His parents are having a fit."

CHAPTER SEVENTEEN

K̲ali left the hospital. She couldn't sit and stare at Ashton a minute longer knowing that Kenny was missing. She drove into the narrow driveway of the Blackmons. Kenny had grown up in a large old home in Germantown where his parents still lived.

Mrs. Blackmon met her at the door.

"Kali," she hugged her. "I didn't want to worry you." She touched Kali's stomach.

"Oh, baby girl. When are you due?"

"Two weeks," Kali couldn't believe how fast time had flown. Nor could she believe how tired she was. Mrs. Blackmon showed her to the living room and helped her ease down on an old worn sofa.

"Who is it?" Mr. Blackmon said, coming down a narrow set of stairs.

"Kali, have you heard from Kenny?" he asked, when he saw her.

She shook her head and then wiped a tear from her eye, "I didn't know he was missing until a couple of hours ago. Why didn't anyone tell me?" she sniffled.

"We know you have your hands full," Mr. Blackmon sat next to her.

"But, but," she didn't know what to say. "When did he go missing?"

"It's been about three days, four maybe," Mr. Blackmon leaned forward on his knees.

"I haven't heard from him in weeks," Kali tried to stifle the cries, but she was overwhelmed.

"We know," Mrs. Blackmon said. "We know. Kenny kept saying he was going to call you. We had just asked him about you the other day."

"I feel bad. I hadn't called him."

"Honey, he was feeling bad, he hadn't called you," Mrs. Blackmon got up.

"Would you like some tea?"

"Yes, ma'am."

"Kenny's business was taking off like a firecracker. He was working some long hours," Mr. Blackmon said. "I fussed at him. I told him he needed to take a break. But, he was working like there was nothing else to do in life."

"Something was hurting him real bad," Mrs. Blackmon came back with a china tea cup and saucer. Kali took the delicate set and began to sip slowly.

"He was sick?" she asked.

"No, darling. It wasn't physical. I think part of it was about Ashton. He was real hurt behind Ashton. It was as if he took part of the blame. I can't explain it. Kenny hasn't been himself for such a long time," she said, patting Kali's knee.

Kali stayed with the Blackmons a little while longer trying to make sense of what was happening. When she left, she pulled into the parking lot of a McDonald's and called Micah from a pay phone.

"Meet me at Kenny's?" she asked. "I want to stop by his house and see if I can figure out where he could be."

Micah showed up with Troy. Kali was sitting in the car as she looked at the metal stairs that led up to the side apartment. She really didn't want to climb them, the baby was weighing her down, but she wanted to find out what had happened to Kenny.

"What are you doing here?" she asked Troy as he helped her from behind the steering wheel.

"Don't you think it's time for you to stop driving around? You need to be at home with the kids," Troy tried to chastise her.

"Did I ask for your advice?" she answered testily. Micah may have forgiven him for arresting Ashton and leading the mob against him, but she hadn't.

"They reopened the case, today," he said.

"Good for them. All they are going to find is that Asa is guilty." She removed his hand from her arm and led the way upstairs. There was yellow tape across the door.

"What's this?" she asked.

"Crime scene tape," Troy said, putting on a pair of gloves.

"I thought Kenny was missing. Do they normally put tape on the door if a person is just missing?"

"No, they don't, not usually, unless…" Troy looked at Micah.

"Give me the keys," said Troy.

Kali handed him the keys Kenny had given her a long time ago.

"Somebody didn't want anybody going in here for some reason," Troy had his hand on his gun as soon as he heard the door unlock. Micah pushed Kali behind him and pulled out his gun.

The door swung open slowly. Troy stepped across the tape with his gun held out, he began to look around. Micah followed him in and held his hand up to tell Kali to stay back. They searched the place and found no one. Micah came back and helped Kali across the tape.

"Don't touch anything," Troy ordered and the three started observing.

"That's Jordan's album, the one with Miles," Kali reached out for it, but stopped short of touching it.

"How did that get over here? You think Ashton gave it to him?" Troy asked.

"Naw," she shook her head. "That album cover has too much history. Just wait until I see that boy. I know he didn't steal that album."

"How do you know that that's Jordan's and not just another copy? You know they sold more than one," Troy grimaced as something else caught his eye.

"It's dog-eared at the right corner. And I bet if you turned it over there's a little flower drawn on it. And," Kali reached for it again, but Micah caught her hand. "I bet that there's a tic tac toe game with hearts and flowers on the sleeve. I thought Jordan was going to kill both of us," she sighed. "Ashton and I used to do stupid little things. He called himself humoring me, but he was just as childish as I was at times."

"So you played tic tac toe on the sleeve of one of Jordan's albums?" Micah pulled out a handkerchief.

"I got it." Troy picked it up with his latex gloves on and pulled the sleeve completely out of the cover. There were about five games of tic tac toe on the sleeve. There were hearts and flowers and no X's or O's. He slid it back in the album cover and sat it back where they found it.

"What about that?" Troy pointed to a tall gold water pipe on the desk near the window.

"Oh, my God," Kali squealed. "I know Ashton didn't give that away. I smoked my first reefer on that thing."

Both men looked at her.

"Actually it was my first and my last," she said defensively. "What is Kenny doing with it?"

"Something tells me my father has something to do with this, too," Micah looked at Kali. "Didn't you say Reggie said Kenny was still seeing him?"

Kali nodded her head, "but I didn't believe her and he denied it. I just figured Reggie was trying to come between us. I didn't want to believe her. So I didn't. I believed him and just let it go."

"Well, your closed circuit tapes at the Banks Building?" Troy asked. "I know you have that building wired down and watched like a hawk now."

"You mean, let's put this stuff in daddy's hands first?" Micah said.

"He was going to the penthouse, and he was probably taking as much stuff as he could, thinking Kali wouldn't have time to notice anything missing."

Kali was waving the air in front of her, she was getting over-heated. The apartment had been closed up a few days and the heat was unbearable.

"Let's get her out of here," Micah guided her through the apartment and held the door open with his handkerchief. As he opened the door, two uniformed officers and a plain clothesman were coming up the stairs. Troy appeared at the door behind them.

"Detective, what are you doing here?" the officer asked as he looked at Kali and Micah.

"We were trying to find out what happened to our friend. What are you doing here?"

The plain clothesman stepped forward. "Hi Detective. I am sorry about your friend. Some kids swimming in the Wissahickon Creek just came across a car down there earlier, and it was your friend. He was still in the car. Looks like he just drove into it."

Kali was surprised her knees didn't buckle from under her. Could it be that she was beginning to get used to bad news? She spent the next few days between home, Ashton, and the Blackmon's.

Her heart sank when she saw pictures of them raising the car from the creek. She couldn't believe he was gone. First Marcus, now Kenny was dead and Ashton was still in a coma. She was starting to feel like a black widow spider. Nothing good happened to the men in her life. They had to do something. She couldn't spend the rest of her life looking over her shoulder or the rest of her life under lock and key. After Kenny's death, Micah had her escorted everywhere she went. She couldn't even go to the bathroom in a public place in peace. There was a bodyguard standing outside the door, sometimes checking the bathroom before she went in. She was more than annoyed. She wanted this over.

Troy and Micah were busy trying to build a case against the Dangerous Duo but they kept hitting roadblocks. All they had was circumstantial evidence, not enough of anything to get Ashton totally in the clear although he was free. There was still doubt out there that would always follow him.

The break came from Kenny's death. Kali went with the Blackmons to gather his personal things from the salon. They had received an offer from one of the stylists that already worked there. The Blackmons had accepted, since they really needed the money. Kali picked up each of his personal items and held each to her heart. She knew Kenny would never have done anything to hurt her or Ashton, not purposely or under his own will. She was putting his things in a box when she came across a letter Kenny had written to Asa.

The baby started kicking as she lowered herself into his desk chair and began to read it. She picked up the phone and called Troy.

The letter was entered into evidence that day, and a warrant was issued for Asa. They couldn't find him, he was on the run.

The letter revealed a heartbroken Kenny who had discovered he had been used by Asa. Asa had convinced Kenny that he was in love with him. Kenny detailed the events that led up to the day of Marcus's death, including the names and addresses of the witnesses. They were all gay men. All of them knew Kenny well enough and loved him enough to help him save his lover from being wrongly, but concealed to them, accurately accused of murder.

It wasn't until later when Asa began to pull away from him that he realized he had been duped and then he had been threatened. Kali would never know if Kenny took his own life or not. All she knew was that he had not written this letter in vain. She copied it and kept it in her end table drawer. Everyday she looked at it and prayed for Asa's end.

The police no longer guarded Ashton; only his own men took turns protecting him. She was tired. Tired of making the trek to the hospital, so she made a decision.

"I'm taking him home," she told the doctor who protested. He was quick to tell her about all of Ashton's needs. She wouldn't hear any of it. She had the doctor order the necessary medical equipment. She hired two practical nurses to cover him full time and she took him home to his bed.

Everybody thought she was crazy. The doctors said she was taking him home to die. She didn't care, as long as she didn't have to go to sleep in her own bed alone anymore. For five days, Ashton lay on his side of the bed in his coma while she and the kids made as much noise as they possibly could, something they couldn't do in the hospital. They danced around him and sang. One of the nurses quit because she would have no part in the madness. But, Kali didn't quit. At night, she cuddled up to him and kissed him and stroked his chest and Taylor. She was doing anything to get a rise out of him. Nothing was changing or happening. Then one morning, her water broke as she was getting out of bed to go check on the kids. She called Chico.

"Again, Kali? You would think you would, at least, want to have this baby in the hospital," Chico complained, but she knew he was on his way.

She waddled around as best she could to get everything ready and dropped it all next to Ashton.

"You are going to remember this!" she knew she was sounding and acting like a mad woman, but they had had so many plans for this pregnancy. She was determined she wasn't going through this alone. She didn't care if he weren't awake.

The nurse came in and screamed.

"What the hell are you doing?" she picked up the phone to dial 911.

"Baby's almost here, darling. The doctor will be upstairs in a minute," Kali answered as she huffed and puffed her way through the pain.

Chico walked in the room and saw Kali had lain on the bed with her knees apart.

"You are serious about this?" he dropped his things and went to wash his hands.

"The baby's head is crowning," the nurse stood at the foot of the bed yelling to Chico.

"She drops them like water," Chico grinned down at a panting and pushing Kali.

"You have no fear, do you?" he knelt down and helped to deliver his new nephew. He threw a towel on Ashton's chest and laid the screaming baby on it. Then they both watched for a reaction.

"One day," Kali said. "I don't know how I am going to top this, but one day."

Kali held the baby for a moment, and then handed him to the nurse who seemed not to care that she was working for a certifiably insane woman.

"We need to clean this mess up," she got out of the bed and headed toward the shower.

"You are insane," the nurse said.

"Haven't you ever read The Good Earth?" Kali got into the shower.

"I need you to go the hospital to have you and the baby checked out," Chico yelled into the bathroom. He was busy cleaning up the bed and turning Ashton as he cleaned him, too.

"In a little while," she yelled back.

"No, now, Kali. Your stunt didn't work. He is still asleep. Hell, he will have a fit if you don't take care of yourself and the baby!"

"I don't care."

Chico finished cleaning up the bed and the nurse handed him a clean little nephew. He reached over to the end table for a tissue and there weren't any. He opened the drawer and found Kenny's letter taped inside. He cleaned up the baby and began to read the letter. It sickened him. It sickened him even more that Billy was calling him saying how worried he was about his missing Asa. Billy kept saying that Asa was being setup to take the fall for Ashton. And then it occurred to him, when Billy called he wasn't just bellyaching about the situation, he was asking questions. He had thought that was his way of showing his concern about Ashton in an around about way. They were questions about injuries, head injuries. Micah walked in the door with Ruby and the kids. Chico handed the baby off to Ruby.

"Get Kali and the baby to the hospital, please," Chico grabbed Micah by the arm.

"Have you been over to daddy's recently?" Chico asked.

"Nah, not since all this stuff went down with Ashton."

"Your mom, you talk to your mom?" he asked.

"At least once a week," he said.

"What does she have to say about all this?" Chico was more than curious.

"Well, you know the drill. She is sticking by her man, no matter what. If Billy believes Asa is being set up to take Ashton's fall, then that's what is," Micah and Chico stopped at the bottom of the stairs.

"When Asa went missing, did anybody go over to daddy's to see if he were hiding there?"

"Yeah, it's under surveillance even."

"All of it?" Chico raised his eyebrows.

"All of what?" Micah wasn't sure what Chico was getting at.

"Didn't daddy have that little closet downstairs? You know the one he used to hide his excess liquor in, the illegal kind, so his lawyer friends wouldn't see it?"

"You mean that hole in the basement?" Micah went to the foyer and picked up the phone. He told Troy where to tell his men to look.

Ruby and Kali left for the hospital with the new baby. They saw Micah and Chico shoot past them in Micah's car.

"Are they in some kind of hurry?" Kali was angry about bringing the baby out of the house so quickly, but Chico had stood by her so she would, at least, follow his directions.

"Probably to get a stiff drink after what you just put that poor boy through," Ruby laughed as they pulled around to turn into the hospital parking lot. Three police cruisers shot past them and then an ambulance, all heading to the emergency room entrance.

"Wow, I wonder what happened?" Ruby was taking care to help

Kali remove the baby from the car seat. They went into the hospital through the main entrance and then Kali laughed.

"I bet we were supposed to go through emergency. Chico didn't tell me who to go see."

"All you need is a pediatrician to check the baby out," Ruby said.

"Well, did we really need to go the hospital for that? I could have just called my pediatrician," Kali sighed, she was tired and wanted to go back home. Her adrenaline rush was subsiding.

"Well, let's go down to emergency. We're here," Ruby led the way back to the elevator and they kept the baby draped away from onlookers.

The two of them got off the elevator as a very pale Asa with a dirty bandage on his head was rolled by on a gurney.

"Shit!" Ruby said. "Was that Asa?"

Kali handed Ruby the baby. "That was Asa."

She turned to follow the gurney when a hand caught her and jerked her back. It was Micah.

"He's dying," he said quietly. "Go take care of the baby and let it go."

"What happened?" she said.

"Here we were thinking he was on the run, when he was in the basement," Micah said.

"Doing what?" Kali asked. "What happened to his head?"

"I don't know," Chico chimed in, "but you know how much he wanted to be like Ashton. I wouldn't be surprised if it was self-inflicted."

"You think he's that stupid?" Kali asked.

"Don't ask," Ruby said. "Let's take care of the baby."

That night, Kali was happy to see her feet again. She sat on the bed next to Ashton talking to him while nursing the baby. Then she heard the children screaming at each other.

She stood up and almost stumbled with the baby.

"What are you two doing in there?" She pulled the baby away from her breast and laid him on Ashton's chest. She figured he wasn't big enough to wiggle out of the bed yet. He was only a day old, but his little legs and arms were waving chaotically, fighting the air.

She ran into the kids' room and dragged them both back into her room by their skinny little arms. She dragged them over to Ashton's side where she could still see the deprived and hungry infant continuing to protest.

"What is wrong with you?" Kali went to reach for the baby and the twins started fighting again.

"I am going to hurt both of you. Now somebody start talking now. Why are you fighting?"

"Cause Grandpa said girls shouldn't play with boy things and she touched my trucks," AJ whined.

"Who said what?" Kali couldn't believe her ears. Billy's short time with the kids had influenced them.

"You see your grandfather?" Kali asked.

"We did everyday before you pointed a gun at him," AJ protested.

"Oh, well, trust me, that was probably the last time you will ever see him," she pointed to the chair. They both climbed in to it together.

"I don't know what else your grandfather told you, but I think he left something out," she kneeled before them. "He left out the fact that he had a hand in what happened to your father. And, that he doesn't like your father very much."

"But," AJ looked puzzled.

"But, nothing. Your grandfather is not a sane man. He's a little crazy. Just a bit," she held her forefinger and thumb together as a sign.

"If he told you to look down, I think you need to look up. You can't trust him. One day your father will wake up and tell you more about him than I can. But, don't listen to anything he said, especially something that makes the two of you fight each other. You have to love each other and hold onto each other. It's okay to disagree, but not to hit each other or try to hurt each other. You understand?" Kali looked both children in their eyes and they began to cry. She thought about the baby who was still screaming. She went back to him to pick him up, but her hands stopped mid-air. She saw a pair of hazel eyes looking up at her.

"Ashton," she whispered, but not low enough to keep the kids from hearing. AJ ran and bounced on the bed crawling up his father's leg.

"Daddy!" AJ yelled in Ashton's face causing his eyes to blink. Katie worked her way between Kali and the bed and crawled up and kissed Ashton on his face. A tear ran down the side of his face.

"You know these two," Kali said. "I want you to meet Adam Kenneth Sperling."

She picked up the squirming child and turned his howling face toward Ashton's. She saw a smile in his eyes.

⸺⫸⫷⸺

"I'm sorry, Micah." Troy said as he followed the doctor to the waiting room where Micah and Billy sat facing each other silently.

"He didn't make it, sir," the doctor was talking to Billy. "He was pronounced dead ten minutes ago."

Billy collapsed in tears and slid to the floor sobbing loudly. Micah got up and walked past him.

"I want to see him," Micah had to see his brother dead for himself. He knew Billy was capable of many things. He still couldn't understand the head injury. Billy claimed he showed up on his doorstep like that. He knew it was a lie, but knew he would never get the truth from his father.

The doctor ushered Micah and Troy into the room. Micah walked up to the machines and saw the flat lines. He removed the sheet from his brother's face. He stared at him hard to see if there was even a slight breath. He leaned forward to his face to see if he even felt a breath.

"Asa Thomas Sperling, may you rot in hell," Micah whispered, and straightened up. Then he was satisfied.

The two men left and went straight to the penthouse. They found Ashton propped up, his feeding tubes removed, and Kali cradling his head in her bosom surrounded by his loving family the way it should be.

LaVergne, TN USA
18 October 2009
161225LV00001B/1/P